Last *of the* Red Hot Poppas

LAST *of* *the* RED HOT POPPAS

A NOVEL *by* JASON BERRY

fall 2006
CHIN MUSIC PRESS — *PUBLISHERS*
SEATTLE ✳ TOKYO

Copyright 2006
by CHIN MUSIC PRESS INC.

CHIN MUSIC PRESS INC.
2621 24th Ave. w.
Seattle, wa 98199
USA.

http://chinmusicpress.com

FIRST EDITION

Design *by* Craig Mod
Cover Art *by* Leslie Staub

The cover art is a work by Leslie Staub that unfolds into a poster depicting the late Governor Rex LaSalle and some of the people he influences from beyond the grave: Reverend Christian Fraux and Henry Hubbell in the foreground; Amelia LaSalle and Sophie Thibodeaux as jewels in his crown. The poster was painted in gold leaf on canvas in Ms. Staub's studio in Durham, NC. The work traveled an unusual route: Durham to Tokyo to Seattle to New Orleans. Many times. It was photographed by a man named Bubba.

Printed and bound by YUSHIN PRINTING, located in the rolling felds of the Kanto Plain near Tokio, Japan. Overseen by Kohiyama-san, a man who knows both his printing and his tennis.

LIBRARY OF CONGRESS CATALOGING-IN-PUBLICATION DATA
Berry, Jason
    Last of the Red Hot Poppas :
      a novel by Jason Berry; design by Craig Mod;
      edited by Bruce *&* David Rutledge.

    ISBN 0-9741995-2-4
    13 DIGIT ISBN 978-0-9741995-2-8

    1. Politics — Fiction. 2. Murder mystery.

ALSO BY JASON BERRY
NONFICTION
Amazing Grace: With Charles Evers in Mississippi, 1978
Up from the Cradle of Jazz, 1986
Lead Us Not into Temptation, 1992
Louisiana Faces, 2000
Vows of Silence, 2004
Do You Know What It Means to Miss New Orleans?, 2006 (essay)

PLAYS
Earl Long in Purgatory, 2002

1 2 1 6 3 1 12
18 18 12 2 30
1 11 6 2 60 48
19 132 132 10
192 2 31 168
108 66 35 252

FOR THE DAZZLING DR. MELANIE MCKAY ...
Every man needs a doctor.

This novel was inspired by environmental reporting I did in the 1980s as Governor Edwin Edwards gave *carte blanche* for toxic-waste dumping in Louisiana. Those policies rewarded certain of his cronies and kin while sending poisonous chemicals into communities of innocent people. Many political sins are forgivable; I have trouble with that one. Over time, as I worked on other books, the idea of nature's fury in response to such poisoning roiled within me. I finished this novel before hurricanes Katrina and Wilma hit in 2005.

It is customary for the novelist to announce that his characters are works of the imagination. That is true of those who prance herein, save for a few historical figures in cameo and another exception. Astute readers will find surface affinities — a roguish Cajun charm — shared by the fictional Governor Rex LaSalle and Mr. Edwards, the only Louisiana citizen to win four gubernatorial elections. Edwards held a well-earned chair at a federal penitentiary (extortion: casinos) as we went to press.

The comedian's mask as a cover for the criminal has become a commonplace in popular culture, but had there never been an Edwin Edwards, there would have been a Rex LaSalle, some comic figure to personify the surreal performance of Louisiana where democracy became a sideshow, diverting scrutiny from the petrochemical industries that used the region as a toilet for their wastes and gutted coastal wetlands that protected us from hurricanes.

I wish to thank Moira Crone, Valerie Martin, Christine Wiltz, Adam Nossiter, Andrew M. Greeley, Mark J. Davis, Jeffrey Gillenkirk, Charles Davis, Don Congdon, Susan Ramer, Deborah Grosvenor, John Glavin, Dennis Maguire, and particularly my wife, Melanie McKay, for informed readings as this work matured. I am also grateful to Rosemary James and Joe DeSalvo, the editors of *Double Dealer Redux,* for publishing a short excerpt of this work when it was still in progress. It has been a pleasure to work with Bruce Rutledge, the publisher of Chin Music Press; his brother

David Rutledge, a writer and editor who teaches in the English Department at University of New Orleans; the art director Craig Mod; and the grand artist Leslie Staub, a friend whose work I have long cherished.

I took the title from the late Governor Earl K. Long, a theatrical populist to say the least, who called himself "last of the red hot poppas." He carried on a torrid 1959 romance with a stripper from Bourbon Street name of Blaze Starr and won a Congressional seat from the Pentecoastal woodlands the following year, despite public knowledge of his ribald ways. His death, a few days after that election, gave impetus to my play, *Earl Long in Purgatory*.

To live in Louisiana pits the civilized mind against a tradition of politics and religion that often seems downright bizarre. Figures like the Longs, Edwards, Jimmy Swaggart and others one could name challenge the literary artist to do reality one better. That can be quite an imposing task. I have taken a few factual liberties. There is a civil parish, but not a town, named Avoyelles. I have never spent a night there and have no personal connections to the area.

Lastly, I am unaware of a sixty-foot statue of Jesus in Rapides or any other civil parish of Louisiana. However, if one were to surface, I would not be greatly suprised.

JASON BERRY
New Orleans
March 30, 2006

By and large, people in the South still conceive of humanity in theological terms. While the South is hardly Christ-centered, it is most certainly Christ-haunted.

FLANNERY O'CONNOR

In the top floor bedroom, the First Lady dreamed of making love with Rex beneath the arms of a muscular oak. Her body, cupped by the earth, moistens in feathery rain, the sky explodes with a quickening rhythm of water on leaves, and then they fall, sinking into hot muck, lost in a magic and sinful state at the bottom of America.

At fifty-four, the First Lady wore the same size six as her wedding gown. Her dark-haired beauty was a solvent to the advance of time. A stream of sun rays parted her eyelids. She bolted up from the pillow and wrapped herself in her red silk robe, a gift from Exxon's wife.

Waking Rex was odd duty. She so rarely did it. However long he may have lingered in some assignation hatched after the hustings, he always made it back, smelling clean, for several hours of sleep, his room or hers, wherever prudence deem he camp. She daubed her face with cold water and stepped into the hallway, muttering a Hail Mary for patience.

Each day he wasn't on the road, Rex was head of the Mansion he loved like a human body. His ratings had risen steadily across the years while she installed art works from distant places, purchased with her own money, the more exotic pieces a secret between them. The marble for the solarium came from quarries south of Florence, a goodwill gesture to the state from some now-interred Mediterranean administration grateful for medical supplies, foodstuff and Italo-Louisiana volunteers, dispatched by Rex on oil company airplanes to a village rubbled by an earthquake west of Pisa. That is when Governor LaSalle had gone on TV. He spoke from the Capitol terrace, overlooking the statue of Huey Long, and held up His Holiness's letter: "A gift of stone, blessed by the throne in Rome, affirms the values of our state — *an international state!*"

He was a bawdy man, the most outrageous she had ever known. Down the years he had stretched every tissue of their original love; she was tired of taking him back with stale apologies, of trying to restitch the bond. Part of him, she believed, was driven by a wild erotic charge beyond the circuitry of most men, incapable of sexual honesty, reduced to a tearful display, down on a knee like some black-face vaudevillian pleading *you're the only one I ever loved, baby, nothin', nobody else counts, I mean nobody!* Never had she felt more isolated. His levers of influence functioned more fluidly than those of her daddy, Mayor of Avoyelles for thirty-seven years and still getting votes ten summers after his funeral. Rex wielded power as naturally as some men glide across a ballroom floor. He took three showers a day and was the most spectacular politician in these latitudes since television.

Amelia LaSalle (*nee* Broussard), Queen of the 1959 Sugar Festival, Miss Louisiana runner-up, 1960, had her own issues. Battle scarred in matrimony, she had shifted of necessity to an aesthetic quest, a search for clarity in the paintings, photographs and works of anonymous artists whose carvings from black Africa lined her space in the interior of a mansion that drew more people on guided tours than any other in the fifty capitals.

She had serious money banked in her own name and tolerated his galloping libido for reasons she didn't brood upon with chemical company presidents due at ten and at a quarter past nine the Governor hadn't stirred.

She crossed the hallway and rapped the mahogany door, a gift from Hondurans who flew in every winter, generals and politicians toting weapons into marshes behind camps loaned by the petro-chemical companies, feral men yet sociable in that seamless Latin way, blasting deer, rabbits, nutria, raccoon, anything in a shotgun's sight, trailing bloody boot prints back to the lodges with women who disappeared when TV lights came on for our good neighbors to the South. Partners in free enterprise type guvment.

Turning the knob, she advanced into the smaller room and pulled back the curtains, shedding a diaphanous glow on her husband of more than three decades. She shook the Governor's foot. "Rex, honey." *He's fifty-five. Running around like a yard dog. Lord, Jesus: help me salvage him ...*

"Come on, *dear*. Time to get *up*."

She jostled his shoulder: an arm flopped, hand on the floor. His eyes were wide open.

They still talk of how her screams cascaded down the banisters, streaking over portraits of long entombed governors, Mayan figurines and a Harlem painting by Jacob Lawrence, walls tremulous with echoes of her voice hitting the downstairs reception hall, startling a florist who dropped chrysanthemums, scattering yellow blossoms on the floor.

Mitchell Mudd, the Governor's confidential assistant, had just sat down in the foyer of the boss's office where Colonel Lawson Bellamy, the chief of state police, had come to lobby for a better pension package. Mudd was lean with dark hair; Bellamy muscular with a crew-cut the color of wheat. Popping out like springs, they raced up the stairwell in the wake of her screams, bounding into the room where the First Lady had collapsed over the body, sobbing.

Mudd cupped his fingers on her shoulders. "Miss Amelia, let me see."

"Jesus God, Mitchell: he won't wake up!"

Mudd cradled her shoulders as she pulled up from the bed. She covered her mouth. Colonel Bellamy held the Governor's wrist, studied his watch, put an ear on Rex LaSalle's chest. Bellamy pulled out his cellphone. The First Lady shut herself in the bathroom, faucet running to quiet her sobs, washing her hands in reaction to the feel of his dead skin. When Mudd cried *"you all right in there?"* she emerged from hot vapors, scowling at the men.

Bellamy barked into the phone: "We got a critical emergency with Governor LaSalle. I need a cardiac unit *immediately!*"

Out in the world, cirrus clouds hung like gauze in an azure sky. Autumn was the season Rex loved best: festivals at harvest time, football nights. For fourteen days the heat had been so brutal that people could not work outside in the middle hours. Economists were being interviewed about lost labor time.

Amelia LaSalle left for the master suite. "I need to change."

"Absolutely," asserted Mitchell Mudd. "I'm keepin' track."

The bedroom swallowed her in the silence of a crypt.

She was alone: two daughters on their own, her mother living sixty miles away, her charming half-mad rogue of a spouse gone forever. She pictured Rex's hands reaching up through misty clouds, only to be pulled down by hairy Satanic paws. Dead: why? She murmured a prayer for the soul freed from the body down the hall where Colonel Bellamy had his eyes trained on the medical men like amoebae under a microscope.

"Well, was it his heart?" the Colonel demanded.

The young doctor and his younger paramedic perspired in green smocks. "I can't document cause of death," said the physician. "But his lips are blue, his fingernails are blue, and he has an acrid smell. I'd be speculating to say he's poisoned, Colonel."

An exposed sheet revealed the Governor's right leg. Lipstick smears ran down his knee and thigh. The sheet was folded over his equator.

"You saying he didn't die of natural causes?" muttered Colonel Bellamy.

"I'm saying it's not my job to produce forensic data."

"Looks like somebody visited," stewed Bellamy.

Mitchell Mudd's black eyes glared at the Colonel. With other men present, every word was adhesive.

"We don't know enough," grunted Bellamy.

"Gentlemen," put in the emergency physician, "you need to call the Coroner. And since the Governor was Roman Catholic, you should call a priest."

"What's your opinion?" Bellamy fired back.

"His vital functions ceased operating several hours ago."

"He was vital at some point," said Bellamy, eyeing the lipwork on the dead man's leg.

"Goddamn," growled Mitchell Mudd. "Can't y'all clean him?"

"The Coroner should deal with the corpse in its present state," said the doctor. "I grew up here and don't need an order to keep my mouth shut."

"Cause if it opens, you're in a sea of burning shit!" snapped

Mitchell Mudd. He threw a cold glance at the paramedic, who said: "It's all private!"

"That's right," said Mudd. "What a man and his wife do alone is sacred. Reporters have no morals."

The four men stared at the body.

"Y'all take the servants' elevator," ordered Bellamy. "Stay in the kitchen till the Coroner comes. Nobody leaves till we got control of the physical plant."

"We're on call," stated the doctor.

"We'll get you people out," reported Bellamy. "Won't be long."

The medical emergency team left.

"Media's gonna crawl up our ass," said Mudd.

Bellamy faced him. "What's your story, Mitchell?"

Mudd ran his fingers through dank hair. "He was fine on the way back from New Roads last night. I didn't see him sneak any female up here. And his wife sleepin' down the hall? Nanh-unh."

"My night guard would have a record of any visitor," said Bellamy. "Rex didn't smoke, didn't drink, and he waddn't overweight." Bellamy sniffed a glass on the night stand. "Scotch! Any idea how *this* got here?"

Mudd shrugged. He was gazing glumly at the body.

Bellamy went to the window. Wooden posts of a side gallery, lined with palm fronds, supported a private balcony facing the vast back lawn and ridge of trees along Capitol Road. "I'm six-foot one and a hundred-ninety pounds," reported the Colonel, "but even I could get out through this window. We need fingerprints on the sill, floor photos, big time forensics."

"Not the FBI," said Mudd, a lump moving north in his throat. "Governor hated the FBI! Sez they're worse than the mob. Goddamn, I loved Rex." Mudd choked. "He gave me the best job of my life. This is assassination!"

"Unless a woman did it."

"A woman kill him for what?" squealed Mudd.

"All the ones he had, possibilities multiply."

The body loomed as a personal disaster to Bellamy: a Governor dies on your watch. "Mitch, I got to call the Federals."

"Nobody needs to know about this man's state," simmered Mudd. "You call the Feds, him like that, those people feed the media and Rex is dirty forever. That ain't fair. We don't know what happened. We need a probe we can control."

Bellamy had a Purple Heart from Korea. Although he considered Rex LaSalle a political genius, he had been stunned by his sex life. Since Clinton had gone to Washington, Bellamy had been mesmerized by stories of Arkansas troopers leaking dirt on the big man. At dawn Bellamy had been strategizing how to boost his pension when he met with the Governor. Now the need to cut distance from an ugly death moved to the foreground of his thoughts.

"City homicide has trouble solving passion crimes, Mitchell. This means fiber samples, a zillion tight shots, plus meshing gears with the Coroner."

Mudd's chin was speckled red from shaving cuts. "The Feds are cannibals, Bellamy. They eat anything they find. Humans, rugs, cars. They eat it raw."

Bellamy rubbed his brow. "I'll call Attorney General Abadie. He was the Governor's ally. Oscar's smart. Plus he's got good lab connections."

Mudd wiped his eyes.

Bellamy stabbed his cellphone. "Good mawnin'. This is Colonel Lawson Bellamy of State Police. I need to talk with General Abadie. Mm. He's where? Tobago. Which is — Trinidad, I see. So, who's minding the store? Benton's in court upstate. My my. Who's the General's next best? No I haven't. He did? And Oscar knew his daddy. Well, all right. Yes, ma'am, I will." Bellamy cupped the receiver. "Oscar got a lawyer went to Harvard. Someone Hubbell."

Mudd nodded vacantly.

"In the legislature," said Bellamy into the phone. "Thank you."

Bellamy punched the buttons once again. "Hullo, this Colonel Bellamy of State Police. Please, ma'am: give me the Sergeant-at-Arms *immediately.*"

Mitchell Mudd sat slumped in a chair.

"Mike boy," said the Colonel into his cellphone. "You know Henry Hubbell?" Bellamy's eyebrows went up. "*Good.* Get him for me lickety-split. I am holding and it is critical. Thank you, sir."

Mitchell Mudd cradled his head in his hands. He was wheezing. Poor bastard, thought Bellamy: his life just got cut down the middle.

It was 10:02 AM.

POLITICAL SCIENCE 2

Hubbell found himself in the rotunda, the great floor between House and Senate chambers. Erected by the ruler during the Depression, the Louisiana Capitol was an Art Deco phallus of thirty-four stories that dwarfed the green grounds, elegiac oaks and a lake that curled around toward the Governor's Mansion. Down on the center of the vast lawn, the bronze force of Huey P. Long, square-jawed and immemorial, peered up at his creation.

This is where Henry Hubbell, the Assistant Attorney General for Constitutional Affairs, began each working day: at the elevator, watching tourists and school kids hover around the spot where Long was gunned down that night in 1935. Many times Hubbell had caught himself staring at those onlookers, envious of their wonder. Like excavators on some dig, they were thrilled to touch the bullet scars on marble, to feel some property of the past.

Today only adults were present — about three-thousand of them swollen into the rotunda like cattle in a boxcar. Word had leaked from the Speaker's office: debate was about to begin on the flag-burning bill. If the motion passed, the masses would roll across to the Senate side for the spectacle of a one-two punch into law. Hubbell, by virtue of his job description, would have to draft his boss's defense of the bill for the inevitable fire-fight against the ACLU, of which Hubbell was a member. Up before dawn, ramrod straight in his underwear, fixated on the computer screen like an assassin at the trigger, he drafted his resignation letter. He tore out of his home and sped to work on a hollow gut. At the rotunda he fell into line for the House gallery. All these cheery bureaucrats, sweetly sprayed and come for the show, left him stewing in the malicious joy that overcame him when Louisiana was at its worst.

He had gone away for college, farther still for law school. Having sworn never to live again in the state where his father died, he was midway past thirty, aglow in Paris when the pull of familial duty yanked him back to the land of bayous and sweet wisteria. It was two years now since his father's funeral. Possessed of a mortgage, health club membership and a politically connected job, Hubbell joined other state servants as witness to the titans of the legislature.

White curtains shimmered like taffeta gowns, shrouding the forty-foot high windows. Four chandeliers, sheathed in bronze cones, cast a halo over the floor. He imagined himself an invisible sociologist, spying on a Belle Epoque bordello: politicians sprawled on couches black as petroleum, waiting greedily for the naked dance.

As a boy, the awareness had come upon Hubbell that his father was making bitter enemies. The patrician attorney had secured the family financially; he had put all three of them on the good side of history with his work for civil rights. Shunned by his white peers, Henry stood on graduation day 1973 at a small high school forty miles outside the capital — his mother serene, his father in a wheelchair, the mouth a zippered smile — and gave the valedictory address praising Thomas Jefferson and Stanley Kubrick.

In the House, a state trooper dispensed people into seats. Hubbell was uneasy that so many folk were downright friendly; the verbal niceties, so natural, chafed against the force of childhood images: TV news bleeping out bellowed profanities of a mob, his father emerging from the courthouse flanked by US marshals, the boy in the den seated next to his white-knuckled mother, murmuring words like "honor" and "dignity." Even the black people Hubbell met seemed lights years away from the anger and fear on the mental screens of his past.

Many people were too young to remember Forrest Hubbell, much less the stroke that in midlife had split him into a ghost of his former self. Older people had forgotten the hatred, which left Henry feeling cheated. He wanted everyone to know that the darkness of a state on which his father had trained his light was still dark, not past. He sat at night, dazzled by the windsprints of TV news, the latest old son, hands caught red in the kickback tray, joining the parade to criminal court. The guilty hid their faces; the people mainly laughed.

He stared across the room at the white-maned Speaker of the House, seated at a massive oaken desk raised behind the podium. Six-and-a-half feet tall, Walter Sutton was one rugged septuagenarian; he walked a little slower now, but his mind was sharp as a scythe. Sutton had never been indicted, which burnished his aura, and it was public knowledge at the Capitol how he savored life in the legislative season away from his wife on the farm.

Late the day before, debate had begun about an injection well in a distant town that was pumping oil-field waste deep into the ground. In some states it was illegal to use injection wells to eliminate muddied toxins and heavy metals left over from the petroleum rigs. Louisiana had 2,800 of these wells, plunging away, their place in the economy fortified via an army of lawyers fed by big oil.

A group of black citizens from the town of Avoyelles, where Governor Rex LaSalle had gotten his start, was irate about an injection well said to be polluting a trailer park. The accusation was perfectly plausible to Hubbell. The protestors had not contacted the Attorney General's environmental department, which was a statement in itself. Instead they had gone straight to the House, crying environmental racism.

So it was on the first Friday in October of 1993, before a chamber bulging with petrochemical lobbyists, that Speaker Sutton rose with the authority of his years and announced in honeyed baritone: "This water cleaning bill oughta fall under local control. Whatever, we goan take that up later. *And now …*"

And now the Speaker nodded to Representative Little Joe Du-

Bulio, who had crafted a bill that network producers assured him meant a national spotlight should it become law. Cameramen were in place to record the opening move. DuBulio would call for a $25 fine levied on anyone who assaulted a person or persons caught burning the American flag.

Because the bill had no provision regulating the degree of bodily harm on the flag-burners, an acerbic *Times-Picayune* columnist had proposed a schema: Begin with a floor fine of $25 for simple assault; a boost to $75 for a patriot who broke the jaw of a flag-burner; $150 fine for two limbs riven in democracy's defense; $300 for maiming; with a wellcap at $500 to punish full homicide.

As Hubbell had bolted out of sleep to compose his resignation letter, dreams of eros had dissolved into dread. What if some hothead lit a flag and got his brains kicked in? Sanctioning homicide was a cockleburr to these bill-crafting cavemen. With no report of a charred flag at any time on Louisiana soil, most members of the House saw it as an easy vote. Swatting off volleys from editorial writers and the ACLU, Little Joe DuBulio told the hostess on Channel Nine's coffee show: "We talkin' *values*. That's my position. Values."

DuBulio wanted one shot at the House. A straight up-or-down vote: pro-flag or no.

To DuBulio's moment the crowd had come.

Speaker Sutton yawned.

A Channel Five anchorwoman passed Hubbell, smelling good. He turned as the aromatic wave dissolved in the crowd.

Hubbell had the raw material for a good image: naturally white teeth, sandy brown hair and a six-foot two physique hardened by years of five mile runs, the composite sight of which made the Speaker of the House across the room fantasize about flaying him with a bullwhip. Sutton had despised his daddy. On top of that, Henry Hubbell had never, not once, given Walter Sutton a nod of recognition. Whenever Hubbell passed into Sutton's view, the Speaker was reminded of a show his missus had dragged him to see the time they went to New York, back during Nixon — *Man From LaMancha*, a musical about an egghead on muleback lugging a lance, singing about impossible dreams. One day Hubbell had locked the keys in his Mazda. The Speaker halted his limousine driver and gleefully watched the Assistant Attorney General pay a House page five dollars to pop the lock with a coat hanger. Avoiding Sutton's gaze, Henry got in his vehicle, cheeks red, and sped off. The Speaker roared with laughter.

Hubbell's aloofness signaled his disdain for men of the legislature. All that baggage plus his membership in ACLU made Sutton want to thrash him.

The Assistant Attorney General for Constitutional Affairs hung in the back of the standing room of the House chambers as he watched the real-time waddle of Little Joe DuBulio, five feet five inches, 235 pounds, dark strands curled over the gleaming bald head, a grandson of Sicily and the second largest Toyota dealer in the South, beefy arms squared at the podium, a man come to his moment, waiting for silence.

"Mist' Speaker," rasped DuBulio. "I rise to defend" — controlled cadence — "*the flag*" — eyes pan across the room — "of the U-nited States … of *Amurca!*"

"And shit on its Constitution," growled Hubbell.

"Hush-up, boy!" muttered an old man, elbowing Hubbell in a rib.

DuBulio paused for momentum.

Hubbell could barely move in the crowd. Scanning the faces of people in the balcony, he saw Reverend Christian Fraux, the mortician who owned a Negro ward in the town of Avoyelles. His father had been Fraux's ally in wars of legal principle long gone. Fraux, slender and silver-haired with mahogany skin, cut a dapper figure in his pinstripe suit. The scowl on his face telegraphed a stake in the injection-well debate dislodged by DuBulio's ascendance.

For months Hubbell had told himself to call Reverend Fraux, invite him to lunch. For some nebulous reason he had not. Now he wished he had.

"I thank God," puffed Representative DuBulio, "for mah freedom."

DuBulio's page and three secretaries applauded.

How many idiots does it take to elect a DuBulio? Hubbell wondered.

Perhaps God had forgotten Jefferson Parish, where the fat man held his seat on ties cemented to the mob.

3 REX IS DOWN

Speaker Sutton's telephone lights blinked through debates, and he enjoyed fielding calls above the din, especially from bookies on college football. As DuBulio hit his stride in oratory, Sutton's mouth opened in response to words from Mitchell Mudd: "It's fixin' to hit media right now."

"You are telling me that Governor LaSalle is positively, factually dead."

"That's correct, Mr. Speaker. I feel like a zombie my own self."

"Sit tight, son. I'll call you back."

Speaker Sutton engaged a tiny TV monitor at his knee and peered down as if through a telescope to a live shot of state police vehicles swelling the parking lot at the Governor's Mansion. A spasm hit his shoulder. The world was about to divide, and Sutton had to get ready.

"I beg pardon of the distinguished lawmaker at the podium," announced the Speaker, cutting off DuBulio's microphone with a button usually reserved for punishment. "Ladies and gentlemen, *silence!*"

DuBulio scowled at Sutton. A strange pall descended on the room.

"It is my tragic duty to inform all here that Governor LaSalle is dead!"

A huge gasp erupted from the floor and gallery seats. Then everyone began talking. Sutton pounded his gavel. "*Come to awduh! Come to awduh!*"

Decisions of a democracy tilt when the big man dies abruptly.

Sutton wanted to quote scripture but lacked the recall. Politicians scrambled for telephones, reporters poured into the aisles, and state troopers forced them back to the press table. Summoning the authority of his years, Speaker Sutton slammed the gavel with a crack. He ordered the Whip to beckon Senators from across the rotunda for a brief joint session "to honor Governor Rex LaSalle … a man of courage, a man of honor, a man of fair dealing, the man who made our state the *international state!*"

In the Speaker of the House, Hubbell suddenly saw an interesting man.

The constitutional line of succession began with Lieutenant Governor Hall, an alcoholic without parallel among his peers. Once known for traveling to ends of the earth for ribbon-cuttings, Hall no longer got invitations. His body toxicity made men hide in bathrooms when they saw him coming. One raw struggle was looming. Hubbell wondered how the Speaker would maneuver.

The next figure in the line of ascent was the President of the Senate, a porcine investment banker named Clifford Atchison who inhaled Pall-Malls and stalked legislation like a predator. Atchison was in court this very week on charges of extortion. Hubbell imagined the reverberations in federal chambers a few blocks away: Atchison's lawyers trying to elasticize time, stall testimony, keep the jury from deliberating so Atchison could assume the governorship. But Hubbell could not imagine the high Senator beating a jury vote. Atchison was tainted meat, his guilt a given.

Next in line stood Speaker Sutton. The Mansion was within his grasp — if Lieutenant Governor Hall could be dislodged, and if, as widely assumed, Atchison got marching orders to the penitentiary. Hubbell cracked a smile.

As the parade of eulogists passed beneath his hickory hammer, Sutton's moment-of-history frown belied a deeper discontent. The Speaker believed in obedience and money. The majority of both houses had years of debts owed to Rex LaSalle. The petrochemical lobby, now in hot caucus off the House floor, packed their money into officials approved by the Governor. Only a few of the clean land people spurned such largess and their votes counted little. In this vacuum, untold liabilities were building interest quick.

The Speaker coughed and sent his page for water.

His next telephone call was from the First Lady. "Amelia, he was my friend," said the Speaker soothingly, eyeing the clock that said 10:55 AM. "Such a magical man. Words can't —"

"*Walter.*" The Speaker sat forward. "Walter, give me your word that *no other soul* will hear what I am about to say."

"I make my business guarding privileged information." Sutton had his phone system swept for listening devices every Monday morning.

"He didn't die of natural causes."

"That's a heavy charge, Amelia."

"Oscar Abadie is in the Caribbean. Can you divert the press?"

"I can and I will. Now tell me what happened to Rex."

"What about Joe Hall?"

Sutton frowned at the mention of the Lieutenant Governor. "Man pee-pees Johnny Walker Red. What are you saying about Rex, Amelia?"

Her voice was steely: "I think he was poisoned."

Sutton swallowed. Before he could press her for facts, Amelia LaSalle ran on about people needing to "realize all the *good* Rex did." Sutton, who had accepted $37,000 from Rex in her presence, agreed that the FBI belonged nowhere near the situation "right now."

"Or ever," she shot back.

A long life had taught the Speaker how emotions flare when people die. "We're here to help," he said courteously.

"Nobody knew how much Rex had going on, Walter."

"I do believe that. You got to be strong for yo family, Amelia."

"Do something with the media."

"I'm fixin' to."

"I'll call you back." Then she hung up.

Sutton smoothed his eyebrows with a crooked finger. The last time he'd had an opponent from Ascension Parish was 1967. His

1991 election cost chump change: $155,000. A Governor had to raise staggering sums. Sutton wondered how much it would take to survive an emergency of this scope.

As the Speaker sat with resolute bearing, Hubbell watched men and women weep. Melancholy permeated the pitch and roil of the House floor. LaSalle meant something to these people, Hubbell realized. His own distance from the tidal sentiments made him uneasy.

At that moment, Sutton was glaring at Hubbell, fantasizing his skin bloody from the lash as dark wings circled above. A corpulent figure appeared at the Speaker's elbow: a glum Representative DuBulio. Shorn of his moment in media, he moaned: "Walter, what you thinkin' ?"

"Goddamn," muttered the Speaker. "Rex was a good boy."

People were streaming down from the balcony as Hubbell collided with Christian Fraux. "Rex was against that injection well!" blurted the undertaker.

Hubbell felt the paw of the Sergeant-at-Arms on his shoulder: "Emergency call, son."

"I'm sorry about your bill," he called back to Fraux.

Suddenly he was alone, in someone's empty office, holding a telephone, listening to Colonel Bellamy: "Tell no one and come *immediately.*"

Christian Fraux was gone as the bodies massed in the rotunda, rolling past elevators and phone booths, a stampede across marble that shoved Hubbell against a wall, tightening his abdomen. He took the stairway to the basement as people thundered into the parking caverns. Blocked vehicles, exploding horns and a cacophony of voices mingled with exhaust fumes.

State troopers cleared a swath for the towering Speaker, flanked by DuBulio in plump polyester and a man with curly straw hair and wire rim glasses whom Hubbell thought he recognized. Television crews sprinted up as the trio jumped into a limousine. A guard saluted the Speaker. His black vehicle rose into a sea of sunlight and disappeared from sight.

Hubbell cut through the basement past a blind newspaper vendor, huddled over a radio in his kiosk: "Lordy-Jesus … Not Rex!" He passed the folk display of saddles made in Eunice where each Mardi Gras masked men rode horseback through Cajun hollows. He stepped outside. The heat hit him like a furnace. Peeling off his coat, he traversed the long footpath past the lake behind the Capitol, making his way toward the Governor's Mansion. White pillars shimmered in the distance. Ducks in the lake napped in the shaded, oar-like roots of cypress trees. *Memory is a curse,* he brooded in the echo of Bellamy's "come fast …"

To the west loomed Exxon's petrochemical complex, an empire of pump stacks spreading smoke over land where remains of slaves sank deeper each year beneath the iron and concrete of a transmogrified sugar plantation. He moved in long strides, cursing the cycles of power that grind people down, perpetuating poverty as the lawmaking wheels roll on.

Three years of law in Cambridge, MA, do not remake a man, nor a decade more ascending in a venerable Boston law firm. Save the dough, quit and vault to juris *etudes internationales* at the University of Paris and Marie-Nicole, the best girlfriend of his life. A day carved in time: rock flats in a bluff overlooking Cote d'Azure, her glorious sun-pinkened bottom, his own proud nudity in the spent energies of afterlove. Twilight at the hotel WESTERN UNION AUX ETATS UNIS: YOUR FATHER DIED IN HIS SLEEP STOP PLANS ON HOLD STOP COME NOW STOP LOVE MOTHER. May 1, 1992, Feliciana, LA.

Marie-Nicole, attends. Je retournerai, cherie.

Twenty-four hours on trains and air bridges brought him back, wondering what did that man mean to me? Of course I loved him: he was my father, but no longer a full man after his stroke sundered my adolescence. He buried his society long ago. What is the value of truth when it mocks those who seek it?

"A man unlike others," eulogized the Episcopal priest. Hubbell stood with his arm around his mother, her elegant stoicism a counterpoint to his fidgety exhaustion. Henry lowered his eyes, unable to cry. "History revealed him a prophet," the priest continued. "Now he finds truth of a higher realm, and we ask God's blessings on his dutiful wife and son." *Am I dutiful?* he wondered.

Following the service, thirty people Henry had not seen since the eighth grade filled the parlor of their house, a raised white Creole center-hall on the National Register of Historic Places. Built in 1840, renovated in 1962, just in time for the revolution. His mother was positively radiant after years in the shadow of a great man gone to wheelchair. Greeting kinfolk and forgotten acquaintances, she was sleek in Navy blue. He saw her long silence lifting. The night before, paging through scrapbook photos, Henry inspected Forrest Hubbell's marriage, law career, himself as child-boy-man. Sepia news clips of the violent years: *Feliciana lawyer 'NAACP stooge' say House leaders.* Loneliness of the two people he loved most ebbed into all that he left behind.

He had forgotten the Southern custom of parties after funerals. Voices enlivened the old house. He realized the place needed a paint job. My father meant something to these people, he thought. He was doing his best not to come apart when at his side materialized Attorney General Oscar Abadie, a barrel-chested former blocking back at LSU, once his father's law partner.

"Your daddy was some fine man. For his sake, try not to be angry."

"Contemptuous is a better word. This state is primitive."

"Yeah, we got that. Plenty of decent folk, too."

Abadie draped his hand on Henry's shoulder.

"Please don't touch me."

Oscar Abadie removed his hand and gazed at the gazebo, mummified in green vines and Arabian jasmine, shaded by palmetto fans. Oscar's friendship with Forrest had been a backdrop to Henry's formative years. Then Abadie stopped coming around. Although the two men spoke by phone, the relationship became invisible, like the family's bonds with most people they had known before the civil rights movement. Later Henry learned that Oscar had extended a generous severance agreement when Forrest was felled by the stroke. Oscar stood five foot ten and filled his space like a sumo wrestler.

"I'd expect a man of your background to grant an older fellow the courtesy of a dialogue," the Attorney General said softly.

"Certainly," Hubbell heard himself reply.

The sagging flesh beneath Abadie's eyes betrayed his physical intensity. Henry did not remember him being so short. "Your daddy paid a supreme price for his integrity. Losing that friendship is the regret of my life. Most people thought of him as a firebrand liberal. Not me. Was he brave? Positively. He'll stay in the case law for that. He was also the most detached human being I ever met. Took me to lunch at the country club, sez: 'I've decided to represent the NAACP, Oscar.' 'Don't be a jackass,' I sez. 'Those people have lawyers.'"

Henry pictured his father, hair beginning to gray, breaking his news to the wife and son. *The Negroes need local counsel* — in no way preparing them for the ferocity of what was to come. "He drew out divisions of the law firm on an envelope," continued Oscar Abadie. "Felt like the wind knocked out of me. It hurt more when he quit seeing me. Things about him I had never appreciated. Over time, I believe we'd have patched our differences."

"He didn't know how many people were going to hate him," said Henry.

"Maybe." Oscar Abadie sipped his drink. "After the stroke I came here one Sunday totin' a ham, sugar-glazed the way he liked. Your momma thanked me up and down the porch. Said he wanted no company. Would not let me in this house. I wrote letters. Called. I tried, son. I seriously tried."

"Well, he was paralyzed."

Abadie let the comment pass. "As you get older, life presents more mysteries than solutions. Human beings *change*. And institutions react to people. This is not the state you left. A third of Rex's cabinet heads are black. We need intelligent minds to uplift this state. Come home, Henry."

"I have legal opportunities in France."

"You can earn big-league dough with a super firm. But will it make you a *better human being*? I need a constitutional expert. You can start at $75,000. That's fertilizer compared to Paris but the experience you'll get litigating against the Justice Department is a ticket to any law firm in the world."

The state and federal governments were fighting over severance taxes from oil revenues extracted out of beds in the Gulf of Mexico. Washington wanted the money. So did Baton Rouge. A cool billion slept in escrow.

Christian Fraux stepped onto the side porch, slender in a black suit, club tie, blue shirt and cufflinks as silver as his hair. "I hope I am not intruding."

"Rev, what you know good?" smiled Abadie, clasping palms.

During the violent years, Fraux had been one of the few periodic visitors at the home. "I have come to pay respects on behalf of many people."

"Thank you, sir," said Hubbell.

" 'Sir' makes me feel older than I am," the black man smiled.

"Everyone older is too old," reported the Attorney General.

From the living room came laughter, something Henry could not remember in his parents' house. Abadie gripped the rail. "So, Chris: is Assistant AG a good base for this young man's electoral career?"

"I don't want to run for anything," snorted Hubbell.

"You enter any campaign with two assets," said Fraux. "Downtown law firms would provide money, and black ministers would open doors to our folk. The hurdle would be young white people. Too many have gone Republican."

"I appreciate that, Reverend Fraux. But even if I had ambitions, I doubt that my father's reputation would carry weight among black voters today."

"Pentecostals and black folk vote with their preachers," reported Fraux.

"Thank God Catholics don't," affirmed Abadie, a pro-choice usher at Our Lady of Prompt Succor.

"Your father," said Fraux, "was one of the finest men I knew."

"Thank you, Reverend," whispered Hubbell.

Fraux gazed at pink crepe myrtle, tangled with honeysuckle. "I remember these aromas. I drank my first old-fashioned right about where we stand."

Henry's mother had prepared an old-fashioned for his father every evening before supper. For all his father's idealism, Forrest had not had many friends. Fraux winked: "The Attorney General needs a few good men."

"Amen!" proclaimed Oscar Abadie. "Amen, I say!"

A few moments later Fraux said his farewell.

"That man had no desire to walk into a houseful of white people," said Abadie. "He felt the call of duty. So should you. It'll take three years for our offshore royalties case to work up the appellate ladder. Every mineral lawyer in America knows we're headin' to the Supremes. We go to Washington, you argue the case. That's a promise. Your name in law books, just like your daddy."

Oscar Abadie handed him a card. "Call when you get back from Paris."

Six weeks of letters and transatlantic phone calls to the bosom of France. One son, one mother: foreign lovers wait only so long. Marie-Nicole ... *Marie-Nicole!*

He stepped onto a jogging path beneath oak trees that shaded Capitol Road and went, as instructed, to the rear gate of the Governor's Mansion. A car waited with a man behind the wheel.

4 REX IN REPOSE

At 11: 15 AM the First Lady sat numb in her bedroom. The weight of Rex's death cut hard. Pounding a velvet armrest, she wondered, what monster would kill a man over politics? Her secretary had located Oscar Abadie in Trinidad. It would be seven hours before the Attorney General crossed the Gulf of Mexico, and she wanted his help desperately.

She knew via a final conversation with Rex that Oscar was traveling with Doctor Nobby, moneybags to one and all. Nobby and Rex had been arguing and making up since college. Nobby's latest marriage was in a meltdown, which made him need Rex more than ever. Senate President Clifford Atchison, who loathed Rex, was on trial for extortion. What motive could he have?

"Nobby uses your name too much," she warned at lunch the day before.

Rex stabbed a crawfish from the *etouffe*. "Nobby's in desperation mode. Usually happens 'round the Alabama game. Starts thinking about his knee."

"Cocaine plantation won't fix that knee."

Rex nodded. He had few facial lines. Mild sunlight gave his face a bronze hue, lightening the auburn hair, flecked silver at the temples. He had a galvanizing grin on the hustings; his smile and upcurved eyebrows bespoke to her a cheery *can you believe we made it here?* His manliness was reminiscent of her daddy, Mayor Bobby Broussard, who had guided Rex's early career.

"I worry about the people Nobby wants you to see, Rex."

"Little Rompy," grunted the Governor.

The Rompallo family's vegetable contract for school cafeterias was a good piece of the rock. The arrangement had quietly passed down from one administration to the next, like oral history, preserving equilibrium with the mob. In a French Quarter warehouse, Big Rompy had built the South's largest tomato empire with ledger sheets shrouding topless clubs, landfills and control of video poker at seventeen-hundred truck stops. Rompy eluded FBI agents while his son Luigi Jr. prospered with a four-star restaurant and hands ostensibly as clean as they come.

Then, in a striking accident of law enforcement orchestrated by a small town prosecutor name of Joe Hall, the old man was nailed for bribing a rural sheriff. Big Rompy landed a five-year seat in the state penitentiary. In an even greater accident, Joe Hall ran around the state promoting himself as a mob prosecutor and got elected Lieutenant Governor. He had been drunk ever since.

"Little wants Big home for Christmas," smirked Rex.

"What is Nobby's cut if you let Big Rompy go?"

"I'm not supposed to know."

Amelia hissed: "You pardon Rompallo, Rex, and Joe Hall will

find an hour of sobriety for a press conference and all he'll need to harpoon you good."

"The infidel is at my door. A hunger loose upon the land."

"Rex, this is serious!"

"Day comes I can't control Nobby, pa-tooie: cut him out." He folded his napkin. "When people get too close, you build a circle, slow and quiet. Position yourself outside, then squeeze 'em till the grapes run dry."

Years of women had circled her marriage! All kinds he had pulled from coffee parties, rallies, even strippers off Bourbon Street about whom she learned from informants who wanted to hurt him, and so told her. As the media pounded Clinton for bimbo eruptions, she stewed about Rex's secret pages.

In happier times she had relished their carnal rites. Rex always put on music — Doo Woppers in their twenties, the Moody Blues in their thirties, Dr. John's lazy rasp as they forded middle years, laced by standby ballads from Elvis and Otis Redding. Alone in the bedroom, Rex pranced around like a ballerina, eliding into pirouettes; she'd laugh as he wrapped a yellow towel around his hip, knees pumping like a can-can girl, then tear it off and peel her down, massaging, nibbling, layering her with sensations that rose to his probes until she squealed, thighs thrashing and then they were all over the bed.

For months now, waters between them had gone dry. Her skin held a memory of the chill in his study the winter before last, heat from the fireplace drawing them close to the grill; they were wrapped on the rug as Arctic winds whipped the state on the coldest recorded day of the century. They dressed quickly as the logs ran to ash; he caught a helicopter to False River where National Guardsmen were evacuating people on houseboats.

His affairs, such as she knew of them, had materialized in the mid-eighties, after her daddy died. The prominence that once fed her pleasure ducts sated her less and less. And *Vogue* had just pronounced her "the most attractive woman in American political life" — an encomium earned by more than her well-kept looks.

The art works she had arrayed through the Mansion bestirred culture writers to praise her aesthetics. She owned a gallery in New Orleans which was making enough so that she didn't have to pilfer Rex's slush fund.

The erosion of marital love sent her into a trading frenzy. With the first two floors earmarked for the Mansion's permanent collection, she stripped the third floor of photographs by Man Ray and Cartier Bresson and a small John Singer Sargent scene of Venice; she flew to New York where she sold them for $480,000. She put $240,000 away for future buys and bought six Dogon masks, deep-eyed visages of a West African psyche. The austere beauty left her breathless. At night, lights down, she gazed at the sleek dark patinas of the masks in mottled shadows, the eyeholes glowing like tiny black planets that made her wonder if the spirits infused in the masked rituals had infiltrated her uncertainty, a self quaking to be set free.

The Governor's Mansion was a requisite stop for anyone seeking high office or regional gain. In an age of tabloid hunters, she met wives of governors, senators, congressmen and others who enjoyed the paintings and sculptures subtly lit on soft-hued walls of the public floors. When she showed her private collection on the top floor, the urgency of those carved faces moved women to share secrets of their own bruised alliances. She was buying more masks when the Associated Press in Montgomery reported an opinion poll of born-again Alabamians who had determined that thirty-eight percent of people in their state were going to go to hell. If Alabama's governor cheated on his wife, he sure as shinola knew the risk. From her own sample of spouses of the powerful, Amelia LaSalle concluded that seventy percent of political wives had cheating men, thirty-two points higher than the percentage of Alabama souls earmarked for eternal damnation.

Every woman knew that a display of teeth was part of the ticket: celebrity, big house, wardrobe, travel, intellectual stimulation or good works as desired, the power rush, parties to the wall. Amelia admired Hillary Rodham Clinton for fending off popular angst about the shifting gender roles in public life exacerbated by her husband's promiscuity.

Tribal masks opened a zone away from Rex, the hunger for something more authentic. The craving had come over her gradually as she poured through art journals, flew off on gallery visits, came home with more art. When the news broke that she owned masks, an upstate Pentecostal preacher complained about "heathen morals in the Democrat Party!" The story made the wire from a town of 2,800 souls and turned into national headlines.

"Get rid of the stuff," ordered Rex.

"Shut your stupid gubernatorial mouth."

With network TV crews in tow, she traveled by motorcade to the Rapides Parish church (the viewfinders pausing en route for shots of the sixty-foot statue of Jesus in the Big Woods), and in the preacher's pews she passed out masks for people to touch with their fingers. She did a PowerPoint presentation, comparing Renaissance icons and deities of the Ivory Coast. They gave her a standing ovation. "A cultural bridge builder," sang *The New York Times*.

She returned to a bedroom of roses from the Governor.

And an anonymous female on her voice mail: "Rex is doin' it with Joanie Charlot of Channel Five." She confronted him immediately.

"Don't believe dirty rumors," he replied.

"Are you claiming fidelity to me, Rex?"

"I'm claiming that message is false."

"What about all the other times?"

"There's never been a woman competed with my love for you."

Struggling to shape a new life, she brooded. *Marriage is like democracy, an imperfect state yet the most workable plan our species has devised. We are mammals. Men roam.* Still she prayed for him to come back.

Her own infidelity had come late, pulling her between surges of freedom and despair. Stephen had come from Chicago to run a gallery in New Orleans. He was installing a piece at Saks, Canal Place, on a thunder-pounding afternoon while she looked at maternity dresses for her younger daughter. Stephen had long eyelashes. When he suggested "a more earth color tone for a woman with child," she thought she would melt. They passed hours in a dark lounge, talking about art; he ruminated on his divorce, his move South and a new start, the son he loved off at college.

Five days later, with Rex on a hunt in the Yucatan, she visited Stephen's gallery. She took tea in his Royal Street apartment of exquisite taste. Through kisses and caresses that began gently, he touched her like a sculptor, molding energy from flesh, kneading spots that aroused her as if he had planted erotic memories, and when the shaking subsided, she began to sob. He held her quietly for nearly an hour. After each of their visits, she drove to an empty church in Prairieville; a young priest heard her confession. When, finally, he asked why she kept repeating her sin, she said: "I can't decide."

The reality of Stephen caused her to hate the decay of her marriage even more; yet she was unwilling to halt a journey into the interior, to some uncharted zone where a new way of living might find form. "That's when the dreams began," she told her psychiatrist a week before the murder. Rex beckons her to a mountain ledge; they dive like perfect shadows into an oceanic sky, a shimmering plane of liquid silver that pulls Rex toward a blinding light, her legs kick in scissor-strokes, *keep your head down, Amelia*, swept ahead by a school of dolphins that rock her, gently, as Rex dissolves.

"What do you associate with dolphins?" the therapist asked.

"Beautiful creatures I can't touch."

"You are saying something about your husband, no?"

"I've always been fascinated by dolphins."

"But in this dream what do dolphins suggest?'

"That I need a buffer."

Plugged into a Walkman, Rex danced in upper halls of the Mansion, grooving to zydeco. *He's thinking of someone else*, she thought. *But so am I.*

Amelia married Rex in another autumn, bedded in luminescent memory. Thunderheads pulled warm air currents off the Gulf, breaking into torrent lines that dragged across the southern parishes, flooding the wetlands cupping the coast. By the end of October, a dry cool had settled. The town of Avoyelles simmered with the sour-sweet scent from the syrup factory. Boys on bicycles trailed alongside the trucks laden with sugar cane rumbling past St. Joseph Square, past the bronze soldier's statue commemorating sons of the parish lost in two world wars. The highest stalks, dripping light, spilled onto the asphalt, making splayed designs beneath crunching tires as the boys on bikes scooped up the cane shards to suck them for the thick malt flavor.

Mayor Bobby Broussard and his wife Miss Della hosted the rehearsal supper at the big house with silver service, seven courses, Bordeaux wine, priest, kin and bridal party humming through a litany of toasts that ran on as servants brought coffee. Now the floor was occupied by Domainge Nobby, a big boy with slick red pompadour, boosting the volume on his transistor radio as Jake Gibbs punted for Ole Miss and Billy Cannon caught the ball deep in LSU territory, breaking through four tackles as Nobby roared, the uncles veered closer, Nobby turned up the announcer's stentorian bullfrog voice, the room hushed as Cannon hit midfield, churning past Gibbs in the sprint of his life when magically, like a sign from the gods, the stadium exploded and moaning sirens far from the feast filled the room via radio. Domainge Nobby erupted in a war hoop; his fist shot up, showering brandy on Miss Della's carpet: *Cannon scored! Tigers up! Sombitch that ole boy went all the way!*

Thirty years later, Dr. Billy Cannon, dentist of Baton Rouge, went to prison after burying counterfeit money at his horse farm.

Amelia heard a rap on the door. Then the voice: "It's me, Mitchell."

"You may enter."

He was twenty pounds heavier than Mitchell Mudd, the garage mechanic making $75 a week in 1966 when Rex hired him as a driver and won State Senate. His eyebrows were thick and dark, the rest of his face a mess from crying. Mudd sat on the pink couch from Sotheby's. "I don't know what all this means, Miss Amelia." He mopped his face.

"Who was she, Mitchell?"

"Who was who, she?"

"The floozy who killed him!"

"Miss Em, we don't know that. A woman? I don't believe it."

"Explain that damnable lipstick! And the cocktail tumbler!"

"My bet is, it's planted. You ever saw a woman up here?"

"Of course not!"

"Me neither." Mudd pulled fingers under his chin. "I got a weird smell in my nostrils. Whatever happened in there was a set-up."

And me sleeping in the next room, she thought with a shiver.

"What time did you bring Rex back?"

Mudd straightened. "About three AM. It was lights out."

"Retrace his steps from New Roads."

"Yes ma'am. First off, he met with the colored undertaker from Avoyelles."

"Christian Fraux."

"That's right. In the New Roads parking lot. They talked. Then we drove to the air strip, flew on to Baton Rouge. Stopped in Port Allen for a cockfight around one. He was fine. Then we come in." Mudd shrugged.

Her anger was on him like a searchlight. "He came in *alone?*"

"I'd never escort a bimbo up here. That's not only dumb, it's wrong."

"Your ethics are comforting. So then: who has seen the bedroom?"

"Me, you, Bellamy and the two medics. They won't talk."

"I hope not. Thank you for that." Mudd nodded. "Our priority, Mitchell, is to see that the Governor is given a proper wake and burial. In the meantime we have to find out who committed this hideous crime — and why."

"I am right with you."

With swollen eyes, Mitchell Mudd seemed a spent force; yet she resisted a show of empathy. Mitchell had helped facilitate Rex's sexual encounters. The tension between them lay coiled like a spring. With her, Rex had confided about money. For years she had shared with Mitchell Mudd a tacit corporate morality of protecting Rex, preserving power. Each knew things the other didn't.

"We need a plan, Mitchell. My freedom is limited."

"Bellamy called a guy in the AG's office. Someone Hubbell."

"On the line, Mitchell: you know where Oscar Abadie is?"

"Oscar went to Trinidad."

"You know who is with him."

"Doctor Nobby. Which means the Feds'll be tracking Oscar before he knows."

"Who is this Hubbell?"

"He sounds like a virgin. Bellamy thought it was better'n callin' FBI. I support him on that, Miss Em. FBI is vampires."

Two blunt thuds hit the door. She nodded. Mudd opened the door.

Colonel Bellamy saluted, crossed the rug and knelt by her chair. "Miss Amelia, I want to express my personal sorrow and the sympathies of everyone at the State Police to you and your family on the death of our statesman."

"Thank you, Colonel."

"The Bishop has come to administer the last rites of the Roman Church."

"Momentarily, Colonel. Please stand."

Bellamy rose and faced Mudd. "Mitchell, would you give me a moment of privacy with the First Lady?"

Amelia LaSalle's eyes trailed Mudd with a bead of defiance that made him look down in shame. His boss was dead. He turned and shut the door.

The First Lady stood behind her chair.

"Sit down, please, Miss Amelia."

The rawness in her eyes made Bellamy's sphincter tighten. A

woman like this, no telling how she will take to jagged news. "I've never been a man to mince words, ma'am."

"Don't start mincing for me, Colonel."

"Looks like he had female company."

He had gone to homes to tell people about kinfolk killed in automobile accidents and once about a little girl who drowned. He had never confronted the arched eyebrows and face of regal fury, which froze him at the knees.

"And?" said the First Lady.

"Lipstick is evidence. I think the Governor was murdered, ma'am."

She took her seat. "Sit down, Colonel."

He lowered himself onto the sofa like a pilot sinking into a cockpit. Feet apart, elbows on his thighs, he met her gaze head on: "My officer's oath says if somebody broke the law, I got to see justice done. Then again, I worked close to Governor LaSalle and recognize the need for a practical approach."

"I trust you will conceal details of marital intimacy, Colonel."

The Superintendent of Louisiana State Police wanted more.

"This is *obscene*, Colonel! Whoever killed my husband wanted to disgrace him and *I won't let that happen!* Finding out who did this is vital. But I won't be shoehorned. My priority is a dignified funeral, *and that* means no dirty press!"

"I would certainly want that part."

"What about this Hubbell?"

The topic shift caught him off guard. "Wull, he's Assistant AG. Went to Virginia undergraduate. Harvard Law. I only made three calls on him. Seems real clean. Episcopalian, speaks French. They say he's brilliant. His daddy —"

"Was Forrest Hubbell," she said in a synapse of memory, picturing the patrician lawyer who shocked people when he took desegregation cases and made his wife quit her membership in the Daughters of the American Revolution. Amelia remembered the national news: the tall, lean man with sandy-silver hair standing with Christian Fraux of the NAACP and US Marshals amidst roaring crowds at the courthouse. Rex, then a State Senator, muttered: "Guy knows the law. Which is a lot for our cavemen to handle."

She saw Forrest Hubbell's impact as Rex made his own subtle shift well before other politicians: quiet favors to the Negroes, money to the Reverend Christian Fraux. "One day this'll mean votes," said Rex after their covert meetings. Hubbell was paralyzed by a stroke when Rex swept into the governorship on a pro-oil, anti-Klan platform that surged with black support. The old man's last twenty years were silent.

"That's right," said Bellamy. "Forrest Hubbell's son."

"The Governor often remarked about your talents of command. Forgive me." She turned her head and choked.

Bellamy felt like an invader. "I'm sorry, ma'am. Real sorry."

Her eyes flared. "*Hubbell must be made* to understand that in this investigation he is serving *my family*, and that means keeping it quiet!"

"Well, with technical matters, criminal implications ..."

"Our task is to give my husband a fitting burial and preserve his honor."

"Miss Amelia, I told Hubbell that things here are delicate."

He felt himself breathe. Each time she spoke, the complexities grew more stark. He was relieved when she stood. He stood, too. "How long, Colonel Bellamy, do I have before the FBI breaks into my house?"

"Nobody's going to break in here," he bristled. "Soon as the Coroner issues cause of death, my job is to coordinate with higher-ups."

"You coordinate with me first. So we are waiting on Dr. Willoby?"

"He's on his way."

"I am concerned that those federal agents who sought to persecute my husband when he was alive will heap scorn on him in death. Rex LaSalle was smart, Colonel. But he had his enemies. In this state nothing is impossible."

"With all due respect, ma'am, if the Governor was murdered,

then by God we will use all available manpower to find the killer."

"Innocent people get hurt when power is abused. I want you to consult me before speaking with other authorities, Colonel."

Bellamy looked at the door. "Bishop Ott is waiting. The sheets are pulled over the Governor."

"Do we have an understanding about this, Colonel Bellamy?"

Bellamy sighed. "Yes, ma'am."

"Thank you. Please stay close at hand."

She was alone with the Bishop and her husband of thirty-four years. The Bishop extended his hands to her shoulders. She threw her face into his chest, screaming her sobs, biting his gold ecclesiastical chain, wailing her fury at God without actual words until the Bishop pulled back and turned her toward the window. They stared at the Mississippi River. He told her to breathe deeply as he invoked God's mercy on her husband's soul. She followed him in prayers, but all she could think of was dolphins.

BEDFELLOWS 5

Hubbell gave his name to state troopers at the rear gate of the Mansion and entered the waiting car. "Mitchell Mudd," said the driver, exuding body odor. Hubbell shook his moist hand and sneezed in the car chill as they shot up the road. A state police vehicle passed them followed by an ambulance.

Across the field of sun-starched grass he saw a car at the front porch out of which stepped a man with a black bag who was engulfed by news cameramen. Mudd eased in behind the big house. Hubbell followed him up the stairs. He caught a glimpse of white-uniformed Negro kitchen workers, peering into the foyer as the Coroner arrived, flanked by state troopers keeping reporters at bay.

Mudd moved along the narrow back porch and pulled Hubbell into an alcove. He locked the deadbolt and pressed a button. Metal doors opened, revealing a sign: *No more than four people at one time.* "Servants use this elevator," said Mudd.

Which Hubbell knew from its resemblance to the *ascenseur* that carried him to his flat on Rue Pascal the day he had returned for his belongings and made love with Marie-Nicole in a blue glow as the lights came on over Paris. He asked her to marry him. She shrugged: "*Mais, ta vie est dans la Louisiane, et pour moi, c'est ici.*" No, no, he cried: my life is not back there; it's here with you!

The elevator deposited them on the third floor of the Mansion.

Mudd led him down a hall lined with carved faces from tropical Africa and deposited him in the Governor's study, which had a desk, small bookshelf and long polished table. What kind of man is Bellamy, he wondered, and why am I here with him and this Mitchell Mudd? The TV showed pictures without sound: reporters surrounding the Bishop, with upslanted brow. Cut to Rex LaSalle's oath of office, First Lady holding the Bible, daughter Regina beaming.

Bellamy: "So. How'd a young man with your credentials end up working for the General?"

"Roots, I guess. When my dad, died I hadn't lived here in a long time. The offshore tax case intrigued me. I also had great respect for Mr. Abadie."

"Everyone respects General Abadie," said the Colonel. "And your daddy showed us all a thing or two about the law."

"I'm surprised you brought me in the back door."

"The time for bull shootin' is over," replied Bellamy. "I am speaking as a fellow servant of the law. Mitchell is here on behalf of the LaSalle family. This does not look like natural causes. We suspect a conspiracy."

Why are these people on the phone cursing you, father? Are you really a traitor to the South?

"I don't understand why you want me, Colonel."

"With General Abadie out of state, we want you to help launch an investigation."

"District Attorney sucks media," added Mitchell Mudd.

"The real problem," said Bellamy, "is that city homicide is not equipped for what we need: state-of-the-art site documentation and lab samples."

"That's the job of the FBI," replied Hubbell.

Mudd: "In this state politics is rough, only some people are more rough. General Abadie and the Governor were like brothers. I can certify that his political enemies were feeding the Feds a crock of dung about Rex. Read me?"

"You bet."

"The First Lady wants him buried right and proper. So do a bunch of folks who loved that man and don't know what we do about the body. We can't turn this over to the Feds without our own facts, and we cannot tell the media. A lot of forces are at play; we need a legal line and we need it fast. You with us?"

"Of course I'm with you."

With you because the moment was like no other on a life-curve out of an only childhood that had ruptured into adolescence as race wars flared and girls had daddies who would not let them be seen with you. Forrest was paralytic when his son drove off to UVA. The arc of life soared at Harvard: his father's name was in case law books. *You must have gone through hell down there, Henry*, a professor said. *Well we did, but things are different now.* Thinking: that state is an unnatural act with history. Stoicism will shield me from idiots of this earth.

Paris was his golden dream. Then the old man expired, and the arc pulled him back like a boomerang. His mother pleaded that he stay. She was serene now, welcomed back at the country club, with a gentleman caller for whom he was grateful. Bellamy and Mudd equaled the manhood of those who never let you around their kids. Whiskey in the duck blinds; poker games in hunting camps; righteousness of a blind Bible; a way of life built on black peonage.

Bellamy, jittery with Salem cigarettes. Mudd, oozing sweat. Take away the antique chairs, put these two in LSU Tiger Stadium of a Saturday night — hear the heels throttling steel, feel the mesh of liquored bodies. Only now their leader lay dead, and questions filled their space like acid rain. Mudd was an avatar of bellowing rednecks on TV news in his father's study. Security guards posted outside their driveway. Four years of holy war. *There is a heritage to uphold, son. A fund of liberty is our trust. Thomas Jefferson was a Southerner and we owe him a defense of the Constitution.*

But what do you want, father? That is what people ask me.

I want them to be civilized — ah, obey the law.

Mitchell Mudd was flushed: "Lipstick smudges ..." (Don't beat around the bush, Mitch: everyone heard about the governor's lust. Who'd ya say he was popping last night?) "... and so we have this problem with the body."

Bellamy: "First Lady thinks a political motive might be behind foul play."

The big man peters out with Revlon tattoos: any wife would call that foul.

"She wants to see you," said Bellamy, stamping a cigarette in the porcelain tray. "Mitchell and me got to meet the Coroner."

"Stay in this room," warned Mudd. "Reporters are crawling downstairs."

"I need to see the Governor's bedroom."

Bellamy folded his arms. "Let's walk before we run."

"Gentlemen, if you want me on your side I've got to see the body and scene of the death with my own eyes."

Bellamy hitched his hands on his hips. "This is a shock to Mrs. LaSalle and her family. Before you see things, she wants to meet you. I mean, there's a certain decorum at work. From her standpoint, you're a total stranger."

"Of course." He winced, thinking about his father.

Many years later he would retain a mental imprint of the gubernatorial study with duck decoys lining one wall. Above the desk hung the governor's BA and law degrees from LSU; photographs of Rex shaking hands with Carter, Reagan, Bush, Clinton, all signed. Smaller photographs of the state's Congressional delegation and scrawled lines under an older photograph of Senator Russell Long: "To Rex, Governor of the great state, and brother under the skin."

Another picture, cut out of *Life Magazine* and framed in gold, showed a beaming Oscar Abadie, hands on hips, tie askew, sleeves rolled up in a gleeful grin next to Rex in a deep bow with his arms outswept like Nureyev. Audience hands reach up for the two politicians along the bottom of the photograph.

"Envirement" was Oscar Abadie's tap dance. He had three staff attorneys who dealt with pollution cases, most of which resulted in modest fines to the petrochemical industries. In civil cases, the defense lawyers used stall tactics on poisoned plaintiffs; oil companies moved on to new dumps with fresh permits from another state agency, Natural Resources. Hubbell the constitutionalist had no role in the dispute resolutions which he despised.

From the gubernatorial window, he gazed down at the huge cypress trees dotting the lake that girded the Capitol. Two days earlier at lunch time a six-foot bull alligator had crawled up the shady slope, homing in on a picnic blanket where a secretary from Agriculture was making out with her boyfriend. The crunch of teeth on a box of Popeye's Fried Chicken sent the lovers screeching toward the Capitol. WBRZ TV's lead story that night featured the couple's breathless account of how the saw-toothed creature hauled the blanket down the slope; the camera tracked a trail of shredded cloth and cardboard shards to water's edge. The next day, from his office, Hubbell gazed down on Governor LaSalle and Colonel Bellamy standing by water's edge, Rex grinning, the Colonel pointing as state troopers roamed the banks with rifles and nets. "Gator Flees, Lovebirds Okay," read the headline of the *Baton Rouge Advocate*.

A large photograph above the desk showed Regina LaSalle: wavy black hair, starlet smile, Ralph Lauren bathing suit with *Miss Tri Delt* emblazoned on the sash traversing perfect breasts. He calculated the image was taken six years before his encounter with Primo Daughter, as clucking law clerks called her.

Poured into black leotards, sleek legs on a stationary bike, Regina magnetized iron-pumpers in the health club where Hubbell worked out. Affecting none of the cerebral traits he sought in women, Regina with brassy laughs and unvarnished sensuality had the subtlety of a boxcar. The night LSU lost to Rice 14-3 he discovered her at midnight, three sheets to the wind in the parking lot of an upscale body emporium called Bayou Fever. Searching for her vehicle. "Talkin' a silver BMW but some Mister Someone maybe left it at the stadium." He offered her a ride. She sank into his Mazda, exhaling Scotch: "I'm divorced."

"Ah —"

Babbling about the Tigers' turnovers all the way to her condominium, she invited him in and started shellacking his chest with sulfurous kisses. In his quest for meaningful love, Hubbell had cleaved to a quaintly chivalrous code, which that night snapped like frozen taffy. Regina punched a stereo button, igniting the *bump-bamm-bah-bump-bamm* bass line and then Mick Jagger singing "I can't get-no ... sa-tis-*fac*-tion." His eyes popped like poached eggs when she pulled off her dress, twirling the bra in a lasso of improvisation that pulled him toward nipples so plush he spilled across the bed, her tongue burrowed into his ear and he rocked to wiggles of an ass so glorious that at the supreme moment he let out a great Viking war hoop.

She passed out cold.

Spine tingling, buttocks drenched, he extracted himself as she snored — long, serrated brays that made him feel like a paparazzi on rooftop shooting movie starlets in topless sunbath. Yeah, whispered his inner child, but a photographer feels no guilt. He stood in a nimbus of confusion. Designer dresses were strewn across Regina's bedroom. The kitchen sink was clogged with Lean Cuisine trays. He tried to rouse her. Not a chance. He took a shower, got dressed. She was dead to the world. He hung two of her dresses in the closet. She had another fifty in piles. If he hung them it might leave a good impression. He considered leaving a note but decided he didn't want to leave any impression. He slipped out like a thief in the night. Since then he had seen her twice, at Bayou Fever, without making eye contact.

The Governor's bookshelf featured leather encyclopedia volumes, biographies of Napoleon, Huey Long, DeGaulle, *Profiles in Courage* and *Ducks Fly South*. "This state swims in caca," he muttered. A smaller bookcase next to the swivel chair contained two biographies of Elvis, a book on Cajun music and *Up From the Cradle of Jazz*. On the far wall hung photos of Fats Domino, Clifton Chenier and Aaron Neville with Rex LaSalle flashing full teeth in each frame.

The door opened and in swept a black-clad Amelia LaSalle, blue eyes watery and red. She extended a hand with refrigerator fingers. "Mr. Hubbell."

"Yes, ma'am."

She stood behind a chair of oak and leather with a gathering of emotion that hit him from the blindside. Governors sold off the minerals and served the state supine. Suddenly, he of all people, was facing the widow. Hubbell was transfixed by Amelia LaSalle, the dark eyebrows, high cheekbones and slow melancholy turn of her face. She was nearly two decades older than he and one of the most exquisite creatures he had ever seen. Regina was a bare reflection of the First Lady.

"Your father took a valiant stand when others were afraid, Mr. Hubbell. When his death was announced, the Governor told me, 'That man showed us honor.' I wonder what you think of honor."

"Well," he began (thinking: what manipulative skill!), "my father was a man of honor, but — "Her eyes waited, hungry for a reciprocity of pain, a hunger so demanding he felt almost naked. He wanted to shout *it's none of your goddamn business, lady!* but she was right there, listening. Some ineffable force was driving him toward her. "After his stroke the relationship lost vital elements. By the time I was sixteen, he was not very verbal. Civil rights showed me his virtue. It was the man in him I missed."

"I've only started missing my husband," she sighed. "He had his flaws, Mr. Hubbell. But Rex was a man of vision who led our state out of bad times into prosperous ones. He cultivated leadership in others, a quality few people appreciate. I hope you are strong, sir, because what my family needs will not be easy."

"Whatever it takes," he said manfully.

"Let's sit down. You tell me about yourself."

He took a deep swallow and began a verbal resume, assuming she knew some of it but wanted clues to his personality, body language, signs of who he was. "Mr. Abadie is on vacation, so when Colonel Bellamy called —"

"Oscar's not on vacation."

"You know more than I do."

"I need to know even more. Someone just killed my husband."

Her eyes brimmed. He had never seen such aching beauty. He searched her face for signs of fear, weakness, hints of fraud. "I offer you my condolences, ma'am. But I'm curious why you've turned for help to someone you don't know."

She stiffened. "I need someone outside the sharks."

"Is my boss one of those sharks?"

"Well, now." Her voice lowered an octave. "I would not classify Oscar that way. But it concerned me to learn he went to Trinidad for a transaction with Doctor Nobby. Nobby has a serious habit for trouble."

Her words hit him like hot water in the face. Oscar Abadie in a conflict of interest? Goddammit! He checked himself: don't draw judgments without facts.

"Yesterday," she continued, "the Governor informed me that Doctor Nobby's dealings had come under heavy scrutiny by Federal authorities. The same agents, I will tell you frankly, who hounded my husband unscrupulously."

"They went after him pretty hard."

"They pretty damn well did!" Her eyes narrowed. "People probe a man's life. They dig like dogs and find nothing to indict. So much fodder for the media. Some people get ruined. But not Rex LaSalle, Mr. Hubbell."

"Why are they after this Doctor Nobby?"

"Toxic waste, cocaine — something. Nobby's money is dirty."

"I can't believe my boss would help someone launder drugs."

"Nor do I. But whatever Nobby is doing in Trinidad is no good for Oscar, let me tell you that." She stared as if he were in a jury. "They are airborne and expected this afternoon. When I know more, I will tell you. In the meantime —"

"In all deference, Mrs. LaSalle: if you want my counsel, then we have to level with each other. Was Oscar Abadie's absence in some way linked to this?"

She was staring at the empty fireplace. He spoke more softly: "If you think people had reason to hurt the Governor, I need to know who, ma'am."

She turned toward him. "Tell me how you see all this."

He paused before her evasiveness. "I have not seen the body or the room. I understand an autopsy is under way. That should guide us." He took a breath. "It appears, or I have been told, that he had female company last night."

"How genteel, Mr. Hubbell. So it does appear."

"Ma'am, I know this is painful."

"*He never brought a woman into this house!*" Cheeks flushed, fists clenched, she cut across the room to the Governor's desk. "I won't stand here and claim Rex was at all times faithful. How many men are? But he did not flaunt — I mean, he cared for me, he loved me, and he was not cruel. Do you understand? Bringing some bimbo up here with me in the next room just does not compute. When I found the body, it was revolting enough. But this other part does not make sense. We shared the same bed many a night. He slept in the smaller bedroom mainly when he came in late. Or if we had a fight."

"Was that often?"

Her fingers drummed on a copy of the state budget. "Is it only the absence of a wedding ring that tells me you're a bachelor?"

"I would have asked, regardless. Yes, I'm single."

"*Of course we had fights.* Like every couple since Adam and Eve. I need someone to block the FBI and investigate. Whoever killed my husband had other things to hide."

"Like what?"

She wrung her hands. "I've been speculating all morning. I need facts."

"Is there any person you suspect?"

"He was sleeping with a tramp named Sophie Thibodeaux."

"You think she murdered him?"

"*Get that girl and grill her!*"

"That can be done. Tell me why Sophie Thibodeaux wanted him dead."

Her eyes closed in pain. "I couldn't say," she whispered.

"Someone must've had a reason. Who hated your husband?"

"State Senator Clifford Atchison. He loathed Rex."

"Atchison is on trial for extortion. The evidence is overwhelming. He's heading to prison. What would his motive be?"

"*I have no idea!* Get me information on how he died."

He backed off a beat. "I can get the best commercial investigating unit in the state. If we do it on the Attorney General's budget, the media will demand the findings. If you pay privately it will preserve —"

"How much?"

"This isn't my department but I can easily make the call. It may depend on what they find. Keeping people quiet can cost."

"You *are* smart. Good. If it takes twenty-thousand to line up your ducks then go ahead. Just be careful and move *fast*. What about your fee?"

"I have no desire to quit my job, ma'am."

"Who said anything about that?"

"But that would be a conflict of —"

The exasperation in her face stopped him like a pupil being scolded by a professor.

"Mr. Hubbell, can I trust you?"

"Absolutely, ma'am. But there are rules I have to live with. My job as a government attorney precludes moonlighting on private cases."

"I expect to pay for services rendered."

"Let's not worry about that, Mrs. LaSalle."

"Don't patronize me, Mr. Hubbell. Your job is to guard every shred of fact and report *only to me*. Strictest attorney-client confidentiality."

"Certainly. I've just never thought about fee terms because my job —"

"*If I don't pay you, then how can I trust you?*"

"I work for the *state*! We're on the same side!"

Her body was teeming with anger. "I need you to drop the rest of your life until this is resolved, be my silent hand and *keep the wrong people away.*"

"Like the FBI."

"Yes, sir. I am concerned about whether you can do what I need."

Hubbell leaned forward, elbows on thighs, fingers clasped. "I can do whatever I need to as long as you don't hide information from me."

"What do you want to know that I haven't told you?"

"How my boss might be implicated."

"Oscar's ties to Nobby are risky business. Oscar bore a heavy campaign debt. The banks had become impatient. After Trinidad, with federal agents burrowing in on Nobby, their interest in Oscar will follow right along."

"What were they doing in Trinidad?"

"All I know is Oscar needed financial help."

Hubbell scowled. "Explain Nobby to me."

She rubbed her forehead. "His knuckles are in everything: campaigns, rock concerts, oil leases, waste deals. He has a streak of wild charm, but he has greed like you never saw. No children. His fourth marriage is a volcano. Yesterday my husband told me Nobby has ties to the underworld."

"What kind of ties?"

"He mentioned the name Rompallo. The Governor said, 'Anyone who deals with the mob is a danger to state government.' "

"Meaning Doctor Nobby."

"That's right."

"What kind of medical practice does he have?"

"People started calling him 'Doctor' after LSU when he got involved with rock bands. He changed his name."

"So he's not a real doctor?"

"Oh God no."

"His first name is actually 'Doctor' ?"

"I believe so. No one calls him Domainge any more."

"Rompallo is in the state penitentiary at Angola."

"Rex said he still controls his operation from Angola. It was a passing comment, the kind we would have picked up on … later."

A vein throbbed, discoloring her creamy forehead. She folded her arms and shut her eyes. He resisted a wild urge to take her in his arms.

"I know this is hard, ma'am. What did the Governor say about Rompallo?"

"That his son wants him out of prison."

"What did they offer the Governor?"

"My husband did *not* traffic in prison pardons, sir!"

"Are you saying Nobby wanted the pardon for Rompallo."

"I'm saying I believe that, but I don't have proof."

"Ma'am, I realize the Governor had battles with federal agents over his finances. But the Bureau should investigate if an elected official is murdered."

"*Do you think the FBI knew nothing about the murder of Dr. Martin Luther King?*" she exploded. "Can you muster curiosity as to why this 'bureau,' as you so innocuously call it, is value-neutral about shipping guns to thugs in Latin America, while keeping a hit list on certain US public servants? We lived with that investigation for three years! They combed every line in my checkbook. Like being raped, young man! I'm sorry. The federal forces arrayed against Rex are not welcome in this house, and I am paying you to keep them out!"

"Are you prepared to testify in court?"

"I am prepared to say whatever is necessary to defend my husband's honor. I'm counting on you to keep it out of court. Right now I want to find out who killed him."

"Where does the girlfriend, Sophie Thibodeaux, fit in?"

"She works for zydeco musicians. I don't know what else."

"Are you positive she was involved with the Governor?"

"Too many people told me."

She turned to a filing cabinet, twisted a combination lock, withdrew an envelope and counted money. "Here," she said. "Ten-thousand dollars."

"I don't know that I need that now."

"Yes you do. It takes money to get things done."

She nudged him aside, and with a tiny key unlocked the top drawer of the Governor's desk. Inside was a tape recorder and earphones. "Every line in the house is secure," she said. "The blue button connects you to the conference room one floor below us. The red button is for record. Rex used ninety-minute tapes. The light flashes when the tape has two minutes before halting. The bottom drawer has a box of blank cassettes."

She laid the earphones on the table. "Lock the door after I leave. If Mitchell or Colonel Bellamy come for you, put the earphones in the drawer, lock the drawer and let the recorder run."

"Who's in the conference room?"

"Members of the legislature."

"You want to tape their conversations."

"That's what the red button does."

"You think these men plotted to kill your husband?"

"I don't know. But I need to know what they're plotting now."

She left him alone in the room.

Hubbell was dumbfounded. *The guy taped people — like Nixon!* If anyone knew that, the motives for murdering him multiplied. Using this machine was probably against the law. But she turned it on. She wanted clues about her husband, why he was murdered. That could be defensible in court … probably.

Hubbell hated lying. In the Governor's sanctum, he understood his task as concealing one layer of truth in advancing discovery of another. The realization threw his thoughts back to the eight years of sixty-hour weeks in Boston, poised to make partner in a big firm when he had a crock with the legalized mendacity of corporate life and packed off to Paris for higher studies on money saved and visions of teaching. By habit he researched all sides of a conflict before mapping his move — until an hour ago, when his long-held notion of life as a struggle against boredom evaporated with a phone call from Colonel Bellamy. *Why are you doing this? You don't really know these people.*

He was mesmerized by the First Lady, a voyeur to her struggle. If character is destiny, Amelia LaSalle was snared by an obsession to impose her will on a broken cosmos. His leverage lay with facts to be found in the bedroom down the hall. The stillness of the lake outside evoked a *deja vu* of his teenage years, a long melancholia relieved by reading. Now he was in the wings of a ripping human event. Here's a person in trouble. She needs the kind of help I'm qualified to give. The law is my weapon.

The earphones beckoned.

The photograph next to the Governor's desk showed a wild-haired Jerry Lee Lewis on piano, laughing.

6   ISSUES AND ANSWERS

Back home in Ascension Parish, Speaker Sutton went to First Presbyterian as political duty. Rarely did he contemplate God. Behind his limousine's tinted windows, Sutton sat in the parking lot of the Mansion. State troopers formed a wall between the car and the media. "I need it to be — spiritual," said Sutton.

"Somepin' like a prayer," agreed Little Joe DuBulio.

Representative Frampton, whose district encompassed half of the capital, hunched over a laptop. "Our time on earth is a brief transit," he proposed.

"That sounds good, son," said Speaker Sutton. "But keep it short."

Frampton's wire rims tilted down his nose. He scratched his curly straw hair and handed Sutton the printout. "Mmm," said the Speaker. "Good job." Sutton slipped the paper in his coat pocket. "Awright, boys. Let's do it."

At the driver's signal, a state trooper opened the door. Sutton stepped into the glare, raising a hand to shield his brow. DuBulio and Frampton followed into a storm of questions. As they disappeared from Hubbell's sight at the window of the Governor's study, he turned on the TV, which magnified their images.

"*Where is Lieutenant Governor Hall?*" called a reporter. Sutton ignored the smart ass. His hawklike gaze moved on the AP photo wire fifteen minutes later. Looming over DuBulio and Frampton, Sutton said: "A great man, a beloved leader has fallen. It was an honor for us to serve with Rex LaSalle. We come to pay respects to the First Lady." He paused. "I have a proclamation."

Hubbell watched Sutton withdraw bifocals from the pocket of his blue seersucker suit. TV made the Speaker appear more intimate and menacing. A wisp of white hair curled down his forehead. "The state of Looziana is in mourning," he asserted. "State workers are hereby dismissed for the weekend. All flags shall be lowered to half mast for a period of thirty days."

The porch of the Mansion bulged with people watching the Speaker. Flags of state and nation hung from the balcony, listless in the torpid heat.

"I have asked the President of lsu to cancel tomorrow's football game with Alabama," Sutton declared. He lowered his eyes to the paper in his hands. "We dare not question the Creator's ways. Our passage on earth is a short transit. I ask, all here, bow your heads for the man who built this house."

Hubbell searched Sutton's face for hints of guilt.

"Thank ya now," said the Speaker throatily. Flanked by DuBulio and Frampton, he trudged up the stairs through a volley of unanswered questions.

Sutton and his comrades joined other legislators in the foyer. Cars were flooding the parking lot. Sutton smiled at the stuffed leopard Rex had wangled out of the ambassador from Kenya; it was his favorite piece in the house. The men fell in behind Bellamy, lumbering up to a second-floor conference room.

"Miss Amelia asked y'all to wait here," announced the Colonel.

Bellamy left. Frampton shut the door.

"Coffee, Mr. Speaker?" prompted DuBulio.

"Not yet, thank you, Lil Joe."

One floor up, Hubbell marveled at the taping system. How many conversations had Rex bugged before making calculated appearances? He pictured the Governor, flush with covert intelligence, greeting smiles with a coy grin. Hubbell felt the dead man's presence like a silent partner. Frampton telephoned his secretary. Listening to Frampton's humdrum instructions made Hubbell feel dirty. Frampton, thirty-three, touted himself as "a moderate and darn proud of it." Hubbell prayed no one would discover him plugged into the nerve center.

Speaker Sutton pulled back curtains. To the east stood the thirty-four-story Capitol, the city's tallest building (by Huey's law, none could be built higher). Sutton's eyes ran along the ridge of chemical plants hugging blotched Mississippi docks. Pillars of gray-brown smoke from Exxon's vast complex ventilated a sweet blue sky. Across the Mississippi River Bridge, green flatlands stretched on toward Acadiana, where they would bury Rex.

Sutton tapped his pipe in the ashtray. A crowd of men sat at the long table. "Let's take stock," commanded the Speaker. "Woodruff, and you, DuBulio. We goan need a committee to raise funds for Joe Hall's retirement."

DuBulio took orders like a loyal German. Hubbell knew that DuBulio was close to Rompallo. Joe Hall had put the Mafia don in prison. In a strange way, raising dough to expunge Hall might help DuBulio.

"Joe Hall's my friend," purred DuBulio. "I help my friends."

"Me too," said Woodruff, close-cropped brown hair and medium build perfectly shrouded in a beige Armani suit. Woodruff's daddy developed shopping malls. Woodruff, who spent $20,000 a year on a speech coach, had emulated DuBulio with a bill coming out of committee that would empower local prosecutors to raid stores that sold immoral music on CDs and cassette.

"What kinda retirement for Joe Hall?" groused Frampton.

"End-of-today kinda retirement," retorted the Speaker. "If he wakes up sober, we're in pickled shit."

DuBulio snorted and put Equal in his coffee.

"Sounds right to me," said John Burns Logan in his trademark baritone. Logan was six foot three with piercing black eyes and fair brown hair. At thirty-nine, he was the richest man in the room. His law firm wrote prime mineral leases, and he woke up every morning with a headful of maplines and money.

Hubbell heard the cigarette lighters click like popcorn bursts. He made out voices perfectly. *Why am I doing this?* he worried. *Because you have to, or enemies may appear as friends ...*

"Maybe we can use Hall till next election," averred Frampton.

"His brain needs three months in dry-dock," said Woodruff. "That's why Rex let him run for Lieutenant. Nullify the threat from below."

"Woody's right," said John Burns Logan. "Hall is polluted."

"John Burns," said the Speaker. "I'ma need a short, intelligent letter of resignation for the lieutenant guvna."

"No problem," said John Burns Logan.

"Can we do this?" put in Frampton.

"Help him exit gracefully," smirked Woodruff. "Or — make him admit he's a Scotch addict, can't fill his duty in a time of tragedy for our state. Ha!"

"Shorter you make it the better, John Burns," offered Buzby, an independent oil driller from Avoyelles. Small, wiry, silver crewcut, Buzby smoked Merit Lights and loved the surrogate testosterone in deal hammering.

"No problem," said John Burns Logan.

Beaconfield, a CPA from Shreveport with bulldog jowls, blew a haze of menthol smoke and said something ending in "momentum."

"Wait!" fumed Frampton. "Hall signs that letter in a fog and wakes up without a job! He draws sixty-five a year as Lieutenant. It's a part-time job, for him even less. Still, he did get elected. And we stop his checks?"

"That's why he needs a retirement committee!" boomed the Speaker. "He should get some decent money here. Let's see. This is October. He was elected twenty-three months ago, means he's … Help me, y'all."

"Twenty-five months left," said Beaconfield, "comes to $137,500."

"Plus he's gotta buy into the state health insurance plan," said Sutton.

"Five-hundred a month," said Beaconfield. "You're talking another $12,500. Total comes to $150,000."

"Joe Hall goan need more'n dat," volunteered DuBulio. "He's puntin' out two years of pension."

"We'll grandfather him," said Woodruff. "Do a law for state officials hadda resign reason-a health setback, unique facts, bluh bluh."

"Woody's right," said Sutton. "Pension won't be a problem long as we give him a bonus to get the hell out. He's goan need two-hundred-thousand. Now Joe Hall got good money from Shell, BFI, Freeport, who-all last time he run."

The Speaker paused. "And we need to get this money *quick*. By supper time."

"You need money," reported DuBulio. "We need Nobby."

Silence fell on the imagined triangle of Little Joe DuBulio, the godfather Rompallo in the state pen and the bearish Doctor Nobby.

Sutton scowled. "I don't want Nobby on this. No way to control him. Do bidness with Nobby, everybody knows yo bidness."

Nobby is stronger than Amelia let on, thought Hubbell. *Sutton fears him.*

"Awright," said Speaker Sutton. "Frampton, I nominate you as chairman of the finance committee for Joe Hall's safety net."

Frampton tugged at his bow tie. "I don't like the smell of it."

Goddamn right, stewed Hubbell. *I voted for you, Frampton.*

"Frampton," said the Speaker, "if you can't run with the big dogs, then stay on the porch."

"And if you do," piped Buzby, fingering a fountain pen, "I know certain oilmen, teachers and union folk who paid good money to put you in the House, brother Frampton, and they'd be some sad to see your bills go poo-poo."

Woodruff intervened. "I second the nomination of my friend Frampton as treasurer of Joe Hall's retirement committee."

A chorus of voices backed Frampton.

"Awright," said Sutton. "Frampton needs men to help squeeze money."

A barge floated down the Mississippi with a foghorn blast. Hubbell tried to picture Frampton's complicity. Did he nod, smile, tell his wife in bed tonight?

"Question," said DuBulio. "We knock Hall out, who's Governor?"

"The constitutional line of succession," said John Burns Logan in basso profundo, "goes to the President of the Senate."

"Whoa!" exclaimed DuBulio. "Atchison's goin' down next week."

"Atch becomes Governor," chuckled Buzby, "he'll fight that conviction!"

Laughter erupted. Every man in the room detested Clifford Atchison.

"After Atchison," continued Logan, "comes the Speaker of the House."

Hubbell pictured the men: coffee, ashtrays, gravitas bearing down on hunched shoulders. His jaw dropped as Sutton said: "I don't want guvna."

"Constitution says you got to take it, Walter, " hissed Buzby.

"I wear a pacemaker. I'm near eighty. I don't need guvna."

Woodruff cleared his throat. "We need Walter as Speaker. Atchison's conviction'll throw the Senate up for grabs. We can't be scrambling for a new Speaker, a new Senate Prez, plus a governor.

That's chaos. Next week we face a bill to outlaw injection wells. Crazy bill like that passes, I know some silver-dollar lobbyists who will target all our gonads."

"I don't see the connection," said Frampton.

"He's talkin' about Atchison," sneered Buzby.

"I sure am," said Woodruff. "Atchison sank heavy campaign money into five state senators. We know he extorted contractors to give those five boys dirty money. His lawyers won't let him take the witness stand. Once the jury votes to convict, Atch will grovel for a reduced sentence. When those five senators go to the grand jury, you're looking at a line of Fifth Amendment dominoes."

"Goddamn," said John Burns Logan, who paid for his own elections.

"Hold on," said DuBulio. "If the senators haven't been subpoenaed to testify against Atch, why would they be called this late?"

"US attorney is laying groundwork for perjury," said the Speaker. "Feds are stretchin' the investigation to see how high the money reaches."

Several men coughed. They hated talking about money. It was more private than their sex lives.

"But if our friends don't know how Atchison got the money he gave them," reasoned DuBulio, "they've committed no crime."

"Plenty people get indicted for things they don't know," said Sutton. "Each one of those guys will be lookin' at three-four-hundred-thousand in attorney's fees. And media coverage will be awesome. You can't predict behavior when a man *knows* that the folk back home are watchin'. Most days we snuff a bill, it could be in Bostwana for all people know. These senators are on Natural Resources committee. Anyone of them takes a powder on a hot vote, it opens the gates for every goddamn clean-land bill you can invent."

"They're already sweatin' blood that Atchison won't spill his guts before the conviction," said Woodruff.

"He don't have guts to spill," snapped Buzby.

"He would spill," said Beaconfield, inhaling a Salem, "for a lighter sentence. Federal judges can be mean."

"Goddamn," said John Burns Logan.

Then DuBulio said: "Atch can't afford to spill."

Silence followed. Everyone knew DuBulio was the mob's man in the House. His words telegraphed some implicit linkage between the indicted senator and imprisoned Rompallo. Hubbell wondered what Atchison owed the mob.

Woodruff refocused. "A floor battle to elect a new Speaker means the clean-land people will close ranks with the born-agains. Those Jesus people vote like sheep. When we were dealin' with that abortion crap, I had preachers calling me till midnight. We lose Walter as Speaker, you talkin' civil war in the House. The Senate'll be hemorrhaging without a President. Plus five votes on the Natural Resources Committee — those boys who took Atch's money — goan be peeing in their pants. Bird-lovers'll run radical bills while we're fightin' over a Speaker to please the born-agains *and* the Afros. You talkin' pollution editorials, national press and the Sierras carryin' torches at midnight."

"That's not a healthy bidness climate," said John Burns Logan.

"Tell me," said Buzby, animated by the constitutional issue, "how do we do an end-run on the succession?"

Beaconfield lit another Salem. Logan gazed at the towering Capitol outside the window. Frampton checked his watch. DuBulio waited for more.

"We do a state of emergency bill," said Woodruff. "The House, more than at any time in our state's history, faces a crisis of unprecedented scope."

"Civil War was worse," smirked Frampton.

"We might could change that," Woodruff huffed.

"Pass coffee," said DuBulio.

Woodruff continued: "We accept Lieutenant Governor Hall's resignation with sadness. We suspend the legislature till Atch's verdict. Absent a full acquittal, we cannot accept him as Governor. The Speaker has unselfishly offered to remain our leader in this crisis. The legislature will select an interim Governor until an election for Governor and Lieutenant Governor."

"You forgot to ask for the Crown Jewels," chuckled Buzby.

"Oh fuck off, Buzby," growled Woodruff.

"Calm down," said the Speaker. "We can change words as we go along. Let's get the basics nailed down fuhst."

"Mister Speaker," said Frampton. "I agree with all that you wanna do. I'm just powerful concerned about the legality of it."

"We can do it!" exclaimed DuBulio. "I know we can!"

The assumptions of wealth gave John Burns Logan a serenity during emergencies. His parliamentary prowess had exterminated countless bills seeking regulation of the petrochemical industry. When Logan spoke, which was sparingly, people listened: "The wake and funeral mean we can't convene till Monday. My recommendation would be Tuesday, Walter."

"So ordered," said the Speaker.

"The state Constitution," resumed Logan, "has a clause saying that the line of succession follows, unless — here's verbatim, Frampton — 'there should arise illness or dire provocations.'"

"When they wrote that law?" interrupted DuBulio.

"Eighteen seventy-six," answered John Burns Logan.

"They didn't pay nothin' to be Governor then. Now, it's a good payin' job."

No one responded. DuBulio blushed.

"What the Sam Hill does 'provocations' mean?" snorted Buzby.

"The footnote," continued Logan, "talks about 'interventionists at bay in these proceedings.' Carpetbaggers trying to dominate a succession crisis."

"Reconstruction!" cried Frampton. "A black US Senator and ex-slaves controlled by Yankee moneymen. The framers needed leverage, just like we do."

Logan: "I'd say we need a definition of 'dire provocation' to match Woodruff's motion. Walter turning down the governorship could ignite an impeachment call — failure of the Speaker's oath in upholding the line of succession."

"Nobody wants that," said Woodruff quickly.

"No, no, that'd be bad," said DuBulio.

Clutching the earphones, Hubbell tried to imagine the men's eyes. Any one of those bastards would love Sutton's job.

A weird sensation of warmth crept over Hubbell. The loneliness of his personal life was melting in a furnace of emotions all around. The system he despised had suddenly exposed a drama of tearing loss and craven appetites. Listening to the politicians made him eager to play his own role, beat them at their game. In an odd way, he felt happy.

DuBulio shook his fist. "It damn sho *is* provoked when Rex is *dead*, Hall *quits*, Atch is goin' to the *pen*, and Walter *don't want the goddamn job!* Now that's *mighty* fuckin' provoked in my book!"

"John Burns is talkin' about the language," hissed Buzby. "How do you pee in a bottle and sell it as champagne?"

"Media's fixing to eat our lunch," muttered Beaconfield.

"Not if we give them Hall," said John Burns Logan. "You saw those reporters outside. They want raw meat. They know Hall's a drunk. We throw him down, they'll carve him up for barbecue. If we have the votes, the news will play out."

"Niggers and the bird-lovers goan raise bloody hell over this," said DuBulio. "Fuckin' ACLU, too."

"Let them," rejoined Logan. "Our enemies don't want Walter to become Governor. They'll be fighting a *process*. Does Walter bear an onus for unselfishly denying himself a position most politicians covet? Won't wash. If we sacrifice Hall, we deny the opposition a clear target and protect our flanks."

"That word 'provocations,'" considered Frampton. "We better be dead on the money with that definition."

"Meantime," said Sutton, "we need to find the right man for guvna."

"It's gotta be somebody we can trust," said DuBulio.

The air vessel rose into noontide sky and Nobby looked down on Trinidad, biting his lip to stabs in the right leg. Curse of an interrupted man. Silver-spangled tin rooftops receded into a mass of palms. *"Red sails in the sunset,"* came Fats Domino's sugary tones on his earphone. *"Oh, carry my loved one ... hooome to me."*

Music is the sovereign antiseptic. Nobby carried the Fat Man on cassette in his briefcase: Jerry Lee, Dr. John, Gloria Estefan, too. When you're three-thousand feet high, painkillers gobbled, no reefer or blow, Jack Daniels must service the throb where surgeons restitched his knee strings. That was October, his junior year at LSU.

Listen to those ivories syncopating, hear that magic voice! *"Yes it's me and I'm in love again —"* Rolling time back to Tri Delta chickywawas singing on Amelia's sorority house porch, night before the Bama game. Luscious girls, rockin' to Fats Domino records, and Rex-the-ever-nimble conductor leading one serious meat block of chorus boys (two guards, two tackles, plus Nobby), singing: *"Ain't had no lovin'"* — reach down low — *"since yuh-hew knowww when!"*

Waves beneath the airplane rippled out in emerald billows.

The night after the Tri Delt songfest, Domainge Nobby, six-foot three tight end ("magnet hands" Coach called him) soared toward stadium lights. Reaching for the twirl of the pigskin, riding a roar of sixty-thousand Tiger fans, he heard them gasp at the *crack!* of a red Bama helmet that hit him midleg so hard it sounded like a cherry bomb up in the press box. He lost the football.

Out of the hospital, the big boy was on crutches for six months.

"You go back to moments like that," he ruminated ten seasons later (night of his thirtieth birthday) with a bass player's chickywawa curled in the crook of his arm, "and ask yourself how life might've turned out for a pro ball player." Loins glistening under the whir of a ceiling fan in the deluxe suite of Nottoway Plantation, they sipped champagne. The silver bucket stood by the satchel holding seventeen-thousand fraternity row dollars chained to the bed.

"Way-ulll," she said. "You do pretty good bookin' bands, I'd say."

He pictured the bass player cursing over his vanished chicky-wawa. "The Rhythm Doctor never sleeps," he hummed. "Everybody needs a doctor, sugar."

"Do it to me again, Nobby."

Nowadays his silver hair was so curly that bad heat melted the pompadour into a Medusa's mane. A trail of cobalt light danced along the wing outside his window. Positioning his stogie in the ashtray on the armrest, he poured a toddy from his flask. He still hit the big concerts (had his photo taken with Elton John at the Superdome), and when the bass lines bulged and percussions went to rolling, Nobby would stand and clap, meaty elbows moving like an accordion, shoulders slanted as the good knee swayed to the beat of the band.

The other passenger, putty-faced in a white linen suit, came out of the john into the cigar fog. Oscar Abadie slid into his seat across the aisle.

"You got the turistas, General?"

"What I got they got no name for."

Bearer of bad tidings, stewed Nobby. *Serves you right.*

Abadie peered out the window. "How far to Yucatan?"

"Fifty minutes, General."

"You could kill someone with those cigars."

"Tobacco never made a rich man po."

"Until it hit his lungs."

Nobby coughed without irony. "They packed us a whale of a lunch."

"You start. I'll eat when the air clears."

Nobby stuffed out the stogie. "Mm. Stuffed chicken ... stewed plaintains ...Those're good people in Port-Au-Spain."

Abadie stared at Nobby. "I miss Rex somethin' awful."

Nobby opened red wine. "Me too."

By the time Rex made Governor, he had learned the value of music. *"We need each other as silent partners, Nobby."*

Come midnight Rex would saunter into a club, hair slicked back, wearing pointy sunglasses, gyrating like Elvis in his own contained space. They'd duck into a back room and divide the money. Nobby sweating like a horse, Rex grinning while some new girl waited outside in jeans so tight it looked like her thighs were sewed into them. *Politicians can't birddog today cuz press is in yer underwear. Look what they theowin' at Clinton. Rex was a genius at disguises.*

The big boy was running rockarolla bands from Lafayette to Biloxi when Rex guided him into landman work: negotiating rights-of-way for drilling leases in the oil patch. But Nobby wasn't rich on accounta those jelly bean leases. In time he saw the drillers had a problem: where to put the crap left after they drilled.

Arabel came along when some damn woman divorce lawyer was hunting down his money. Arabel pulled his lever up and down the Gulf Coast. In Port Arthur they broke a bed in a Days Inn. Sex solves a lot of problems so long as it's not creating new ones, and Nobby knew how to hide money. He put one big diamond on Arabel's finger. Fourth time you better make it good, boy. Arabel was heavier now, and truth be told Nobby was no Cupid on tiptoes either. Arabel been sayin' quit cigars, bleach the teeth. "Polish yer image, tootie."

Arabel, his best wife.

Attorney General Oscar Abadie shut his eyes and woke up to cotton-mouth. Nobby was snoring with his teeth and throat exposed, wine guzzled, the empty plate on his lap. Abadie scowled at him before prying a Coca Cola from Nobby's ice chest, trying to ward off sensations of vine growth in his intestines.

"Hey, Nobby. We're startin' down."

Doctor Nobby stretched. "Don'tcha think it's hot in heah, Gen'ral?"

Abadie said nothing. When they landed, the Attorney General

wobbled down the stairs onto the tarmac of the air strip at Quintana Roo.

Nobby popped open his briefcase, removed an alligator-skin address book and adjusted the Walkman. *I'm walkin till you come back to me!* Sing, Antoine. *What you gonna do when the well runs dry?*

Nobby limped toward the lobby, cogitating: *Injection wells are the answer.* EPA was onto landfill dumps. A week earlier Nobby did tell Rex: "We need Senator to pass us a bill in Washington, secure injection wells for time immemorial. Erect an injection well in the lobby of EPA. A shrine to free enterprise type guvment. Give those boneheads up dare somethin' to drink coffee from."

Rex laughed. He was so proud. Their roles kept changing.

If pressed, Nobby would say that, yes, Rex helped me substitute rockarolla money for football dreams and then oil patch for rockarolla. But Nobby did his own quantum leap into the big money: making oil waste disappear.

"If everybody made a wholescale conversion from dumping pits to injection wells," he told Rex at the Mansion, "you wouldn't hear the farmers and bird people squawk after it rains."

Absorbed in a Zydeco Flames CD, Rex nodded.

"Pits overflow," Nobby declared in Trinidad. "With an injection well, you push the goo down so deep, the cows won't get sick. Grass don't die neither. Nobody's come up with proof to the contrary. *Don't kill cows no kinda way!*"

Black men with British accents, big time politicians on their soil, they looked at him until Oscar Abadie said, manfully: "Doctor Nobby means that these wells are scientifically tested. We are moving in that direction in our state. We have a lot of wetlands and marsh to preserve. Y'all have beaches and rain forests."

The men in Trinidad bought five injection wells. Oscar the envirementalist. Pfft! Rex had star power, woulda sold 'em ten. Still, Oscar put those Trinidadians in a comfort zone. Oscar wouldn't win prizes for a weight-bearing brain, but he knew how to impress muckety-mucks.

Between meetings, Oscar sat by the hotel swimming pool and

read the *Wall Street Journal*, erecting a wall around himself like he was a country club. But Oscar wasn't old money. Hell, if Oscar had scratch he wouldn't be lap-dogging in Trinidad. Which supported Doctor Nobby's creed: Money is the great leveller and the great protector. It makes the high-born and low-born come up equal. A man must use money as a tool to make more. It don't matter if your money is young or old: it's what a man does with the money to make it procreate.

Suppertime last night, Oscar turned quiet. Back home, he's such a newstown whizzer. Nobby expected a real spokesman for free enterprise type guvment. But Oscar *turned down the dinner invitation* from the guvment people in Port-Au-Spain! Said he had jet lag. They did not extend a solo invite. Oscar was the dignitary. Next thing, back at the hotel, in the grill off the swimming pool, Oscar sipped Scotch, poked at his swordfish. "Nobby, I don't like having to moonlight."

"Shut mah mouth, Oscar. Here I bring you forty-thousand potatoes for a quick tripa smooth talk with tropical Negroes, and *you don't like moonlighting?*"

"America pays public servants too much like servants."

"That's what yer friends are fer," smiled Nobby. "Every man needs a doctor, Oscar. I'm yo doctor."

Abadie gave a lame grin. It was Nobby's first sustained exposure to the Attorney General, one on one. Oscar was way more quiet than he had imagined.

After supper, Nobby went jiving down streets behind a steel drum band to a club where they danced like no tomorrow. Everybody was black. He picked one in a red dress. A young, full-breasted woman. "Dating?" said she. He: "After the roosters." She ran a finger down his thigh: *oh* that felt good. "Roostahs?"

"Cockfights," he said. "Show me where."

She took him to an old half mansion turned into a B-grade hotel. Vines in the shutters, a lizard slithered across the lobby. In the parlor, two coffee-colored women played cards with an Afro giant who trained his eye on Nobby. The galpal at Nobby's side whispered to the giant, who led them out back to a corral, and you could smell the money. Men bunched together along a rickety fence, watching the flutter of feathers and bloodspew screech as the loser bird went down.

Nobby's daddy had disappeared when he and his momma went to live with Uncle Dudley. Dudley never went to church, but he did take the boy to cockfights. At LSU Nobby took Rex to cockfights, hooked him like a trout.

Trinadadian man with shiny gold teeth had a winner cock. Nobby watched it demolish two tough roosters and bet fifty dollars against him the third fight; the bird went down and Nobby won a hundred dollars on the spot. They did not like that much. He made like he had to leave. Goldteeth man said: "How much, Mistah? Betcha some big money, see what you do this-a time." Nobby gave him two-to-one and bet another hundred. A smaller bird on razor-wrapped ankles spun like a trained ballerina, slashing the other into screaming ribbons. Lo, Nobby won again! *Coal Black Missy in the rose dress looking now like my name is Trump.* Somebody swept up the bloody rooster, and they rolled out a blanket. *Man with the dead fighter cock crackles dice, asks do I play, I say yay. Put down a hundred: other dude lays down so many bills so soggy it coulda been less, anyway I lost, which prob'ly was good because in a foreign country you can't be winner take all and expect to feel safe.*

It was time. She took him upstairs to a room with a mammoth bed and wind-billowed curtains, and shut the door. He stuffed five twenties down her bosom. She counted quick while he unzipped her and began pawing those melons, got hot quick and lay down nude. Sky outside blacker than a million barrels of oil.

"You don't move much, Mistah."

He sat up and spread his legs. "I pay you for that."

She started licking his thighs and he felt la-la-la *Good God almighty a cock's beak slashed the moon.* Nobby laughing as blood burst across the sky: a wheel of fire charged his body, rolling him around and around. He shut his eyes, heat pouring out of him like an electric river, but the bleeding moon was too painful to watch.

He lay on the bed, panting, a hand on the floor. She went to the washstand. Brushed her teeth. "D'ya see the red out thar, gal?" Her gleaming ass turned to the window. "No-ho," she sang. "I see black sky and a fat moon."

He told her you can build an injection well for three-hundred-thousand and work your payments from day of delivery of the first waste. Because a good injection well will bring fifty-thousand a month. Fourteen months' good bidness and you are clean amortized. After that, gravy. (I doubt they'll make money that quick in Trinidad. For one, guvment's involved. Number two, they need wider roads for the vacuum trucks. The big sixteen wheelers.) Eight trucks haulin' to one of my Looziana wells equals twenty-four-hundred a day, net.

"I don't know about those things, Mistah. Time to get movin' now."

"There's talcum powder in a lil envelope by my shoe. Dust me real nice."

"I can't make you feel clean, Mistah."

"I'll pay you twenty more."

Damndest thing: a whore turning down more money. Her clacking heels emptied down the hall. He washed, powdered, dressed and went to his hotel.

With injection wells, he told Rex, "Shit won't come up in our lifetimes."

"Maybe so, Nobby. But it ain't an investment for me."

Truth be told, a pipeline was the most profitable way. Spend more up front, he told Rex, but you're talking primo profit down the stretch. Tough part is your leases: negotiate each landowner for a strip of turf to run contiguous with the pipe tunnel. "Rex, you sold that big pipeline cold brilliant."

"Yeah, but natural gas is our state's product, Doctor. Sticking a toxic waste pipeline under folks' land is a scheme out of Dick Tracy."

"Follow the existing pipeline! Lay another one fifty yards away. Double-trunk the sucker! Renegotiate leases with the same people. Save *beaucoup*."

"But there's *natural gas* in those pipes, Nobby!"

"It's all in the control of yer flow, Rex. See the engineering specs. They guarantee the pipe casing. Plus, on this deal here everyone's insured."

"Insured? One burp from your commode pipe and we blow up a pasture full of Farmer Brown's cows. Two hundred insurance companies can't re-elect a politician for ruining a man's land."

"Won't happen, Rex. This chipahoona flies under radar."

"Sorry, Nobby. It's a dirty lollipop."

Nobby smirked. It was all so simple and so brilliant: a pipeline to dispose of toxic poo, routed along existing tunnels of the natural gas pipeline, Rex's signature industrial achievement. "Podna, this will pull two-hundred-thou a week. Minimum. Your pipe casing is fortified, guaranteed secure. These engineers aren't like lawyers. They do real work. Chemists monitor everything goes in them pipes. It's all in the control of yer flow. You build a fan of pipes and shuttle the glunk by computer. You're lookin' at sixty-seven miles as the crow flies to reach the discharge pipe at Burnside."

"Where?"

"Ascension Parish."

"I carried that parish twice. Why make it the anus for a dump line?"

"It's just the leftovers. You burn the worst stuff in the big incinerator."

"Tell me where the leftovers go."

"Miss'ssippi River. Where all them refineries dump anyway. Look at these blueprints, Rex. It's all in control of your flow. When the incinerator complex runs at full volume, you're discharging the grease, not the lard. That's way less bad than what-all they are crappin' into the real estate today. On that I agree with the Sierras and bird-lovers: too many landfill dumps. So what you goan do? Two choices. Stuff it underground with injection wells. Or burn the poo into smoke. You shuttle waste from the other plants to this big incinerator, pump effluents into the River. It's a filter system by fire. It'll earn you a million a year."

"I don't have enough illiterates in my base of support."

Nobby had to laugh. Rex knew how to deal it back. "All right, I just want you to think about it."

It's wrong to pressure a man in yer preliminaries. Meantime, he told the Governor, think of this other thing here. Rex looked at his watch. You had to have the numbers down waterproof to keep his attention. Rex switched on a CD of James Booker singing "Junko Partner" and began fuming over a Lil Joe DuBulio bill about hippies burning flags. "This is a legislative hemorrhoid, Doctor, and *I am dealing with the threshold!*" Nobby listened. The man did have a trip-hammer mind. Besides, any self-thought DuBulio bill was a potential train wreck. Even Luigi Rompallo in prison had told Nobby it was a dumb bill; Rompy didn't want to hurt DuBulio's feelings. People despise Rompy for being in the pen, but he's an American and plenty of Americans do time for whatever reason.

"Hey, baby bubba: ever been to Trinidad?"

Of course Rex said no. Underneath that perfect face, he was a coonass from the bayous. But slick: oh, did Nobby know that. When they met, fall of '57, Rex was guitar-tuning on steps of the Kappa Alpha house before his combo played, and Domainge Nobby saw a man as cool as the other side of the pillow.

"Fly to Trinidad with me weekend yonder. I'll put good material in yo pocket for an afternoon's work. Cash money. Come back Monday before the birds chirp. Bring Sophie. She'll warble for a month."

"Takes a lot to make Sophie warble. What you peddlin', Doctor?"

"Injection wells."

He knew Rex would say no. But it was important to let him know he always had first bite on any Doctor Nobby investment. Rex understood Looziana economics like nobody's business; he was catty about his own stakes. Nobby knew not to make Rex feel back-to-the-wall. Nobby wanted his calls returned.

"I can't go to Trinidad," Rex said in a trail-away voice. He was studying the blueprints of the pipeline.

"Mebbe I should inquire of Oscar."

"Oscar?" Rex traced a finger over the pipe grid on the blueprint.

"Hear tell he needs financial aid, Governor. His bankers have halitosis."

Rex, absorbed in the blueprint: "I wouldn't mess with Oscar on that. His environmental department has to prosecute the bad-poo truckers."

"Seems to me this quickie-gig in a foreign country is somepin Oscar might could handle. I don't see no kinda conflicta-interest type crap in that."

Rex rolled the blueprint and used it like a scepter, tapping Nobby on his noggin. "Burnside is real congested. It's an awesome big plant you got here."

Nobby beamed. "Incineration is the top industrial toilet known to oil. They burn shit you can't imagine over Houston all the time."

"Texas is a foreign country," reported the Governor.

"Your doctor can get you land options on those blueprints, Rex."

Rex's lips thinned into a tight smile. "I believe that."

Nobby reached for the blueprints, but Rex put his index finger up and shook it like a teacher telling a pupil no. "These things interest me, Doctor."

"They're my only blueprints, Rex!"

"Get a duplicate. This might have potential, Doctor."

He thought Rex was bluffing, but he didn't want to snatch the blueprints for fear of offending high power. Rex had often made him feel special, anointed, on the inside; other times, Nobby left feeling like a slave. Until Sophie, Nobby had never sacrificed a chickywawa to Rex. Sombitch could act like God.

Nobby was dreaming of a woman spread-eagled over Trinidad

when his door exploded to the sound of Oscar's banging paw. Nobby limped across the rug in his underwear, turned the knob and saw Oscar standing like a small pathetic gorilla: "Rex's dead! Amelia's office just called. Rex died last night!"

"Whaddya mean batterin' the door to tell me somethin' like that?" Nobby glared. "Well, come in." He walked to the window, knee shot with pain, and saw the beautiful Caribbean Sea. "You sayin' Rex actually died?"

"Durin' the night." Oscar gnawed his lip, face all tear-spattered. "Prime Minister'll have us a plane in one hour."

"My knee hurts Jesus-awful. How'd he die?"

"No announcement yet. My secretary sez it's all over TV."

The plane was refueling at the airport in Yucatan when Attorney General Abadie emerged from the men's room with a face looking like split-pea soup. Nobby had the cellphone in his hand with numbers in his head.

Come, Oscar. I will show you the way.

8   BLEEDING HEARTS

Reporters surged against the cordon of troopers as a state police car deposited Regina at the mansion. Colonel Bellamy guided her up the stairs. On the porch she turned, for a peerless moment, allowing the cameras to capture her furrowed brow, shielded by designer sunglasses, without a word to the pitch of questions. At twenty-eight, she had the same dark eyes and brushed features of Amelia. A famous spread in *Vogue* had showed the mother and daughter who looked like sisters. The text had no hint of the epic quarrels during Regina's years of copulating through LSU till Amelia evicted her from the Mansion.

The media drama turned next to Kay, the raven-haired younger sister, who had evaded the mother-daughter warfare while Rex disappeared to points unknown. Kay was a junior at LSU when Regina eloped with a scuba diving instructor who was history ten days later. A Tri Delt in the footsteps of her mother, Kay married a bond attorney the month after graduation. They had fifteen-hundred people to the reception at the Mansion. Willowy in her final term of pregnancy, Kay scowled at the reporters and clutched Colonel Bellamy's arm.

"Your sister already went up," he uttered in a ragged nicotine voice.

Her husband was in Atlanta on business, leaving Kay alone at the worst moment of her life. She loathed politics, adored her mother and was five years in therapy over issues with her daddy that trailed her into the big bedroom.

Amelia stood like a statue with folded arms.

Regina, flushed red, was jabbing her finger at the First Lady: "*Well what happened, mother?*"

"She didn't do anything wrong!" cried Kay.

"The Coroner is in with daddy now," simmered Amelia.

Kay hugged her mother and guided her to the bed.

"Daddy was too healthy to *just die!*" squealed Regina.

The television threw out a low hum of anchorpeople pattering to live shots of powerful persons arriving downstairs. Amelia sat on the edge of the bed. Kay lay back, propped by pillows, hands crossed on her womb.

Regina leaned on the bedpost, gnawing a knuckle.

LauraLee arrived with a tray of beverages and stack of telegrams. She had been with the family twenty-four years, the first decade running the big house in Avoyelles under Miss Della and Mayor Bobby Broussard, since then at the Governor's Mansion. A reedy, blue-haired African American widow, each of whose five grandchildren attended a different college in the state on scholarships arranged by Rex, LauraLee earned $67,000 a year for management of the family's emotions. She placed the tray on a bedside table and stood behind Regina, kneading her taut shoulders, whispering as if to a child.

Speaker Sutton's image dissolved into speculation among the

news anchors. Regina threw up her arms: "This is out of control!"

"Regina honey, don't get fussed," counseled LauraLee.

"So what *happened*, mother? Why can't you *just tell me*?"

"I woke up and he wasn't breathing! What else to tell?"

"I want to go in there with Dr. Willoby!" she cried.

"Regina," moaned Kay, "have some respect for momma *and* daddy,"

Regina clenched her teeth: "I want to *see him,* mother."

"Be patient, darling. Please!"

"Come on, baby," crooned LauraLee. "You got to give it time."

"When was the last time you saw him alive, mother?

"Regina," intervened Kay, "can you just be *appropriate?*"

Amelia bolted out of the room, clutching telegrams from the Clintons, Al and Tipper, Governor George Bush and his daddy, Lady Bird, Jimmy Carter, oil presidents, union leaders, the New Orleans archbishop: saddened to hear/our prayers with you/hearts go out/please advise if anything we can do …

If only they knew.

From the pink snow of phone message slips, one drew her gaze. *Stephen is concerned. Call when you can. 11:45 AM.*

Concerned! Thrilled, more likely. She imagined his serene delight at the prospects of seeing her more frequently, in time squiring her around the art world. How convenient for Stephen, who never complained about Rex. I never really wanted Stephen, she steamed. *Oh, Jesus, Mary and Joseph: why am I in this infernal mess? Lord, help me through this.*

She paused before two Dogon masks, their tiny, planetary eye sockets like placid pools as the rage within her swelled. She wanted blood from Sophie Thibodeaux! Electrocute the bitch! She was balling her fists when Mayor Bobby Broussard's words wafted down a memory duct: *Never make an important decision standing up.*

Her mama still prayed to daddy as a spirit capable of lighting up the night. What explains such enduring love? A decade after his death, Miss Della doled out turkeys and hams along Christian

Fraux's bayou to make sure Bobby Broussard still got black votes each time Avoyelles had its mayoralty.

Take time to take stock. Daddy's words came straight out of her youth. *Use your prowess. Never let people know you're angry.*

The rage hit so suddenly, she lost her grip on sadness. Anger at Rex, fermenting for years, surged through her like a burning river. That slutty girlfriend. Whoever killed him: so much filth feeding her fury. Back to the wall, she sank to the floor, pulling her knees close, the telegrams scattered as she sobbed, blotting her eyes with a silk cloth. The hall window threw back her image: black hair in a taut bun, two strands framing her cheeks like curled ribbons. She traced the silk around mottled mascara. How can the predictable surface of life just cave in, leaving you an inch shy of madness? First you pick up. Then what?

She gathered the telegrams. An image invaded her thought field: Rex in a pool of silver quicksand up to his waist, reaching for her, crying open-mouthed but words she couldn't hear. *Rex, baby: I wish I could!*

She opened the door and crossed the rug on cat feet.

Hubbell, hunched over the desk, was listening on earphones.

"What are you finding, then?"

He jumped out of the chair. "Those men are conspiring to defraud the Constitution of this state!"

"I reckon. What did they say about Doctor Nobby?"

He was startled by her face, so vulnerable, so harsh. "DuBulio suggested Nobby help them raise money to buy off Hall, but Sutton said no."

"They want Hall out — that makes sense."

"Oh, yes ma'am. They don't want Joe Hall one damn bit."

Hubbell wondered why Rex LaSalle had let a woman like her sleep alone. Her fusion of grief and scheming jolted him like an erotic charge. With a dead man down the hall, her mobility was shackled. What did she know, what did she truly fear? He knew she wanted to control him, master the information that he found. He was leaning toward her, against his better instincts, driven to help in a perverse way so he could pull back the rock and examine worms feeding on the innards of a system. How deep in it was she? Helping Amelia LaSalle meant matching her, wit for wit — fill in her mysteries. Nothing like this had ever happened to him. His excitement was almost promiscuous.

He reported to her the details of what he had overheard.

"Those men didn't talk about the circumstances of your husband's death," he said solemnly. "If any of them know, they concealed it from others."

"It's time to meet with Dr. Willoby," she replied, smoothing the sleeves of her dark silk dress. "First, I want you to tell the Speaker that I asked him and the others to adjourn and wait in the reception hall."

"Certainly."

He followed her out of the room, wondering if his fifteen minutes with the taping system was a felony. She headed toward the bedrooms; he descended the stairway. At the conference room, he gave the door a hard rap. Frampton opened it. They had passed acknowledging glances at a bar association dinner but never formally met. "You too?" blurted Frampton.

"A message for Speaker Sutton," he replied passively.

Sutton filled the doorway with his towering frame, surprised to see a nemesis in the house of power. The attorney conveyed the First Lady's request.

"Come on, men," the Speaker called. "Time to head down."

Frampton threw him a sour look as the others moved down the stairway. Sutton hung back. "Hubbell, I didn't know you were close to the family."

"Life doesn't always add up."

When the others were gone, Sutton glared. "What are you finding?"

"Not much. Coroner just arrived."

"I want a full account." Sutton pulled a card from his wallet. "That's my suite at the Hilton. Safe phone. I want an update every two hours. We clear?"

"I'm not sure I can do that, sir."

"What the fuckdog ain't you sure about?"

"Anything I say has to be cleared by the First Lady."

Sutton was three inches taller than Hubbell. His jowls ran pink to purple as he stabbed Hubbell's lapel with a bony index finger. "This is a *crisis,* Hubbell." *Pop* went the finger on the chest. "Amelia and I are allies" — *pop* — "and you work for the state. The Looziana Speaker just gave you an order. Mess up and you're in deep shit. I'm your ally." *Pop!* "At the Hilton. We clear now, boy?"

"We're on the same side," Hubbell said, fighting an abrupt urge to defecate.

Sutton's blue eyes bore down like pincers. Hubbell realized how the man passed bills. "Nobody knows what this holds," the Speaker muttered. "You goan need me just like I'ma need you."

"I'm holding the ball till Oscar gets back."

"Oscar. Hmph. What time's he due?"

"Late today."

"I expect to hear from you, Hubbell."

He searched for something to say that would draw more out of Sutton without revealing his own shaky grasp on things. Nothing came.

"Mr. Speaker, I know we'll be talking."

It was now 12:45 PM. Six-hundred people jammed the reception hall, waiting for the Coroner's announcement. Warren Rutter, the Governor's press secretary, had spent a decade at the *Baton Rouge Advocate* before joining Rex for ten-thousand a year more. Circulating among politicians and old podnas in the press, Rutter did his best to patch over the silence from the upper floors. A sullen mood was coagulating in the hall. Rutter was livid with Amelia for keeping him out of the loop. He tried not to look slack-jawed when Joanie Charlot, a shimmering red-head for Channel Five, buttonholed him on live remote: "Is there any reason why you, as press secretary, don't know more than we do?"

"Joanie, that's very easy to explain." Bourbon drums from the night before pounded Rutter's temples. "I'm not a next of kin."

"Did the Governor show signs of ill health yesterday?"

"None whatsoever. This comes as a total shock."

Watching TV upstairs, Regina and LauraLee and Kay gazed at Rutter's craggy face. Joanie Charlot (Rex's honeysuckle of 1991) held her earpiece, poking the microphone at the media's link to the top: "Speaker Sutton has arrived and we're about to go to him. Meantime, Warren Rutter" — here it comes, harpoon-sharp — "what about funeral plans? The whole state is waiting."

"So are we, little wench," hissed Kay.

Regina gnawed her index finger. "I need a drink."

"CoCola be better," opined LauraLee, grimacing at Joanie Charlot.

"Bourbon," reported Regina.

"Lemme go see. Kay, darlin'. Howzabout you?"

Kay shook her head as LauraLee left the room. Moments later the First Lady returned, flustered. "The media is like an army. This is a nightmare! I have to meet Colonel Bellamy. Are y'all praying for daddy?"

Regina stood up. "Mother, you're not blocking me out of this!"

"Regina, for once in your life, *shut up*!" retorted Kay.

"Kay," admonished the First Lady, "be understanding with your sister. Regina, there are logistical problems with so many people downstairs. No one is blocking you. Don't make this harder than it is, honey. Pray for your father."

Regina slumped in a chair. "This is the most miserable day I can remember."

LauraLee returned. "Here's your highball, sugar."

The First Lady met Mitchell Mudd and Bellamy outside of Rex's bedroom.

"Have you been briefed by Dr. Willoby?" she asked the Colonel.

"Not yet, ma'am. He wants to speak with you first."

Henry Hubbell joined them. "I have a lab-site unit on the way."

"They're in an unmarked vehicle," said Bellamy. "I got a two-car escort holding. Miss Amelia, I can't get those technicians into this building with suitable cover till Willoby goes down to brief the press. I am real concerned about security. It's an anthill down there. Unless we clear people out of this house, the press will mob those lab people the moment they hit Dodge."

"Thank you, Colonel. Would you please wait in the Governor's study?"

In the bow of Bellamy's head, Hubbell saw a man relieved to be out of the orbit. What the Colonel did not know, officially, he could not be forced to testify about under oath. Hubbell followed the First Lady and Mitchell Mudd, feeling the ten-thousand dollars in his pocket with a hand of muggy guilt.

He recognized Arthur Willoby from his TV spots. His career as a Navy doctor had taken him to places like Guam, Manila, Pensacola, San Diego. At sixty-two, he had returned with good pension to the city of his birth, run for Coroner and won by a whisker. He had sandy gray hair, thick eyebrows and a freckled face that looked painfully grave.

"Arthur," said the First Lady. "Mr. Hubbell and Mr. Mudd, my advisers."

"How do," said Willoby, distracted by his clipboard.

The Governor, shrouded on the bed, made Hubbell think of his father.

"If you please, ma'am," said Dr. Willoby, motioning her to sit. Mudd put his elbow wing on the mantle piece. Hubbell stood next to Amelia's chair.

"It breaks my heart to talk about this," said the Coroner.

"Hurts us more," grunted Mudd.

"By law, an autopsy must be conducted at the morgue or a medical facility," began Willoby. "From the surface examination, I am convinced the Governor died by poisoning and on that basis I want a thorough anatomical review with the necessary surgical procedures."

"Oh my God!" exclaimed the First Lady.

"Tell us what the procedures would entail," demanded Hubbell.

"Removal of a kidney, blood samples, portions of bone marrow, in this case part of a lung, open view of the intestinal tract and then some. The face would in no way be defiled. The embalmers customarily prepare things so that with the body clothed, mourners see no sign of incision."

The First Lady closed her eyes, shaking her head.

"Amelia," stated Dr. Willoby. "I know it's hard to embrace news like this, and my heart grieves with you."

Hubbell spoke: "How did Governor LaSalle die?"

Willoby read from a clipboard. "Cause of death: ingestation of a compound with cyanide as dominant property. Patches found in throat, on his tongue, lips, plus flecks in the nostrils. He got hit hard and quick with a heavy dose, bringing on cardiac arrest. I surmise he died in about two minutes. Approximate time of death, 3 AM. There were definite signs of sexual activity."

The First Lady went white. Her eyebrows curled in twin arches toward her hairline. "Rex must not be disgraced, Arthur."

Willoby tugged at his collar. "That's my report. By law —"

"Arthur," retorted the First Lady. "We *must* decide how to deal with this."

"We object to references of any intimacy between the Governor and Mrs. LaSalle," said Hubbell. "It is immaterial and an assault on their privacy."

A cold silence filled the room.

"Okay. I'll agree to that," said Willoby, striking through a paragraph on the clipboard. "I'll have to write up a new report."

"Thank you," said Hubbell, registering Amelia's nod.

"Wait before you write," said the First Lady. "If we oppose an autopsy, how significant a loss of information would that be?"

"Very significant. We don't know if the compound that entered his system was mixed with other chemicals. How'd he swallow it? I was careful not to put my fingers on the whiskey tumbler by the bed. I saw no sign of regurgitation. People often vomit. How much did he eat? What kind of fluids did he imbibe? I don't mean to be crude, ma'am, but there is evidence inside that body, and if I can't get in there, key questions may never be answered."

Mitchell Mudd drew his thumb and index finger down his chin, rubbing whisker patches that his morning shave had missed.

"There are suspects," said the First Lady. "Your findings confirm things — leads. But if the media get this, it hurts our chance of catching the murderer. This must not be made public, Arthur. Not yet. Trust me."

The Coroner met her gaze. "I took an oath on the Bible, ma'am. I got elected on the basis of thirty-five years in the Navy. I took out the appendix of the Vice President at Subic Bay. If I falsify an autopsy, I might not get re-elected. And I might get indicted, too."

"No one gonna do that in this state," Mudd said dismissively.

"Of course not," said the First Lady. "Should this go public, you will be covered. I give you my word, Arthur. Rex's reputation — and catching the animal who did this — hinge on a swift, private probe. Don't destroy our chances."

"It's against the law, Mrs. LaSalle."

"Don't lecture me about the law, Dr. Willoby."

"I just don't think I can go that far."

You shouldn't, thought Hubbell.

"What about the promissory note?" said Amelia.

Willoby coughed. "Say again?"

"The thirty-thousand dollars from Rex you spent on final TV spots."

"Rex swore me not to enter it as a campaign contribution."

"A grand jury cannot subpoena my husband, Dr. Willoby."

Hubbell had a client to represent. "A loan of that size could demand some rethinking," he said with a toughness that surprised himself. "On the other hand, the financial arrangement can continue, in a fashion amenable to all parties, if you honor Governor LaSalle's faith in you."

Willoby sat with elbows crossed on his thighs. "I never did anything like this. The money — I can pay you back, *Missus* LaSalle. I just need more time."

"Arthur, you are trampling on a dead man's reputation!"

"Dammit! I already agreed to strike the lipstick reference. Why does the fact that he was poisoned have to be covered up?"

"*Because we want it that way!*" bellowed Mitchell Mudd. "This is politics, not the Navy! Whoever murdered the Governor wants it known. If it's not announced, someone'll try to get the word out, and when they do, we can attack."

"And you, Arthur, will be a hero for assisting us," said the First Lady.

"Start a manhunt!" countered Willoby. "Check the outgoing flights! Paper it over, you give the killer time to clear out."

"He has a point," said Hubbell, mulling his own position in the widening net. "It could give the killer or killers a big jump."

"And bring the FBI right up our ass!" barked Mitchell Mudd.

Willoby raised an eyebrow. "FBI still digging on Rex?"

Mudd shot back: "Look, Willoby, we're tryin' to be nice. You took money and it's illegal. If the Feds strap you on a grill, we can say the bunch Rex gave you was all above board, with documentation to back it up."

"What about his signature?" snorted Willoby derisively.

"I know my husband's signature as well as my own," the First Lady said impatiently.

Willoby scowled. "How come it wasn't illegal for Rex to give it to me?"

"That depends on how you registered the money," said Hubbell, turning on a dime.

"I did what Rex told me," whimpered Willoby.

"*Yeah?*" snapped Mudd. "Well he's *dead!*"

"Arthur," said Amelia. "As God is my witness, it is in your best interest to assist us. The federal agencies have a dragnet going after political money. Senator Atchison is the first one snared. They are probing Doctor Nobby."

"Dirty, dirty people," muttered Willoby. "How you supposed to know in a state like this if a man gives you tainted money?"

"You took money from Nobby," marveled Hubbell.

"Who didn't?" shrugged Willoby.

"The FBI wants Rex's records," said the First Lady. "I am a suffering woman, Arthur. My husband is dead, my daughters are at a breaking point, I need time and air and space and *I don't need you getting in my way!*"

Willoby hung his head, holding the clipboard. "Wonder what to say."

"Massive cardiac arrest," rejoined Mudd. "His daddy died of one at fifty. Tell media if it'll help. The rest stays under wraps till we give the signal."

"Then you don't want me to work on the body."

"I need to think about that," said the First Lady.

When they entered the Governor's study, Colonel Bellamy rose to his feet. "Dr. Willoby wishes to speak with the press at his office," said the First Lady.

"Yes, ma'am." Bellamy cocked an eyebrow. "What's the verdict?"

"Heart stopped cold," muttered Willoby. "Damndest thing."

Bellamy's mouth formed an O.

"Dr. Willoby has agreed to coordinate his departure with a public statement from the family," said the First Lady.

"I want out," said the Coroner.

Bellamy escorted the Coroner into the hallway where a state trooper led him to an elevator. Bellamy returned to the room, ravenous for a Salem. His official knowledge was based on what he had been told. Bellamy's charge was protecting the family. Forensic responsibility was shifting toward Hubbell, who imagined chains being strapped on his chest. The First Lady leaned against the brickwork of a cold hearth. "Colonel, how many troopers in the house?"

"Sixty-four. I have men posted at the first-floor landing, in the kitchen, solarium, the reception hall, front and rear exits, plus sixteen vehicles."

"Mr. Hubbell, these lab people you called … "

"Site Analysts Inc. They reconstruct plane crashes, accidents, criminal entries. The US Attorney in Lafayette used them on the Panamanian drug-smuggling murders."

"And where are they as we speak?"

Bellamy: "Parking lot of the Kopper Kitchen two miles away. Waiting with an unmarked escort. Course, if it wasn't homicide we don't need them."

"For my own peace of mind I want them to inspect the room. Should they find something the Coroner should know, we'll tell him. Colonel, wait just a second. Mr. Hubbell, come with me please."

He followed her down the hallway lined with tribal animist masks, like visages out of some netherworld, dark eyeholes peering made him think of his father's gnarled white brows, staring at TV news from his wheelchair.

"It wasn't fair," he said.

"No, Mr. Hubbell. It most certainly was not."

She opened the door to Rex's bedroom, handing him the report Willoby had defaced. He folded it into his coat pocket next to the envelope with cash.

"What now?" she said.

"We should weigh the facts after the technicians finish their work. If you want evidence — and prosecution — an autopsy is inevitable."

"We'll talk about that. Right now, you monitor the technicians. Don't let anyone else, especially my daughter Regina, into this room."

"Then keep her and anyone else downstairs as long as you can."

"I'll do that. What is your concern, Mr. Hubbell?"

"Keeping people quiet is harder than making them talk. Bellamy, Willoby, Mitchell Mudd and two medics know it wasn't his heart. That's five people."

"If Willoby keeps quiet, the others won't jeopardize themselves. Let's do what we have to do."

She shut the door and left him standing over the body beneath its rubber sheet. He took a silver pen from his pocket, hooked it under the cover and gave a delicate tug, exposing the face, ashen with a patch of green on the left cheek. The lips, thin and blue, were shut tight. Only then did he notice how cold the room was. He wondered if hell were cold. Did warlords, tyrants and prostitutes of democracy swim in sewers of the damned? Is it our final measure of justice that the depraved won't see God? All of a sudden he felt a sea change in his intestines. He left the bedside and faced the window, calmed by the sight of a manorial lawn dry beneath the merciless sun. And then some power grabbed him, pulling him toward the bed like invisible arms connected to her mysterious African faces — *sonofabitch his eyes are open!*

Hubbell blinked.

Rex LaSalle's eyes were closed. His lips held a crooked smile.

Did I imagine it? Tiny lesions marked the lips, dotting the chin like an abused patina on a mask. *This is what you wanted: to understand their kind.* Forget honor. Are you up to this, pilgrim?

His belly was rumbling. Then the old man's words came to him: Courage is something most people don't understand, son. *You have to be afraid before you can be brave.*

Hubbell leaned over the body. He pointed a finger in its face. "I'm gonna do this. But not for you, Governor. You hear that? *Not …for …you!*"

He reached the toilet before exploding.

In the downstairs reception hall, Speaker Sutton had become a magnet to the media. "Lieutenant Governor Hall is runnin' a bad fever, but in discussing the situation, we agreed that this state is officially in mourning for Rex LaSalle. I know y'all are interested in succession matters, but I have to say, the real issue here is the family, their needs, and just how we can assist …"

A current rolled through the room as Amelia LaSalle came down the curve of the stairwell, fingering pleats of her midnight dress, flanked by state troopers shouldering their way into the crowd. In the swivel of heads, cameramen lurched for positions. Colonel Bellamy led the advance with Regina and Kay following the First Lady and four troopers bringing up the rear.

A surge of energy crackled through the room. Lights flashed in the jigsaw of elbows; microphones stuck out like spears. "*Y'all give these people room!*" Bellamy shouted as the family inched ahead in the crush of the crowd. "*We got a lady with a baby comin' through!*" Kay moved forward with arms crossed upon her chest. "Ease it on back!" commanded Bellamy while upstairs in the Governor's bedroom Henry Hubbell watched as Elvis Banks, the forensic genius, and his younger brother, a technician, trained high-definition lenses on Rex LaSalle's naked body: they photographed his mouth, his chest, his penis, his legs; they wore rubber gloves and turned him over, combing through hair on his thighs and ankles and his equator with a tiny raking device that extracted fiber samples they hoped to match with sheets they stripped off the bed; they lathered dust across the floor and the nightstand for 167 print impressions and with a tiny blade took filigrees of lipstick from the leg, knee and thigh along with chemical sediment on his lips in a process Henry Hubbell had never seen before.

In the reception hall, Amelia LaSalle braced the podium, confronting the forest of microphones. Her poise filled the television screens in a portrait of sadness, stilling the hunger for facts with a suffering, personal and pure. Flanked by Regina and Kay, she said: "Ladies and gentlemen, Governor LaSalle is dead." Cameras clicked like machine guns. Her eyes were moist with tremors of the heart. "There are medical terms, but let me say it simply: my husband's heart gave out — that golden, gallant heart."

Muffled coughs suffused the crowd. "It should be obvious that the family is in no condition to receive visitors. And yet I know that that is what Rex would want, for all of you who loved him as we did to gather here in the house he built and cherished. I thank Speaker Sutton for his declaration of official mourning."

Chin erect, eyes welling, she caught a sob and said: "I would only add to the Speaker's declaration that every citizen of Louisiana is welcome at the rotunda of the Capitol tomorrow afternoon for a wake ... a wake to mourn his death and celebrate his life. The burial will be Sunday in Avoyelles. Here ... at the Mansion … Bishop Ott has been consoling. My mother is expected shortly from Avoyelles. The family will remain in privacy until the services. Hundreds of you have called to express condolences, the telegrams … the flowers. Thank you, each and all, from the deepest layer of my heart."

She saw servants, staff and a few reporters crying, and then Sutton, calculating; red-cheeked Frampton; DuBulio wiping his bald spot; John Burns Logan beady-eyed; Woodruff faceless; Buzby leering; Beaconfield pinch-lipped.

At that moment, the black man caught Amelia's line of vision as he entered the foyer far back from her podium: Reverend Christian Fraux.

"I know the members of the media have questions," she continued. "I would ask you to respect the family's need for our own time in this terrible ordeal. Dr. Willoby will meet with you at his office downtown."

A roar rose out of the room. "*Let her speak!*" cried the press secretary.

As the rumble subsided, the First Lady continued. "Please understand that *I* asked Dr. Willoby to leave for his office. We must sleep here tonight with this awful weight. And I want everyone, all the citizens of this state, to know that we shall bury Rex LaSalle in full honors of his office. He was my h-husband" — and then the resistance broke, her tears flowing into the hearts of viewers riveted to TV that night and the next morning, her words replayed over ensuing days — "and he was a Governor who led us with dignity and distinction.

"At this time, I ask the ladies and gentlemen of the media, the friends and elected officials here assembled, so many of you who have been with us on campaigns and functions in the past — please respect the LaSalles in our time of grief. I ask this of you as friends and citizens. I am not in any condition to take questions. Thank you. God bless you. *And may God bless Rex LaSalle!*"

On the day of the assassination, Christian Fraux had arisen at dawn and put on his best silk suit. With damp hair combed like a silver yarmulke, Fraux had prospered in the business of burials. Checking his oil stick at the Avoyelles station, he saw Mayor Bobby Broussard's yellow Cadillac pull astride the pump, a 1979 with garish bumpers driven by his widow who endowed the behemoth vehicle with a strange kind of grace. "G'morning, Miss Della. How are you?"

"Slightly vexed, Rev'nd Fraux." She was a slender lady with a porcelain face and ruffled gray hair. "Not a tin of cat food in the house."

A Cajun in a Saints T-shirt emerged to feed her tank with gasoline.

"A brochure came in the mail," she stated. "It wanted money."

"Some charity?" Fraux replied.

"There is nothing charitable about the Republican Party."

"Computers don't think the way people do, Miss Della."

"The Mayor would be livid."

Fraux smiled, wondering if among white folks she spoke of him as Mayor Bobby, Bobby or The Mayor. "I'm headed for the legislature. Second day, now."

"Good luck," she said. "Will you see Rex?"

"It's a strong possibility. We met last night in New Roads."

"If you do see him, please tell him I found The Mayor's champagne coil."

"Mayor Bobby drank champagne from a coil?"

"No, he used it in a tree."

"I shall tell the Governor," Fraux smiled. "G'bye, Miss Della."

The buttery radiance of her automobile hung in his rearview till he hit the outgoing road. When he had occasionally asked her support of causes, Miss Della gave generously. Fraux never took white folks' money for granted. After each mayoralty, some reporter went out to see her at the big house, asking how does a dead man keep getting votes? Forty for Mayor Bobby after this election, 85 the one before, a fat 250 (out of 950 cast) in the special election after his death. Miss Della was sweet and coy with the press. Everyone assumed she kept voting for her husband. Mayor Bobby's other supporters were a mystery.

In violent years Fraux led people, hungry for justice, over horizons their forebears barely imagined. "*Everything changes*" — began the previous Sunday's sermon by a distinguished preacher from Atlanta, come for the thirtieth anniversary of bloody marches at the Capitol — "and nothing is changed." *Yes-Lawd*, murmured the congregates, fans fluttering in hand, while Fraux, whose mortuary duties left little time for reading much less preaching of the Lord's letter, brooded over red-green sludge stinking up ditches behind the trailer park.

Avoyelles had been a village between sugar plantations in 1863 when his great-grandfather, a free man of color, purchased fifty-seven acres on the outskirts. The town grew and the annexed area came to be called Blue Line. Fraux's father gave him the original deed. Framed above his desk, its look of yellowed parchment conveyed the authority of time. Ex-slaves, Indians and latterly Cambodians had settled into pockets sold down the ancestral line. Fraux Mortuary covered a knoll that stood five blocks from St. Joseph Square.

And so on a morning of record autumn heat, with poisoned sewers flooding his thought field and no inkling that the Governor was dead in bed, Fraux climbed the Capitol's forty-eight steps (one for each state, save belated Alaska and Hawaii) and entered the rotunda, waiting in the whoosh of cool air for his son, Robert Lincoln, a sophomore at LSU. Christian Fraux stared at Huey Long in bronze defiance on the lawn below and wondered how much he stole.

Momentarily his boy appeared in a dark suit under the arch of oak limbs, eons removed from the beaming child on a hobby-horse when his father came in smelling of formaldehyde. Robert Lincoln had strapping shoulders and the rusty crinkled eyebrows of his mother's people; he had come in his own car lest the arrival of a hearse draw cackles from white boys in dormitory windows.

Christian Fraux and his son had begun their quest the afternoon before, Thursday, watching debate in the House gallery.

"In an age of shrinking revenues and principled attacks on our taxation system," Speaker Sutton had intoned, "we are mandated to weigh each dol-lar, each *dime*, to assure its cost-effective use. Now, before us today —" *Negro legislation*, ruminated Fraux. Everything changes, nothing is changed.

To Robert Lincoln, the sole son and middle child of three, the sight of lobbyists buttonholing their bill shepherds, as the hum of voices wafted up the chamber, was pure spectacle. It was no longer a secret that Buzby, whose legislative district included the town of Avoyelles, drew a monthly retainer of fifteen-hundred dollars from the vacuum truck company that hauled waste to the injection well behind Blue Line. Asserting that "if there's one sure thing, Clyde Buzby is the envirement's friend," he filed a bill seeking funds to test the groundwater.

"I am a Jeffersonian Democrat," stated Frampton, with the neutrality of a weather forecaster, "but communities with dirty water are a health debt this body will be forced to pay off in ten years, so I say, let 'em have the money."

Fraux whispered to his son: "What are you finding?"

"Frampton's the only honky besides Buzby on our page."

Fraux rose. They moved down the seats, muttering "'scuse me" to a burly watchdog for the Louisiana Good Government Petro-Chemical Coalition who was bunched next to an evangelical circuit rider who that day was lobbying on behalf of waste disposal companies — polite, blow-dried men with the starch of smiles, shitbirds of democracy like peas in a pod.

The hearse broke out of late traffic, heading for New Roads. A radio newsman said that summations were expected Monday in the extortion trial of Senate President Clifford Atchison. "You think they'll convict him, poppa?"

"I hope so. But expensive lawyers are capable of anything."

The newscast said that the House had adjourned without decision on an appropriations bill "with a controversial rider benefiting the town of Avoyelles."

"It wasn't a rider," frowned Robert Lincoln.

"White folks still in the lead."

You will learn more painful lessons, thought Fraux. At least you will have money and the benefit of education. I pray you are shielded from violence.

"Mebbe a bill would pass if you were in Buzby's place, poppa."

"Mebbe you'd like working at the funeral home if I was in Buzby's place."

"But even white folks know Clyde is in bed with polluters."

"True. But I supported Clyde before we knew that, and now is time to make him deliver on something for our folk."

Twilight drained into dusk.

"How long have you known Governor LaSalle?"

"Hmm, 'bout thirty years now. Rex was a new legislator when Mayor Bobby Broussard brought him to our house one night. The three of us had coffee. And I could see he wasn't a John Kennedy liberal or a man with a dream. When politicians talk about money, always listen. When they speak of ideals, open the window. Rex handed me an envelope with three hundred dollars. I said, 'What is this for?' Thinking, why bribe a man who can't vote? And he sez, 'Bail money.'

"Your sister was in diapers. Students 'bout your age were gettin' thrown in jail. Rex said: 'I can't afford to represent those kids.' 'No politician can,' pipes the Mayor. 'But,' says Rex, 'I figgered I could help you folks with bail money.'

"Some liberal," Robert Lincoln said with a smirk.

"He wasn't even an admitted moderate then. I told Mayor Bobby that if any more kids got beat, they'd see reverse Klukker tactics — burnin' buildings, raving in the streets. That Mayor's eyes looked like poached eggs. But Rex LaSalle had X-ray vision: 'I know you're angry, Rev'nd Fraux, but I can't believe a minister would stir violence. We're trying to cool tempers, not enflame 'em. There are white people in this parish who realize change must come.'

"*Who?* I sez. And he sez, 'They are here, b'lieve-you-me. This money's a start. These marches and beatings ain't solvin' nothing.'"

Robert Lincoln knew the general story his mother and grandmother had told him, his sisters and cousins: how teachers and preachers (so tiny a class in Avoyelles!) pressured white folks to pull down barriers; how President LBJ pushed Congress. *We have come so far*, his mother would say. *And we have so far to go,* his grandma would echo. Robert Lincoln addressed his father: "You told me Bobby Broussard was the first mayor to give black folk jobs."

"Among Cajuns, at least. He was no hero, but his instincts were all right."

The morning after that meeting, Fraux's wife had taken the baby to New Orleans for Thanksgiving; he would follow in several days. Christian Fraux had been faithful over urges stirred by female freedom workers. In blue jeans with bobbing Afro haircuts, citing books of Frantz Fanon, they were unlike the ladies at Fisk where he had met his Creole wife. The sexiness and wit of those civil rights girls, wanting to converse rather than listen to men talk of their exploits, intrigued him. They slept with male activists in a rooming house paid for by the NAACP. Church elders fumed: what if the press finds out? Amidst stormy discussions, Fraux said, "The young people protest in ways we cannot because we have families to support. Let us back them, and admonish them privately."

In truth, he envied the boys' freedom and fantasized a geometry of hot sex with the girls. One night, driving with a shotgun on the floorboard and a young woman next to him in the dented truck, he experienced a raw surge from his loins that nearly sent him off the road. Who are these beasts, he thought, that beat our young people? What blood runs in the white man's veins? Not once had he touched a girl — and how many times he hungered for it!

The night his wife left, he had driven across the prairie under a bosom moon, past swampbottom and marsh to an oil depot on soggy land, thickened by bulldozers, overlooking the Gulf of Mexico. The place was not even on the map. Men who worked the offshore oil rigs departed and returned at the pier. He felt now he hated the white man. He beseeched the Lord to reveal His way. Where do white and black meet? What are the terms of our common humanity?

Steering down a gravel road girded by wooden-slate sidewalks, he saw a liquor-and-canned goods store opposite a bar with a Regal Beer sign. Empty oil drums lined the outside wall. Paper trash followed a ridge of earth streaked with chemicals that ran up a bluff to the pier. A dirt road trailed off the gravel into a murky warren. Kerosene lamps flickered in shacks. It was true. People actually lived here. When rain pelted the depot, the gravel turned to slush and the hill became purple mud. When frost descended, the truck tires cut sawtooth patterns into icy sludge under the Regal sign.

It was the ugliest place he had ever seen. A UPI reporter described it as "a strange admixture of racial tolerance and oil patch bravura, a frontier where Negro and white know fewer differences than in most Southern towns." Fraux would never tell his son of the night his car pulled into the parking lot of the barn. He had learned of its infamy from an indignant preacher on a fishing trip in Vermilion Bay. It was less a barn than a big metal cave. Yellow light powdered the trucks and cars outside. He sat in his vehicle, palming the pistol in his pocket, anger rising against the white race. Never had he paid for sex. Bounding up the stairs, he found a wizened Chitimacha Indian at a table with a strongbox. A blanket covered entry to the maw beyond, with moans and whoops.

"Twenty-fi'e dollars fo a bed," said the Indian. "Ten dollars for the wall. Be 'bout half-hour for a bed."

"So I take the wall," Fraux replied.

"You kin put yo money down for a bed. Drinkin' room yonder. Buy yo'self a place in line."

"I could do that," he said, flexing shoulders of his one hundred and seventy-six pound frame, "or I can pay ten and see if this joint's all it's cracked up to be."

"Make no difference to me no kinda way."

He handed over the bills, wondering if the performance of coitus standing up was more exciting or simply more economical given the price of rent in this hell lot. The man pointed down a hall. "Take number three." Fraux followed a greasy wall on the other side of which cries rose from squirming mattresses. Outside the cubicles, muddy jeans dangled from wooden pegs over shoes and boots. A sign said: *Keep wallets and valuables!* In the glare of a bulb, he checked ends of the hall, stuffed wallet and pistol in his shoes, and entered the stall, buck naked, hooking his shoes with his fingers.

Enclosed by thin partitions, the wall facing him had a hole at the level of his waist. He stepped forth, trembling, trying to ignore moans in the space to his right. He stared at the hole, big as a catcher's mitt. *I should have waited for a bed.* From below, a voice beckoned softly: "Come ... closer now ..." Peeling away his fear, he followed his erection to the hole and felt the caress of fingers, then hot moisture: his flanks went taut, his legs tightened, he couldn't see her lips but a warm titillation engulfed him and suddenly he was standing on tippy-toes when the man in the next stall bellowed: "*You a man! A gawdamn man!*"

Fraux's head swiveled as a splintering crash caused the stall on his right to collapse and a voice shrieked, "*Wait! Wait!*" A white man hit the floor behind Fraux, pulled himself up and lunged back into the shattered room, fists battering wood, and Fraux felt the buckling of his neighbor's wall to the sound of fists pounding flesh and someone shrieked, "*You doan unnerstand! Stop! Stop!*" and then a new voice said: "Jesus Christ, he's gonna kill that fag."

At which moment Fraux realized he knew nothing of the other, down there working on his member. Was it a woman — *or ...?* Oh, no! Oh, *God!*

Feet thundered down the hallway as the fight rose in volume to his right. Fraux pulled back, rocking on his feet. Out of the hot hole came a soft coo: "Put that sweet potato right back heah." Stiff as a sword he back-pedaled, spilling his shoes, and the trigger snapped POW! POW! POW! Fraux jumped up and down avoiding the bullets with his member spewing like a garden hose.

A naked white man bolted into the hall, grabbed his clothes and ran for the door, fuming, "Cocksuckers got guns here." "*Who shootin?*" yelled a Negro. "*Niggers!*" cried someone. "*Faggots!*" yelled one more. And another: "*Po-lice!*"

Fraux snatched his clothes as another man tore past, bare bottom churning. Fraux hopped to one foot, sliding into his trousers, feeling eyes of a white man beating down his neck.

His shoes were gone.

He lunged back into the stall, groping on all fours in the sticky darkness until he found one shoe and leather-blasted remains of the other, and made for the door, forging into the mesh of limbs. Someone cut the lights. Women shrieked, men pushed in a surge for the door; a guy toppled over the stair rail, bouncing off a car hood like a piece of tuna, and two women scrambled down the gravel toward the swamp. People poured out in terror, some half-clothed, several naked as jaybirds, others carrying clothes as they streaked into the black swamp. Fraux jumped into his car and gunned the engine.

"Turn on the light," commanded the voice of a white man in the back seat. "And do not think about touching that gun."

This is how it ends: Fraux saw his life split into images of those he loved and the scandalous ruin he had made of freedom work and himself. Sweat-lathered, he turned the knob: the vehicle lit up: the rearview showed cool eyes.

"I would like to join the NAACP," said Rex.

"Abraham and Moses!" cried Fraux, melting like an ice cube.

As warring bodies raged inside the bordello, the politician laughed, one belly whoop upon another so contagiously that Fraux assessed his bare foot, the shirt-snagged pants zipper and he chuckled, hitting the accelerator with Rex LaSalle howling: "*The shame of it all*, mah friend!"

Fraux drove to the oil pier. "Why'd you shoot up that joint?" prompted Rex. Fraux's truthful reply ignited more LaSalle laughter, causing Fraux to giggle over how he had scared the beejesus out of his own state representative in a nearby stall. "Did you know," said Fraux, "… about — the wall?"

"I *think* it was a woman," howled Rex. "I sure *hope* it was!"

Fraux looked anew at Rex LaSalle, the first white person with whom he had laughed. Two men, not yet thirty, parked at the bottom of America the day before Jack Kennedy was shot. In the months that followed, as the killings mounted in Mississippi and Alabama, a passion for civil rights swept Washington, assaulting the self-styled sovereignty of the South. As the first Cajun to campaign in black churches after the Voting Rights Act, Rex LaSalle sought his people's support and Fraux the pragmatist gave it. The scandal of Christian Fraux's corporeal journey became their secret, never mentioned. In 1967 an envelope arrived with a photograph of State Senator LaSalle lined up with politicians and oilmen: the ribbon-snipping with a new town's Mayor (owner of the barn) — the place was named New Enterprise. The slip of paper had no signature beneath the scrawled line: "Here, surely, is progress."

As the years passed and tales of Rex's wayward pecker followed him into the Mansion, Fraux had come to see the night as a diversion to Rex, one among countless erotic episodes, while Fraux's fidelity grew in ratio to his night of sin.

The evening before Rex's death, Robert Lincoln had fallen into a doze as his daddy steered the hearse into New Roads. Reverend Christian Fraux had years of loyalty to Rex LaSalle: delivering Blue Line's vote, covering the backwater wards with kids nailing signs on trees, voter cars on election day. Jaded though he was about politics, Fraux knew that if Rex gave his word on something, you got it. In the parking lot, father and son donned their coats and strode into the A-frame building with a cypress roof peaked above a big fan blowing air into the hall. White people sat at newspaper-covered cafeteria tables with mounds of shrimp, crawfish, ketchup and lemons; the rosy hills of spent shellfish in saggy cardboard boxes put out a tangy aroma as older folk danced to a Dewey Balfa waltz on the jukebox. Governor LaSalle moved down the row of tables, shaking hands, kissing women, slapping men on the back. Behind the Governor trailed an aide with oily hair and a five o'clock shadow.

A white state trooper said: "Y'all lookin' for someone?"

"Reverend Fraux from Avoyelles. Here to see the Governor."

"He's talkin' to some folks now. Is it critical?"

"We have driven from the legislature."

The trooper motioned toward the crowd. "He'll be done in a few minutes. Y'all want some food, some beer?"

"No thank you." Fraux had nothing to prove to these people.

Sleeves curled at his elbows, tie loose, patting sweat with a small towel, Rex worked the rows, pressing the flesh. His aide made eye contact with Fraux, and whispered to the Governor. Rex looked up, and waved. Fraux waved back.

Finally, the Governor blew kisses to late applause and stepped into the night heat with the state trooper and his aide called Mitchell Mudd.

"Who's the movie star, Chris?" asked Rex, pumping Fraux's hand.

"My son, Robert Lincoln."

"Pleaure to meet you, Governor."

The Governor engulfed the young man's hands and looked him in the eye: "My pleasure to know *you.*"

"Our limousine is air-conditioned," said Christian Fraux.

"Lead me to the banks, Reverend."

The student followed them across the gravel lot. "Robert," said Fraux, "take the driver's seat so Governor LaSalle and I will have room in the back."

Engaging the motor, Robert Lincoln's first impression of the ruler was the smell of crawfish. He lay his right elbow over the front seat as the two men huddled in the back. "Whew," said Rex, reclining in the cool cushions, "those coonasses eat like they just discovered food. No bodies in here, huh Chris?"

Robert Lincoln laughed.

"Just ours," said Fraux. "Miss Della reports that she found Mayor Bobby's champagne coil."

"My daddy-in-law was an expert." Rex's smile drew out the lines around his eyes. "So. What brings y'all to nether regions on a Thursday night?"

Robert Lincoln leaned against the door, idling the engine with a foot on the floorboard. The Governor looked at his watch.

"It stinks," said Christian Fraux.

"Say again, Chris?"

The boy's calves tightened. After all the nasty jokes about black people smelling, he couldn't believe his father would rib the Governor about his odor.

"My backyard," said Fraux, "your backyard, the whole of Blue Line. Stench. Strange chemicals creeping toward St. Joseph Square. Rotten, shitty ditches and some gutsick, prime-time TV black folks."

"What'd Representative Buzby-what's-his-first-name do?"

"Clyde. He spoke without influence today. The poo-truckers own him. We're facing Third World diseases, Rex. An injection well behind the mobile home park is shooting toxins into the soil. The stuff is filtering back up."

"Dang tough to prove cause and effect in court."

"We have to shut down the well and clean the water."

"What about your Mayor?"

"He's no Mayor Bobby. Said go get money from the legislature."

"Stupid prick, he's got discretionary funds."

"No," said Fraux. "See here. The bill is step one: test the water. Step two is aborting the permit at Department of Natural Resources: kill that well. These actions in Blue Line are *evil.*"

"Evil?" Rex LaSalle raised an eyebrow. "That's a big word."

Fraux pulled an envelope from his pocket. "Here, fifteen-hundred dollars. A token of appreciation from The African-American Voters League of Acadiana for ongoing efforts in our behalf."

"Manna falleth like gentle rain," said LaSalle, taking it.

Robert Lincoln was startled by his father's move.

"You in business with yo daddy?" asked the Governor.

"Nawsir. I'm a sophomore at LSU. Poli-sci major."

"They call it science," the Governor muttered.

Rex tossed the envelope into the boy's lap. "Now your father is an honorable man. Well regarded among the people. Bein' an observer of democracy yourself, Bob, you appreciate ramifications of our dialogue. First time I ever did pow-wow in a hearse. But Robert Lincoln, I ask you: is fifteen tomatoes enough to convince me I need to strong-arm some sorry-ass appropriation bill? *I am dealing with the threshold!* You're lookin' at one of the USA's seventy-five busiest men. Is *this* the threshold? *Tell me,* Bobby Fraux!"

"I don't know about that. But you ought to do it."

"*Do* it, you say! And *why?*" squealed the Governor.

"Your political base could be hurt in your hometown." Then he shut up.

"Astute young man you got here, Chris."

"We try, Rex. We try."

"Well so do I. Rob't, the envelope please."

The boy handed the envelope with the money to the Governor, who stuffed it in his pocket. "Thank you, Chris." Pump-shaking their hands, Rex stepped over his ally's knees. "And remember: y'all got this one for a Hershey bar."

The sweat on his back resembled a spectacular inkblot as he walked to his car. Mudd sat in the front. A young woman in a blue shirt with stars on the shoulders scooted over in the back. The red taillights dissolved into the night.

Fraux deposited himself in the front passenger seat. Driving down the road, Robert Lincoln said: "You think the bill will pass?"

"Today I thought not. Tonight I will sleep less fitfully."

"Then the money —"

"The money is like seafood. In this state everyone eats."

That night Fraux had dropped his son in Baton Rouge and driven on to Avoyelles, bedding down at 1 AM. Up again at sunrise, he drove back to the Capitol to sit with his son in the House gallery, waiting for the delivery. When DuBulio rose for his flag-burning atrocity, Fraux wondered if Rex had given Speaker Sutton a new schedule, allowing the Governor time to line up his ducks. Instead, Sutton shocked everyone in announcing Rex's death.

As the hearse followed cars out of the Capitol parking lot into the tropical heat, Robert Lincoln punched radio dials. Fraux guided his vehicle around the lake toward the Mansion, the chill of the cooling system entombing them as choked voices on the radio eulogized Rex. *What happened after we saw him?* brooded Fraux. State troopers, sweating like horses, were directing vehicles down the road to the Mansion. When they saw the hearse, two troopers immediately cleared a lane. Fraux, who had come like so many others out of bewildered sympathy, forged ahead to steps of the Mansion and in the state's hour of emergency parked there like he owned the place, nodding to guards who assumed he had come for the body, striding upstairs with his son into the packed hall where the First Lady was speaking at the podium.

After the speech, a pulse linked people in the hall, trying to connect with Amelia LaSalle. Reporters gathered along the circuitry, pulling notes from officials and specialists. Fraux counted ten cameras in a radius of the LaSalle women, boom mikes hovering like building cranes among sobbing well-wishers.

A tear rolled down Robert Lincoln's cheek. Christian Fraux squeezed his bicep like a vise: "Do not cry."

"He would have helped us!" the boy blurted.

"I know that!" hissed Fraux, eyes darting. "Comport yourself."

"Aren't you sad?" his son mumbled. "Last night, and all —"

"Of course I'm sad." He tightened his grip.

Tear wells receded in the boy's eyes; confusion etched his brow. Long tutored to show white folks that we are superior to hate, the younger Fraux wanted to shout: Don't show emotions? A man going to help us died!

"Watch people," whispered his father. "Listen to what they are saying. Give away nothing about what we know." Black women in white uniforms were gathering coffee cups and beverage remains. Pockets of black men wearing expensive suits were talking and gesturing amongst themselves or with white men the boy recognized from the legislative lineup. In the buzz of voices, Robert Lincoln stood alone, assuming a pensive mask.

Christian moved to a corner of the room and paused, head down, murmuring to LauraLee, nodding as the family servant whispered. Robert Lincoln wanted to hug his poppa, tell him how much he loved him. Fraux returned, muttering: "Such deception."

"What do you mean, poppa?"

"Mendacity!" seethed Fraux through clenched teeth.

"What is it?"

"The evidence of things unseen."

"Father, we must leave this house!"

"Not until I pay my respects."

The worst place to put Della Lee Broussard in a crisis was the back seat of an Avoyelles Sheriff's car. She still moved with that trademark gait — the head-forward tilt, arms swishing in rhythm with her hips. She popped her rosary beads as they peeled across Atchafalaya Basin bridge. "Please go *faster!*"

"Hold on now, Miss Della," said the deputy driving.

The siren moaned like a wounded animal.

She knew the pain Amelia would feel. The ghosts of love dawdle. My poor daughter: why this? Lord, *please* accept Rex.

"Home stretch now, Miss Della," said the second deputy.

Bobby's orchestration of the wedding reception bubbled out of her memory vault, his arrangement of the seating grid with tables on the lawn; the food canopy in LSU purple and gold; the gazebo for Dewey Balfa's band. And then he plunged into telephone inquiries until he found an old man, lo in New Iberia, who came puttering in a dented truck with the coveted thin tubings.

Ma fille va a mariage, Bobby explained. *My first born.*

The old man held the ladder as Mayor Bobby climbed the oak, hefty and old as the ages. Squat hams straddling the joint of limbs, the Mayor of Avoyelles drew forth the tubing from his helper and laced the lines through branches. As twilight fell, the old Iberian marveled at the coil's gyre-like track along winding branches already lined with — Christmas lights! With the sway of a nimble ape, Mayor Bobby swung down, hit the earth on a stomp and adjusted the nozzle, testing the speed of water through tubular veins. The next day hundreds of guests hovered around the tree as foam rose from a silver fusilade, wedged in a hole carved out of a gigantic ice block. Children were mesmerized by the magical lights, red, green, blue, up in the branches as black men in white jackets serviced the glasses for adult guests, chirping the mantra: "May Bobby got a champagne tree run clean from de root to de vine."

Biggest party in the town's history. Eight-hundred people. Two suckling pigs, apple-mouthed and seasoned with cayenne. Fandangoes of dancers left bare patches on the lawn by the bayou. By dusk all were gone. It was dark when Miss Della found the last guest, snockered, the big boy whose mother had succumbed to tumors that would curse other families as the oil boom spread: Domainge Nobby, weeping under the champagne oak, gazing at the moon.

A famous picture hung in the hallway of the big house: the sheer white of Amelia's dress beneath an elegiac oak, Spanish moss in tiers of breeze-blown symmetry with her hair, dark and full like a flag. The bride's hands clasp his left elbow, her smile dreamily content. Rex wears white tails, that Napoleonic eye on the lens, the luckiest man in Louisiana with a smile to beat the band.

The Avoyelles Sheriff's car stopped at the steps of the Mansion.

"Thank you, gentlemen. I hope I have not frayed your nerves."

They both said "no ma'am" as she opened the door, shielding her eyes from the glare.

"My God, it's hot," she mumbled.

Cameramen burst onto the porch. Christian Fraux followed them out of the front door and witnessed the self-drama of Regina, tearing down the stairs yelling "oh gran-mumeeee" into a swallow hug that nearly knocked Miss Della down. The old lady made it up the stairs for hungry cameras with Colonel Bellamy supporting one arm, Regina the other. The cool foyer was ablaze with roses, chrysanthemums, sesanqua and goldenrods spreading aromas so sweet she muffled three sneezes. She embraced Amelia next to the stuffed leopard from Kenya. "I heard your speech on the radio," she whispered. "Daddy would be so proud."

"Help me with Regina," whimpered Amelia.

The old lady turned to make a greeting. "Oh, Reverend Fraux, an eternity has passed since this morning!"

Fraux gently took the old widow's hands in his own: "We are grieving, Miss Della. My son Robert Lincoln and I. For you and Miss Amelia, the entire family. Rex was my friend. We share the burden of sorrow."

"Thank you," she sighed. "I am not in as many pieces as I may seem."

Fraux withdrew his hands. "Miss Della, you are just right."

Christian Fraux felt himself shrinking in the circle of people and cameras around the First Lady. In Amelia LaSalle's eyes he saw fear. "The Governor was my friend, ma'am. I will pray for him, and for you."

Cradling her mother with one arm, the First Lady used the other to swat away a protruding boom-mike. "I need your help," she whispered. "Please wait."

"Yes, ma'am," he replied calmly, as if life had prepared him for this moment, betraying no scintilla of the fear stirred within him by the sight of so many state troopers, the mind reeling back to bigot howls and billyclubs cracking young bodies while the human line winnowed down to Miss Della and the First Lady and her daughters at 2:15 in the afternoon.

Dr. Willoby's decision to make his stand at the morgue set the tone for a surreal news event. With reporters assembled, the Coroner trudged past the metal holding-lockers for cadavers, pausing to confer with a black assistant in a rubber smock who smiled gold teeth for the cameras while up and away in the gubernatorial bedroom forensic investigators were reconstructing the crime scene. Hubbell sat in Rex's study, watching TV coverage with a gnarled gut and premonitions of media stalkers hiding behind the azalea bushes in his yard.

"Massive cardiac arrest," announced Willoby.

"Any indication," said a reporter, "of what caused the heart stoppage?"

"Naw-sir. At the family's request there will be no autopsy."

"*Dr. Willoby!*" erupted voices.

"Y'all let me talk!" huffed the Coroner. "The First Lady was insistent on 'the sanctity of the body' — her words, people. When a person expires you often find next-of-kin opposed to an autopsy. Religious reasons, as a rule."

"Any indications of foul —"

Willoby shook his head: "I can't say that."

"— or any activity that may have caused —"

"No again. At some level, every human body is a mystery. I'm told his daddy died at fifty. When you have an early mortality like that in the ancestral line, a genetic factor could be at work. But that's only speculation."

The reporters' circling questions reminded Hubbell of vultures over carrion. "Who was the last person to see him alive?" said a radio voice.

"His wife," replied Willoby, shrugging his shoulders.

Goddamn! stewed Hubbell: now she'd have more explaining to do.

Joanie Charlot, star of Channel Five: "Dr. Willoby, did the Governor undergo any undue exertion yesterday?"

Muffled snickers spread among reporters for whom Charlot's season with Rex was hot oral history. Happily married now, a new mom to boot, Joanie trained her sights on the man of the moment and never blushed.

"No exertion that I could tell," remarked Willoby.

"Where was the Governor last night?" asked Joanie in bold follow-up.

"Come back from a rally in New Roads, I'm told."

"What time?" demanded the Associated Press.

"After midnight, is my understanding. Look, my job's to examine the dead. The First Lady was unable to wake him this morning."

"Dr. Willoby," asked a reporter, "where was the body found?"

Willoby opened his mouth. The silence trickled like an IV into a body fighting for life. Hubbell glared at the TV: *Say something, you idiot!*

"There are some ... details." Willoby shook his head. "Imagine waking up to find a man in the prime of life, just lying there — not even a whisper."

Good, thought Hubbell. But watching Willoby lie on a stage where his persona was the selling job made the attorney jittery. Would they believe him?

"Y'all be considerate," said Willoby. "The LaSalles are suffering and this state is sufferin'. That's all I got to say. Thank you now."

Willoby's exit tossed the coverage back to an anchorman who summarized the statement with gravitas in the pauses: "Every human body ... a mystery ... just lying there ... not even ... a whisper. We'll be back after a message."

Backup media trucks lumbered out to Fishy Hall's house in the suburbs. The Lieutenant Governor's wife called the AP to say Joe was down with flu, there would be no further statement, and would someone tell the media to please leave? The news potential in waiting for a drunk to open his front door dissolved; however, reporters for the *Advocate* and *Times-Picayune* kept vigil in the hot shade.

Television showed the last mourners leave the foyer. WBRZ cut between a sullen Regina and Kay's bulbous body, intimating a continuity of life over death. Hubbell wondered how he would have shared the grief of his father's death with a sibling, much less on TV! Della Lee Broussard's arrival made him root for the First Lady: stall everyone, you can do it! Now the viewfinder did a slow reverse zoom as the First Lady climbed the stairs followed by Regina, the grandmother and Kay. At the first-floor landing, dominated by a huge painting of Napoleon in Egypt, his client's real time dissolved into Joanie Charlot, outside the morgue, recapping Dr. Willoby's statement.

Hubbell bounded down to the second-floor landing, which was shadowed by a massive Yukon bear that Rex had shot in 1979 and paid a man in Anchorage two-thousand dollars to stuff. Then came Regina: wired up, feline, eyes dripping. "I know you," she rasped. "Bayou Fever."

"Yes." He blushed. "I'm terribly sorry about —"

She clenched his forearm. "Take me to daddy."

"Really, I can't. The men are … preparing —"

Regina's nostrils flared. "This person is an *obstacle*, mother."

"Mr. Hubbell is helping us, darling."

"Why can't I see daddy?"

"Regina, please."

"Mother, cut through it."

"That will be enough, young lady," interjected Miss Della, hooking her arm through Regina's elbow. "We owe your father some civility."

"Somebody owes *me* an explanation."

"Darling," said Amelia. "I think you need a sedative."

"She needs a muzzle," growled Kay.

"You're jealous because you're fat!" barked Regina.

"You two *stop this!* " hissed the grandmother.

"Mr. Hubbell will speak with us in the dining room," said the First Lady.

As he followed the family, Hubbell tried to expunge thoughts of the hulk of Elvis Banks, counting the first five-thousand the attorney had given him while his humpback younger sibling lifted the death-stiffened leg for a thirty-five-millimeter lens that never lied. In the dining room a Negro trusty from the penitentiary, wearing servant's white, stood at the long table with place settings and andouille gumbo as first course.

"Come back when I ring," Amelia told the prisoner.

The black man left.

"I need a drink," declared Regina.

"In the cabinet," sighed Amelia.

Regina poured Wild Turkey on ice and stood at the window, framed by white afternoon light, goose bumps on her arms.

"All right," said Miss Della. "Let us remember who we are. I did not spend sixty torturous minutes on the highway to come be an umpire. This is a time of mourning, Regina. Not recriminations."

"I want to see daddy before they cut on him."

"Regina! We do not need this at table!" cried Amelia.

The old lady called the switchboard. "Hello, this is Della Lee Broussard. Please send up some of those floral arrangements and make sure y'all keep a list of names on the cards. Mm, thank you so-much."

"Mr. Hubbell," said Amelia, "how soon before Regina can see her father?"

"Shouldn't be long. Let me go find out."

"Do that. And please speak with Christian Fraux about preparing my husband. I want him to take charge of that."

"Yes, ma'am."

Regina disappeared into the bathroom.

Hubbell headed downstairs, his shoulder brushing the thick fur of the Yukon bear, a creature so out of place with the art works Amelia had arrayed through the great house that he imagined an explosive argument between the Governor and First Lady over the hairy mammalian presence.

He found Christian Fraux in a corner of the reception hall, seated alone, sipping coffee, as servants cleaned.

"Well, well," said Fraux, rising. "I had not expected to see you here."

"Nor I you."

Fraux's eyes had a strange sparkle.

"Mrs. LaSalle is with the family right now," reported Hubbell.

"Naturally."

"The Governor will lie in state. She wants you to handle the body."

Fraux raised a quizzical eyebrow. "She requested my services?"

Hubbell frowned. "I assume she discussed this with you."

"Not in as many words, though she said she wanted information. But under the circumstances this certainly makes sense."

"She's under severe stress. What information did she want?"

Fraux dismissed the question with a wave of the hand. "Oh, how the community might participate at the wake. No matter. We're happy to assist."

Robert Lincoln appeared. "They want us to move the hearse."

"Who?" demanded Hubbell.

"Policemen with an ambulance."

"Robert Lincoln," said Christian Fraux. "This is Henry Hubbell. His father was my friend and an ally of our people. We have been retained to provide services for the funeral. Tell the police we will follow them to the mortuary."

"She doesn't want it that way!" parried Hubbell.

"No?" said Fraux with his curious eyebrow.

"We need a coffin," said Hubbell in sudden recall of his father's casket descending into the earth.

Two policemen entered with a gurney.

"Embalming is usually done at a funeral home," explained Fraux. "You realize my place of business is sixty miles from here."

"Bear with me, Reverend Fraux. I'm new to this kind of task."

"What exactly does Amelia want?"

The black man's use of her first name struck a note of solidarity. "She wants you to take control of the body," said Hubbell. "She needs more time. She doesn't want cops upstairs. She wants the body removed in a coffin."

Robert Lincoln stood ramrod straight. "What kind of coffin?" asked the elder Fraux with a grave brow.

"A silver one," blurted Hubbell, remembering the coffin he had chosen for his father.

Colonel Bellamy met the policemen with the gurney.

"Hold on a second!" called Hubbell.

Bellamy frowned. Hubbell crossed the large room and pulled Bellamy aside. "The First Lady wants Fraux to handle the remains. I assume the police will provide an escort."

Bellamy glared at Hubbell and finally nodded.

Hubbell left him with the police and returned to Fraux and son.

"Reverend Fraux," said Hubbell, "can you select an appropriate coffin and come back here in two hours?"

"If you call Schoenbaum Funeral Home on Earl K. Long Avenue and tell them the state will pay for the coffin, I will select one there. Schoenbaum is top of the line."

"I'll certainly do that."

"Tell Mr. Schoenbaum that at the First Lady's request I shall prepare the remains. Unless there is an autopsy."

The strange curl of Fraux's mouth sent a telegraph to Hubbell: *He's toying with my inexperience.* "You trusted my father, Reverend. I want to trust you."

"Trust is based on mutual need. Avoyelles is being poisoned by an injection well. You saw what Sutton did to our bill this morning."

"The Attorney General can intervene on well permits. I don't have authority in that department but I'll help you with the Attorney General."

"You have a deal," said Fraux. They shook hands.

As the mortician and his son departed, Colonel Bellamy confronted the attorney. "Hubbell, I got men outside with nets huntin' a bull alligator that almost ate two kids on the lawn yesterday. On the Governor, I got inertia."

"I think the First Lady is working on a blueprint. Give her time."

"I'm glad you're confident."

A thin smile masked Hubbell's fear as the Colonel did an about-face and made for the front porch. Hubbell raced for the elevator, praying that the Banks brothers would soon be done and that he would not end up like a reptile overgrown its habitat.

II CHECKS AND BALANCES

The first courier reached the Hilton at 2:00 PM, slipping a tote bag to DuBulio and bitching about the walk up nine flights of stairs. With reporters in the lobby, the routing system had to rely on stealth.

The outer room of the Speaker's suite, his command center, featured turkey, ham, potato salad, slaw, bread, mustard, soft drinks and bottled water in addition to the bank of telephones the men stopped using to watch Willoby's press conference. The Coroner's brow dissolved into a wide shot of Capitol Hill as CNN captured Senator Breaux in Washington for sonorous reflections on "the sorrow we feel for the loss of this man — a visionary, a family man, a builder, a master of the legislative process, a great Loozianian!"

"Cut through it," said the Speaker. "We got work to do."

The bags and padded envelopes kept coming. At 3:45 Woodruff entered the Speaker's cavernous bedroom. John Burns Logan sat on one of the two king beds, counting bills in neat columns. Beaconfield wore bifocals and worked a calculator. Woodruff smiled: "How we doin', Mister Speaker?"

"Seventy-five-thousand plus change," muttered Beaconfield.

"This one could put us over," offered Woodruff, opening a briefcase. Logan put his hand in and came out with swatches of money.

"We need more," said the Speaker. "Anybody stonewallin' ?"

Gazing at the sea of bills on the bed, Woodruff said wistfully: "Uh, Canton — he's up in Alabama somewhere at his daughter's college."

"Canton?" said the Speaker, brooding over Hubbell's silence.

Woodruff and Logan in unison: "Gulf Exploration and Marketing."

"Right," said Sutton nebulously. "Who carries his bills?"

"Buzby," prompted Beaconfield.

"Only fifteen thousand in this package," said Logan. "Who sent it?"

"Peele," said Woodruff, turning red. "Chem Waste Management."

Woodruff was going to say something derogatory about Peele, but he saw the Speaker's attention drift as the old man stared at the Capitol, looming like a dark monolith in the heat. The mounting years yielded moments when Sutton's words lagged in his attempt to verbalize thought. Still, he was their Speaker.

"We got feelers out all over," reported Woodruff.

"John Burns, anybody you hadn't called?" said Sutton.

"There's a few," the younger man sighed.

Two quick knocks hit the door and before anyone could respond DuBulio's dark, fleshy face protruded into the room. His eyes widened at the vista of bills on the bed. "*Awrigghht!*" he beamed.

"Shit," said John Burns Logan.

"Shit is right," said Sutton. "John Burns, why'ont you make a round of calls? Lul Joe, you come in here and help Beacon with the tabulatin'."

"President's comin' on CNN," shouted Frampton from the main room.

Beaconfield's face pleaded; Sutton nodded.

Logan and Beaconfield followed Woodruff and DuBulio into the main room to watch Bill Clinton praise Rex LaSalle as "a son of the New South, a true leader of his state, a man of vision, a man I was proud to call — *mah friend.*"

Sutton sipped Coke in his chair.

The phone rang. He answered wearily: "Speaker here."

A rush of air filled the line. Then: *"Tell me about it."*

"Hold on," said Sutton. It always began that way: no "hello, Walter" or verbal niceties — just the hard, guttural *tell me about it.*

The Speaker shut the door to the outer room and returned to his chair, hooking one knee over the armrest. "Where you at, Nobby?"

"Oscar and me are refueling in Yucatan. Goddamn this a bone-chiller. What happened?"

"They say his heart gave out."

Nobby repeated the information to Oscar Abadie, whom Sutton pictured standing next to Doctor. "What about Joe Hall?" demanded Doctor Nobby.

"Scuba diving in Johnny Walker Red."

"Yeah, but he's runner-up. Somebody got to talk with him."

"Say again?" parried Sutton, despite perfect audibility.

"*Oscar says this a major constitutional crisis.*"

"That's a valid viewpoint."

"Who all's doin' what?"

"It's complicated."

"*I'm payin' for this fuckin' phone call.* Oscar and me're standing in some Mexico airport."

Sutton paused. "*Speak … louder,* Nobby."

Doctor Nobby was no dummy. Like all men in the show, he knew how federal tentacles oozed into uncountable phone systems. His voice rose: "I said, if they get Atchison, you're the one. We need to meet. This evenin' when I get in."

"Go ahead."

The Speaker heard a muffled exchange between Nobby and Abadie. Then Nobby: "I'll come to your hotel at supper time."

"Whatever works."

"Hold on. Oscar wants to talk."

Sutton had known Abadie for years and never heard his voice sound so aged or fearful: "Walter? You talk to Amelia?"

"Indeed I have. She's bearin' up in a bad situation. You got a ton of work cut out the moment you get back."

"How's that?" came the Attorney General.

"Hubbell. He's your man, right?"

"Sure. He was in top condition last time I saw him."

Sutton understood: Oscar was blocking information from

Nobby. Sutton paid well for clean phone lines, but this was Nobby's cell call. "I'm glad you think he's top," the Speaker told the Attorney General. "Hubbell is helpin' Amelia with a probe. Bellamy called for you and got Hubbell."

Seconds passed. "At least she's in good hands. I am sick over Rex."

"This state's in a fryin' pan, Oscar. Be careful who you talk to."

The long recess of Oscar Abadie's pause certified his predicament. No one applied pressure like Doctor Nobby. The Speaker pitied Abadie for hours alone in an airplane with Nobby. Oscar's approach to the real estate was less muddied than other men's. With twenty-thousand oil waste dumps scattered across marshes and prairies, Oscar took money from law firms in lieu of their shit-truck clients. Abadie was lucky his office cost less, campaign-wise, than legislative tracts of deep mineral wealth. Oscar had no responsibility for oil-related bills. For once, Sutton envied him that.

"Soon as you break free, call me. And contact that Hubbell."

"By God, Walter! Rex was my *friend*. This is horrible."

"In more ways than you think, podna."

"It's me again," came Nobby over the line. "What you need?"

"The feeling that God has a plan."

"Banks goan be closed time we get back. Got us a phone right chere. You need somepin financial, say so now."

"I don't reckon."

"Suit yourself."

"Mm," said the Speaker.

Nobby hung up, as always, without saying goodbye.

Sutton rose and peered down at television trucks with satellite dishes. Nobby's last comment struck him as brazen. He wanted Oscar to know he could get money to the Speaker. But Oscar was no stooge. Without inquiring into amounts, he would focus on details of a succession bill he'd have to defend if the ACLU protested. Sutton wanted Hall's ouster to be smooth. Cash growing on his bed meant equity. Why did Nobby force the question? Maybe he had turned snitch for the feds: entrap the boys he gave money to to save his own bohunkus. Whatever Oscar and Nobby had cooked up in the Caribbean interested Sutton less than the fact that they were so coupled. A part of him pitied Oscar.

Five days earlier Sutton had had his Monday lunch with Rex, just the two of them at the Mansion. Over coffee they got down to the meat: Senate President Atchison. "Feds have him strapped on a barbecue pit, Walter. Atch wants me to get Leon to go soft on sentencing," Rex said tartly.

Judge Leon Carter, once a lieutenant of the Rex LaSalle machine, was the presiding judge in Atchison's federal trial. Fifty years in politics had taught Sutton the value of silence.

"Help me uncloud this picture, Mr. Speaker. Atch does a shakedown of construction companies. He takes their dirty money and he channels it to five sapsuckers in the Senate. Press calls that influence-peddling. I thought being President of the Senate gives you plenty to peddle. Why give big dollars to five yamheads who would never vote against you on major legislation anyway? *What does he get for his money, Walter?* The Feds haven't indicted the five Senators. They will drag each one before the grand jury if Atch doesn't snitch during his pre-sentence phase. Cooperate, he gets a lighter sentence. What will Atch do: drag five baboons down in the outhouse — or eat his own waste?"

Sutton raised doleful eyebrows. Money irritated the Speaker. He knew how to get the material (you don't become Speaker without magnet hands), but he needed sparse funding for his own campaigns. Rex's alchemy was different. Money galvanized his imagination. Speaker Sutton respected that.

"What Atch did doesn't offend me, Walter. But it sure does *puzzle* me. He got his bohunkus indicted for squeezing contractors who owe Rompallo."

Sutton's mouth dropped.

"You didn't know the contractors were tight with Rompy? Funny thing. Neither did I — till Atch came over here, begging me to twist Leon's arm."

Sutton spoke commandingly: "Did he really say, 'twist Leon's arm?'"

"Nah, nah. He blubbered on what his wife and children and banker goan do, his life's a shambles, could I do this erranda mercy bluh-bluh-bluh."

A curious emotion had come over the Governor: exasperation.

"If he just kept the material *himself*, Walter. Used the money cuz his daughter needed a mortgage or face surgery — even college tuition. People in our state understand larceny if it's for the family. Leon could be sympatico over a crime of personal desperation. But this shakedown scheme's a cold hamburger, Mr. Speaker! You think chasin' pussy caused a crisis in my marriage? Shee-it. Try bein' stalked three years by FBI flesh-eaters and Amelia wailing about having to sell off some of her Juju masks. *That was serious*. She kept the art. I ate five-hundred-thou in legal fees. Which made me a smarter politician. Last session we spread out road contracts like spaghetti to keep DuBulio's money bags happy. Once a month Lil Joe drives up to Angola prison with a stuffed turkey for ole man Rompallo. Lil Joe owes his seat to Rompy, so he does things for him. Food. Errands. A piñata for the grandboy. I am starting to snore. Allasudden here comes Atch, shakin' down Rompy's contractors to bribe five Senators. He needs them for groundwork on something. It has got to involve Rompy. I bet it's big, too. No one said Atch has a mushy brain stem."

Indeed. Lack of intelligence was not a trait the Speaker associated with his Senate counterpart. Sutton shook his head. "Atch is a glutton."

"That's exactly right, Walter." The Governor paused. "You and I are normal men. We can stop eating. We understand limits, how things balance."

Sutton was in that season of life where friendship and political ties mature coterminously. He liked the way Rex's mind worked. Rex had an innate curiosity about power, how far to stretch the tissue, the limits people would tolerate. This inquisitiveness competed with the sensuous smile, the open pleasure on his face.

Rex's first election had coincided with the discovery of a

mammoth natural gas field sweeping down a vast subterranean fan from Tuscaloosa through Mississippi, broadening beneath the Cajun prairie. The legislature's job was to divvy up the tax relief. At a stag dinner in 1973 with fourteen oil, gas and petrochem barons, Walter Sutton watched the boldest power grab of his life. Rex announced that he would personally guarantee tax moratoria on new exploration sites. In return he wanted veto power over what they paid legislators. The ensuing silence was as awesome as Rex's audacity. Finally, bull-chested Robey Canton said: "I sank a hunnert-thou into yo campaign, Rex. And I don't believe what you just said."

"I don't want any tamperin' with the real estate," Rex shot back. "We now have Negroes in the legislature, Robey. The leasing race begins at midnight."

In the geometry of so many creased foreheads, Sutton had a revelation: *They don't understand niggers.* Sutton assumed that with proper guidance, the black politicians would take money just like the peckerwoods. What did Robey Canton know?

"Spread your donations on selected officials," said Rex, "and on the major action everybody is gonna be hungry. Who do you give to? Give to the wrong Afro, you insult a big gorilla redneck. Pipe it through me, nobody loses. My crystal ball shows many roads to your wellheads, roads that need to be cleared. I see a maze of districts. Who has the final say over *how much* asphalt gets laid. That map is *mine*, gentlemen. *I am dealing with the threshold!*"

Sutton had just read a newspaper story about the bicameral mind. He imagined the oilmen as a collective brain: a tableful of niggers at one lobe, oil derricks spewing green money at the other, and Rex in the middle.

Robey Canton glowered. "We never had to do it this way before."

"How many times you been visited by EPA?" Rex said casually.

Canton scratched his jaw.

Sutton sized up the economics. If Rex delivered, every man in the room was looking at huge profit escalators. No taxes and free roads to their wells!

"The other problem," continued the Governor, raising a water pitcher and pouring himself a glass — "is your waste. Y'all got enough dumps littered across the real estate to bankroll defense lawyers till rapture comes at the end time. Imagine what is *in* those purple lagoons, Robey Canton! Department of Natural Resources needs guidelines on this disposal bidness." Rex took a drink of water. "I could ask the Sierra Club for help."

One week later he had two million in Colonial Bank. Key men in both houses assimilated the facts. Energy was the governor's domain: lock, stock and barrel. Money flowed like wedding wine. Sutton became Speaker of a happy House. News coverage turned on moral-fervor blacks and segregationists reborn as fiscal conservatives. The segs lost on social bills but stood with Rex on industrial development. Rex doled out money to black officials who marched with him on legislation benefiting big oil. Years after the initial two million dollars had replicated itself many times over, the waste pit regulations Robey Canton had confected were mired in litigation with the Sierra Club. No dump site targeted for prosecution by Attorney General Oscar Abadie belonged to a major player.

Sutton thought back to his last encounter with Governor LaSalle and remembered the anger, so rare a trait in Rex's molecular composition.

"*Atch took mob money and spent it like a dufus*! He won't rat on old man Rompallo. That's intelligent. You wouldn't want your wife waking up to dead poodles in the swimming pool. Don't fault Atch for defending Rompy."

Sutton emitted an intelligent sigh.

"Atch gave money to those five Senators so they'd be in his pocket for something, Walter. He's goin' down next week. If he won't say what that *something* was, he's got no leverage with Leon for a light sentence. In which case, the Feds start carving on those five Senators in grand jury. Question: will one of them burp? Po silly me wonders what the fuck was Atch tryna do."

Rex loved to leave matters hanging like a question mark. Sutton had assumed they would pick up the thread at their next Monday lunch. Instead the Governor never got out of bed on Friday.

Amelia said Rex was poisoned, Sutton brooded.

Coroner said heart attack.

Where was that goddamn Hubbell?

12 FALLING

Mitchell Mudd had no inkling of Rex's hideaway on the eighth-floor studio in Capitol Towers where Sophie Thibodeaux awoke that afternoon to songs of angels at the throne. Head throbbing from scripture dreams she kept trying to expunge, she raised a hand, shielding her brow to white glare slanting through the blinds. She imagined Mitchell out there, somewhere, blasting his Lincoln down a road, wind running shrill in his ears. Staggered by it all. What do you do when the world caves in? Ride that car into the void, Mitchell.

She shuddered at another memory deposit. *I saw an angel come down out of heaven*, so her stepdaddy had preached, *and I saw a new heaven and a new earth*. That was when he bought the Buick. A car shiny green that evoked hums and approving nods from the 250 church folk full of pride for the pastor who was building the great statue of Jesus, with his own hands, alone.

And so it registered: she had managed to sleep. Since noon. Four hours. She turned on TV. Droning, replays. Nothing new in the news since Willoby.

Sophie was still in the jeans and black T-shirt she'd pulled on in the middle of the night. She drew her legs up, forehead resting on knees, and wondered if Rex could see inside her mind. Fear and hunger rose within her.

She pushed off the bed with a personal stench of death. Long before she let him touch her, Sophie had turned Rex's private logo

— *"the great power is to make people think that something false is true"* — into a prism on her scripture-sodden past. What do you believe once you decide what you can't believe?

In a choking reverie, she visualized Rex listening with gentle eyes as she told him what happened the day before Easter when she was eight, in a white gown, knee-high in Big Woods bayou, the beauty of those rolling harmonies sung by Pentecostals on the shore, her sweet stepmama standing by ladies with their smiles. *Are you saved?* cried Reverend TJ Thibodeaux *Yes, daddy, I am saved, I know it's true I am!*

"We Roman Catholics never got in water like that," Rex had ruminated.

Sophie stepped into the shower. Heat sizzled her skin, steam rising to the fusillade of mental echoes. Mitchell Mudd, screaming.

She slipped into the sundress Rex bought her on their trip to Yucatan and sat on the couch. Too spent to cry, she watched the sky turn indigo.

A cone of light rose within the memory crypt, followed by Doctor Nobby, skittish in Jerry Lee Lewis's dressing room at the LSU Assembly Center. Ten PM. Jerry Lee on the phone to Vegas. The warm-up act, the Boogie Kings, was all done. Nobby: "Natives getting restless out there, Jerry Lee." Jerry Lee shut the door for privacy on his call. Nobby laid out white lines on a mirror: "How 'bout some, sugar?" *Not for me, Doctor.* Nobby's nostrils inhaling like a rocket in reverse. He licked that little mirror and stuffed it in his pocket. Good thing. The door flew open and the Governor of Louisiana filled the room: white suit, white shirt, white buck shoes, a scroll under his arm tied in a bow as red as his tie.

"Came to make Jerry Lee an honorary Colonel on my staff, Doctor."

Rex's eyes turned on her with a force that made her blush.

Nobby: "Jerry's back there on the phone with an expert. He's late on stage, guvna."

"I want to do the Colonel proclamation on stage."

"We're committed to make that happen, guvna."

Rex smiled. "And in whose exquisite presence do I have the privilege to bask?"

Those eyes of his. She giggled. This man was unreal.

"My assistant, Miss Sophie Thibodeaux," said Nobby. "This here gal has better R&B recall than Oldies One-Oh-One."

"My, my, my," said Rex. "Who sang the Popeye song?"

"Oh come on, Governor. That was Eddie Bo. Ask a hard one."

"A *hard* one she says?" Hands on hips. His eyebrows so playful! Nobby yelled: "*Jerry Lee!* Governor LaSalle's here."

Jerry Lee opened the door, cradling the phone on his shoulder, smiled at Rex, pointed an index finger and pulled it like a trigger.

Rex winked at Jerry Lee and turned his gaze toward her: "Awright Miz Lady, answer this one. In 'Baldhead,' where'z the woman lose her wig?"

"She loses that wig at Lee Circle's Park."

"Ho, this gal knows her Professor Longhair!" Then, smiling: "And would you be related to Senator Cecil Thibodeaux of Calcasieu Parish?"

"No, sir."

"*Good.* Who's yo daddy?"

"He's a preacher for Assemblies of God. You don't know him."

"Try me."

"I don't want to."

Jerry Lee came out, smelling like Bay Rum.

The following day, against her better instincts, she went to lunch at the Mansion. Regina and the First Lady were getting their pictures taken in New Orleans for some magazine. Kay was in Hilton Head. *Want a job at the Capitol?* No, thank you, Governor. *Call me Rex. What about a car?* I'm not that kind of girl, Governor. *You must be the other kind.* What kind is that?

The kind ah like! smiled Rex LaSalle.

I am not going to jump in bed with you.

I didn't expect you to.

She had accepted the limousine ride out of wild curiosity about a Governor and the house with the famous paintings and sculptures. He told her what people believe is made of information other people control, which got her thinking about religious matter she wrestled with in therapy. They met two days later at a bench in the park, as natural as two people could be. He told her all about his drunk daddy. She told him music had been her sanity through adolescence: "When your stepdaddy builds a sixty-foot statue of Jesus on a bluff above the black top in Big Woods community of Rapides Parish, it alters everything." A thousand and one nights in her room, plugged into the mystery train from Fats to Roy Brown singing "I'm a Mighty Man," on to Elvis, back again to the Flamingoes crooning clouds of Doo-Wop heaven while Reverend TJ Thibodeaux snored after each day's toil on the scaffolding by himself, high up, constructing Jesus in the Big Woods.

"I saw his picture in *Newsweek* when he finished," said Rex.

"He framed the letter of congratulations you sent."

"I'd forgotten that," frowned the Governor.

Her stepmother began coughing as Reverend Thibodeaux soldered the joints at the waist of the mighty statue; Molly's hacking worsened as TJ completed the elbows. He was making Jesus' hands when they learned it was tumors in the lung. TJ dropped Sophie at school in the morning, sat with his wife till ten, up on the statue hammering till dusk. A deacon gave Sophie a ride to the hospital after school. TJ joined them at night, praying over Molly, beseeching Jesus for her healing, for their salvation. Molly was one year deceased when Reverend Thibodeaux began courting a widow in Pollack.

Bibles in so many languages came to the post office for Reverend TJ Thibodeaux's Chapel for International Bibles lodged in a pinewood pentagon he had built with funding assistance of Reverend Marvin Gorman, who preached on TV from New Orleans, as Sophie moved from DH Lawrence to Virginia Woolf, hiding paperbacks under her bed. She was relieved to be alone with *Mrs. Dalloway* and cassettes of Little Richard, which by the fall of Jimmy

Swaggart you could get for $4.99 a tape in Alexandria, the seat of Rapides Parish. Little Richard in the K-Mart. Imagine that.

"Fantasy allows us to live," she wrote in her first-semester term paper on Virginia Woolf. "Full truth means stealing from the dream life we need in order to survive." *Great!* wrote her professor at LSU.

Rex was like a movie. Days dissolved into months of telephone calls and walks in the woods, her telling him *you just can't remake your life like this, you are the Governor of the state* and he kept materializing in zydeco clubs where she was dancing, wearing different disguises, sometimes even Nobby didn't recognize him, advancing like an army of charm. Months passed before she got hip to the proximity of Mitchell Mudd in a car with tinted windows near the vehicle Rex drove, a precautionary motor purring in the event of an emergency to beat a gubernatorial retreat. Which never happened. She dated several boys but by junior year was in a sea change beyond all comprehension. She feared the reaction from her stepdaddy, discovery by the First Lady. But when a man tries to remake himself, "to create a counterself so that you are not trapped into some permanent definition by the forces that made you," as Rex put it, she heard her own thoughts being spoken.

Jesus, You know I resisted him, I resisted him for months.

Tried every way to stiff-arm him, in point of fact. But Rex offered tenderness like cloud formations unseen in her experience of the sky. All of his power, squared into stories about how we search for love, love you can't understand when you marry the daughter of a big house in flight from the numbness of a drunk-as-sin deputy sheriff daddy. *Ville Platte was the worst town on earth to grow up in, Sophie. A town where there are no secrets.* His yearning to escape his persona mesmerized her, a life-quest that reverberated with her desire to go back like a science fiction time traveler and find her biological parents. How did TJ locate me? "We create ourselves with what is available," Rex said in a canoe on the lake at Chicot State Park one afternoon, "and move on from there."

His love came raining down, swirling, lifting her into the idea of a woman forming, a self apart from the man who built Jesus in the Big Woods.

Rex having a wife and children made her feel dirty, but his curiosity — "to find myself on the other side of these zydeco disguises, sugar, you don't know how I want to escape these oil pirates at the threshold" — was a sweep of energy that left her breathless each time she saw him. The sheer drama of his personality provoked some essence in her own development, waiting to be released.

Now she was awake-and-dreaming: Rex tears off the red tie and white suit, his hands wide like Our Savior on the cross, the blinding blue light crests in a halo above his face as angelic incantations rain down:

Swing low, sweet char-iot,
Comin' for to carry me home …

His halo dissolved in a cry from somewhere buried deep. She wanted forgiveness for his obscene death, but had trouble knowing how to ask.

Bolting off the couch, she rummaged through the closet for her things. If *po*lice find this place, they will see my skirts and blouses hanging by his shirts and trousers, they will root through the chest-of-drawers looking for our underwear. I have to escape this wicked city. Where do you go with a hellhound on your trail?

PSYCHE'S DIRGES **13**

When the table was cleared and the last trusty gone, Regina sprang for the door. "I'm goin' to see daddy!"

Caressing a Valium, the First Lady followed Regina up the stairwell in a back draft of acid memories: Rex, waving off her pleas to tame Regina's sexual hurricane; Rex spoiling Regina with cash, rescuing her credit cards, lavishing the buttery praise, Regina my pretty one, Regina my lul queen, till the night she called from Belize, shit-faced, with news of her marriage to a scuba teacher. The Bishop arranged an annulment. At the third-floor landing, Amelia watched her wild daughter totter, tilting back in a swoon of Wild Turkey.

Amelia steadied Regina to the gaze of Kifwebe, the wall mask from a leopard society in deep Congo with furrowed cheeks, flared nostrils and a tubular mouth, pursed out. *Bet that bucko could do a heap of damage,* Rex had cracked when Amelia hung the mask. She loved the geometric purity of the scarification lines even if Kifwebe lacked the cool mystery of her favored Dogon pieces.

Startled by the mask, Regina hiccupped.

Kifwebe's energy radiated into Amelia, a force of resolve. The wars with Regina suddenly seemed small; what mattered was that they brace together for the life ahead. She tried not to picture the husband she had had.

Regina halted at the bedroom door. "What's that chemical smell, mama?"

"I don't know."

Regina turned the doorknob. Amelia swallowed the Valium.

"*My God, mother!*"

White powder coated the floor, splayed with shoe tracks. Bed sheets were gone. The body lay spread-eagled beneath a green rubber cover.

Regina covered her mouth.

The First Lady went to the bathroom and pulled six towels out of the closet. She ran water on three towels and began working at the bedside, rubbing dust off the furniture. Regina stood frozen. Amelia threw a towel on the floor, stooped and began mopping the white powder.

"Help me, Regina. For your father's sake, help me now."

Lifting her hem, Regina knelt next to Amelia. "They put all this dust for fingerprints because someone killed him!" she whimpered.

"Help me, Regina. We can't let the maids see this!"

"You're right," she muttered. "They'd tell everybody."

"I can't do this alone, Regina!"

Regina took a towel and wiped large circles on the floor, absorbing the dust, erasing the residue of white whorls. Amelia wiped dust off the bed stand. On and on the women worked, rubbing out swaths of powder in large circles on the floor, one hand with a wet towel, the other gripping a dry one. Regina fetched more towels. She knelt, splitting her panty hose. Smoothing the floor to recover the cypress sheen, she worked away, panting in a conspiracy of love. Dizzy from the bourbon, sweating, toiling, the sight of the room proof to her suspicions, Regina recoiled from the patina of her own smooth flesh exposed by the stocking rip. Watching her mother on her knees like a maid, she swallowed her questions, wiping away at the smell of death. The stark outlines of her father beneath the rubber shroud sent a voltage of sorrow through her body, pain racing into her temples. She stood up, wobbly, wondering what to do.

Amelia stumbled toward the bed. Her slender fingers felt obese and numb as she tugged at the rubber sheet, exposing Rex's leg.

Regina saw the lipstick on his flesh and squealed: "Oh *no!* He didn't. Oh Jesus-God, not up here. Momma … *Oh, Momma!"*

The First Lady's grace had been a pillar of sovereignty in Regina's life. She resented her mother's savoir-faire even as she bumbled in its emulation. The abrupt image of black curls falling over Amelia's forehead opened a quick vista, the track of silver dots along the scalp the dye could not reach. Amelia worked a towel along Rex's leg, pressing hard to erase red smears on his skin, stuffing a cry of rage to reach all the Kifwebe masks ever carved when the passion rose and she hurled a fist on the chest: *"Rex, goddammit, why did you do this to us!"*

"Don't hit him, Mama!" Regina wrestled her away from the bed. "He's dead, don't get mad, don't fight, we don't know what happened!"

Regina pulled her hands around her mother's shoulders. She felt the force of Amelia's face, sinking between her breasts, drenching her with sobs.

"We need to get out of this room, momma. Leave daddy be."

"I can't let Reverend Fraux find Rex this way! Help me clean daddy."

Regina grabbed the towel and squeezed the reddened surface,

unable to erase the memory of Fats Domino playing in the Assembly Center and the man in the far corner, in sunglasses and rockarolla threads dancing with that Sophie creature over whom half the football team lusted *that is my daddy over there I just know it is*. When she confronted him the next day before an AFL-CIO speech, he shook his head: "Sugar, you got to keep off of drugs."

"I cleaned him, Mama. No one can see the lipstick. Let's get out of here."

Regina clutched her mother at the waist and led her into the hallway. Regina was fatigued. She felt a hundred years old from the death room.

"Don't tell your sister or grandmother!"

"Mama, I won't tell a soul."

At that moment, the elevator opened and they encountered Miss Della, LauraLee and two trusties working toward probation as servants, all of them laden with flower arrangements, a rainbow of colors. The grandmother led them to the master bedroom. Fragrance suffused the hallway. Amelia sneezed in three staccato bursts. "God bless you," everyone said at once.

Kay was lying on the big bed with a box of Kleenex, eyes swollen, watching TV with the sound turned down.

"My stockings are ruined," said Regina, opening Amelia's closet.

The trusties left by the stairway.

Della Lee Broussard walked with LauraLee to the elevator.

"Did Rex seem ill to you?" the matriarch asked.

"Yesterday he was his usual self, vim and vigored like a champion. This ain't like when May Bobby died, Miss Della. Mens were in that other bedroom."

Miss Della frowned. "What were men doing in there?"

"Testing the body. See how he died, maybe."

"I thought he had a heart attack."

"That's what the Coroner say."

"Don't play coy with me, LauraLee."

"I only know what my eyes see. I ain't been in that bedroom."

The elevator opened.

"Excuse me, ma'am."

Della Lee Broussard cast a cold eye on the room with the body. Eighty years of the proper life formed a wall of resistance to peeking in. She returned to the master bedroom. Amelia sat by the window in a mauve haze, her dress damp and streaked with white dust.

In the bathroom, Regina was getting sick.

Della Lee Broussard stood by Amelia. "I think you need to go in a quiet room, honey."

Amelia nodded. "Will you be all right?" she asked Kay.

On the bed, Kay nodded.

The First Lady followed her mother down the hallway to Kay's old bedroom, now a guest quarters with off-white walls and two photographs by Man Ray. Amelia lay on the bed. Her mother sat next to her in a rocking chair.

"He had company last night, Mama."

Della Broussard stiffened. "Had that gone on here before?"

"Once that I knew of. We had an awful row. He swore never again."

"Disgraceful!" hissed the old lady. "Rex put you through a lot, honey."

"He did," she whispered. "He certainly did."

"Do you know who it was?"

"I have my ideas." Kifwebe loomed in Amelia's thoughts like a god demanding supplication "I tried so hard to make him happy."

"Everyone knows that, honey. God rest his poor soul."

"I didn't want Kay to see the mess in the room."

"No, a woman carrying doesn't need that."

The sun drifted behind clouds as bells on the university commons tolled four. Amelia's eyelids closed to an image of her daddy on the porch of the big house in Avoyelles. Sophomore year, Thanksgiving, she came home from LSU with her boyfriend, not knowing then that her daddy had called the Ville Platte sheriff. Who said: "Rex LaSalle would be Maury's boy. Maury was my deputy back ten-some year. Died on the job. Likeable fella, yes-sah. *Mais*, he had a weakness for the skirts, him. And he was a serious boozer. But I'ma say it straight, Mayor Broussard: Maury La-Salle was a *damn* good deputy shar'ff."

The gene pool worried Mayor Bobby the day Rex walked around and opened the door for Amelia as if the Pontiac were his. Then Bobby saw the mustache, so much blacker than his sandy hair. Rex followed her up the stairs. She melted in her father's arms, that hug-hold he cherished to his soul. She stood back, prim ladylike: "Daddy, this is my boyfriend Rex." He set the suitcases down.

"It's a pleasure to make your acquaintance, Mr. Mayor."

"Likewise I'm sure," said Bobby Broussard, shaking his hand, thinking that he looked like a buccaneer.

What does a drunk, tomcattin' daddy do to a boy? The Mayor and his wife wondered. But he stood when ladies entered the room and he had perfect table manners. On the porch, Bobby sipped Jack Daniels; he asked if Rex had anything against libations. "I prefer my soda straight, sir." Amelia insisted that Rex simply did not indulge. The way he walked into a room ignited Mayor Bobby's curiosity, dazzling everyone in his radius as if he owned the patent on charm. His intelligence on Rex came via ten-dollar payments to Dudley Ardouin, whose nephew Domainge Nobby was the boy's friend at the college.

"He play in a combo," Dudley reported. "Domainge say dey sing like on de radio. Trumpet, drum, banjo. Heh-heh." What's funny? "They got no accordion."

The day Amelia met him, The Bayou Devils were rocking the lawn at an SAE rush party, Rex on guitar singing, *"Jim Dandy to the rescue ... Go, Jim Dandy! Go!"* A band with black jeans, black T-shirts, berets and sunglasses: the first beatniks in Baton Rouge. She felt his wave of heat across seventy-five feet of twilight barbecue, head bobbing, his body gyrating like Elvis. The band took a pause for a worthy cause; her date went to the john. She turned. That smile: "I am Rex LaSalle, matriculating in prelaw with one question in the world."

"And what would that be?"

"The boy you're with: does he understand a woman's *mind?*"

Alone with his daughter, Mayor Bobby asked if she thought that singing in a combo was the way for a man to make his mark. *Just what do you mean by that?* she shot back. Remark of a casual bystander, he muttered. Her eyes flared: *Daddy, you don't have a damn right to snoop in my life!* Mind you, daughter: no sass. *Daddy, I don't peek through your keyhole and I will thank you to keep your nose out of my interpersonal relationships!* She was about to cry. The Mayor shifted somberly in his chair: Don't yell daughter. *I mean it, daddy. That's the meanest thing — spying on me! My girlfriends like his band.* Well, said the Mayor, why does he have that hair stripe radicalizing his face?

Her eyes sparkled. "It makes him look so *distinguished.*"

"Not to me. Not to lawyers. Not to bankers."

"He didn't have it when we met. One night after a Tyrone Power picture show I said, 'That's the handsomest man in Hollywood.' He said, 'Better'n Clark Gable?' I said well, maybe. He didn't call the day after that. Or the day after that or the day after that. *Ten whole days* passed. I never lost a boy *in my life.* You don't know the hurt I felt. Well, Wednesday at midnight Carol Sue Jennings starts squealing and every girl in the house went to the windows. Down on the lake behind sorority row, Rex was on a raft with five football players holdin' torches, he had his guitar and Tyrone Power mustache, and he got up on the shoulders of this big boy Domainge Nobby — and daddy, Rex *serenaded* me. He came under my window and sang 'Heartbreak Hotel' with all the Tri-Delts watching. My sorority sisters say the mustache enhances his sex appeal."

"That worries me."

"Oh, daddy. I'm nineteen."

"The mustache looks scheming."

The next time they returned to Avoyelles, Rex had a used Studebaker, buffed bright green, the whitewalls clean — and no mustache.

"Well, now," said Mayor Bobby. "That there is some ve-hicle."

"A man needs four wheels he can trust."

"All right now."

Through many a limpid bayou dusk, Mayor Bobby and the suitor sat on the porch, bantering about cars and football before Rex steered the talk to politics. The Mayor drank Jack Daniels in his rocker. Rex sipped soda in the swing, tasting advantages he had never known. The arriviste strain bothered Bobby, but with the mustache erased he put a five dollar bill on the table.

"What's that for?" said Rex.

The Mayor gazed across the pasture. The sun lay in a low ridge, the color of rust. "Politics is the movement of money. The money useta come from land. Harvests and darkies, that whole bit. Farmers don't have the big money now. I know fifteen mineral leases in a thirty-mile radius of where we sit. Any one could be worth a thousand head of cattle *per annum*. If you want power, real power, know where the oilman sups and find a place at his table. What those men want — tax breaks, leases, zoning — that's where this state's headed. Four refineries are goin' up on the River below the Capitol. Fifteen years from now, we'll be looking at the Ruhr Valley of the South."

"What about relations between the races?"

Bobby Broussard frowned. "This Supreme Court bidness is just the start. It'll get bad before it gets better."

"We need rock and roll concerts."

"What the hell for?"

"Bring youth together. Promote harmony for a new society."

"Good luck," said the Mayor gloomily.

"Music makes people happy, Mayor Bobby."

"Money makes 'em happier. When some buster palms you the cash, be damn sho you can deliver." He slipped the five toward Rex. "Now, a future elected official needs gasoline for his automobile."

"You're a generous man."

"Not at all."

"I appreciate your vote of confidence."

"Are you sleeping with my daughter?"

"Love is more complex than a one-word answer."

At the rehearsal dinner, Mayor Bobby searched the furrows of Mrs. Ruth H. LaSalle's brow. The boy's mother was not much older than Della, but how she had aged! In the candle warmth of Cajun sup, softened by the Mayor's time-tested jokes, the little woman confided that she was a Hunkie from Yallaboosha, Mississippi, as if they owned the hardware store. Yallaboosha is hill country near Memphis. Tough scrabble soil. Nothing like the alluvium of the Delta or the fertility of French Louisiana. Hard-shelled Baptist. A dry county: you buy likker from the sheriff's friend. What kind of name was Hunkie? A *poor* name.

Her eyes conveyed the pain of a long-buried scoundrel of a husband. The boy, losing his daddy at thirteen, roaming as teenagers do. A small house, those years, her life's prison. It happens to widows of no-account men in these little Southern towns: in church they atone by their mere presence, living vicariously through the child or moving to a town where tongues won't wag. Ruth Hunkie LaSalle had stayed in Ville Platte. No one said it would be easy. At rehearsal supper, Rex doted over her with a courtliness that had the Broussard aunts humming.

Stories shape a family, the tellings and retellings give memory its tone.

As time passed, Mayor Bobby's confidences seeped into Amelia. She imagined her mother-in-law pining for escape from those drear Mississippi hills to the merry lowlands of crawfish dances, only to learn her husband was a whiskey-fueled philanderer. Ruth died a year after the wedding.

Della Lee Broussard heard a rumbling on the stairs. Amelia was sleeping. The old lady peeked out the bedroom door. For what seemed an eternity, she watched Christian Fraux, his son and two state troopers maneuver the coffin into the hallway on portable wheels. They lifted the silver vessel with hard breathing, grunts and pushes, turning toward the stairs.

It's over now, the old lady thought. *Both men dead.*

I4 REX IN A FREEZER

Hubbell's intestines were churning as the van thundered down River Road. Elvis Banks wore goggle glasses. His hands cradled the steering wheel like webbed wings. The forensic consultant's hair was a plaster of sweat. He was one of the strangest human beings Henry Hubbell had ever seen. The attorney belched as they bounced past an oil refinery. Elvis cut down a street of sagging shotgun houses; green sedge sprouted through cracks in the pavement. Hubbell felt like a milk shake as the van reached the warehouse inside of which hung Elvis's laminated degrees in criminology and chemistry on cypress walls.

In the back sat Brother, a humpback a few years younger and full foot shorter than his sibling. Hubbell had studied Brother, gnomelike, in the death room, wheezing through maneuvers of the photographic gear, sweat rolling *plink!* on the floor while Elvis, arm veins glistening like marble, used surgical tweezers to uproot fibers from the bed, the body, the sheets, the works. Hubbell saw that Regina and Kay fought like cats. The Banks' dug into dirt worth money. Surely they would guard secrets; Hubbell had no siblings as a gauge.

"Pointa entry tru an open mouth," asserted Brother.

"Don't say nothin'," ordered Elvis.

"Rex's mout hadda be open. Only way dey coulda popped him."

"Who said *they?*" snapped Elvis.

"Dey, he, she, it. Somebody hosed that man's adenoids."

"Shut up, Brother. We got nothin' confoimed yet."

"Dey shot it into his mout like a seltzer bottle outa Fred Astaire."

Elvis exploded: "*Never talk* till we know what we fount!"

"Whomy talkin' to but you and client heah? What I saw was a

mout —"

"Only mouth open is yours so shut it."

"I saw what I saw."

"*You like this job?*"

"Yeah," suffered Brother. Then: "You know what I like about you, Elvis?"

"What?"

Brother smiled: "Everyteeng."

The warehouse lay behind a cement wall crowned with broken bottles that threw off green-blue spangles of light. A metal gate opened and shut behind the vehicle as it stopped. Elvis checked his Rolex. "I'd say three hours' lab work for your preliminary report. Tomorrow, you get disk 'n spreadsheets."

Hubbell nodded. "About seven, then."

"Plus or minus."

Brother opened the back of the van. He closed his fists on the strips, pulled four sacks of gear across his shoulders and hobbled into the cavernous warehouse. Hubbell felt an edgy optimism. "My brudder won't talk," said Elvis.

"You told me that three times," replied Hubbell.

"I'm not as smart as you. This is more'n my brudder ever made for one day in his life. Tonight, we leave out for a safe place so FBI no-can-find. You oughta see the toys when I go portable. I respect Missus LaSalle."

"Respect the terms."

"One and the same. Let's have the other ten-thousand."

Hubbell reached into his coat pocket and handed him five-thousand dollars. "Here's another five. Give me an invoice for the last piece."

As a youth enslaved to severe myopia, Elvis had loathed the frogman persona of his binocular lenses. Now in the swim of midlife, the goggles made clients squirm. In these moments he savored capitalism as a personal art form.

"Whoever clipped Rex had someone on the inside. Penetrating security, kiss on his leg, steal out the Mansion — that's big boy logistics. The money went into that hit, you could use to make a movie. You and I don't deal on that level, but we're too intelligent to argue. Get me cash, bubba. Before we leave tonight."

"Let me see what I can do."

"That's a good idea."

Elvis unloaded the boxes and carried them into the warehouse. Hubbell stepped into the office. The temperature was sixty degrees; the receptionist in a red sweater watched CNN. Her name was Henrietta. She had grown up in the Ninth Ward of New Orleans. Her hair was a silver beehive. She smoked Salems. "Lookit that po Miz LeSalle. Some poise, huh? 'magine ya husband dies like dat and all dem cannibals axin' questions. You a lawyer, hon?"

"Yes, ma'am."

"Personal injury?"

"You bet."

"That's nice, hon. You want coffee?"

"No, thank you, ma'am."

He gazed at CNN's replay of events, fixing on Sutton's somber face and silver eyebrows as DuBulio whispered in his ear. As they cut to the First Lady at the podium, he wondered what Sutton had said as he checked his watch.

"That po po woman," said Henrietta, knitting in a menthol fog. "Rex buttonholed a girlfriend-a-mine's niece, then gave her a job in Commerce. Screw 'em and hire 'em. This town got more secretaries owe jobs to Rex than the Labor Deparatment. But Amelia! Now that is class like Princess Grace."

He crossed the street to a diner where he sipped Diet Coke and brooded about the FBI. Elvis's line about leaving town was a telegram: prepare for a fire-fight if the Feds find the Banks brothers. The brothers wouldn't talk without a subpoena. Or would they? *Get the money, Hubbell.* If the Feds cornered him, he had attorney-client confidentiality as a shield. Attorney General Abadie would stand by him. Unless the Feds had dirt on Oscar. If the FBI went after Hubbell, they'd have to get Colonel Bellamy, the Coroner, Mudd and the First Lady. The Feds could not do all that. He stepped outside, swallowed by sulfurous air, and put coins in a pay phone. That was safer than using his cell.

"Governor's Mansion," said the female voice.

"This is Henry Hubbell calling the First Lady."

"One moment, sir."

The feeling of power, new and provocative, gave him a sensuous tingle.

"Mr. Hubbell?

"Yes, Mrs. LaSalle."

"What have you found?"

"At least two people entered the room. The technicians are working as we speak, matching shoe tracks and fingerprints. The fiber sample work is more involved, but I'll have a preliminary report in a few hours. Mr. Banks agreed to fifteen-thousand dollars with conditions I wrote on their laptop."

"These people are reliable."

"Yes, ma'am. But they want cash, and I don't have to tell you how unorthodox this is. Mr. Banks is afraid of a documentary trail on checks."

"A man dies and people want cash."

"I gave him the ten-thousand dollars."

"Where did Reverend Fraux take Rex?"

She seemed unable to think of her husband as a corpse, which saddened Hubbell as her battlefield strategic mien pressed on. "Schoenbaum Funeral Home. Fraux will prepare the Governor for tomorrow's wake in the rotunda."

"I am thinking maybe we should have an autopsy."

"It's a hard decision but the right one, ma'am. The procedure must be done before any embalming."

"Yesterday I had a husband and now I have embalming. All right, I'll work on the money. You make sure Reverend Fraux gets Rex to the Coroner, without Willoby blabbing."

"I'll do that. Mitchell Mudd might be more persuasive with Dr. Willoby."

"Mitchell will go to the morgue. What time will you see me?"

"About 8 PM, I reckon."

"Thank you. Good-bye, now."

A gust of hot wind snaked up his legs to the groan of an eighteen-wheeler. He had written the mortuary numbers on the back of Christian Fraux's professional card. In another moment he was put through to Abraham Schoenbaum. He asked to speak with Reverend Christian Fraux.

"Oh, well, he went to lunch."

Hubbell pictured Abraham Schoenbaum, tall and aquiline with a mane of silver hair, from his newspaper visage: Big Brothers, United Way, the Anti-Defamation League, Ducks Unlimited.

"Do you know where he went to lunch, Mr. Schoenbaum?"

"Why should I? This is most disturbing, a total breach of protocol. I have always been considerate of Negroes. But I have never gone to another man's house of business to prepare a body. This Fraux arrives, and at your request we provide a coffin. We *never* send coffins out. This is not a Popeye's Chicken. For Governor LaSalle's family, we make an exception. So this Fraux drives into my garage, locks the coffin in his hearse, has the cadaver put in our cooler and orders my staff: 'Don't let anyone touch the Governor!' And then goes off to eat with his son. Do you understand I am not pleased by this one damn bit, sir?"

"Mr. Schoenbaum, we apologize."

"This is more than an inconvenience!"

"Whatever costs you incur the state will cover, sir."

"Cost! Well, sure. I have two colored men who prepare bodies and they stand by the freezer on orders from some politician down the bayou. Elected officials come into our parlors every night to pay respects, be remembered. This Fraux doesn't hold any office and *I have a dead Governor in my freezer, sir!*"

Hubbell smiled at the thought but maintained a serious voice. "This is awkward for everyone, sir. I'm really sorry. It was difficult getting the First Lady to let them take Rex out of the Mansion in the first place."

"What use would she have of him there?"

"I'm not a psychiatrist, Mr. Schoenbaum."

"We remove bodies on a gurney from hospitals and homes every day. So do the police. Why did she want a coffin delivered?"

Realizing that his own ignorance and impulsive decision had sent Fraux for the coffin, Hubbell said: "People get irrational when grief comes down hard. Mr. Schoenbaum, I must speak with Fraux before he leaves."

"Oh, he's in no rush," huffed Schoenbaum. "Is there a problem?"

"Ah, just a small … something —"

"Jewelry?"

"I'm not at liberty …"

"The body is unclothed, sir. We keep a record of the state in which every cadaver arrives. There is absolutely nothing missing from our end."

"I just ask your patience."

"You know we delayed a service once because of a missing brooch. You'd be surprised how paste diamonds become real when someone dies. The insurance people make us send jewelry with the family after a wake. I've seen people suddenly want things at the cemetery. Wedding bands. A Confederate stickpin. One man, we almost had to saw off a finger to get the ring to the daughter."

"Please take my cellphone number, sir."

"Why are you using this man Fraux?" he said coldly.

"It wasn't my decision. It had something to do with politics."

"I don't like to mix business and politics, young man."

The Hilton had the largest bathrooms in the capital, and with his long legs, that was important to Speaker Sutton. He was on the john reading the *Times-Picayune* when a wall phone rang above the toilet paper. "Speaker here."

"Walter, this is Amelia. Can you talk without being overheard?"

Sutton drew in his abdominal muscles. "Things are hectic, but yes, go ahead."

"The combination to Rex's safe is in the bank vault. I can't leave the Mansion. My daughters are a wreck. Do you have access to cash?"

"That's my job. This is rather awkward, though."

"Of course it is. Hubbell needs five-thousand for the site examiners."

"*Hubbell!*" Sutton squirmed uncomfortably. "Amelia, I wouldn't let that boy near a serious investigation! He's not some-one —"

"I have confidence in him."

Sutton paused, setting up gravity in his reply. "That makes one of us."

"*Walter, I don't need more grief.*"

"I just don't want you put in a vulnerable position. This boy is very untested, no proof of loyalty to anyone."

"He's a direct line to Oscar and he's working for me. I don't want this request to put a wedge between us, Walter."

"You and I are allies, Amelia," said the Speaker softly.

"Then don't cross-examine me. I'll pay you back on Monday."

"He needs five-thousand dollars cash?"

"That's right."

"Where's he at?"

She gave him phone numbers which Sutton scribbled on the sports page. "All right, Amelia. I'll handle this. But you and I need to sit and talk."

"This has been one day from hell, Walter."

"It hadn't been a sugar bowl for me neither."

"Just a second." She cupped the phone. "I have to call you back. Is this matter with Hubbell under control?"

"Well, yes. But I was —"

"Thank you, Walter."

Damn woman cutting him off! His haunches tightened.

The cellphone shattered Hubbell's fantasy about stained glass windows in the cathedral of Chartres. "Would that be *Mister* Henry Hubbell?"

"Yes."

"Speaker Sutton here."

"Yes, sir."

"I gave you an order, Hubbell, and you didn't call me back."

Because you're a rotten bastard, thought the attorney. He replied: "I haven't been near a phone, sir."

"Is that your wang-dang-doodle you holdin' in your hand, boy?"

"Mr. Speaker, this has been hard. I just did speak to our friend."

"And what the goddamn what?"

"I'm on a cellphone, sir."

"I pay real money for a clean phone. Give it to me straight. How did it happen?"

"Cyanide mixed with potassium chloride. Direct entry into his mouth. You can get a full briefing after the lab results are complete. It looks like two people entered about 4 AM and used a device to shoot poison into his mouth. I don't have word one on suspects."

"He died in his bed, you say."

"That's their conclusion, yes sir."

"Was he clothed?"

"Not exactly."

"He was nekkid."

"He was unclothed, yes sir."

"Stop the horse shit."

"Buck naked."

"Buck naked," repeated the Speaker. "Do I infer a female was involved?"

"My client is upset about intimacies being misconstrued."

"I'd imagine." Sutton smiled. "What time you comin' to see me, Hubbell?"

"I should get to my client about eight and be there a good while."

"It don't matter whether it's ten, midnight or 2 AM. You come directly to the Hilton after. Is that understood, Hubbell?"

"Loud and clear, Mr. Speaker."

"Mm-*hmm,*" sneered Sutton.

He wants me to beg for the money. Goddamn hillbilly beanpole prick.

"So then. Word has it you are in need of an infusion."

"For the technicians."

"But I need assurance about your political smarts."

"I'm just an attorney."

"Goddamn, boy. You're in this as deep as the rest of us. If I send a bag of groceries, I wanna know what time supper starts."

"You want me to report back with information."

"The phone can be so impersonal. I wanna feel a good base of support."

"The moment I leave my client's, Mr. Speaker."

"How much you need?"

"Five-thousand dollars."

Sutton let his silence sink in. "That ain't chump change, Hubbell. These boys know that the choir don't sing?"

"They certainly do, sir."

"You realize if *one thing* goes wrong, you are in some deep shit trouble?"

"That possibility has never left my thoughts, sir."

"Tell me, slowly, where you are."

A line of blue light was fading behind silver girders of the bridge that crossed the Mississippi, heading south toward fecund prairies of Cajun country. The tedium of legal research that ruled his days seemed light years away. He felt like an astronaut stranded on a distant planet, forging a strategy of survival. Taking money from Sutton to pay for forensic research was not illegal so long as he had no direct knowledge that it came from the slush fund for Joe Hall. To that Hubbell could swear.

His cellphone rang. Hubbell opened the receiver: "Who's there?"

"Call for Henry Forrest Hubbell," came the melodious tenor baritone.

"Reverend Fraux!"

"At your service, sir."

"It seems we need anatomical work."

"This should not be undertaken on an empty stomach."

"Your friend with the freezer was upset when we spoke."

"One doesn't like to wear down a welcome mat, but these are strange times, Henry. I sketched a silhouette of the grieving lady. I tried to underscore my humility in requesting a box from his store. I would not call him pacified, but mollified — well, ahem. My son has gone to his dormitory. Where are you?"

"A bit of a drive away. I have something to wrap up here."

"I'll come get you. We can catch up on old times."

In the Hilton's executive suite, Speaker Sutton handed an envelope to DuBulio and asked Frampton to accompany Little Joe on an errand. Frampton was relieved to quit a room where hundred dollar bills grew on the furniture.

They drove silently in DuBulio's Toyota van. In the draining twilight, the heat was so bad most people were still inside. DuBulio pulled up to a curb. Hubbell stepped out of the diner. Corpulent in a burgundy suit, DuBulio stuck his head out the window. "This Hubbell Street?"

"Sure."

Hubbell saw the diamond ring on his left pinky finger. *Sonofabitch has an unconstitutional flag-burning bill and he's the Speaker's bag man.*

He saw the man in the passenger side staring at him with beady eyes: his very own state representative, Thomas Frampton. Wonderful.

DuBulio gave him a thick envelope. "Need a lift, podna?"

"No, thanks," said Hubbell, turning toward the diner.

The Toyota wound its way back to the interstate. Frampton simmered. "You know who that was, DuBulio?"

"Personal frienda the Speaker."

"Sutton told you that?"

"Nunh-unh." DuBulio lit a cigar. "Only a friend or a lunatic takes the tamale in daylight. Capone and dem never did drop-offs like that."

"I thought we were collecting for Joe Hall."

DuBulio chuckled. "Money walks, nobody talks."

15 BAD MOON RISING

In the ragged holding pattern, Nobby absorbed the engine hum in his knee. Lear jets hovered in arcs, waiting word from air traffic control. Big shots coming to pay respect. Hail, Rex! Governor of Governors and royal highness of rockarolla! Twilight, full and blue, soaked the sky outside his window.

"Oscah, yo! We fixin' to head down."

With food and gas at war in his belly, Abadie peered down. "Too many satellite dishes, Nobby. A media feed is serious bad for me."

"Yeah, we don't needa get skinned and salted for dem peckers."

Nobby pulled his bulk up the aisle and conferred with the pilot. Abadie closed his eyes and tried not to think about throwing up.

"We changed the plan. He's fixin' to land across the river in Port Allen," said Nobby, piling into his seat. "Won't be no media over dare."

Abadie nodded with his eyes shut.

"Pooh-wee, Oscah. Trinidad plum did you in. We et in the same hotel. You et swordfish and I et bouillabaisse. How come you got sick?"

"Shut the fuck up, Nobby."

"That's no way to talk to yo doctor, Mistah General."

"I need a real doctor."

Nobby drew a bead on the silvery light of a hearse threading along Airline Highway. *Every day people die, the world keeps turning, Proud Mary keeps on rolling* … Rex, what I'm goan do? Nobody made the wheels turn like you.

The airplane landed. Oscar Abadie ran to the hangar like a bat out of hell. Nobby hoisted his briefcase and struggled down the steps, favoring his game knee. He saluted the black man who had flown them from Trinidad. "You done good, Buster." He handed the pilot five one-hundred-dollar bills and palmed two more to the steward, who toted their bags out front. The hangar lay on a curve of the Mississippi next to a grain elevator.

The sun sank behind a purple ridge.

Nobby stuffed the shirt tails into his pants and mopped his brow. The heat made Trinidad seem cool. He popped a mint and called a taxi on his cellphone. Moments later Abadie joined him, redolent of washroom soap.

"Feelin' better, General?"

Oscar pulled his bags to one side. "What feels better when your good friend dies?"

"I meant your personal system, how you feelin' physically."

"I know what you meant. The answer is I feel like garbage."

"Called us a taxi."

"It's time to travel in separate vehicles."

"I don't see FBI or paparazzi trackin' Yellow Cab."

"In this state you never know who's watching you." Abadie's eyes crinkled. Across the river the bronze monolith of the Capitol blocked a full view of the Governor's Mansion. "I can't believe he's dead. Poor Amelia."

"Yeah it's tragic." Nobby shook his head. "Think of all he did. It was a lot, you know?"

Abadie looked at Nobby and then threw his eyes in another direction. Just then the taxi arrived. Nobby pointed to his bags. The cabby put them in the trunk. "Liable to be twenty minutes before they get another taxi cab out this-a-away," chimed Nobby. "Whyon't you ride to my car, Oscar? My treat."

"We're following different roads now."

"Suit yourself."

Nobby deposited his corpus into the back seat and slid another mint beneath his tongue. The taxi hummed into the night. "Got me a Cadillac parked at Metro Airport. Reckon we bettah go fetch it."

"Yes, sir."

"What they sayin' about the Governor?"

"The wife gave a speech. Talk about."

The cabby boosted radio volume on a Cajun newscaster trying to shed his flattened vowels with a nasal wine. "Hotels are rapidly filling as dignitaries flood into the capital. Not since the death of Huey Long …"

Rompy needs a piece of paper with your signature, Rex.

Dumb blob got snared by Joe Hall.

That's history. Gettin' out the pen is real important to him and his boy.

He's a real PR asset to me, smirked Rex.

You can't afford a no on this one, Governor. Serious bidness hangs on it.

You threatenin' me, Doctor?

No, sir. Just warning you.

So's your friend Senator Atchison.

Atch? Warnin' you? About what?

Oh, piddly things, said Rex in that cagey, above-it-all way so infuriating to a man who had known him longer than most NFL players been alive.

What kind of piddly things was he sayin', Rex?

That Senator's scared of his lord and master up at Angola prison farm. Atch isn't accustomed to so much silence. Makes him sad. Makes him edgy.

Atch is too hot for Rompy to call.

No one calls Atch anymore.

His phone is dirty. Agents track him. How you know he didn't wear a body mike when he saw you, Mistah Guvna?

Feds would've bought him a house for what Atchison told me.

He was tryna entrap you, Rex!

At Metro Airport, he paid the cabby and got in his car. Beyond the parking lot, TV cameras crowded around some muckety-muck. The dashboard went luminous as he drew a puff on his stogie, paid the attendant and glided past a string of no-tell motel neon signs. Sutton, John Burns Logan, Lil Joe DuBulio — what were they up to? Nobby knew he couldn't call Oscar so soon. The plane ride had petered into long silences as Abadie got sick and sulked.

Nobby's house lay in a subdivision called Royal Oaks, a clover-leaf design with cul-de-sacs where everyone had a big carport, plenty of trees and room for a swimming pool. He had closed the book on ex-wives and hard years running rockarolla bands after broken pigskin dreams. Nobby liked seeing the bricks piled up by a new foundation, the two-by-fours in stacks bound with metal strips and the barrel fires where workers huddled on chilly mornings, blowing steam off coffee in white cups. He liked driving past roofers laying tarpaper on beams for different hues of slate, his nostrils taking in the scent from whirring saws.

On the CD deck, Chris Kenner sang "Land of a Thousand Dances," the *na*-nah-nah-*naaa* refrain that Sophie Thibodeaux was singing the night Nobby spotted her at Bayou Fever, waitressing. What a chickywawa! Hair the color of natural honey, flawless teeth and doe-eyes to stop a train. Nobby slid onto the stool nearest her as she waited for the bartender to fill an order. *You know that song on the rebop. I could read your lips.* "Wull, yes," she said in a sing-song voice. *Ever considered a career in music management?* "Not rilly. I just love to sing." *Young lady like you could go far in music bidness. Take my card. The Rhythm Doctor'll double what you earn here. That's a guarantee.*

She stared at the card like it was a UFO.

"I'm majorin' in English literature," she said finally.

Keen to his predilection for lust, Nobby introduced Sophie to his wife Arabel right from jump and made sure they spent enough time together so his missus had no cause for complaint. His fourth marriage had coincided with geysers of cocaine and the greatest sex partner of his life. At times he fantasized Sophie naked, served supple to him every which way. But lumbering across the half-century line, he rationalized his chastity toward her as a mark of business maturity. You don't let a chickywawa with a body of gold waste that potential in a bar like Bayou Fever while Rex, the last singer in the Bayou Devils band, was taking too long to return his kimosavee's phone calls. Biding his time, Nobby invited Rex backstage to see Jerry Lee Lewis, promising "a lil lagniappe if you keep yer shoes on."

One week later Nobby was back in Rex's orbit. So, of course, was Sophie.

He drew to a smooth stop in the driveway of his five-hundred-thousand dollar suburban castle, Normandy-style with exposed pilasters, all designed by Arabel. When *Southern Living* ran her picture in the house, she was happy as a coed in a spanking new Corvette. The carport door was down; he didn't bother with it. Pulling his suit bag and grip, he almost tripped at the front door. Porch was dark. With twenty keys on his chain, he struggled to find the right one; his hot rod was ready for Arabel. "Goddamn front poach light needs changin'."

He opened the door, flicked on the light, set his bags down.

The living room was empty. He looked around. There was literally nothing in it. He walked through the house in a daze. The floors were a smooth sheen, but furniture had evaporated. He trundled into the den that overlooked the patio and swimming pool. The chairs and table in that room were gone, too. Photographs of rockarolla concerts with him and Arabel were gone. Color TV, gone. The aquarium, his favorite footrest, the CD system — gone. He ran to the stairs bellowing *Arahbelll ... Arahbell ...* but she was gone and the Persian rugs were gone, the china cabinet with expensive plates, and the only thing left in their bedroom was the bed. He tore open his closet and an avalanche of clothes fell on him. He kicked a *Penthouse* and pawed the closet to see what she had left: his wardrobe and a mound of unwashed T-shirts and boxer shorts.

"YOU GODDAMN CANNOT DO THIS, ARABEL!"

He lunged for the telephone and jabbed the buttons. The voice of the answering service came on, young and female: "May I help you, please?"

"This Doctor Nobby. You holdin' a message from my wife?"

"One moment, Doctor. Let me see. Senator Atchison called at

five-thirty today. Senator Atchison called again at six-thirty, asking you to call back. At eight-fifteen, Senator Atchison said it's important, please call. His num —"

"I got that number. What about this afternoon, this mawnin', yesterday — my wife Arabel."

"No other calls, Doctor."

He hung up wondering how in hell she moved everything out in forty-eight hours. That was fast! No, not fast: premeditated. She was a rockarolla cash collector who knew how to make club owners pay when the gate was down. First night they made love, she worked him like a corkscrew with her *derriere* on a pillow, tightening her Garden o' Venus each time he pumped till she had him yelping like a moon dog. *This exit musta been on her mind, she was waitin' till I left.* The maid, she would know — Nellie: Nellie what? Some black woman been their cleanup lady for years, but Arabel paid her.

He stalked into the bathroom. Nothing on the sink stand he always left messy with toothpaste and aftershave for her to clean up. At least the medicine cabinet contained his toiletries; he carried his pills every day and night. Their talk-talk had gone down like a fading light bulb in the late nights of surfing cable TV streaked with cocaine. "If we made love every night, yo weenie'd fall off," she insisted. He smiled manfully. But after months on the snow trail, they were having roaring fights intercut with sex so throbbing he got hard in the Caddy driving home, forgetting battles of the day before. Arabel, back on Kools, was brushing her teeth ten times a day. It had been two weeks since the night her nipple bled; he figured they'd put that behind 'em.

"The neighbors will know," he said aloud. "Someone — Jack Angelle over there." But he did not touch the phone. Avoid embarrassment. People see moving vans. She'd have had an excuse. Arabel, you will pay for this goddamn somepin awful! Get my lawyer in the mawnin'. Put bloodhounds on yer trail. I'll get it back: every pillow, every chair, every spoon. Desertion. Abandonment.

Terminator! Liquidator!

He noticed light in the kitchen. That was strange. He went to the fridge and when he saw the floor he shrieked out loud. "*Oh my God oh Jesus!*"

A man's fingers, all ten, severed, oozed in blood on the checkerboard tile.

Nobby's whole body began shaking. He pulled his hair roots. "*No-no-no-no!*" Circling the red gore, he exploded back in thought to the night he was eight years old (before his daddy left) and fifty townsfolk in the hamlet ran to the levee where a lunatic in white pajamas tried to jump into the river as hospital guards cornered him in a pathetic spectacle. Nobby *felt like that man musta felt.* Tryna scream but throat all hollow.

They goan think I chopped off them fingers. But I was with Oscar!

He pulled the pistol out of his pocket and searched the house and backyard. Not a soul on premises. Maybe it's bait. They tryna trick me. See what I do about these dead fingers on my flo. They fount out. They tryna scare me now.

He went outside, took a shovel from the shed, and under the moon's torpid heat dug a hole next to the azaleas Arabel had planted in June. He went inside, put a towel under the severed fingers, and dumped the hairy reddened strips of flesh down the hole, hoping other body parts were not nearby. He shoveled the dirt back and tamped the garden bed down flat, padding the earth with his foot and the shovel. Back in the kitchen he mopped up the blood with a new towel and buried that towel in the garden behind the swimming pool. He kept his gun in his hand and carried his suit bag to the trunk of his car, and then returned for his valise, making sure no one was watching.

When his things were safely in the trunk, he activated the garage door, but Arabel's car was gone. Maybe they did something to his wife! He careened down Oaks Circle, leaving rubber streaks as he barreled onto the interstate.

Nobby knew he was marked. Men who chop off fingers don't wait. He telephoned the Avis rental office in Lafayette, forty-five minutes away, reserving a vehicle under the name and credit card of Joseph Benbow. He telephoned the Lafayette Hilton, on Vermilion Bayou, and made reservations for Benbow. Rex would appreciate his ingenuity.

He had to get situated. Get back on track. Find out what-all went on. Find Arabel. If she can be found. He made an abrupt turn and fired down the interstate toward outskirts of the capital, his mental vistas racing with pictures of Arabel naked and a man's fingers being chopped, but then the CD tray clicked, and on came Roy Orbison crooning Nobby's number one all-time favorite song, "Blue Bayou." And the rhythm doctor began to sing.

THIS PARISH IS NOT FOR SALE **16**

At 8 PM the doors of the Hilton elevator parted. The Speaker's aorta fluttered as the men gazed into the lobby. No one saw them. Woodruff pinched the *close* button. The compartment descended and they stepped into the basement parking lot. DuBulio opened the rear door of his Toyota van. The men hoisted the suitcases into the back.

"You think media's on to us?" muttered John Burns Logan.

"Petrochem people don't leak," said Speaker Sutton.

DuBulio's van, silver with tinted windows, stopped at a red light. "You feel confident, Mr. Speaker?"

"Nothin' predictable about this situation, Lil Joe."

At sunset, when the other men had returned to their rooms, Frampton met alone with Sutton amidst the detritus of drinks and food from the day's fundraising. The pressure to corral money for Lieutenant Governor Hall had gotten under Frampton's skin. The young representative was anxious to head home to his family. Sutton sipped Wild Turkey as Frampton fumed: "Why are we routing some of Hall's money to that Henry Hubbell?"

"Attorney General Abadie got tied up."

"I didn't know Hubbell was political, Mr. Speaker."

"Everybody we talk to is political."

"Mr. Speaker, I did things today I never dreamed I'd do. Hubbell lives in my district. If he has eyes on my seat, I need to know that."

Sutton roared with laughter. "No *way*, son! Hubbell owes me forever."

As DuBulio's van glided into the night, Sutton brooded about the succession. He was tacitly leaning toward the man in the seat behind him: John Burns Logan. John Burns had serious wealth and that was important to the Speaker. Install a man without material and he'd be scrambling for it in sixty days, such was the nature of the office. With environmental wars heating up, no one would dictate political money as Rex had. John Burns had good nostrils, he stood tall with the serious chipahoonas and he would rely on the Speaker to maintain control.

To preserve order, Sutton was tight-lipped about his inclinations. He had not even told Logan. The Speaker was a generation older than the three other men in DuBulio's vehicle; he demanded deference to his authority. He was glad Frampton had gone home; the boy was squeamish, too much a pussy. Sutton was delighted at the First Lady's request to rescue Hubbell with five grand: money to Hubbell meant money to Oscar Abadie, which cemented the Speaker's interests with the Attorney General. Oscar wanted to be Governor like any number of them. His disadvantage was Trinidad and that was large.

The Governor's Mansion came into view, pale and spectral in the night.

"I still don't believe he's dead," mumbled Woodruff.

"He had it all," said John Burns Logan, "and he was a kicks guy."

The van floated past the entrance with the long row of magnolia trees that Amelia had planted when Rex was first elected, sturdy trees now. The white pillars were lit up like a spaceship with two state troopers on the porch in rocking chairs. The estate stretched on beneath a golden harvest moon.

"*May the Lord have mercy on our brother,*" intoned Speaker Sutton.

"Amen," said DuBulio.

"Amen," echoed John Burns Logan.

"Amen," came Woodruff.

Soon, DuBulio halted at the corner of a medium-wealth suburban street. Woodruff cracked his window.

"Any vans?" said Sutton. "Cars with reflectin' windows?"

DuBulio scanned the street. "Naw-suh."

"Looks clean to me," said Logan. "Clean and quiet."

"Which house is Joe Hall's?" asked Woodruff.

"Yonder left, brick colonial with pot plants on the porch," said Sutton.

Little Joe DuBulio steered into the parking slot by the driveway where Hall's Town Car with state license plates was installed behind his wife's Crown Victoria. The porch light was a gas candle sheathed in glass.

"Listen up," declared Sutton. "Y'all don't take any political talk by me in there as gospel. We got one job. He'll forget half what we say anyway."

Sutton turned to DuBulio. "Lil Joe, keep this vehicle purring. Anything happens out here, call Woodruff's cellphone."

"Yessuh."

"All right, boys. Let's do it."

Sutton, Woodruff and John Burns Logan quietly shut their doors. DuBulio popped open the rear panel. The younger men withdrew suitcases and fell in line behind the Speaker of the House on the porch. Before they could ring the bell, Mary Hall opened the door. She was petite with frosted brown hair and pouches beneath her eyes like bags about to burst. Her smile was familiar, a signature at innumerable of her husband's redundant speeches where she had sat, rapt like Nancy Reagan, through each one. John Burns Logan had twice eaten lunch with Joe Hall when the Lieutenant Governor was sober; he had given fifteen-hundred dollars to Hall's campaign. For some reason Hall called him Butch. His wife was loyal, though. John Burns Logan could see that.

She led them into a den composed of encyclopedias on the shelf, color paintings of marshes and ducks, and a huge stuffed swordfish that dwarfed the television set, which was an imposing size in itself. The Lieutenant Governor, short with sandy brown hair and mottled purple cheeks, sat on an antique couch. He bore scant resemblance to the robust persona of his TV spots: "The man who beat the mob! *You can depend* … on Joe Hall!" Then the dissolve into an American flag.

Three chairs surrounded the couch and coffee table, which was set with china cups, a pot, lemon cookies, tiny spoons, linen napkins. Hall stood with outstretched hands. "Can I offer any y'all a cupacoffee hour of bereavement?"

Woodruff swallowed and shook hands. "Mist' Joe, how you do?"

"Good evening, sir," said Logan, shaking Hall's clammy hand.

Sutton gave Hall a perfunctory hug. "Always a pleasure, Joe."

"Walter," said Hall, raising a hand to the Speaker's shoulder.

Sutton paused, respectfully, gazing down on Hall.

"Walter," sighed Hall, tipping back onto the couch.

Mary Hall invited them to sit; she poured coffee. She took a seat next to her husband on the couch. She said: "Y'all, Joe has something to say."

Sutton nodded.

Joe Hall's eyes were swimming beets. He put his hands on his hips, the gesture of his campaign posters, and cleared his throat. "Ah loved him, boys. Now I know it's true. Rex kept me at arm's length: not too nice, b'lieve-you-me. No, not the way he done. But there waddn't none of us — I mean, who could see? Well, shit. This is plumb awful."

"We all agree on that," said the Speaker. "This is a real human tragedy. It affects you and Mary, me, Woody here, John Burns, the whole legislature plus the 'lectorate. The boys are concerned, Joe. You always dealt straight and we feel you're behind us now. God knows the state of Looziana needs he'p."

Woodruff folded his hands thoughtfully. John Burns Logan glanced at the big swordfish on the wall. Mary Hall looked at the coffee cup balanced in the perfect curve of her hands on her lap.

Sutton cleared his throat.

"Rex liked me to tell how I nailed Rompy," cackled Hall.

Mary Hall rolled her eyes.

"You did the state a service," said Sutton. "Now, then — "

"Law-n-order," piped Hall. "Everyone's lips."

"Yes," said Sutton gently, "crime protection is vital."

"Sheriff down in Lafourche Parish couldn't keep his zipper up," announced Hall. "I got tape recordings on that old pecker *delicto.*"

"Joe!" hissed his wife. "Don't talk that dirty talk."

Sutton folded his arms.

"I put a mike on a hooker in the female jail!" chortled Hall. "Sheriff couldn't keep his hands off her. I tole that shariff I'd give his wife the tape unless he gave me Rompallo."

"Goddammit, Joe!" snapped his wife.

"Rom-pal-*low,*" smiled Hall, stretching the syllables for effect.

"Joe, take the high road," said the Speaker.

"I'm Governor," announced Hall.

Woodruff said oh-shit to himself. Logan looked at his watch.

The Speaker spoke: "Bo, a lot of us don't think that will work. You controlled the ball down in Lafourche Parish. On this field you ain't got the same footing."

"When Rompy came by to make payday, I had that shariff wired!" beamed Hall. He slapped his thigh. "Same body mike I used on the hooker!"

"Talk *business*, Joe," scowled his wife.

Hall pulled his shoulders back.

Sutton: "Time waits for no man, Joe. You'll face killer opposition as Governor. I know you're not rich. Nobody in this room is."

Woodruff and Logan, multimillionaires, nodded in unison.

"And to meet the challenge you would need big money, real bad," said Sutton. "Dump trucks of money."

"I got strong support," retorted Hall, "from St. John the Baptist, Feliciana and St. Tammany Parish. Plus Harry Lee in Jefferson."

"That was last time," said Sutton. "This time, you got a serious health problem. Everybody knows you can't say no, Joe. Governor's a job that packs hard material. You'd need five-million to start. You got nowhere near that."

Joe Hall smiled like a playful grandfather.

John Burns Logan spoke in baritone: "Think of your place in history, Mr. Joe. Think of the issues you stood for, and how you'll be remembered."

"Butchie," said the Lieutenant Governor. "You the man I want."

Woodruff intervened. "Mrs. Hall, would you stand please, ma'am?"

Mary Hall withdrew from the couch.

"May we clear the table?" said Woodruff.

Watching Woodruff's courtesy, Sutton registered the training of old money.

Mary Hall removed the sauces, cups and pot. Woodruff lay the first suitcase on the coffee table and its companion next to Hall on the couch. He popped them open simultaneously. Fields of money riveted everyone. Woodruff opened the third valise on the rug between the Lieutenant Governor and the pixy feet of his wife.

"A hundred-and-twenty-thousand dollars down on your salary for the next two years," reported Sutton. "Another hundred next week at First Bank of Nashville. You can get he'p up there. We grandfather your pension. You buy into the state health plan at $425 a month, and in your condition, that's a bargain, Joe. This here is a solid package. A plane is waiting at Port Allen. Your resignation, Joe, is critical."

Hall opened his mouth at the vistas of cash. "*Whoa now,* Mary girl!"

She hugged him. "Oh, Joe. I never dreamed —"

"No ... no ... yes, well ... Ah-ah-ah-*henh!* Ah-henh *henh-henh!* Yes-*sah!*"

Hall cupped his thighs, elbows akimbo. He shook his head to see if the money was a mirage. It was not. He sank back on the couch, staring glassy-eyed at his future arrayed on the couch, table and rug.

Woodruff retreated, hands behind his back.

Logan sat with clenched fists. Sutton folded his arms.

Hall popped to his feet. "You boys join a drink! This calls a celebration!"

Sutton's long right arm met Hall at the shoulder and pulled him back on the couch. "No drinkin' over the money, Joe." Sutton nodded to Logan.

John Burns Logan opened his briefcase and withdrew a document. "Mr. Joe, we have a letter for you to sign, plus a legislative order mandatin' Walter to remain as Speaker of the House, a suspension of activities till Tuesday with an interim Governor to be chosen jointly, requiring a simple bicameral majority."

Hall made Logan repeat the information, slowly, five times.

After a vast silence, Hall said: "What about Atch?"

"Atchison's a zombie," said the Speaker.

"I never liked Atch," snorted Hall. "Atch don't like people enough to be Governor. In politics, man got to *like* the people. Remember the people, Butch."

"The people," said John Burns Logan, nodding.

"The people," echoed Woodruff.

Hall rubbed his palms. "Buy TV spots early, we do a saturation. All that identity, what'em-a-call-it …"

"Visibility," said his wife for the ten-thousandth time.

"Sho nuf visibility! Money means visible. Y'unnderstand that, Butchie? *Money … means … visible!* Yes," continued Hall, cracking his knuckles, "this gives us a jump. Knock out some of dem peckerwoods teenk dey can tryta beat Joe Hall."

Logan fingered the documents. Woodruff looked at the swordfish.

"Joe," said Sutton. "The money is not for you to campaign. It's payment to step aside, keep out of the pack. To quit. We'll handle the succession."

"Not to run?" Hall rubbed his forehead. "Whoever heard …"

"Take it, Joe," said his wife. *"Take* that money."

"Success, success, suc*cession,*" said the Lieutenant Governor.

"Look at it from a fresh angle," counseled the Speaker.

"One thing," said Joe Hall. "It can't be … Lester Dutreaux."

John Burns Logan frowned.

"Mist Joe," said Woodruff gently, "it's goan be somebody sure higher up than Lester."

Sutton's mind ran blank. "Who is Lester Dutreaux?"

"Sheriff of Lafourche Parish," Logan and Woodruff said together.

"Naw, naw," rumbled the Speaker. "Joe, this is a big league deal. Oscar Abadie's got the inside track."

Woodruff and Logan turned toward the Speaker.

"Oscar's got a clean image," stated Sutton. "When we open the special election, he can scramble with the others."

"Oscar get elected rest of his born life," groused Hall.

"Mebbe," said the Speaker. "But mebbe not."

"Well, what I say when media say, *How come Joe Hall quit?*"

"They won't do that," said the Speaker. "Your problem's no secret, Joe. We got you pre-registered at a blue ribbon detox center up in Nashville. Place called Cumberland. Secretary of State of Arizona went there to dry out. CEOs are in the client base. Green fields, top medical people, no media. Look, Bo: people do recovery all the time. It's a health issue. You need to duck the limelight. Lay low, beat the hooch. Next go-round, you might could run again."

"That's right," said John Burns Logan.

"I second that," said Woodruff.

Hall beamed. "Mary girl, we are movin' into the Mansion!"

"*No we're not, Joe!* You turn down this money and I'll stick you in Salvation Army. I paid my dues. This is the best deal we ever got."

Hall scratched his scalp with two hands. "Man works all his life. What they do? Rex liked me. Sombitch kept me on a leash. Rest his soul."

Logan lay the documents atop the money in an open suitcase.

"Joe," said his wife. "Tell 'em what they forgot."

"Who?" said Hall.

"You know, what we talked about. *Rrrruummmmmmm.*"

Hall perked up. "Like I said, you talkin' seventy-thousand miles. Rex was behind it. He said wait till after the election. Mary has an old one, and I get one automatic for being Lieutenant."

"What is this?" said the Speaker.

Hall pulled his shoulders back. "You don't get a rebate when they go that high. *And I made every dang trip.* Sleet or slop. Bunkie … Cut Off … Lul White Lake. Places never saw a mob prosecutor! I'm talking Dry Prong. Only Lieutenant Governor *ever* went to Dry Prong. Kiwanis Club. Makes perfect sense."

"What makes sense?" fumed John Burns Logan.

"I'll pay for the phone," said Hall.

"I think he's talking about his vehicle," said Woodruff.

"That's a Lincoln Town Car," ruminated Logan.

"Suffering Jesus," said the Speaker.

"Walter," said Mary. "We have come this far."

"Joe," said Speaker Sutton. "That ve-hicle is the property of the state of Looziana. Switchin' it over to a civilian —"

"My daughter-in-law does title transfers in Motor Vehicles," said Mary.

"Nobody in Looziana buys a car with seventy-thousand miles unless they're out of office!" thundered the Lieutenant Governor.

"Walter," shrugged John Burns Logan. "What's a car?"

Speaker Sutton gazed at the ceiling.

Joe Hall made a fist with his right hand and shot up the index finger: "And I said to jury: *Ladies and gentleman of Lafourche Parish. You have it in your hands to make history. Tell the world, tell yo chirren and grandchirren, and tell Mistah Romapallow dat DIS PARISH IS NOT FOR SALE!*"

Speaker Sutton sighed. "Joe, you hold on to that car. Just don't drive it till you get back from Nashville."

Hall nodded.

Everyone waited while the Lieutenant Governor read the documents that John Burns Logan had prepared. Hall read slowly, his lips moving. "Everyteeng seems to be in order. A holiday, I see. *And* a special session in thirty days. Mm-*hmm.*"

Speaker Sutton held his breath.

"So," smiled the Lieutenant Governor. "Who got a pen?"

Christian Fraux sat in the hearse at a Tastee Donuts parking lot. The tape deck hummed "Rambling Rose" by Nat King Cole: "Where she *wannders,* no one knows …" Rex, the libertine who wandered too far, lay in the coffin in the rear of the vehicle. Fraux could not bring himself to pass judgment on a murder victim. His memory held the fresh wound of Abraham Schoenbaum's ire: *You take a body from the freezer without preparing it! What do I say if they ask where the Governor's remains have gone?*

This is an affair of state, Fraux had shot back. *Tell them nothing!*

Hubbell appeared in the muggy nightglow. Watching him revived ancient thoughts of Henry's father in strategy sessions with NAACP attorneys from New York, hammering out arguments that Forrest Hubbell mowed through like a timber saw. Secretaries retyped motions through the night. "Your Northern friends despise me," Forrest had sighed. "It doesn't seem to bother you," replied Fraux, curious about the man who had played surrogate judge with such imperial disdain. Fraux told him that he assaulted the Northern lawyers' arguments in a way that seemed to mock the movement culture, the solidarity and bonds of struggle. "It bothers me that they misread my motivations, the logic behind these rehearsals," Forrest replied.

"Oh they understand the logic," Fraux had countered. "It's the motivation that bedevils them." Thinking: *this is the strangest man, white or black, I have ever known.* The next day Forrest suffered a massive stroke. When Fraux next saw him, his mouth was contorted; months passed before he could speak.

Henry Hubbell opened the passenger door of the hearse and slid into the seat, gripping a black binder. "Sorry to keep you waiting, Reverend Fraux."

"We're used to waiting."

Unburdened of thoughts about the Governor, Fraux sent the hearse into motion beneath a creamy sky, lit up by a mammoth moon. "*No one clings to,*" rose Fraux's silken lilt, "a ramblin' rose."

Fraux seemed serene to Hubbell. He wondered if the mood was conditioned by years of working with the dead.

The hearse pulled into the parking lot at Jimbo's Creole Kitchen, an eatery-cum-watering hole that had grown with the oil boom after the civil rights years, the restaurant consuming two adjacent buildings, adding hallways and banquet rooms in a pentagon of profits. Jimbo's was discovered by *The New Yorker* in 1970, "before any of our folk had made it into office," explained Fraux. "It was a positive story on the cooking, with a zinger: they named white politicians who made it a pitch stop for votes. *That* made the *Advocate*. Big Jimbo went to the legislature the follown' year."

Hubbell frowned. "Jimbo Junior has had that seat for years."

"That's right. The daddy gave him the seat before he passed on."

In the dense-packed parking lot, Hubbell counted fifteen license tags that featured the red monolith of the Capitol. The legislative black caucus was in Jimbo's. Hubbell wondered where Sutton's wolf-pack was eating.

"I don't like leaving Rex in the back of this vehicle," said Hubbell.

"Safest place in the world," said Fraux. "No one breaks into a hearse."

A white-shirted valet approached. Behind him, a black policeman sat on a stool by the door. "Leave ya keys in the car, please," stated the valet.

"We have a very expensive coffin back there," Fraux reported solemnly. He handed the valet a five-dollar bill, and another to the cop.

"Nobody goin' near that vehicle," said the cop, palming the fiver.

Clutching the binder with Elvis Banks's report, Hubbell had a second thought and asked Fraux to open the hearse. He slid the binder under his seat; Fraux locked the vehicle, entrusting the keys to the valet. Hubbell followed him inside with a mental image of Rex, kicking and yelling, *Let me outa here, you bastards!* That made the attorney grin.

The bar was a sprawling kidney-shaped affair with stained glass lamp shades bearing logos of Seagram's and Coca-Cola. Black women in radiant dresses, perched on stools, reminded Hubbell of the exotic females in the island dresses of Gaugin. The men cajoled one another with élan, entertaining their ladies as Ben E. King filled the jukebox with "Stand By Me."

Fraux and Hubbell took stools in the lounge at a raised table, studying the menus. Surrounded by African-Americans, Hubbell felt naked, as if they knew his thoughts, how he wanted to feel innocent among them. Then, deep in the dining room, he saw three black male supplicants arrayed around Senator Clifford Atchison, whose dank hair was parted down the middle in a razor line. Stabbing a cigarette in an ashtray that a waitress swept away, as if on cue, the corpulent leader of the upper chamber stood shoulder-tight with State Senator F. Robert Lenton, whose outstretched arms drew a dignified elder couple into the white man's hands and an enunciation so perfect you could read Atchison's lips a hundred-and-fifty feet away: *God bless you!*

Next to Hubbell materialized a man with baby brown cheeks, burgundy suit, a floral tie and bare fringe of gray at the temples. He had a pumping handshake and the grin of a winner at life: "Jimbo Jenson Junior. Whatcha drinkin', Mister Hubbell?"

"Henry, please. Bourbon with a twist of lemon."

"Wild Turkey for mah friend," he told the waitress. "Chris?"

"An old fashioned," said Fraux. "Decide on food, Henry?"

"Turkey with oyster dressing."

"Oyster dressing's precious," cooed Jimbo Jenson Junior as Fraux placed the orders. "My momma and my sisters and my auntee make it from my daddy's recipe. We got a page in *Southern Living*. Miss Amelia ordered a five-pound tray for the Mansion over Labor Day when Rex had them Mexicans." Jenson shook his head. "Rex was good people, man. This is a sorry sorry day."

Hubbell stole a glance at F. Robert Lenton snaring people for introductions to Senator Atchison.

"Atch's last parade," snorted Jenson. "Y'all heard about him in court today?"

"No," they said together.

"Judge announces the Governor died. Recess the court! Atch starts *bawlin'* like Jesus said no at Judgment Day. Sobbing big time! See Atch now."

"He sure is visible," smirked Fraux.

"He comes in here with For Rent Lenton and professional Negroes makin' introductions. It's a hunt for one juror. *All month* Atch been watching four black folk on that jury: a mailman, a seamstress, a plumber and a nurse. Tonight Atch shook six-hundred hands. Did he find the nurse's auntee or the plumber's brother? Atch is so sweet to us Aframericans, us blacks, us darkies. Atch lays his head on the pillow each night, thinking *I just need one nigger to flip*. Bingo. Hung jury."

"Feds have him balls to the wall," muttered Hubbell.

"I think so. But they got a bookie named Myron over by LSU giving three to one the jury will hang."

Fraux leaned closer. "What are you hearing on Rex?"

Jenson hunched forward. "They say a chickywawa popped Rex. What a waste, huh? Regina called about the wake. She been calling Lake Charles, Shreveport, all over. Wants everybody behind Rex comin' to the funeral. Outpour affections, outstanding showa strength. They're organizing gospel choirs in Seventh Ward New Awlins. Be more black folk at Rex's funeral than anybody counted in Looziana."

Hubbell lowered his voice. "Regina said a woman killed him?"

"Nah, that's the word on the street. Regina was choked up, said how much this restaurant meant to her daddy, how much my friendship meant to her. I told her how much Rex meant to me and said she was my friend, too. I always have liked Regina. My supporters *will* be at the funeral."

"Hear tell where Rex died?" said Fraux.

"Flat on a mattress in the big house. Chickywawa skipped."

"Where'd you hear this?" said Hubbell.

"You know Regina?" parried Jenson.

"Absolutely."

"Regina's kicks, man. You never know when Gina gonna pop up, but when she do, that's a hurricane. First time we had Super Bowl in the Dome, she came in here with OJ Simpson and that dude Krofferman — you know, the cowboy singer?"

"Kris Kristofferson?"

"Could be. They brung a portable keyboard and we had one stomp down party in the back room. Regina got up on the table, shimmyin' , singin' 'Pretty Woman' — *whoa*, I like to have video on that."

The waitress brought the drinks. Hubbell handed her a twenty and waved off the change. She thanked him and withdrew.

"Rex cared," said Jimbo sadly. "He really made the show roll."

Fraux: "All these rumors. Any speculating' on who did him in?"

"Ask the satin who stained the sheets, Mister Chris. I know plenty women Rex harpooned, but they liked him. It just takes one too many. What you gonna do: round up every chickywawa in Looziana and have a lineup? Pooh. ACLU be chuckin' spears and the *po*lice chief have a scandal. Nobody knows who packed Rex."

"Media hasn't had any reports like that," said Hubbell in the tone of a question.

"What can media do? Joanie Charlot told me they all think Willoby's lying but they got no proof. Channel Two camped out at the hospital till some e-team doctor comes out, sez we ain't go no statement, y'all go ask the Coroner. Then come Willoby sayin' cardiac arrest. This deal is clamped shut."

The waitress brought two paper sacks of food. "My treat," said Fraux, settling the bill.

Jimbo Jenson Junior whispered to Hubbell: "Watch your back side, little daddy. Your phone might be dirty too."

"Thanks. How do you know?"

"I don't. But this town is oozin' with rumors. They got six FBI agents in this dinin' room watching Atch and not one is white. They see you, they see me, they see who-all behind the tree. Plenty folk wanna know what you know."

"Thanks for the tip."

"A friend of Chris Fraux is my friend," said Jenson, shaking hands.

Atchison and his entourage were moving through the lounge, the Senate President following For Rent Lenton's gray mutton chops, shaking hands and saying "how do, ma'am?" and "it's a pleasure" to spouses and significant others down the line. Fraux thanked Jimbo Jenson Junior as they made for the door. Hubbell felt a paw hard on his shoulder and turned into the nicotine breath of the high senator. Atchison's teeth were butter brown: "Where did Doctor Nobby leave Oscar when they returned?"

"Laying bets with a bookie named Myron over how many years you'll get."

"You smart ass prick," hissed Atchison.

"*Henry, meet my good friend F. Robert Lenton!*" boomed Jimbo Jenson, the intervention diplomat, turning Hubbell to the black senator.

"Mah man!" sang Lenton in a scent of Johnny Walker Red. He gripped Hubbell's hand with the warmth of assured money, regardless of Atchison's verdict. "Tell General Abadie his ole podna F. Robert Lenton sends a *big* hello!"

"I'll do that," said Hubbell.

"Oscar and me go back to when he was DA of Feliciana," purred Lenton.

"He told me he indicted you for vote fraud, but the key witness recanted."

"That's right!" beamed Lenton. "And now Oscar and me are *friends!*"

"I'm sure he'll be happy to hear from you."

"I know that's true. Lemme buy you a nightcap."

"No thanks. I'm late to meet friends."

"Jimbo," said Fraux, opening the door. "We thank you as ever."

"Come back soon!" chirped Jimbo Jenson Junior.

The last thing Hubbell saw was Atchinson, lips wet and down curled, lighting a Pall Mall.

They stepped into the night air, hot as coffee. Fraux drove away on aromas of garlic and oysters from the bag between them on the seat. After a silence, the undertaker said: "Why'd you provoke Atchison like that?"

"Closet prosecutor in me had a power surge."

"I never make an enemy unless it's necessary."

"Atchison's not worth having as a friend."

A ribbon of asphalt ran through dusty shotgun houses and honky-tonks, a version of the back street in Blue Line where Fraux had met with people whose water wells were poisoned in the field behind the injection well.

He wondered if the peonage of slavery's descendants would ever ease. His own water drew from a well on a hill above the poverty. At a railroad crossing, the guardrail descended to staccato rings of a warning bell. Boxcars bearing chemicals passed before the windshield.

"I'm starving," said Hubbell.

Fraux tucked a paper napkin over his tie and withdrew barbecue ribs. Hubbell dug into oyster dressing with a plastic spoon. "Mm, Jimbo was right. This stuff's terrific."

The trail lumbered past with clanging bells. The men popped soft drinks.

"You don't seem upset about Rex," said the attorney.

"When you see other people's bereavement as a matter of daily business, it takes a while to deal with one's own emotions."

"Were you close to the Governor?"

"I was fond of him. We were friends, in the political sense." Fraux nibbled on the rack of meat. "Rex was a man of great charm and persuasion. Most of the time I enjoyed him. With someone that powerful, I assumed he did things that would upset me if I knew about them."

"What things?"

"Pollution. Women. Money."

Fraux dabbed his lips to remove the barbecue.

"He had no scruples," said Hubbell, spearing a slice of turkey.

"That's a bit harsh. He cared about racial harmony. He was sensitive to poor people. I knew I could depend on him for certain things. Like last night, after we met in New Roads about the injection well."

"Who was with him?"

"Mitchell Mudd." Fraux lifted another rib. "And a girl."

"Can you identify her?"

"I only saw her from a distance. She looked like mid-twenties."

Hubbell surrounded the incident with questions that Fraux patiently wore down, offering what little he knew. When the arms of the train crossing rose, Fraux wiped his lips and resumed the drive. A half mile down the road, they stopped at a trash can to dump the food bags. Ten minutes later they reached the City Morgue. Fraux eased into the back parking area.

"Wait just a minute," said Hubbell, studying the two cars in the lot.

"FBI uses Taurus cars," said Fraux. "*Po*-lice unmarked are Crown Victorias. I see no vehicle of concern."

He backed the hearse next to the platform where a set of double doors disgorged Dr. Willoby and Mitchell Mudd onto the loading dock. Freshly shaven, secreting body odor tinged with Old Spice, Mudd wore a crisp tan suit. Eyes hooded in fatigue, he bit his lip on seeing the coffin. Willoby, wearing a green surgical smock, said casually, "That casket got a wheeler?"

"Of course," said Fraux.

"There's something positive," muttered the Coroner.

Fraux and Mudd pulled the coffin out of the hearse and set the wheels on the staging area. Mudd gripped one handle, Fraux the other, as they pushed the vessel into the chilly room. The walls were lined with photographs of Willoby's naval career. One of them showed Willoby, with impish smile, standing on a destroyer next to the craggy grin of Vice President George Bush.

"This way," said the Coroner.

Mudd and Fraux guided the coffin down a hallway smelling of ammonia. Hubbell wondered what secrets of Baton Rouge lay in the metal drawers that stored cadavers. They turned through a set of doors with red letters AUTHORIZED PERSONNEL ONLY.

Surgical tables beneath arc lights formed parallel islands by a glass-enclosed cabinet with three shelves of instruments. Willoby began scrubbing his hands. The soap gave off a sweet aroma that calmed Hubbell. Here was order, direction, duty. Fraux removed his coat and joined Willoby at the wash basin. Willoby slipped on rubber gloves. Mitchell Mudd blew his nose.

"Under the laws of the state of Looziana," said Willoby, laying out scissors, vials and scalpels, "the parish Coroner uses qualified personnel. My job is to certify the remains. A licensed mortician may be present. No other parties permitted. But hell, boys. I'm no cop. I was reminded of that today when the FBI sent a young agent named Jack O'Connor to see me."

"You didn't tell me the Feds came!" roared Mitchell Mudd.

"In fact, that's what I just did do," snorted Willoby.

"What did the FBI say?" asked Hubbell.

"O'Connor asked about you," said Willoby, chin jutting toward Hubbell. "Wanted to know your motivations, who was orchestrating things at the Mansion. Asked point-blank if Rex was murdered."

"What'd you say?" grunted Mudd.

"I said my report is public and if he wants to grill me I stand by right to counsel. He threatened me with perjury, malfeasance plus five other counts he said so fast I forgot."

"Perjury for what?" said Hubbell.

"Cause of death."

"You mean lying to the FBI."

"I guess it's one and the same."

Mudd: "They can't prove that."

"Not until autopsy," said Willoby, folding his arms. He stared at Hubbell. "Once the document exists, a subpeeny can hook it.

Subpeeny Arthur Willoby and watch his balls twist in the wind. How 'bout it, Mudd — Hubbell? Someone enlighten me."

"Did the FBI agent tell you the Governor was murdered?" Hubbell said.

"No-sir. He said they have strong reason to believe Rex did not die of natural causes and wanted me to confirm. I told him what I just told you."

"What else?" demanded Mudd.

"It's all about money," sneered Willoby. "Feds are tracking everybody. Run for office in this state, your life turns into a hunt. Weird people, the kind you'd never eat with on purpose, turn up. You call 'em supporters. The money I spent, God knows where we got half of it. My cousin's a bookkeeper. We called him campaign treasurer. He's been in treatment for ulcers ever since I won."

Hubbell: "Did the FBI agent ask if you falsified your report?"

"Yes he did and I said my report was official and he asked again, real mean, and I said I would not answer questions without benefit of counsel. O'Connor talked about who owed what campaign money to who-all and how Rex fit into the mesh. He told me he was comin' after me like a freight train and then he left. I guess this is what public service is all about."

"Did he tape you?"

"Not to my knowledge. But what's that worth?"

"We're all in this together," said Mudd.

With the binder under his arm, Hubbell circled the room, thinking out loud. "O'Connor may have the morgue under surveillance."

"I won't lie under oath," reported Willoby.

"Of course not," said Hubbell. "But law enforcement needs probable cause to secure an order to wire-tap telephones."

"Probable cause, probable cause," sang Mudd with a grin. "Rex used to sing them words to tune of 'Amazing Grace' when IRS was after him."

Willoby sneered. "Well, should I commence with our procedure?"

With three men present, Henry Hubbell knew that every word he said could be interpreted by others, under oath, with no guarantee that any of them would accurately report what he actually said. "A subpoena demands documents or testimony," he announced.

"An autopsy is the record of what I find," said Willoby. "If I don't write down what I find, it's a waste of time and blood."

A buzzer blasted the room like a cannon, giving all three men a jolt.

"Shit," fumed Willoby. It was 7:45 PM.

The Coroner crossed the room and stabbed a button on an outsized telephone console. The buzzing stopped. He engaged the speaker phone: "City Morgue. You're talking to the Coroner. Who is Arthur Willoby talkin' to?"

"*Baton Rouge Police Car Fifty Five, Officer Rendon at Exxon Wharf. We got a floater down here, all messed up.*"

"Define messed up."

"Decapitated body of a white male approximately thirty-five years old."

"Y'all found the head?"

"Negative. We got a dive crew en route. Plus somebody sliced off the fingers."

"Has there been a search of the area for anatomical parts?"

"Ongoing. Chief is sending for more detail. We're coming back with the body now."

"Roger," said the Coroner. "Over and out."

Willoby hung up. "This job's a lot more interesting than the Navy," he said to no one in particular. "Somethin' ugly happens, nine times out of ten it's a full moon. My wife is heavy into astrology. Some of it makes sense."

Hubbell, Fraux and Mudd stared at Willoby. The Coroner scratched his neck. "A chop job on the River is going to stink up this place somethin' awful. I got to put Rex in a cooler while the *po*lice wait for this other work."

"I don't want Rex in a cooler near the cops," insisted Mudd.

"I can see your position," said Willoby dryly.

"Let's get him back in the hearse," said Mudd.

Fraux looked into the confusion of Hubbell's eyes.

"Unless our lawyer has any objections," came Mudd.

"I don't object to that," replied Hubbell nebulously. He turned away as Mudd and Fraux placed the body in a rubber shroud and moved it from the metal table into the coffin. They rolled the wheel carrier back through the hallway to the receiving platform. Fraux dashed outside, unlocked the rear door of the hearse. With a mighty shove, they lodged the coffin in the vehicle.

"Y'all git the hell out of here," ordered Willoby.

Mudd's fingers formed a claw on Hubbell's forearm. "Miss Amelia's waiting to see you."

"I know that. Give me a moment with Reverend Fraux." Mudd kept his fingers in a vise. Hubbell pulled his arm away. "Do you *mind,* Mitchell?"

Mudd glared. "I didn't know we had any secrets here."

Fraux turned away. Hubbell scowled at Mudd.

Finally, Mudd said: "I'll get my car."

"That's very thoughtful. I'll be right here."

Mudd departed. Fraux withdrew a handkerchief, fingers shaking in a spasm of memory from the night a pickup truck chased him after a civil rights rally. The truck ran into a tree and he got away. For years he had dreams of men hiding behind trees, ambushing him on the road.

"Reverend Fraux, I swear on my father's grave that I will stand by you if anything happens. I will back you with anything you need."

"To do exactly what?"

"Take control of the body. Make sure nothing happens. Get him to the wake on time tomorrow."

"What about the autopsy?"

"I'm learning a new alphabet, Reverend."

Fraux nodded. "I will secure the Governor's remains. I want Amelia to know my role. If anything happens, I will call you. Here are my numbers."

"Don't hesitate to call." Hubbell took the card and gave Fraux his own.

"You're on the edge of quicksand, son. Be careful. Whatever they want, don't lose hold over who *you* are."

"They?"

"The whole sorry gaggle of them," snarled Fraux.

An image of Fraux's eyes, hot as coals, stayed with Hubbell as the taillights of the hearse dissolved into the night. The mortician had been silent during the crisis in the morgue. At least someone was showing moral outrage.

Mitchell Mudd pulled up next to Hubbell in his Lincoln. Gripping the binder of the forensic investigation, the attorney got into the passenger seat and inhaled the pungent odor of Mudd's body that cologne could not camouflage. Hubbell loosened his tie. At the first intersection, they saw the flashing bubble of a squad car followed by a police van, heading for the morgue. "That sounds like an ax murder," said Hubbell wearily.

"A mob job, more likely. Them guineas fight. Where you parked?"

"Basement of the Capitol."

Mudd looped under the interstate to make sure no one was following. The empty streets gave Hubbell fleeting comfort.

"What did Elvis and his brother learn?" queried Mudd.

"Regina's got one big mouth."

Mudd's eyebrows turned into a gnarled frown. "What you mean?"

"She asked Jimbo Jenson Junior to turn out troops for the wake."

"That don't hurt nothin'. Woman needs somethin' to do."

"Word at Jimbo's is that a bimbo clipped Rex."

"Oh shit," moaned Mudd. "The niggers know?"

"At least Jimbo does, though he doesn't know who. He didn't say that Regina told him, which leaves open the possibility that someone else did. I met Senator Atchison over there. He was looking for Doctor Nobby."

"General Abadie been talkin' with Miss Amelia. What'd Atch

say about Nobby?"

"Only that he was looking for him. So I'd know they had been together."

"Atch is a garbage truck."

"All I have is a reputation and a case heading to the Supreme Court."

"Attorney-client covers your butt."

Mudd slipped a plastic card into the machine at the entrance to the basement parking lot and drove to the second level where Hubbell's Mazda was the sole car on a Friday night. They got out of the Lincoln simultaneously.

"Let's take a look what you got in that binder," said Mudd.

"Who was the bimbo, Mitchell?"

A dark vein throbbed on Mudd's forehead. "You don't grill me, Hubbell!"

"I don't report to you."

"I brung you into this, fancy boy."

"Amelia's my client. How much did you tell her about the girl?"

"What I tell Miss Amelia —"

"— *is my business, too*, Mitchell."

Mudd lunged for the binder. Hubbell pulled back. Mudd grabbed his tie and as the force yanked his neck, Hubbell shot his forehead into Mudd's chin, spilling him onto the cement. Mudd was flat out. Jesus, thought Hubbell, I cold-cocked him. He knelt. "You okay?"

The force of Mudd's knee ramming his groin knocked Hubbell onto his back, pain shooting through him like an electrical charge. He rolled over on the asphalt with the binder under his belly. Mudd jumped up, arms dangling like a gorilla. Hubbell gagged. Fire burned between his thighs, pain he had not felt in years, red spots swirling his sight of Mudd's shoes.

"Lemme see that report or you ain't leaving here like you come."

Hubbell pushed off the asphalt, kneeling on the binder, and got his balance with a grip on the fender. "You know a ton, Mitchell. And you need me more than I need you. Amelia wants the girl."

"I can get you to the girl."

Hubbell lay the binder on the hood.

Mudd opened and began reading, hungrily, scanning lines with his index finger, mumbling as he read: "Heel prints … exit routes … Mm, Banks is good."

Hubbell lay his coat in the back seat, fired the starter and let the cool air bathe his body. The pain in his groin had lessened to a dull ache. Mudd pulled into the passenger seat. "Banks is saying two people got up there."

"Did the Governor get sick in New Roads?"

"Nah."

"On the plane coming back?"

"Nope."

"When you left him at the Mansion?"

Mudd smirked. "You don't know much about politics and I don't know much about you. A Governor has back channels to secure his privacy. Rex was a genius at that."

"I believe you. Is Sophie Thibodeaux on state payroll?"

"Rex was too smart for that." Mudd made a sucking noise through his teeth. "I know what you think, Hubbell — and it's true. Some of us are here to do things the nice folk won't do. Because there wouldn't be no system without the likes of Mitchell Mudd. Media laughs behind our backs and we have to suck up to 'em every day. But the lights come on, the bridges get built, the teachers get paid. It all meshes together and no one is innocent. I got kids from three marriages spread across this state. You don't think I miss them or a warm female in my bed at night?"

"I'm sure you do."

"You're so proud," jeered Mudd. He held up shaking fingers. "After years in AA, I want a drink so bad I could scream. Rex taught me that I can't afford that. Who taught Hubbell to be Hubbell? Hanh! You think those eye-fried baboons, raping women, wasting night clerks at convenient stores, care about old man Hubbell for civil rights, or Martin Doctor King? Myself and you are standing in the real world. It takes dirty fingers to grease an engine. Kill a Governor and the machine goes down. Somebody made a real grab."

"Does Sophie rely on him for money?"

"Sophie works for Nobby and Nobby pays good."

"Tell me why she's innocent."

Mudd shrugged. "She respected the terms of his life. She's the last person who would have hurt him. Don't be a Boy Scout, Hubbell."

"People in love do crazy things, fits of passion — you know that."

"I *do* know that," said Mudd. "She's young and she ain't dirty. If I thought she was, I'd strap her in a chair and use a blow torch to find out why."

"Jesus," muttered Hubbell, picturing the image, "I believe you would."

Mudd studied the document. "He was alone in his bedroom when I left last night. About the girl, I told Miss Amelia what I'm tellin' you: Sophie did not harm him." Mudd ran a finger down a page. "The shoe with the slice on the heel, that's mine. Boot heels prob'ly belong to Colonel Bellamy. The other shoe track — those are some suspects."

Everyone is holding back on something, thought Hubbell. The First Lady wanted forensic data before giving him more personal information. Fraux's silences suggested annals on Rex unwritten. Mitchell Mudd knew all about the Governor's sex life. To get at that, Hubbell needed him in the same room with the First Lady.

"I'm sorry for hurtin' you just now," blurted Mudd. A bead of perspiration trailed down his dark stubble.

"Sophie met us at New Roads. But she didn't stay with him in the Mansion. Not once. That's a fact. Someone is tryin' to make it look that way."

"Who?"

"I don't know. This thing hit me like a tidal wave. I am trying to get my own understanding. After New Roads, we flew to Baton Rouge and I personally brung him back to the Mansion. Sophie was hysterical when she found out. She was a mess this morning, but I think she'll talk to you."

"Who could penetrate security at the Mansion?"

Mudd rubbed fingernails through his scalp. "That's where I get stumped. You need Bellamy to track leads in this report."

"Anybody knees me in the nuts is suspicious."

"That shouldn't have happened. My mistake. I said I'm sorry."

"You're holding back on me, Mitchell."

"We're working toward trust." Mudd gave him a business card:

SOPHIE THIBODEAUX

Music Management and Consulting

REPRESENTING: *King Artile and the Zydeco Flames*

22 Duckbill Lane, Baton Rouge LA 70072

CELL: 504-865-7522

"I'm going home and try not to think about the life I had. Wake up tomorrow, go to the wake: a chunk of the machinery trying not to rust."

"I need more from you, Mitchell."

"We'll talk tomorrow."

Mudd left the binder, got in his car and drove into the night.

Mitchell wants to avoid a collision with the First Lady, reasoned Hubbell.

He got out of the Mazda, casting his eyes around the area, wondering if someone had seen them. The place was empty. The huge silence made him think of hell, a special inferno for the most powerful, the opposite of crowds and the roar of affections, a slow, swelling heat under lights so bright a soul could never sleep, and then the ineffable silence, not a cough nor clap nor a cricket's trill, not a mechanical sound: just nothing leading to nothing and no other soul to share the boredom and lonely terror. He guided the car to the exit, slipped his plastic card into the slot and watched the wooden rail go up like a guillotine blade waiting for someone's head.

Christian Fraux guided the hearse into his garage in Avoyelles at 9 PM. He hoisted the body bag out of the casket, rolled the Governor onto a rubber mat atop a metal table on wheels, and paused. The freezer of the mortuary had room for five souls. In a town as small as Avoyelles, Fraux had never had more than three at one time. Tonight, the cold interior contained two teenage males felled in the latest blast of the crack wars. Should the families come early, as country folk sometimes did, for a traumatic last look before the embalming, he did not want a view of Governor LaSalle in that space.

Fraux rolled the table next to a horizontal freezer, which was padlocked. He whipped out his roll of keys, undid the lock and, reaching down deep, squeezed a rubber raft into the cooler, arranging it over the frozen bags of peeled rabbit, venison, pork chops and turkey breasts he and his friends had bagged on hunts and which his wife would defrost come Thanksgiving. He deposited the body bag with Rex into the cooler and padlocked the lid.

With coffee brewing, he telephoned the homes of Willie Boy and Juba, the men who worked as hearse drivers and assistants in the embalming, with stern orders premised on "double-overtime pay. And bring a shotgun, Juba!" When the men arrived, Fraux gave them detailed instructions on sleeping in shifts, how to call him on the private line in his bedroom should any person arrive for any reason during the night. He installed them in the climate-controlled work area, with a couch, chairs and cable TV, and locked the door that led into the garage with the mortuary's four hearses.

Fraux trundled up the padded stairs. His wife Angelle sat up in the king-sized bed; she was watching the late news. "Where have you been, Christian?"

"Politics."

Colonel Bellamy was on television being interviewed about traffic routes to the Capitol for the wake to commence tomorrow at noon.

"Politics all day long?"

Fraux stripped off his clothes and entered the bathroom. "The First Lady hired us for the services."

The large mirror above the sink reflected his wife amidst pillows, her dark bangs, the fair brown face and high cheeks that had galvanized him thirty-five years ago in college.

"Terrible events," she murmured.

Fraux scrubbed aggressively, mittens of foam running up his elbows. He took time drying himself. Then he dabbed his chest with cologne and marched to the bedside, nude. She looked at him quizzically. He stabbed the remote, darkening the television screen.

"I heard you clattering down there," she said.

"Rex is in the garage."

She leaned onto stacked pillows, wide-eyed, hungry for facts.

"Things were complicated in Baton Rouge. I must deliver him to the wake. Willie Boy and Juba are downstairs just in case."

"Just in case what?"

"White people," he said, with a wave of the hand.

For the next thirty minutes, she peppered him with questions he dutifully answered, telling her every single detail save for the precise placement of Rex, who would be gone in the morning. The frozen poultry and game birds in plastic sacks would not be tainted, no need to alarm her about that. When her interrogation had subsided, the weight of an assassination hung above them like a storm cloud. He turned off the bedside lamp. She locked her ankle into his, pulled the gown over her head and tossed it on the floor, freeing her breasts in a magnetic flourish. At the moment of conquest, Christian Fraux felt a *deja-vu* of raptures when they were young, and white men more openly dangerous.

On the blackest night of her life, Amelia switched on the lights in the attic. The only place in the Mansion she could imagine Rex hiding his strongbox was somewhere in the labyrinth of yard signs, his archive of political ghosts from campaigns past. The placard with lumpy yellow jowls of Earl Long leaned against a file cabinet. Seeking Governor in '48, Earl displayed a coon hunter's smile, tinged with lechery. Rex had four Earl Long yard signs and two of Huey's. Each one, he had assured her, was "a collector's item worth a minimum $850."

Oh, Rex: you scoundrel. You gorgeous madman. I must focus on survival.

She fell to her knees and made the sign of the cross: *Saint Anthony, patron of souls in search of lost things, help me find the strongbox.* Lord, I want the papers in that box, whatever it was Nobby gave Rex. If there is money, I will give to the poor. Well, some of the money. There may be a lot.

Yard signs, yard signs, a sea of yard signs.

She fixated on the green visage of an old man in a white Stetson hat, a three piece suit and thumbs hooked in his vest pockets. The raised right knee revealed a cowboy boot on an automobile bumper and the legend **Dudley Guglielmo YOUR Candidate for Commissioner of Voting Machines.**

I'd vote for that old coot because of the cowboy hat! Rex had chortled. That night he peeled the poster off a telephone poll near Erath, summer of '71. He hopped a ditch and clambered back into the car. Mitchell Mudd was fuming in the driver's seat as Rex exulted over his prize. Amelia giggled. A few miles later Rex cried: *Stop the car! I want that Jimmie Davis sign.*

You a goddamn state Senator running for fuckin' Governor! yelled Mudd.

That's unacceptable language, son. YOU go fetch that sign.

Mitchell Mudd had squirmed. Mitchell Mudd peered over his shoulder. He jumped out, bolted across a gravel driveway and vaulted the fence. He pried tacks out of an oak tree with his pocketknife and captured Jimmie Davis in a cowboy hat. **The Sunshine Man!** was running in '71 as a segregationist. Mudd tossed the sign in the back of the station wagon, and they roared off like astronauts for Mars.

Mitchell was lying, she knew. Cannot tell me all he knows because his hands are dirty from helping Rex and Sophie.

She reached for the placard of an ancient John McKeithen, with the 1963 motto **Won't You Help Me?** Behind his sandy hair and gubernatorial face she found a splendid-smiling Negro Orleanian **Vote for Reverend Louis Landrum, House District 48: Give God the Glory!** What does Mitchell factually know about Rex's final hours? Mitchell must be sweating.

The attic was hot as a steam bath. She felt water running down her limbs and in the wetness all she could think was *I want Sophie Thibodeaux, I want to twist her neck with my hands.*

She could not remember five things Mitchell Mudd had said before today that were other than a mere parroting of Rex. Mitchell was a cipher. At twilight he had denied again knowledge of any girlfriend. He had also said: "Miss Amelia, I swear I don't know about lists. Rex gave me slips of paper with names and addresses. Each time, I trashed the papers after I delivered the money. Never saw how much was in those envelopes. When I went to DuBulio's house in Metry, he was sunnin' by his swimpool. He smiled, put a frozen turkey in my trunk. Buzby I fount in a warehouse near Avoyelles with a woman hiding in a room behind his desk. I smelt her perfume. He took the envelope, nodded, that was it. His eyes told me to go and so I did. That Buzby's a cold, cold man. Each time I made a delivery was different. One time, Rex sent me to a baby shower. A niece of the Secretary of State. Those people was Republicans. I never asked why."

Rex kept lists of musicians who sent him CDs; he catalogued their promotional pictures with signatures. He kept lists of the people he bugged in the Mansion: sins of the system preserved for leverage. The FBI had never gotten a list of his money contacts. But she knew he had them. Someone killed him for what he knew.

Where was the strongbox?

She found a stack of yard signs with Rex in his thirties grinning and logos of that first run for Governor **Rex LaSalle — Cut Through It!**

Oh, Rex. Oh, baby.

The niggers love you! brayed Doctor Nobby. Big boy of rockarolla and crooked as a corkscrew. Domainge, if you are behind this, I will make sure you get the death penalty even though I don't support it.

You need a band! Nobby told Rex when he announced his run for Governor in '71. *Bring music into them white towns and rockarolla through the cities and niggervilles. A motorcade, flashing lights, pull into the courthouse square — the band plays thirty minutes while you make palm oil with the masses. Go into towns the world forgot: Talulah. Crotz Springs. Dry Prong. They'll talk about you till the eighth graders vote. How you think Jimmie Davis got elected in '44? HE HAD A BAND, MAN. And he sang the records he made.*

If you say "nigger," you are not in this campaign, Nobby.

Negro-negro-negro. I can run a caravan of gospel choirs, Cajun string bands and rockarolla groups. Peg your demographics to music, podna. Won't nobody beat you as long as you run the bands.

How much?

Nobby grinned. *A hundred-thousand watermelons, plus road expenses.*

Nobby hatched the slogan on everybody's lips: Cut through it!

Rex loved his coda on the hustings: "So if you want change, real change, and a state rollin' toward prosperity, put your vote with Rex LaSalle and help me —" The crowds roared back: *"Cut through it!"*

Amelia and Rex had been a golden couple — *Cut through it!* — sashaying around the state that summer and fall, dancing so many places the photographs were published in a book titled *Cut Through It!* One night they swam naked in the pool of a mansion lent by an oil baron off in Arabia, and on a lawn shaded by elephant ears and palm fronds — *we had it, we had it, oh Rex, how did we lose it?* They melted into a single substance, the undulations washed through her, hot wavelets and an afterglow that kept them entwined — shaking, kissing, laughing — for ten beautiful minutes.

Attorney General Oscar Abadie For Your Rights! blocked her view of the corridor leading to the rear of the attic. An hour earlier, downstairs in the parlor, Oscar, sunburned, eyes watering, the saddest Oscar she ever saw, croaked: "We will find who killed him, Amelia. By God, justice will be done!"

"What did Nobby talk about in Trinidad?"

"Besides injection wells, his main topic was the Mighty Sparrow. Said Rex gave him a list of recordings by this Mighty Sparrow who turned out to be their top calypso man. I don't know what the name signifies, but Nobby was fired up to meet the man. Turned out he was on concert tour in Europe."

Oscar leaned toward her, hairy knuckles squeezing the armrest. "If Nobby had a hand in this, he's got a hell of an alibi: Trinidad. That makes me look like a pickle in a pot. But I will tell you, Amelia, everything about him was suspicious from the moment I told him the news. He got mad. And he never could say anything meaningful, or sorrowful, when I spoke about Rex. Amelia, if you have something hard on Nobby, I'll arrest him in five minutes."

"Cut through it, Oscar."

"Cut through what, darlin'?"

"*Nobby's alibi!*"

"His alibi is me. I'll sacrifice my reputation to find who killed Rex. What I'm trying to figure first, why would Nobby hire a hit man, Amelia?"

"*How many reasons do you need!* Injection wells, Rompallo, Atchison beggin' mercy, money to DuBulio and that cretin Clyde Buzby, the whole thieving aggregation of them lined up like polecats for meat!"

"Honey, that's a whole bunch of facts. Frame 'em together for me."

"Nobby *wanted* something, Oscar. And Rex got in the way of whatever he wanted."

"To prosecute someone, you need data tied to a motive. I could see Nobby wantin' to keep Atchison out of the can for whatever reason. But Rex had no control over that jury."

"Nobby was lobbying Rex to give Rompallo a pardon."

Oscar shut his eyes and opened them. "Did they offer money?"

"Rex didn't say."

"Okay, we got Nobby carrying water for the mob. It's still hard for me to picture Rompallo threatening to kill Rex over a pardon unless Rex already owed Rompallo. Joe Hall salted him away for seven years. He's done two. With good time for parole, Rompy's out in eighteen months. I got no pattern recognition."

Rex had often told her that no man knew Angola prison better than Oscar Abadie. The penitentiary was part of his real estate during Oscar's years as district attorney of Feliciana. Oscar okayed every guard the warden hired. The *Advocate* reported that seven people named Abadie had jobs at Angola, which Oscar did not dispute, adding that he was no direct kin to any of them.

"Till Trinidad I never realized the sacrifice it takes to travel with Nobby. I had to hear his master plan for a Rhythm-and-Blues Highway to the Sky. I have trouble imaginin' him orchestrating an assassination."

"Rompallo's people kill their enemies, don't they?"

"Obviously. But Rompy kill Rex for what? Find the motive! Rex never put the spike on Rompallo selling vegetables in school cafeterias. He didn't mess with Little Rompy's restaurant. Rompallo wouldn't kill a man without a reason. People like that understand limits, that you can't trample certain boundaries."

Oscar's knuckles turned purple on the armrest. "Amelia, I will get you intelligence on Luigi Rompallo." His gravelly voice gave her goose bumps.

"Tell me what you know about Sophie Thibodeaux, Oscar."

"I know she exists." He paused. "I never met her. Amelia, I did not make Rex's private life my business." Oscar hunched his shoulders. "FBI's talking to the Federal Attorney about opening a probe on Rex's death."

"Keep those buzzards away from me!"

"I understand how you feel, sugar. And I know that goddamn Trinidad trip is gonna spread all over media. Damn that Nobby. Damn, damn."

"We must have a plan, some strategy, Oscar."

"Feds can't make Hubbell talk as long as he's working for you. Other people they will hammer. Elvis Banks they will hound like a convict."

Oscar, posing hypothetical questions from the FBI to Elvis Banks. Oscar, on how to deflect questions to himself. Oscar, thinking aloud about Hubbell for strategic needs. Oscar, making her wonder why men in power are so exaggerated, so desperate for love and money.

A rat scampered across the attic floor, the long tail pointed like a needle, the visible eye trained on her in a stutter step. She yelped, and fled down the stairs. At the hall window, she saw the Mazda turn onto Mansion Road, headlights charging in and out of magnolia shadows, a streak of silver that stopped when Hubbell shut his car door and began walking toward the porch. A state trooper telephoned: she told him to put Hubbell in the conference room.

Hubbell's groin was throbbing from Mudd's assault when she entered the room in black pants, black blouse, a pale brow and damp hair pulled back in a dark bun. They sat opposite each other. Anxiety folded across her face.

He tapped the binder. "I can leave this for your review, ma'am. I must warn you, the photographs are graphic."

She raised the open palm of her left hand, gesturing him to continue.

"Eight sets of fingerprints were located in the room. Until imprints are taken from Dr. Willoby, servants, the medics and yourself, certain clusters can't be matched with identifiable heel prints. Some patterns have been detected from the floor dustings. The tracks help reconstruct routes that people moved. Do you wear size five slippers?"

She nodded.

"The boot heel pattern belongs to Colonel Bellamy. Other imprints by the bed associate with kneeling positions, and green fibers — probably the medics."

"They did wear green. How many people attacked my husband?"

"Two, apparently. The dominant traffic was between the bed and the closet, the bed and the bathroom, and a march of prints around the bed, leading in and out of the doorway. Two aberrant lines run through all this. Someone walked from the bed to the window: a lady's size seven shoe. There were no prints of bare feet. Rex's fingerprints were on the cocktail tumbler."

"Rex did not drink alcohol."

"I understand. Another person may have used gloves or a handkerchief."

The First lady crossed her arms and shivered.

"The dusting process should be expanded to the gallery and the upstairs hall for a better sense of the sequences."

"Hell and damnation," she muttered.

"About the body — ah, this is difficult …"

"Say it."

"The lipstick colorations are distinct around the knee and thigh, but nothing at the waist or the genital area."

The tenseness in her body eased ever slightly. Her eyes squinted. "This is unexpected, wouldn't you say?"

"That's right. There was no indication of sperm anywhere. My hunch is that Willoby's statement about definite signs of sexual activity referred to the lipstick. An autopsy should give a more definitive reading."

"I thought Willoby was doing that."

"There was a problem, ma'am." He recounted the arrival of the headless corpse from Exxon Wharf, explaining why the Governor was at Fraux Mortuary.

"Are you saying that whoever was in bed with my husband did not have sex with him, and tried to pin him down while he was choking?"

"No, nothing that specific. The investigators found no sign of a struggle."

"Could he have died so quickly?"

"The compound on his lips and the roof of his mouth is cyanide based with potassium chloride. More compounds inside the corpse could be traceable to commercially restricted chemicals. How did he take it in without keeling over? Everything points toward some kind of device that spewed into his palate. Mr. Banks speculates that the killer engaged in some kind of game, possibly foreplay, and used an accelerated water pistol. Whatever it was, he took a mouthful and spattered some onto his chin."

"And the lipstick?"

"It points to companionship before he ingested chemicals."

Amelia LaSalle covered her face with her hands. "Oh, Rex, you poor baby. Why would someone do this to you?"

Hubbell wanted to embrace her, to soothe her, tell her not to worry, that he'd take care of things. But the ache in his groin set off caution lights.

"All right," she said, composing herself. "What next?"

"They need to take more fingerprints. That won't be easy with the medical unit. People are going to find out about the cover-up. The data beg for serious detective work. I will assist you every step; but I don't have special forensic skills. In the meantime, we need to isolate motives, and suspects."

"You believe this bears the mark of professional criminals."

"Absolutely. The question is how to proceed. An autopsy should take two hours. Any licensed physician could do it; however, the FBI can subpoena the findings once they exist. So that is a risk."

She handed him two slips of pink paper. "These are phone messages I received from an FBI agent named O'Connor."

"I'll call him tomorrow." Hubbell stuffed the slips in his pocket.

Her face turned sullen. "What about the girl?"

"I know where she lives. Mitchell wasn't helpful beyond that."

"*Find* that girl and *bring her* to me."

"I will try. Tell me what Oscar said about his trip with Nobby."

"Not much. He was embarrassed. Kept saying how much he cared for Rex and me." She gazed at the ceiling. "I hope you can protect me from being unkind to Oscar, as that would go against my natural inclination."

"Because he was with Nobby."

"Because this whole thing is so *foul!* I have to deal with it in doses. You have a superior intelligence, Mr. Hubbell. Because of Nobby, Oscar has things to hide. You don't. I pressed him on the need to investigate Rompallo."

"What does Rompallo get out of killing your husband?"

"I don't know. But Nobby is too close to Rompallo."

"Mitchell says the girl has nothing to do with it."

"Mitchell has a lot of dirty secrets."

Hubbell nodded. "Speaker Sutton wants me to see him after I leave here."

"Don't do that. Avoid him. After Mass tomorrow I want to meet with you."

"Certainly. Perhaps someone you trust in Avoyelles can do the autopsy."

She paused. "Let me think about that. You go find that girl."

He left the Mansion wondering how much the First Lady was concealing. She was more fearful than angry now: her control was slipping. He didn't trust Mudd. The First Lady and Mitchell Mudd didn't trust each other. What a dazzling hold the power had on them! The power was a silent force, lurking behind every word, every thought, a hunger always craving for more.

He had a city map in his glove compartment. Morbid curiosity pushed him on, to Duckbill Lane, the last street in a subdivision on the edge of the city that backed onto the Mississippi levee. Several vacant lots separated Sophie Thibodeaux's house from the nearest neighbors. The geometry was more like country farms. Flies and moths blotted the windshield as he followed the river, wishing he had stopped at home to brush his teeth.

Out on the water, a foghorn bayed like the slow knell of a cathedral bell. He lowered the car window to a cacophony of crickets. The house appeared like a candle flicker. At the sight of two vehicles in the grass yard, he killed his lights: A silver XL was overshadowed by a late model Cadillac with whitewalls.

Governor not dead a day and already she has rich company.

He eased the Mazda over the incline of the levee and parked horizontally, close to the river, invisible to the house. He left the coat in the back seat, loosened his tie and stepped into the heat, crossing the levee, creeping into the yard packed with rain trees, magnolias and hydrangea. The tangled foliage laid a web of vines over spidery branches of a crepe myrtle. A sheet of mosquitoes blew into his face, buzzing madly; he smashed them with a handkerchief. Perspiration formed a noose around his neck. His cuff caught on a rose thorn.

The house, new and made of cypress, had four long rooms and tall windows, half hidden by curtains. Leaning over the porch, he peeked through the door glass and saw a front-room poster of Gertrude Stein; the words *La Vie du Picasso* triggered a memory of Marie-Nicole, giggling as he chased her across Champ de Mars, shadowed by the Eiffel Tower, an erotic pyramid behind them.

A horsefly stung his neck.

"You sadist!" shrieked a female.

Hubbell darted to the side of the house. He peered over the windowsill. A man in baggy pants dangled an alligator belt from his right hand. The woman lay in a curl, hair covering her face, tanned legs visible to the fringe of her cutoff jeans and a welt the size of a cigarette, fresh and red on her thigh. The man cradled a pistol in his left hand.

"I have no idea where she is!" yelled the young woman.

"Then we need to spend some time together till you do. Git up or I can whip you someplace worse."

"You leave me alone, Nobby!"

He lashed her across the side. Hubbell flinched as she screamed. Nobby grabbed her by the hair and hauled her across the floor, gripping the gun and the belt in his right hand. *"Stop it!"*

she squealed, bouncing onto the wooden porch. He hauled her down the stairs like a Neanderthal, her fingernails scratching his wrists, feet kicking as he dragged her toward the Cadillac.

Hubbell hit him from the blind side, a wedge of shoulders into the meat of Nobby's midsection, spilling both men on the ground.

"Balls-a-fire," wheezed Nobby, flailing the belt across Hubbell's shoulder, a burning pinch that made him yell and roll backwards. Nobby lunged into his car, gunned the engine and shot into reverse, missing his assailant by a foot. Exhaust smoke gassed Hubbell's nostrils as the Cadillac roared into the night.

Shoulder raw from the belt, Hubbell pawed the grass on all fours.

"What are you doing?" came her voice from the porch.

"*Looking for that goddamn gun!*"

"I have it."

Dusting off his pants, wiping his face on his forearm, he stood and beheld her in the light: whorls of honey-brown hair, a shape of ripened youth and deep eyes radiating into the hole in his heart. His mouth opened but in a startling personality break, he had absolutely nothing to say.

She gripped the gun in both hands, a fuse of power. She trained it on him and said: "So talk."

"My name is Henry Hubbell."

"That's a start. What are you doing in my yard?"

"Mitchell sent me."

She kept the gun trained on him. "Keep talking."

"I'm an Assistant Attorney General. I work for Oscar Abadie. Mitchell asked me to help find out what happened. I didn't expect to find you in danger."

"La dee da. Tell me what happens next."

"Miss Thibodeaux, I did not come here to hurt you."

She lowered the weapon, aiming at his chest. "Come up here."

He climbed to within five feet of her. "I am not carrying a weapon. That gun is dangerous. If I get shot, you'd end up in prison."

She stepped back, still targeting him. "Open the door and go in."

The living room was dominated by audio speakers that rose like Amazonian totems to the ceiling. The shelves were packed with CDs, cassettes, books. Her walls featured photographs of zydeco artists, posters of abstract art and two folk art paintings: rural blacks in a river baptism, Jesus in a chariot carrying a coffin into the sky. She locked the front door. "Go into the next room."

In her bedroom, she lowered the gun in her right hand and began pulling dresses out of the closet. "Take these," she said. "Come-on, *come-on.*" Holding the gun, she yanked open a chest of drawers and stuffed lingerie into a suitcase. In the bathroom she swept articles into a valise with the gun dangling by her fingers. They left by the front door, which she locked behind her.

"Oh *Nobby!*" she cried.

Her back tires had been slashed.

"My car's just across the levee," he reported.

They tore through the garden and sprinted up the incline. The burn in his shoulder fused with the sensation of dresses and blouses clutched to his chest, jump-starting his imagination. The Mississippi rose into sight, houses on the far side lit up by the smokestack flare of a petrochemical plant. He unlocked the car, held the passenger door for her, arranging the clothes in the back.

"Just *hurry*, mister."

He steered down the levee with an eye on the semiautomatic in her left hand, guarding the harsh red welt on her thigh. Her calves were flecked with grass. He stole a glance at the brown slope of her legs. "I'm all wet," she complained.

He pulled out his handkerchief. "Use this."

"Much obliged."

Their bodies tensed at the first intersection. Empty. "One block down, then left," she ordered. He followed her directions and reached the Interstate.

Distracted, he looked in the rearview. "Have you eaten?"

"*Look*, mister: if Mitchell Mudd sent you, then you're the man with the plan. This is not how I am used to living."

"Me neither."

"Who *are* you, mister?"

He repeated his name and explained his role in the Attorney General's office. "I'd like some insight into the last twenty-four hours."

"So would I. What did Mitchell say?"

"He said you and Rex shared a beautiful love."

She turned toward the window and covered her mouth.

He drove quietly for a spell, then said softly: "What did Nobby want?"

"Arabel — his wife — knows his business inside out. Nobby said she split and took all his papers. He wanted me to tell him where she went. I have no clue."

"So he tried to kidnap you."

"You're my witness." She pulled out a cellphone. "I wanna call Mitchell."

He slowed the car. "Please don't. I think what you know could help break this case" — he stared at her with mournful eyes — "and I'm in position to keep you out of danger."

She eyed him like a banker with a calculator. "You make one move on me, you threaten me in any way and I will shoot you ten ways to Texas."

"I didn't mean to offend you."

She had the cellphone in one hand, the gun in her other. Tears were welling in her eyes.

"After we talk, I can arrange a hotel or take you wherever you wish to go."

"Just go where it's safe." She put the phone and the gun in her purse and resumed wiping her legs with the handkerchief. "I feel so miserable."

"I know that feeling."

The car stopped.

"What is this?" she fumed.

"It's my home. It's closer than the Capitol where I work. I thought it'd be more comfortable than a restaurant. We can go to the Hilton if you prefer."

"I don't need to hide in a hotel."

Don't lose her, boy. "I thought we might have a conversation first."

"You make it sound so civilized," she said acidly.

He leaned toward her feral beauty, his heart pounding like a fuel pump, without an earthly clue of how much his confusion registered with his parted lips and curled eyebrows. "The last thing I'd ever do is hurt you," he declared.

She put a mint on her tongue. "I take it your shower works."

"My shower?" He straightened himself in the seat. "Of course it works."

"Then I'll go in there."

He carried her wardrobe with resolve. At the doorway he shifted the clothes on one arm, withdrew his keys and unlocked the house. He pulled his American Express bill from the mailbox and cradled her dresses anew.

She stepped into a room with six hundred books. He lowered the thermostat. She followed him down the hall. She entered the guest room. "More books," she said. He arranged her hanging clothes in the closet.

She set her bags down and glanced across the hall. "Books in there?"

He opened his bedroom door like a valet. "Everywhere," he smiled.

"And they all belong to you."

He frowned. "Whose else would they be?"

"Wife, sweetheart, long-time companion."

He looked away. "None of that applies."

"I am supposed to believe you."

"Books are my one addiction."

"Religion qualifies that way for some people."

"I can imagine."

"I doubt it, but you're nice to say so. Are the towels clean?"

"Certainly. They're in the bathroom."

Twenty minutes later, she emerged on a wave of aromatic gel.

By then he had reviewed the voice-mail sputterings of Speaker Sutton and *sotto voce* requests from Oscar Abadie. The world was suddenly new. Her glow and presence pushed his chivalry to the edge of a mental mineshaft. He fantasized tanned flesh, peeled white across the latitudes, Merlot nipples and deep moisture demanding undivided love. No wonder Rex tried to steal her from the world.

Henry Hubbell cleared his throat. "What can I offer you?"

"A real drink."

"Scotch?"

She gazed at the books. "Bourbon, if you have it."

"My pleasure." *Did she really want Scotch?*

He served her on the couch and sat in a rocking chair, gripping his own tumbler of Wild Turkey and soda. She was about twenty-four years old.

"So, Miss Thibodeaux. What kind of work do you do?"

"I'm a fundraiser for the Democratic Party."

He almost spit out the drink. "Oh come on."

She smiled at his incredulity. "Well, it's not my only job," she said defensively. "I'm active on the entertainment side — fundraisers to help candidates. Things like that."

"What kind of entertainment?"

"I manage King Artile and the Zydeco Flames."

"That must be exciting."

"It can be. I also take classes at LSU."

"Graduate work?"

"I'm a little late on my BA."

Goddamn Governor of Louisiana chasing after college girls!

Her eyes were fixed on his books. Perhaps she was innocent of murder, but what did she know about love, love as the genuine article? He imagined her knowledge of the heart could be squeezed into a deck of cards. Sexual hunger stirred his quest. His romantic life in Louisiana (save for the encounter with Regina) had been a sequence of charging careerists whose power arcs had left him pining for some sweet-bottomed honey to make him laugh, make him rock and lure him into the mysterious fathoms of the self.

Sophie fingered the spine of a Mark Twain anthology. "I wrote a paper about robber barons of the Gilded Age."

"This whole state is gilded."

"I guess that depends upon your perspective," she murmured, opening Mark Twain on her lap.

He wanted to cross the rug and fall to one knee like a son of the South, embrace her manfully, assure her that her perspective was his perspective, that he would defend her from all evil, that she was safe here forever and a day. But at that moment, midnight tolled on the heirloom clock his mother had insisted he take from the house in Feliciana, and Amelia LaSalle invaded his inner vistas in a hooded cape, arms arched like a queen in flight and a warning telegraphed in black widow eyes: *You'd better cleave hard, boy, to the party in power.*

20   JESUS IN THE BIG WOODS

Take your shower in a stranger's house, try to wash away the guilt. She opened her purse. Nobby's gun was gone. Nothing else missing: a surgical extraction by this lawyer person supposed to be honorable. In the living room, Hubbell sat opposite her in a rocking chair, so poised, so controlled, surrounded by his books. A rich boy raised on love could not possibly comprehend what passed between Rex and herself. When she had finally told the Governor she was "a Recovery Christian trying to figure out which parts make sense," Rex said softly: "I bet your life depended on doing that." At that she nodded.

Fingers clasped like a judge, Hubbell rocked in his chair.

Rex always said surprise is crucial. "Well, I'm dying to talk about myself and the Governor, Mr. Henry. Could you first tell me why your eyes are sad?"

Hubbell winced. "Don't call me Mr. Henry." The eyebrows rose as if apologizing and settled into a horizontal dispassion. He was not a man of shrewd emotions. He reminded her of pedigreed fraternity boys who think the world owes them — until his cheeks reddened. Lordy, he was *blush*ing.

"Rex's death affects everyone," he stammered. "I didn't know my eyes showed anything special. I'm not immune to feelings."

"Had me fooled."

"My job," he stated, "is to find out who killed him and why."

My my, she wondered: do I begin by revealing that for all of his playfulness, Rex showed a concern for *who I am* and did not start hitting on me the way LSU boys did? We talked days before our first kiss and by then I was in a maze, hating the chain reaction I felt toward him yet unable to stop talking all those times on the phone or country paths we walked so's not to be seen. Boys had been crawling after me for years, but my heart was a secret vessel. *Love changes as people grow older*, Rex told me. The reasons why we love don't change: the expectations do. I said: But don't you love your wife, Rex? *On a certain level, yes. Marriage is like steel forged in the flame. The fire fades and hardness sets in: you get a well-ordered life. The issue of marriage is balance, how to hone differences into compromise.*

In the last few months, as she had cut distance from him, Rex chased her with a desperation that made her back off even more. Pity will kill love oh-so-easily. What bewildered her now was his power after death, a huge force pulling her back to primitive memories, the biblical traumas that melded with his face, his body, his words, mocking the freedom he had helped her find.

"Can you walk me through the events of last night, Sophie?"

She blinked. Hubbell's face was open to possibilities. "Some people have to break down the past in order to give life meaning," she said.

"I'm not quite with you on that."

"TJ Thibodeaux and his wife Miss Molly raised me in the Big Woods community of Rapides Parish. TJ was a preacher for Assemblies of God. Jimmy Swaggart ate supper at our house before his scandal. He too put money into this huge Jesus statue my stepfather built. Molly died when I was fourteen. TJ just last year. My goal is to find my birth mother if she is alive."

Hubbell raised his eyebrows. "That's a lot."

"So are you and whatever you want."

She followed his eye movements like an archer. He did not stare at her breasts, which impressed her. His eyes were green.

She had borne witness to accounts of how the near-dead enter a zone, dim and eerie with spangles of light, that envelope people whose hearts stop, whose bodies organically cease. And whether by some miracle or feat of science, their systems rebound, their minds return with images from the other side, blessed spirits that embraced them on the almost-journey, releasing them back to the world we know. A man from Vernon Parish had so testified in TJ's church. After years of therapy to achieve equipoise with scripture, Sophie felt a sudden visitation, Rex beckoning her from a distant road, calling through beautiful rolling harmonies of her girlhood choir, and then the preacher's voice breaking in like a freight train echo: *Be sure your sin will find you out.*

"It is not my fault, Mr. Hubbell."

"Call me Henry," he said softly.

He was a gentleman, she could see that. But stiff as a ruler. Lawyers are the worst species. "You have siblings?" he asked.

"Not that I know of. Molly switched the radio to rockarolla when TJ went to work. She and I had secrets like that, more in the manner of sisters, imagining a world beyond TJ's word rivers. I mean, the man made steam out of scripture: *Behold! I was shapen in iniquity and in sin did my mother conceive me!*"

"That's from Psalms."

She eyed him anew. "I didn't take you for a so-called Christian. I mean, the books, your artworks —"

"Even an Episcopalian remembers certain things. Did TJ abuse you?"

"Only spiritually."

"You saw Rex as a father figure."

"He was more like Zorro, one man by day, another by night, and a heart on fire that I simply could not put out. He also listened. For a long time before he touched me. He listened with that same heart."

She emitted a sigh so jagged that the glass trembled in her hand. She steadied the drink on the table, swallowing audibly.

"I'm sorry," said Hubbell. "I know this is hard for you."

Be sure your sin will find you out! TJ Thibodeaux, the campaigner for Jesus in the Big Woods, frame bent like a reed at the pulpit, hands waving invisible batons, a pounding morality she worked years to escape, returning now like a collector demanding the balance due.

"If you tell me what happened, I'll try not to ask many questions."

"You tell me how a woman with my cargo explains to *po*lice that Rex and I were no longer lovers, though I of course had great affection for him and I don't know why he died or by who — I mean, whom."

There was no sin stalking her: she understood this from psychotherapy and Rex. Mind over matter. We make ourselves by peeling off the fabrications that build in layers according to certain people in our past. A mother who surrenders a daughter at birth and floats into dreams, faceless, singing so sweetly you waken, begging to see her, touch her, know her — is the mother an angel half-fallen, or a lost part of yourself seeking some essence?

"I don't have siblings either," said Henry Hubbell.

"Are you serious?" she replied, affecting interest.

He nodded solemnly. Who *is* this bronco? Trusting a man is like buying a car: you don't know about the motor until time passes. The phone began ringing. Hubbell ignored it.

"You took the gun out of my purse, Henry."

"I didn't want to risk it going off."

"Afraid I'd use it on you?"

"Nobby's gun is evidence."

"I hope I don't strike you as the killing type."

"I witnessed a man assaulting you. You are reacting from trauma."

"You work for Amelia, don't you?"

"I work for the Attorney General. Amelia wanted me to find

you. I'm gathering facts to help her through all this. She's hurt, just like you."

"Tell me why I should help her."

He made them both fresh drinks and sat across from her again. "Amelia doesn't want a tabloid funeral. On that, your interests and the First Lady's intersect, unless for some reason you want her embarrassed."

She hurled her drink like a fastball. He ducked as it smashed the glass plate of a French poster, spilling slivers on the rug. *"Don't make false charges against me, Hubbell!"*

He set his drink down, brushed glass shards off his forearm, shaking specks out of his hair. A splotch of bourbon stained the wall.

He stared at her in cold disgust.

"What you said about me wanting to embarrass her, that was cheap."

He started picking up glass.

She marched into the kitchen, found a sponge and paper towels and knelt on the rug, gathering big pieces, massaging the rug to absorb broken pieces of glass. She felt the heat as he knelt beside her: his height, the fullness of his body, a force that had abruptly turned from consoling to a threat. "Don't bother," he mumbled. "I'll use the vacuum tomorrow." Reaching past the sponge, his long fingers were gathering pieces when his palm took a puncture.

"You're cut!"

"Call the FBI."

"No, you're bleeding. You need to wash it."

She led him into the kitchen and wedged close to him at the sink. The water ran red rivulets down branches of his palm. Aware of her body, knowing how it galvanized men, she shifted in place so as not to seem suggestive; she held his hand without seductiveness, dabbing a towel to stanch the bleeding. She wondered if the splayed lines of his palm signaled a long life and many children as a soothsayer in the French Quarter had said of her one day. Rex had been stationed on the sidewalk a few feet away, sporting sunglasses, a Red Sox baseball cap and Rolling Stones T-shirt with a red tongue. Pure incognito.

"I apologize for what I just did. I'll pay for the poster. I feel awful about the cut on your hand."

"I accept your apology."

Hubbell, palming a hand towel, leaned against the kitchen counter, staring at this woman who gave off such twisted signals. He wanted her; she could feel it. But he wanted information and seemed unable to reconcile the two. At some point, she realized, people higher up would have to know. He had her in a corner.

"All right, here is what happened. Last night I got a ride with King Artile and the Zydeco Flames to New Roads. They went on to the gig at a place called Creole Majestic. I waited for Rex outside some rally with a bunch of crawfish people. Mitchell drove us to the Creole Majestic, which is down some in Point Coupee Parish, so I could collect the money, pay Artile and the band. Money is the hard part of rockarolla. Rex changed into black jeans, blue denim shirt, wraparound sunglasses. I never know if people recognize him, but he loved the disguises. We sat in the back of the club till end of the set, then drove back to New Roads, where he changed into Governor clothes. We caught a plane at the landing strip, set down at Metro Airport shy of midnight. It was empty. Security guards turned off the lights. Rex told the state trooper to take his limo back to the Mansion. We went to my house in Mitchell's car, the three of us."

"What about the cockfight in Port Allen?"

"I have been to cockfights in Port Allen. Mermentau, too. But not last night. Mitchell left my place about half-past twelve."

"Why?"

"So Rex and I could be alone. After Rex fell asleep I went out back and soaked in the hot tub."

"And before he fell asleep?"

"He was awake. Healthy. His usual self."

"You were lovers."

"We had not *made* love for several months."

"Why?"

"I was cutting distance. We still saw each other. I was working on how to make my life without him, and let me tell you, that was a bear in itself."

"What did he eat?"

"With me, nothing."

"You remember what he drank?"

"Diet Coke at Point Coupee and another at my house."

"No Scotch."

"Rex didn't drink or do drugs. Ever."

She told Hubbell how she had returned from the hot tub to the sudden horror of "his waist on the bed and head on the floor, arms crossed on his chest like a pair of scissors and his mouth was open. I felt this freezing rush. I shook his arms, pinched his chin and then I phoned Mitchell, screaming *come over, I can't wake him!*"

"Let me get this straight. You come in from the hot tub ..."

She shut her eyes. "And ... he ... was ... *dead.*"

"Who entered the house?"

"I have no earthly idea." Her shoulders shuddered. "I saw no one till Mitchell came back. Rex was asleep when I went out back. I was on the deck thirty minutes, max. I never saw anyone enter or leave the house."

"What time did you find him?"

"Three AM."

"Mitchell was gone two and a half hours."

"I would say so, yes."

"What happened before you went out back?"

"We talked until he fell asleep."

"What did you talk about?"

She sighed. "I told him gently as I could that we were no longer lovers. I still had affection but wanted to keep clear boundaries. I needed my own life."

"How did he react to that news?"

"It wasn't news. This was a conversation he and I kept having. He didn't yell or anything, but he wasn't happy about losing his status quo."

"You didn't see anyone else in your house."

"No, sir. Not a soul. God be my witness."

"Then what?"

"Oh, just everything." Telling Hubbell how she knelt next to him, touching his cheeks his hair his arms trying to wake him, sobbing, begging God, whoever God is, please make him come alive, squealing as she shook his lifeless body when Mitchell barged in with burning eyes, shaking Rex so hard she thought his neck veins would pop and then Mitchell starts shouting *how did you let this happen?* Mitchell raving *why did you do this?* which popped her off the bed like a spring but Mitchell toppled her over, pinned her hands beneath his knees, lowering his stinky teeth inches from her face; she hissed, *Damn you to hell, Mitchell Mudd, for thinking I'd ever hurt Rex.*

Hubbell's mouth opened.

"Mitchell pulled me to my feet and I slapped his face. He said he was sorry and hugged me in a burst of fear. We pushed apart. I think we both felt unclean. Rex was dead and we were living. It was the first time I ever really touched Mitchell. So then we brought Rex back to the Mansion."

"You took the body in Mitchell's car?"

"What, you want us to walk? Rex was dead. Plus they ran off with his clothes. Mitchell put him in my sleeping bag."

"State troopers didn't see Mitchell drive around back?"

"One old boy on duty outside. Mitch used a dim-light signal prearranged for privacy. Rex hated having those cops everywhere."

"No wonder Bellamy freaked. His men could not account —"

"*How'd you like your sex life guarded by the Looziana State Police?* Arkansas troopers ratted on Clinton after he won President. Everyone in this state is for sale. That's why he paid Mitchell so well."

"How often were the two of you together?"

"Lately about once a week."

"And in the past?"

"Until July Fourth we averaged, oh, three-four times a week."

"What happened on July Fourth?"

"I went to Pensacola without him."

"Where was Mitchell, all those times you were with Rex?"

"Never more than five minutes away."

"So last night you get to the Mansion."

"And I had only been there once before, right when we met. For lunch. I mean, I respected that part of his life. Mitchell laid Rex out in the back seat in my sleeping bag, and I knelt low, wishing I had said something about love before he fell asleep on my bed. Mitchell deactivated the back alarm. Came to the car, hooked his elbows under Rex's armpits. I took his feet. He was some heavy. Did y'ever stand a dead man in a tiny elevator for maids? Me neither."

And then she lost it, sitting at his kitchen table, all the hours of resistance breaking like a dam swollen at flood tide, wailing sounds that weren't words until she discovered Hubbell on his knees, holding her shoulder, massaging her face with an expensive linen napkin. "I'm sorry. I really am."

The pieces of Hubbell did not add up. Instead of homing in with kisses at her supreme moment of vulnerability, he stood slowly, as she stopped crying, and moved to the bay window of his kitchen, hands in pockets, gazing at the magnolia tree in his back yard. He was not smiling, but she saw what was in him, as detectable as a bonfire, a weird swell of happiness.

"The sleeping bag is what color, Sophie?"

"Navy blue," she swallowed, wiping her eyes.

"Fibers between his toes." Hubbell's mind was racing. "Where is it?"

"Mitchell took the sleeping bag," she answered numbly. "We put Rex on the bed. I tried to pray, which is hard on account of my background. We were up there maybe ten minutes. Then he took me back."

"You think Mitchell killed him?"

"Absolutely not. Mitchell adored Rex. He was brother, father, uncle, running pardner, all in one. Mitchell is going insane wondering who broke in. He tore through my house like a pit bull they forgot to feed. That part is pretty much a blur. He overturned and probed and pulled things apart, while I just sat there crying. Around 4 AM, he got me situated at Days Inn and then took off by himself. I felt like a zombie. Wondering who on this planet can I tell? I couldn't confide in girlfriends, and I hadn't seen my therapist in several months. I mean, this was pure evil. I fell asleep around nine, woke up at noon. Drank Sprite, watched CNN, then slept till four in the afternoon. Caught a taxi home. I was starting to pack when Nobby invaded."

"Packing for where?"

"My plan was to start driving."

"How did the killer know where Rex was?"

"It had to be someone who knew about me, knew his schedule and had contacts close inside. That scares me. Because if I'd come into the bedroom minutes earlier, they'd have killed me."

"You think it was more than one person?"

"I don't know. I'm not a detective."

The muscles on Hubbell's shoulders and arms showed years of work in a gym. Possessing the space at the window, hands in pockets, he stared at the magnolia in the night sky. "They wanted you to find him. Make you the prime suspect."

"They did a good job at that."

He seemed so detached, emotionally removed, and only moments earlier he had been on his knees, soothing, touching her.

"Why did Nobby want to take you?"

"I think he thought he could use me to find Arabel — obviously, she split on him."

"You and his wife were friends."

"We never went shopping or got our hair done together, but I like Arabel. She kept his books on concerts and his wells. She wrote my checks before I started managing the Zydeco Flames. I hadn't seen her since Mardi Gras."

"Nobby has oil wells?"

"The ones I heard about were for waste injection."

"Those things ought to be illegal."

"With Nobby you always have to watch out."

"Does he have one in Avoyelles?"

"That I can't say. I know he has a big one in Calcasieu and a bunch in Mermentau. I never kept up with that end of his life."

"Why would Clifford Atchison be looking for Nobby?"

"They're both political."

The clock on the wall struck 1 AM. Her arms quivered with goose bumps. Hubbell draped a quilt over her. "You're safe here. The house has an alarm system. Nobby has no idea who I am."

She eyed him clinically, remembering his words in the car, how he would never hurt her. He gazed at her with flushed cheeks. "Did you really love Rex?"

The question caught her off guard. He was not asking detective things. "For a good while, yes I did. He was more alive than any human being I had ever met. Just being around him was an exalting experience. We danced every time we saw each other, mostly in my place but sometimes in music clubs when he'd use quick-dye on his eyebrows and hair or wear some cowboy hat and bandana. He seemed so amused by the power to disguise himself, to fool people. He talked on the phone to President Clinton for twenty minutes in my hot tub. But the logistics, the disguises, the wild dreams he lived by — it was too much. He lived for raw energy and, as time passed, I wanted a relationship you didn't have to hide. A house with a garden and down the road the possibility of babies, maybe even some kinda church. None of that fit where he was going."

"Which was?"

"Perpetual motion. The moment defines us. I wanted tranquility. I think that's what love is about. Part of it anyway."

"You made reference to therapy."

"When we met I was doing heavy lifting at the LSU Counseling Center. A stepdaddy who built a sixty-foot statue of Jesus with a crown of thorns made of lights glowing all night — go figure. I was in therapy with a woman who helped me dig beneath the brain pictures, search the fossil record. She practices in the Bay Area now. I go out there several times a year for corroboration of myself. We talked a lot about Rex as an unhealthy surrogate father. I also did consider him a shooting star. All I can think now is why someone would kill him."

"The Governor had some serious enemies," replied Hubbell.

Sophie stared at him with fretful eyes.

His mind went into lateral drift. "My dad was paralyzed when I was growing up. There was a lot of silence in my life. I came to believe that we have to suffer in order to complete ourselves as human beings — change habits, avoid the old collisions. I think it's possible to find joy if you learn how to search."

"Joy." She bit her lip. "I haven't entertained that notion since Molly my stepmomma died. She told me music was closer to rapture than the other arts. I reckon if I can figure out the biology of where I came from, then I'll have a decent shot of making myself into the person I'm supposed to be."

"Perhaps," he pondered, "I'm heading in the same direction too."

Is that so? she reported mentally. She yawned. "I'm pretty worn out."

He ushered her to the guest room. "Wake me if you need anything. You'll get through this, I promise."

Hubbell's politeness did not seem strained. The intensity of his body was transparent: he was working hard to keep his lust in check. A lonely boy-man in his beautiful house. But he had tried hard to comfort her, not like some political spy. His emotions were stuffed deep. Still, for the first time since death had eaten Rex alive, she felt secure in herself. For three years, Rex had been an overriding presence, and then abruptly he was a body drained of life. *Be sure your sin will find you out.* She hated those words, but the echo from Reverend TJ reverberated like a drumbeat. She lay in the darkness, surrounded by books, determined to escape the wicked city of Baton Rouge.

Hot fog rolled across the dark sky at 5 AM on Saturday. Christian Fraux sat up in bed. Rex was downstairs in his freezer. Fraux's wife spooned her legs around his bottom. "Dreaming?" she murmured.

"Champagne in a Las Vegas hotel room," he lied, softly.

She folded back to slumber.

Fraux had been unable to remember his dreams since Reagan went to Washington. He made more money than any black person in the history of Avoyelles, and he could no longer afford the pulpit. The orderly way he had fused church and commerce split a little more each day as women wailed over coffins of teenage boys. His business was booming because of crack cocaine. The killings that had fired his hope lay in lagoons of the past, a quest that anchored his wife in a community that waited word of marches, court battles, the martyrs in Mississippi and events far from Blue Line that joined them in a drama of the dream. This mosaic of memory had stamped his conviction that if good people make common cause, the human heart will prevail.

Fraux was trying to feel sadness over Rex's death. What did he feel toward the man? He had enjoyed his company, the entertainment of his personality. Rex was a transparent sinner, a man with empathy who lived for succor of the system. His murder meant that the balance scales have toppled. Fraux wondered: What does it mean for us, the living?

Fraux ached for the old, heady feeling that the Lord was using him as a cipher in freedom's quest. His midlife was torn by arguments with his wife as politics supplanted civil rights and she grew bored of his home town. Twice a year they flew to places like Seattle, Las Vegas, Toronto and San Diego for meetings in which he had scant interest save to satisfy his spouse. She plotted their itineraries months in advance; they ate in fine restaurants, saw the fundamental sights. On four-star beds, he poured into her loins with waves of intensity absent back home. In Louisiana, his sadness enlarged with the realization that morticians' conventions had become the salvation of his marriage.

His skin softened to the sizzle of the shower.

Fraux wondered if the newly deceased infiltrate our minds, like spies, before we lay them in the earth. People behave in cemeteries because they feel the spirits, those who have gone before, watching, assessing us. It is not God as much as the beloved dead who engender our decorum. The dead know things. What would Rex be thinking?

His wife, in thin nightgown, was ironing his shirt as Fraux emerged from the steam. Her eyes were hot with wonder. "Do you want me with you today?"

"Angelle," he said gravely, "if it were dangerous, I would want you — I would need you." He emitted a minor key of exasperation. "Today is politics."

"I'll watch it on television." She drew his mouth into a kiss. "You've always been so brave, Chris."

He gave a look of consternation. "The Governor has nothing to wear."

Fraux opened his closet and removed a dark pinstriped suit.

"*Christian,* that suit cost four hundred dollars!"

"We'll bill the state six hundred." He arranged the suit, white shirt and club tie on the bed. He set a pair of loafers on the rug.

"Put him in some good shoes, Chris."

Fraux searched the closet and found a pair of scuffed Cordovans.

"I'll tell Juba to shine them," she said, taking the shoes.

"Yes, tell Juba and Willie Boy to make the preparations."

Fraux pulled on a T-shirt and faded khaki pants, spotted with smudges of blood that had blackened from cycles of detergent. He only wore khaki when he did embalming. Now fifty-seven and about to work on his oldest white ally, Fraux had felt his scaffolding of hope come down piece by piece. Black people with stable jobs feared the menace of burn-brained young triggers. "Nihilism!" thundered the visiting minister from Atlanta at Fraux's pulpit the previous Sunday. "A nihilism in those *narcotized, possessed* and bereft of hope! This is our scourge, my brethern. Empty rooms in the Father's many-mansioned house. Call them home, my sisters and brothers. Call them home!"

"Home," echoed the congregates.

But the voices lacked the optimism of freedom days. The people were tired. What most of them wanted was not to call the crackheads home but to clear them out, to prison or an island. This new pendulum of dependency and violence sliced through communities where injection wells and dumping pits leached chemicals into the capillaries of the earth, seeping into water veins that flowed silently into the homes and bodies of unknowing folk.

Christian Fraux went downstairs and out the kitchen, passing through a large garage with three silver hearses. He entered the working area in the back of the mortuary, where his cutting instruments were laid out on a steel table. Juba wore a rubber smock. He was a huge man with coal black skin and veins on his arms that glistened when he worked like train tracks after rain.

"Well, Mist' Chris," announced Juba. "Willie Boy done gone home."

Fraux wrapped his chest in a rubber smock, tied with a sharp tug. The Governor lay under a spread on the table. "Willie Boy sick?" muttered Fraux.

"Willie Boy say he tired stayin' up all night."

"Plenty nights he stay up past dawn, playing that zydeco."

"Willie Boy still vote for ole Mayor Bobby Broussard."

"Man been dead ten years," snorted Fraux.

"Miss Della Broussard give Willie Boy a turkey so he do vote. Willie Boy was sleep rightchere on the table when I brung the guvna out the cooler. I propped the guvna upright, stood behind him, said real deep: *Don't vote for Mayor Bobby Broussard no more, Willie Boy Benoir. Time to vote for ME!*"

Fraux grinned. "Willie Boy thought the body talked?"

"Willie Boy got spooked!" Juba's smile was an accordion of gold.

"You ain't spooked, eh Juba?"

"Nah, Mist' Chris. I never vote for no dead man." Juba smiled again. "But I do take Miss Della's turkey."

Fraux let his smile hang before summoning a stern tone. "Nobody knows who we got here, Juba. Nobody!"

"I hear what you sayin', Mist' Chris."

"Willie Boy know to keep his mouth shut?"

"I'm more 'n sho he do."

Fraux had signed contracts from the two men demanding total confidentiality in their work at Fraux Mortuary. What would he do if either man failed to abide by the scrawled signatures? Fraux shuddered at the roulette wheel of possibilities. He could not think of that now. Embalming was work that required care. He studied the stippled blue of cyanide around the chin and said: "Yellow." Juba produced a canister of cosmetic powder. Fraux mixed it with water. He set a block of pink wax in a pot on the gas range near the table. "Well," said Fraux. "Let's drain him."

Juba handed him a surgical hook for the jugular vein and thirty-six inches of tubing that fed into a bucket. The bottle of formaldehyde contained sufficient volume to replace the blood. The siphoning process would take about forty-five minutes. The precision of a good embalmer left few dots on the neck after the application of cosmetic powder or wax. Fraux slipped on rubber gloves.

The chimes of the front door floated an eerie melody through the building.

"What time is it?" snapped Fraux.

"Ten minutes to six, Mist' Chris."

"No family comes this early."

Fraux tapped the Governor's neck, still cold from the night's storage. "A few minutes yet on this, Juba. I'll go see who's there."

He flicked on the light in the hallway that ran between two reception parlors. Fraux saw a man's silhouette through the glass crucifix beveled into the door window. He had paid a hefty fee for thick glass that afforded a view of inside looking out. He crossed the foyer without turning on the light, crept quietly to the front door and affected a peasant's voice: "Who dat?"

"Calling for Reverend Christian Fraux, please," came the voice.

Fraux studied the shadow on glass. "Who dat wanna see Mist Fraux?"

The figure stooped beneath the glass and slipped a white card under the door.

Fraux read it in the thin blue light of dawn:

James Jack O'Connor, SPECIAL AGENT
FBI Organized Crime Strike Force
Hale Boggs Federal Building
New Orleans LA 70116 tel. 504-329-7522

"Hold on," said Fraux, retreating to the back of the room, knowing the FBI man could not see through the glass. He unlocked his office and stripped off the khakis, gloves and workshirt, stuffed them into a closet and pulled on black suit slacks, a white button down shirt and loafers.

He sprinted to the back of the building. "How is he, Juba?"

"Neck still icy, Mist' Chris."

"I have business up front. Don't puncture the body."

"Yessah."

"Get a hot towel on his neck. And put the fan on him."

"Yes*sah!*"

Fraux raced across the maroon carpet, and collected himself in the foyer. He opened the door. The white man was six-feet tall, wide of jaw with shoulders like carved pine; he had rusty, close-cropped hair and freckles across his brow like mine placements on a military map. He smelled of talcum and coffee.

Fraux peered into sea blue eyes. "Are you James Jack O'Connor?"

"Yes, sir, Reverend Fraux." The agent held up an ID card.

"Picture looks like you."

His suit, dark blue, was suitable for mourning. The attaché case made Fraux think of nuclear codes that follow the President in a Secret Service briefcase. "You may come in for just a moment," said the undertaker.

In the foyer, a room of velvet off-white with tapestries of Jesus and the Apostles on the walls, they sat in opposite chairs with thick armrests. "It's early to call on a man," said Fraux.

"Yes, sir. I'd have waited, but I saw the light go on in the back."

Meaning the FBI is parked across the street. Fraux wondered how many were out there. "I don't like people spying on my home or place of bidness."

"We just arrived, sir. I want insight on what happened at the Mansion."

"It's barely six in the morning."

"The funeral Mass begins in five hours, Reverend Fraux. We have reason to believe Governor LaSalle was murdered by organized crime."

Fraux said nothing.

"We'd like permission to view the remains."

"Mister —" Fraux glanced at the card, "O'Connor. That would violate a sacred tenet of my profession. Your request must go to the First Lady."

James Jack O'Connor — Fordham '69, Notre Dame Law '75; ten years organized crime strike force Washington D.C. when FBI sends you down to bust Dixie mobsters — leaned toward Christian Fraux with searchlight eyes. "I know of your standing in the Democratic Party, sir. The Justice Department has a bipartisan commitment to civil rights."

"*After Reagan and Bush?* Who you shittin', man?"

The flush hit O'Connor's cheeks. "There are career attorneys in Justice who fight turf wars to protect the movement's gains. We had African American FBI agents investigate a fast-food chain for violating open accommodations law. What I'm saying simply is I need help. We think people's lives are at risk. The First Lady is incommunicado."

"Is her life at risk?"

"She's sitting on a volcano."

"Call her lawyer."

"Right. I'd like your take on Hubbell."

Fraux was mute. Jack O'Connor closed his lips. The ridge of freckles curled with the frown of a metallic gaze that met Fraux's eyes head on. "The Bureau compensates individuals who help us gather intelligence."

"That's not my line of work."

"I understand, Reverend. That's why we provide financial assistance for access that makes our work easier. There is no public record. The FBI relied extensively on paid informants to break the Ku Klux Klan in Mississippi."

"Not many Klukkers on our bayou."

"I was speaking by way of analogy."

Fraux folded his fingers on his lap.

"I can give you a thousand dollars cash to let me see the body."

"I'm afraid that's not possible."

"We could make it three thousand."

"I really must ask you to go."

"I have an unmarked van outside with a man inside it named Leo Murdoch. Leo Murdoch can back into your garage, open his van and perform an autopsy in eighty-five minutes. Leo Murdoch is licensed. The body will never leave the mortuary, Reverend." O'Connor checked his watch. "Six-fifteen. At seven-forty you can embalm. At nine you can leave for the capital. Mass starts at eleven. That's an hour plus flex time. You can have an escort if you want."

"That would be just fine!" Fraux bunched his fists on his thighs, elbows extended like thin wings. "You think I'm ga-ga, mister?"

"The Justice Department does not tolerate murder, sir."

"There is not a court in this parish or the entire state of Looziana that would approve of my violating professional canons!"

"Are you forcing me to use a search warrant?"

"The only force here is *harassment!* The town of Avoyelles will protect the remains of our native son!"

O'Connor's thin smile masked mental scenes that made him want to piss — bubble tops at Fraux Mortuary; bad blood with local cops; reporters with spiked clubs and nets. Jack O'Connor needed publicity like a case of hepatitis.

"I apologize, Reverend Fraux." The agent spread his hands on his thighs. "I want an open line of communication."

"Right! And I have two fourteen-year-old boys who also need embalming. Why don't you arrest crack dealers, or the Mafia? That would be a great thing!"

O'Connor rubbed his jaw. "I'm going outside to make some calls. Reverend Fraux, can you give me assurance you won't begin embalming the Governor till I get my business done? You understand what I'm saying here."

"I understand, yes. I will have to make some calls myself. But we move vehicles in and out of that garage all day long."

"We will not obstruct your business, sir."

"Is my phone wiretapped?"

"Absolutely not. I give you my word. Can I ask one favor?"

"You can ask."

"It's better for both of us that local officials are not drawn into this. If we have to explain our position I will, but that makes Mrs. LaSalle a target for hungry media people. I don't wish to upset her."

"You assume local authorities will talk to the press."

"They usually do." O'Connor stood. "My cell number is on this card."

Fraux locked the door behind O'Connor and sprinted to the back room where the fan was whirring on the body and his assistant sat snoring in a chair.

"*Juba!*"

The big man popped up like a Jack-in-the-box. "Mist' Chris!"

An odor of flesh mingled with the tang of yellow wax, scorched on the stove. "Clean up the damned stove, Juba. And *stay awake!*"

"Yes*sah!*"

Fraux went to his office and made three rapid-fire calls to Henry Hubbell's home number, hanging up the first two times the voice-mail message came on, hoping the rings would wake the attorney. The third time he left a message. "Federal visitors are here making demands. Call immediately!"

Fraux poured a mug of coffee and paced the hall, wondering if he should telephone the First Lady, praying for a response to what was the twelfth message on the phone in the house where visions of Sophie Thibodeaux warmed the fields of Henry Hubbell's dreams. James Jack O'Connor orated his own message for Hubbell from his cellular phone in the FBI Taurus behind Fraux Mortuary, and in another moment left the expectant Leo Murdoch with other agents in the van while he tore out on Avoyelles Bayou Road, past the cemetery where Bobby Broussard was buried to a pasture where a helicopter waited in a field shadowed by ancient oaks, bearded with moss.

The chopper blades spun across Atchafalaya swamp like a spider rising in the sun, crawling black and sleek through a web of crystalline rays. O'Connor barked radio commands to a man driving another Taurus that moved out of a parking lot behind the Federal Building in Baton Rouge, up the ramp at Government Street and onto the interstate, moving eighty-five miles per hour past the Governor's Mansion exit, past the Royal Oaks exit and a house denuded of furniture, this ruby of information on Doctor Nobby gleaned by O'Connor from a fellow agent's mother who lived in the subdivision and asked the moving van driver, who said the furniture was Alabama bound.

Ala-fucking-*Bama!* Oh, the South! The Gulf South with its disappearing coastline and arterial pathways for the pot, coke and smack smugglers; the mob-run video poker in truck stops and bars; the political species a parade of diversity, open-palmed moving targets for a Federal hunter: Cajuns, Capos, Afros, Creoles, oil patch cowboys, shanty Irish and now the Cambodians angling for their stake. He pictured these human beings slogging in mudflats left by drenching rains, the sky bursts that thrilled his wife from Rhode Island because she loved to garden; all his wife's flora and all that crime sent Jackie O'Connor into swoons of pleasure with each new spreadsheet matched to dummy corporations, landfills tied to tomato vendors and the prayer running like a mantra in his mind: *Please keep Luigi Rompallo healthy in Angola prison.*

Twenty-five minutes after he left Fraux Mortuary, the helicopter landed on an empty Little League diamond in an innocent suburb of Baton Rouge. O'Connor sprinted with a briefcase under his left arm, high-kicking past home plate and empty dugouts warm in the morning dew to the waiting Taurus of another agent who delivered him three minutes later to the house where Henry Hubbell sat on a kitchen stool in red jogging shorts, wondering how many of the messages on his voice mail belonged to people about whom he cared.

Sophie appeared in the hallway, white terry-cloth robe and haze of honey-brown curls transposable to Boticelli's Venus. All she needed was a shell.

"Your phone sure rings," she yawned.

"Damn thing oughta be outlawed," he smiled. "Coffee?"

"That'd be nice." She took a perch on the stool next to him.

The doorbell chimed.

They both jumped like cats.

Hubbell put an index finger over his lips, and motioned her to follow him down the hallway. "Wait in the guestroom," he whispered.

"Who is it?" she whispered back.

"I don't know. Just stay in here, please."

"How long?"

"Till I come back."

He learned toward her with a raging aorta. "You'll be safe. I guarantee it."

"You better!"

He touched her on the cheek. "Wait quietly."

She removed his hand, gazed at his palm, and said with an

enigmatic smile: "Reckon I don't have a choice."

The front door chimed again.

"*Com*-ing!" he called, darting into his bedroom. He pulled on a T-shirt and jogging pants over the gym shorts to muffle his erection and strode down the hall with his member pulsing like a prize fighter doing jump rope. He peeked through the tiny binocular viewfinder at a man who looked as important as the dark blue Ford in the street. "Who is it?" he said.

"James Jack O' Connor, FBI." The man raised a laminated ID to the viewing glass. Hubbell opened the door and discovered a second man whose image had been obstructed by O'Connor's in the viewer.

"I'm Jack's partner," said the man, holding a badge. "Joe Dymally."

"I'll give Jack five minutes."

"We work in pairs," said O'Connor. "Standard policy."

"My policy is I talk to you alone or shut the door."

O'Connor smacked his lips. "Okay, Joe. I'll have a little chat with the Assistant Attorney General for Constitutional Affairs."

Dymally retreated to the car. As O'Connor entered, Hubbell caught a scent of French body water from his bathroom, a keepsake of his Parisian flame discovered by his voluptuous house guest. The FBI agent followed Hubbell's tightening scrotum into the kitchen. "Coffee, Mr. O'Connor?"

"Black, please."

Hubbell poured two cups and tried not to wet his legs. O'Connor gazed at the bookshelves in the living room. "Impressive library, counselor. You have quite a legal reputation. So did your father."

"Much obliged."

"Friends call me Jack." O'Connor sat on a stool warmed by Sophie Thibodeaux two minutes earlier.

Hubbell leaned his elbow on the counter. "So, Jack."

"You and I share a culture, Henry. Each sworn to uphold the law, both anti-crime. Two honest men. And accidents happen. Good people, bad events."

Hubbell nodded, stirring his coffee.

"I have a man licensed to perform autopsies, waiting in a van outside Fraux Mortuary. We want immediate access to determine cause of death."

"You have no jurisdiction. The Coroner classified death from natural causes. The family wants no autopsy."

"Coroner's a bad witness, bud."

"No one said he was testifying."

"You left the morgue last night before the floor show. We arrived when the cops hauled in that chop-job from the river. One of my men identified substances from a piece of flesh. Willoby blurted out: '*Cyanide 'n potassium chloride, God Amighty!*' I pressed him. 'Miss Amelia wants no autopsy,' he said. That Coroner was sweating tattoos."

"He's old. It's a hard job."

"In my experience what someone won't say telegraphs what he has to say, under oath."

"That's your experience."

"Picture yours after the Federal Attorney hands our grand jury the evidence to warrant exhumation of the body."

"You have no evidence of homicide."

"We have strong leads to organized crime. The Coroner owes the First Lady. You're her shield. Failure to grant us access to the body could be taken as obstruction of justice. That's a criminal act. It could mean disbarment."

"You don't want to pick a fight with my client, Jack."

"Rex had an amazing life. His widow does not want a fight with me."

"You never made dirt stick on Governor LaSalle."

"He died too soon. But we got Atchison. Others are coming. Explain to me why Henry Hubbell, who is heading to the Supreme Court on a federal-state oil tax dispute, is accessory to a conspiracy. What do you get out of this?"

He had a sudden urge to hug O'Connor like a lost brother: he wanted Jack's approval, to have him see that yes, he was an honest man. But Amelia LaSalle and Sophie Thibodeaux loomed as magnetic poles, a feminine energy field radiating love and anger, pushing back walls of the law.

"There are things I'm not at liberty to discuss, Jack."

O'Connor sipped coffee. "Poison permeates skin tissue. We can get some of that with an exhumation but we lose evidence once formaldehyde replaces the drained blood. Study of his innards gets more complicated. As long as fundamental tissues remain, we can track the compounds. You're in way over your head, Henry. Do this the right way, and nobody innocent will get hurt."

"My client wants a dignified funeral."

"Your client? You work for the state."

"This conversation has become mutually unproductive."

"As an officer of the court you have a duty to report anything bearing on criminal activity."

"That discussion belongs in an office with Attorney General Abadie."

"Now that's rich. The General comes back from Trinidad dripping enough of Doctor Nobby's dung to open a fertilizer store. Look, Hubbell. Rex is on ice. I gotta nail the slimeballs who did it. Why are you blockin' me?"

"I can't make any decision before speaking with my client."

"You'd appreciate how our lab people assess fibers and fluids. A true art form. Elvis Banks and his Quasimodo brother have evaporated. We have not yet begun to subpoena, but we will, Hubbell. Go to your broker on it."

Hubbell stared back impassively. The chill in his ankles crawled up the hair on his knees and burrowed into his thighs like a dentist's drill.

"I can lay a Temporary Restraining Order on Fraux Mortuary in thirty minutes to stop that body from being cut."

"You need an affidavit before a judge gives a TRO," snapped Hubbell. "I'll sue you personally for attempted desecration of a body! Inflicting emotional distress by trying to prevent timely burial! Deprive Amelia of her civil rights and Justice will transfer you so far out of this state, they'll have to send you daylight in a jar."

O'Connor scowled. "What do you want, Hubbell?"

"I want you off my back."

"We really are on the same side."

"Then stop threatening me. I took a call because Oscar was out of town. I'm helping a lady work through an awesome tragedy. Normally, you and I might share a joint interest. But this stuff is in a zone all its own."

"How long will it take you to talk with her?"

"I haven't even taken a shower. Couple of hours maybe."

"No! Keep Fraux from draining that body."

"I will make calls. I will not make promises."

James Jack O'Connor handed Hubbell a card with his phone numbers. "I'm waiting to hear from you."

He locked the door after O'Connor left and listened to his voice mail: the first three messages were from Speaker Sutton making threats. Then his mother's quavering voice asked if he had heard the terrible news about Governor LaSalle. He smiled. A cheery solicitation from a young woman asked him to subscribe to the *Wall Street Journal*. Then came a growl from Oscar Abadie requesting immediate contact. Sutton, again: "I wouldn't wanna be *you* if you doan call *me*." Oscar Abadie returned in basso profundo: "Goddamn, boy. It's six in the mawnin'. Where the hell are you? Henry, this is Oscah! Call the moment you get this message." After that came Christian Fraux and then a blunt James Jack O'Connor: "It is critical that I speak with you about Governor La-Salle as soon as you receive this message."

When Sophie Thibodeaux peeked into the hall, he thought of her as a sea nymph, golden hair and aromas of wonder, the pink promises of love in a cove with a waterfall, but she darted back in the room when his bell chimed again.

He opened the front door. Oscar Abadie stood on the porch with clenched jaw and hands on his hips.

"Good morning, General. You missed the FBI by two minutes."

"My lucky day. Get dressed, son. We gotta take a ride."

"I need to call Amelia and Christian Fraux."

"I did that. Nobody's cuttin' on Rex. Put your clothes on."

He cleared his throat. "Would you mind waiting in the car, boss?"

"What, you think I'm contagious?"

"Of course not, Oscar. I, ah, have — company."

Abadie poked his tongue in his cheek. "My motor's running."

"Just a few minutes," said Hubbell, shutting the door.

Sealing off invasions of the world, he tiptoed down the hall and met Sophie standing on the carpet.

"He knew it was me, didn't he?" she said.

"Maybe. But he doesn't control you."

"Neither do you."

"I never for a moment thought I did." With a stirring across his equator, Hubbell touched her hands. She pulled back with an impatient sigh. He pulled his hands away. But she was there, doe eyes, lush lips, morning bliss close enough to kiss. "I didn't mean to touch you," he whispered.

She frowned. "You certainly did. This is no time to come on to someone."

"I take the Fifth. But it wasn't threatening. There's a sense of something real, something promising between us, a moment when a soft touch seems — right, so to speak."

"Well, I think you're a good person, so to speak. You have traits I appreciate."

"When all this stuff is behind us I'd really like to get to know you."

"There's a lot of this stuff ahead of us first. I need to borrow your car."

"My car?"

"Nobby cut my tires, remember. I have to buy a dress for the services."

"You don't belong anywhere near that rotunda this afternoon."

"Now, Henry. I am not going to watch a man I loved get waked on TV. I can call a cab, or phone Willie Boy, the rub board player with the Zydeco Flames. Or you can lend me a vehicle and maybe tonight I'll buy you dinner."

"As long as no one else is there," he heard himself say, "I'll buy."

His hands eased up the soft down of her forearms. She touched his lips with her fingertips. "Be patient, Hubbell. If it's right, it will happen when it's right." His pulse quickened to the mental image of the two of them on an island in lyrical latitudes, all alone, all naked, until she jumped back from the blast on the street where the Attorney General of Louisiana was pounding his horn.

Forty miles outside Baton Rouge, Oscar Abadie's black Lincoln left the interstate for a rutted single-lane asphalt road that ran past miles of brawny oaks and pecan trees with gray-webbed insect nests lodged in the high branches. Oscar never traveled without his driver, who today was absent. The land grew more hilly as stands of pine rose past scattered chimneys demarking sites where houses once had stood. Poverty is never far from the city of power.

With the thickened midsection of a football player well past his prime, Abadie filled his seat right up to the steering wheel. The second week of heat matched the Attorney General's mood. "Why didn't you call Sutton back?"

"He's not my client, Oscar."

"Damn, son! A system turns on spokes that hold. You don't take five pieces of prime from the Speaker and then leave him at the picnic."

"I don't trust that old prick as far as I could spit."

"So what? String him along. Come on, you went to Harvard."

"Things got complicated."

"I hope you uncomplicated them with Rex's galpal in your back room."

"I trusted you, Oscar."

"Meaning the fuck what?"

"What were you doing on an island with Doctor Nobby?"

"Don't answer a question with a question."

"Then tell me what to say when the FBI questions me about my boss."

"For your deniability, it's best we not discuss certain things."

"*Goddamn, Oscar!*"

"What, you think the Holy Ghost comes down to pay off a campaign debt? Time was, everybody went to the barrel and money was money. You got enough, and if you were smart, you won. Know who poisoned that? Nixon! All that Watergate crap. Now you need an army of lawyers and CPAs to perfume the money. You lose money *raisin'* money. Plus everybody's a spy! Feds, media, hidden camera, phone bugs, Internet, Freedom Information — nothing goddamn free about it. You don't know the dough I avoid so our environmental team can do the job. I'm talkin' *big* money! Yeah I went to Trinidad. I don't regulate 'em."

Hubbell stared at the road.

"Tell me about the girl, Henry."

He recounted the night's events, suppressing any mention of the craving for Sophie that had swollen inside him like a fever burning at his temples. As he told Oscar the details, his mind bubbled with Sophie: a preacher stepdaddy who made a gigantic Jesus, the morbid curiosity for her biological mother, an identity quest freed from Rex. He wanted to follow her into some sweet nimbus far from the political tarpits.

"They *moved* the body?" rejoined the Attorney General.

"They moved the body."

"What'd Nobby want with her?"

"To kill her, I think. Make her disappear so people would think she was party to the hit and left town."

The Attorney General weighed the account of Sophie and Mudd, netted in guilty terror, trundling the corpse up the Mansion's elevator at 4 AM. "No wonder Mitchell made himself scarce. How come you didn't tell Amelia this?"

"I learned it at one in the morning. I've been with you since seven."

Abadie grunted affirmatively. "*Advocate* says Regina made a hundred phone calls organizin' the wake. Imagine receiving one. FBI threatened Bellamy. This is fixin' to get real dirty. When Fraux called Amelia, she freaked on the autopsy. I gave FBI ten-minute notice and sent the Avoyelles sheriff to Fraux's."

"An embalmed corpse won't solve this, Oscar."

"I didn't have any choice."

The prison lay in red bluff hills that Tunica Indians once had hunted, an eighteen-thousand acre penal farm on a remote plateau cradled by the Mississippi's harshest currents. There is no back wall at Angola. The River serves that role. No escapee has ever made it across the river. Razor-ribbon wire tops the chain fence where visitors arrive. The lockdown dormitories with metal windows are spaced out on flat green earth tilled by Angolan slaves after the Indians were displaced. Gray cement guard towers break the flatness of the land. Beyond the incarceration camps lie sparkling emerald patches, ribboned with bright rows of squash and yams, cotton and soybeans, where inmates earn a nickle an hour as field hands. Every summer, a prisoner evaporates at head count, and the guards and bloodhounds head for trees and brush along river's edge till the man turns up, sun-scorched or a bloated cadaver.

Attorney General Abadie halted at the entry post, where the guards who search for contraband automatically waved him through. The trail curled past the cell block where twenty men waited for their date with lethal injection. Hubbell hated capital punishment; his blood raced beneath a mental jumpcut to the hooded executioner strapping Rex LaSalle's forearm into the electric chair, condemned for corrupting the bloom of Sophie Thibodeaux's youth.

Abadie drove past gravestones at Point Lookout, where inmates without claiming kin slept in prison soil. He parked behind a three-story edifice of wire mesh cages. The two men stepped into a sea of heat and odors of butter and rooster dung. A black inmate in jeans and hipboots, sweat streaming down his muscled torso, was shoveling slabs of corn-bread into cages that housed Warden Joe B. Carson's fighting gamecocks. A white man wearing khakis and a cowboy hat stood in the shade, resting his hand on a holster with a gun.

"I'm looking for Warden Carson," announced Attorney General Abadie.

"He's in that building yonder," said the guard.

"Warden talkin' with Big Money," said the prisoner.

"Y'all call him Big Money," chuckled Abadie.

The prisoner mopped his face. "That man money be *bigger'n* big. Nobody make more phone calls on cell block. Big Money walk around the yard in general poppalation, he be guarded by a brother on one side, biker with red tattooes the other. Black *and* white. I'm talkin' stone killers, boss. People *fight* to guard that man."

Abadie gazed at the prisoner. "What's your name?"

"Albert Jackson Tremaine. I know what you thinkin'. Why's a good man like Tremaine doin' time? Passion crime, boss. But I fount Jesus and ain't had no confractions at Angola. I'm goin' upta parole board in Janyerry."

"Good luck," said Hubbell.

"I been in Angola since I was baby. Look it up in prison records, boss. Albert Jackson Tremaine. One first offense at fifteen. Now I'm thirty-two."

Abadie: "Who'd you kill, Tremaine?"

"White man in the sack with my chickywawa, boss. Interracial sex! I only shot him once. First cop kilt in St. James Parish since World War II. And they send a baby to Angola. I been here fifty-five percent of my life and I ain't got one tattoo, boss. Say somethin' for me when I go up to parole board."

"We'll take a look at your record, Tremaine," said Abadie.

"Thank you, boss."

"Where do y'all bake the corn-bread?" asked Hubbell.

"Prison cafeteria," volunteered the guard, uneasy about Albert Jackson Tremaine hogging the moment.

Hubbell followed Oscar Abadie through a barn bulging with hay. They climbed a small knoll. In the shade of a sycamore tree, four men in uniforms with rifles guarded a one-room cement building. Warden Joe B. Carson emerged. A thick man with bronze skin leathered by the sun, he wore a ten-gallon hat and saluted Oscar Abadie. "Mawnin', General."

Abadie returned the salute. "Morning to you, Joe B. This here's my assistant, Attorney Henry Hubbell."

"How do," said Carson, shaking Hubbell's hand.

Carson grimaced. "Some powerful godawful news about Rex. I was with him at Port Allen one night last week. He seemed real healthy to me."

"He sure did," said Abadie. "You make much with yo roosters?"

"I do all right with these birds. Got some lawmen over Mississippi come to Looziana where it's legal. I never lost a cockfight to dem peckerwoods. Hanh!"

"World keeps on turning," hummed Abadie.

"Rex admired my birds, Gen'l. You see any shakeup in Corrections?"

"Not really. Rex left a solid foundation. The man ready?"

Carson nodded. "No paperwork on this visit, Oscar."

"You'll do fine with those birds, Joe B."

Carson saluted as Abadie opened the door. Hubbell followed him into the small room, cold as an executive suite and invisible to dorms down the hill. Rompallo sat at the table, a squat pyramid of flesh with lines of gray hair pulled over his scalp from a transplant yet to ripen. Rompallo's furled lips matched the creases of his prison-issue cotton shirt; they were pale blue like the jeans into which his tree stump thighs were packed.

Next to him sat New Orleans Attorney Salvadore Sargassi in a pinstriped suit, lean, swarthy with olive skin and black hair sprouting silver on the curls.

"General Abadie, good to see you," said Sargassi, extending his hand.

"Amen, Sal. How you today, Mr. Rompallo?"

Sour and bullnecked, Rompallo sat slumped in a chair, arms crossed. The two officials took seats across from the Capo and his lawyer.

"Advise my client of his rights," said Sargassi.

"We got no court reporter, no tape, no bazookas, just four home-boys," smiled Abadie. "You understand English, Mr. Rompallo."

"I'm American," he grunted.

"And you want outa this dump," said Oscar Abadie.

Light came to Luigi Rompallo's eyes; he put his hands on the table. Sargassi touched a wrist, and whispered to him in Italian.

"Acknowledge his rights," demanded Sargassi.

"I acknowledge your rights, Mr. Rompallo. Food here is crap. Bikers and Bantus escort you on exercise walks. And the man who put you here —"

"Joe Fock Hall!"

"Calmati," admonished Salvadore Sargassi.

"Joe Fuck Hall is right!" boomed Abadie. "And you know what he did?"

Rompallo watched Abadie.

"*He goddamn quit!*"

Sargassi frowned. "This was not in the media."

"It will be," said the General. "Bet your back pay."

The mass of Rompallo stirred in the chair.

"Somebody clipped Rex. And Hall, who used *you* to get elected number two, he runs. Splitsville. What you think about that, Mr. Luigi?"

Rompallo gazed back with leaden eyes.

"He was afraid. Figgered if they got Rex, he's next. And Senator Atchison, facing serious time when a jury of his peers get done, has got gallstones."

"Nothing at Atchison's trial has implicated my client whatsoever."

"Politicians," uttered Rompallo in cryptic clarity.

"Right!" said Abadie, eyes dancing. "And politicians decide the next man to do Governor's business. You understand that, Mr. Luigi. I know you do."

"Ah unnerstan bidness," came the gravelly response.

"Of course you do," said the Attorney General, folding his fingers like a card dealer. "And *I* understand the business of governing. It is something I trained for, never dreaming it would come down like orders from God."

Sargassi stared intently. Rompallo glowered.

"And my power affects you," said Abadie, warming to his topic. "Where you are today. Where you could be tomorrow."

"Tomarra?"

"Not that quick. But a short time is distinct possibility."

Rompallo murmured to Sargassi in a gruff lyricism of the native tongue. "He wants to know," said Sargassi, "how you sell his release to the press."

"Heart ailment. Waste of public money to keep an old man hospitalized in Angola. He goes home to Jefferson Parish. Old boy sheriff, house arrest."

Rompallo nodded.

"Your son has a restaurant in the French Quarter."

"Lul Lui run a clean bidness," growled Rompallo.

"And he depends on government inspectors to keep the balance."

"Four stars in dem tourist books. *Times-Picayune,* too."

"Killin' Rex upset the scales."

Rompallo bounced in the chair, jowls shaking. He stabbed the air with a forefinger. "Rex LaSalle strongest sonuvabitch govna dis state ever had. Lucky we hadda man like dat do bidness wid. Ran with women, bet on cocks; he drank no alcohol. I like the man. Respec' the man. I never hoit Rex. Hear me? *Never would fockin' hoit Rex!* People hoit Rex, dem people ain't my friends."

"Who clipped him?" said Abadie.

"I advise my client —"

"Shut up, Sal."

"Oscar, this violates statutes so great in number —"

"Mr. Rompallo, do you want to die in Angola?"

"He's served two years on five!" fumed Sargassi.

"I know. And if he knows what I need, but won't say, he'll die here!"

"Fuckin' extortion, Oscar!"

"Talk, Rompallo!"

"How I'm goan git out with Rex dead?" roared Rompallo.

The room filled with the breathing of the men.

Abadie flattened his hands on the table. "I appreciate what you said, Mr. Luigi. Because in this infernal puzzle, you had no reason to put a hit on Rex. He had nothing against you, which meant he could have been passive if you got a ticket out of this dump. Now he's on ice and you, old man surrounded by razors and roaches, old man guarded by rollerheads, your boy can't send restaurant food here. He worries. Your wife, she worries. Your daughters."

Sargassi: "What are you saying, General Oscar?"

"I'm saying Luigi Rompallo has an opinion!"

Rompallo's eyes burned with rage. Hubbell suddenly admired his boss. "Who'd they fish out behind Exxon dock last night?" demanded Abadie.

"What the shit," seethed Sargassi.

"Let your man speak."

Grinding his teeth, Rompallo eyed Abadie like a lion tamer with a whip.

"Somebody did a butcher job on a punk," said Abadie. "We got no head, no fingers. Just a lump, all carved up. Now why'd they turn him into a zero?"

"I advise my client to stand on his constitutional rights."

"Can't incriminate himself off record, Sal. He wants to talk. I can tell. Cause you want out. Right, Mr. Luigi?"

Rompallo parted his lips and stared at Abadie.

"Oscar," said Sargassi, "this is *coercive intimidation!*"

A jaded smile crossed the Attorney General's face. "Mist' Luigi, your lawyer here's implyin' that I want somethin' for nothing. But if I get nothin', I can't *give* something. That's the logic of the market. You been sellin' tomatoes all these years to school cafeterias. Come on, you know business."

"Ah doan know about no dead man crap," he growled.

"I bet you knew the boy when he was alive," said Abadie,

face following thick arms in a long reach across the table toward Rompallo.

Sargassi whispered to his client.

"I don't understand the language y'all are speaking," said Abadie, "but I can guess the topic. So talk to me."

"What kinda talk you talkin'?" the old man heaved.

"Business talk," said Abadie, nostril to nostril. "Serious."

Rompallo wheezed like a muffled accordian.

Abadie sat back. "Business chat can show a change in outlook. Man wants a fresh start. Help his state, help his country."

Rompallo whispered to Sargassi.

"My client says Good Friday is six months from now, a long time for a man with high blood pressure."

Rompallo forked an index finger along his chin.

"Christmas is for family," said Oscar. "Help Rex's wife, she might could help you get home in time to drink egg-nog."

Rompallo scowled. "Some fockin two-bit punk. Lul focking bullcorn yard man."

Abadie shot back: "Bullcorn punk came out which yard?"

"Somebody say Jersey City."

"So you sponsor him down. Kindness of your heart?"

"Puh," rumbled Rompallo.

"An ex-con from Jersey. Why do you reach out, a helping hand?"

"Hard doin' bidness in a place like Angola. Some frien' say, hep a boy back on his feet. So maybe somebody make a call."

"When?"

The old man's thick, silver-black eyebrows curled under the creases of his brow. "Rount a year ago. Maybe more."

"And last night he's fished out of the Miss'ippi River with his hands and his head in sombody's bait box. People don't like the boy. Where'd he foul up?"

Rompallo glared.

Abadie smiled. "Your grandkids like Thanksgiving turkey."

"*Nobby's man!*" yelled Rompallo with a flood of purple to the jowls. "Dumb fock use some two-bit punk —"

"But you sponsored the boy inta Looziana."

"Crazy fock."

"You mean Nobby?"

"— lil cocksuck —"

"Nobby needs Jersey boy for what?"

"Nobby always have plans. Buy, sell, swap, fock."

"How come man like Nobby use a bullcorn boy?"

"Nobby do what Nobby do."

"How many people involved?"

"Objection!" barked Sargassi. "Speculation beyond witness's knowledge."

Hubbell interrupted: "What does Atchison want with Nobby?"

Rompallo squinted at Hubbell with a heavy-lidded left eye. He whispered to Sargassi. Sargassi pondered, ducked down to the old man's ear, and then said: "Labor dealings have never been my client's business or avocation."

Oscar Abadie frowned.

"Atchison's relationship to the Teamsters is not at issue," said Hubbell. "Why did Nobby hire the bullcorn boy from Jersey City?"

Sargassi's eyebrows made a slight rise for Rompallo.

"Man needa man be tough. New bidness hard bidness."

"Waste business," said Hubbell.

"What, he ran a dump?" said Oscar.

"Lul man do what big man say," chuckled Rompallo.

Abadie: "So why's he get sent to the butcher shop?"

Rompallo made a clucking sound.

"Atchison wants Nobby," said Hubbell.

Rompallo strummed his fingers on the table. The strumming lengthened — twenty seconds, forty seconds. Rompallo pulled his fingers off the table.

"Where did the dead man live?" asked Hubbell.

Rompallo squinted. "Where dogs run at night."

"Greyhound track in Mermentau," said Abadie.

Rompallo looked at his fingernails.

"The dog track," said Sargassi, "would suggest a general location."

Rompallo closed his eyes.

"Nobby in Mermentau," stewed Abadie.

"Petro-Cleansers," said Hubbell. "Three injection wells."

Abadie whispered to Hubbell: "Rex's chicky tell you name of the place?"

"No," whispered Hubbell. "There's a challenge to the well permits in your environmental department."

The Attorney General nodded without embarrassment and turned back to Rompallo. "So we got a bullcorn boy working at the black lagoon. Nobby needs an experienced man where the eighteen-wheelers dump."

Rompallo removed a strand of lint from his wrist.

"Still don't explain why the boy got the hatchet, Mr. Luigi."

"My client has been more than forthcoming to your questions," announced Sargassi. "Without a parole document, we have to pack in."

"We need a name," said Abadie.

"We need a hard commitment," said Sargassi.

"Mr. Rompallo knows where I stand."

Sargassi looked at Rompallo. The old man whispered; the attorney whispered. Rompallo shook his head, no. Sargassi whispered again. Rompallo nodded. "My client opines that a certain Dominic Rocca was in the employ of the facility in question. My client emphasizes he gave no order for *any* death."

Abadie made Sargassi spell the name and jotted it down.

"Mermentau's real rural," said Abadie.

Rompallo whispered. Sargassi said: "We are given to understand that a mobile home trailer is located a mile down the ridge from the injection wells."

Rompallo sat back, hands folded.

Hubbell leaned toward the Capo. "You must be pleased with Nobby."

Rompallo narrowed his eyes.

"All the good work Nobby does for you," taunted Hubbell.

"*Fock!*" snarled Rompallo.

Abadie grabbed Hubbell by the arm. Hubbell kept pushing: "It must be comforting to know that Nobby is working hard to help Senator Atchison."

"*Is this some pissant double-cross?*" bellowed Sargassi.

"No!" said Oscar, holding up his palm.

"How can we release Mr. Rompallo to do business with the Senator?" blurted Hubbell.

"Fuckin Atch lucky dey still *in* bidness!" roared Rompallo.

"Basta!" commanded Sargassi, with a clap of the hands. He pulled Rompallo to his feet. "Break your own rules, Abadie, and you're in pickled shit."

"If that's a threat, *your* gonads can move to Angola, Sargassi!"

Sargassi moved Rompallo to the door. "I gave you more credit, General. Parties come, ask questions. Y'all act like he gave different answers. To me that is infinitely stupid, very unprofessional. You want him to say something to fit your theory, or the other dude's, and frankly that is irrelevant to us!"

Rompallo pulled phlegm and spat on the floor.

"This is a deal," said Sargassi. "Like money between the palms. Too many people have heard Mr. Rompallo say he had nothing — nothing whatsofucking*ever* to do with the death of Governor LaSalle. We mourn his death. We send condolences to the widow, to her family. Mr Rompallo has been offered freedom for his help. He has given it and given again. We hope you find the person behind this crime. Either way, we expect a pardon."

Guards led Rompallo back to the prison complex. Sargassi straightened his tie and stepped into the pickup driven by another guard. In the settling of dust from the tires Abadie fumed: "Why'd you get those guineas all riled up?"

"Rompallo's furious with Nobby. He said Atchison was lucky to be in business. He's mad at both of them but didn't want to mention Atch."

"Sargassi said 'double-cross,'" reflected Abadie. "He said 'the other dude.' Somebody came here before we did."

"Must have been last night."

"Had to be earlier than that, Henry. Cops found Rocca's body last night."

"Rompallo sure didn't want to talk about Atchison."

"That's cuz of the trial," said Abadie. "Atchison knew those construction companies he fleeced were mobbed up. He was getting down payments to the five senators on Natural Resources committee — mob money for some kinda deal. But if Atchison says that in court, the blob we just met will never get out of prison. And if that happens, Atch knows he'll get killed, in or out of the can."

They walked through the barn, heels crackling hay that was pungent with manure. At Abadie's car they checked their shoes. The warden met them there. "Ah'm-a-be headin' down to Rex's wake," said Joe B. Carson. "*Times-Picayune* says it's goan go on all afternoon."

"Should be awesome," said the Attorney General.

"Warden Carson," said Hubbell. "How many visitors besides us has Mr. Rompallo had in the last two days?"

Carson shook his head negatively.

"Not even family?"

"No, sir. I do my end to keep y'all's lil powwow off the ledger."

"Thank you, Joe B," said Abadie, shaking hands.

The warden lit a cigar. "We'll check you, General."

The gamecocks were screeching as Oscar fired the ignition. A voice cried: "*Say something for Albert Jackson Tremaine, boss!*"

Hubbell rolled down the window and waved at Tremaine. The car passed through the gate and headed down the Tunica road. "Warden's lying, Oscar."

"Wouldn't be the first time someone gave him scratch to see Rompy."

"Maybe the FBI sent someone."

"I doubt that. FBI's been digging on Luigi Rompallo since LBJ was President. If Jack O'Connor goes into Angola on false pretenses, his probe could collapse. Money for guards is chicken feed. I got snitches at Angola too."

"Maybe Rompallo had the hit man killed for blowing his chances of getting a pardon."

"Dump a carved wiseguy in the Mississippi is a messy way to exact punishment. A gamble, even. Rompy is pissed off about his shot at a pardon."

"Maybe they killed the guy to threaten Atchison."

"Could be. But why the river dump? Photos of body parts work better."

Hubbell wondered who had gotten into Angola before them. Murdering the hit man had been orchestrated with Rompallo — or using information on Rocca that the mob boss provided. But dumping a body in the river was not smart planning. It also suggested a serious mistake in the murder of Rex LaSalle. Rompallo was angry about Rex's death. His lawyer's willingness to let him meet with two attorneys underscored his lack of motive. In killing Rex, someone had double-crossed Rompallo.

Twenty miles down the hill from Angola, the Attorney General pulled into a garage pump with a rusty Jax beer sign. He pointed to his car phone. "Wonderful instrument for a busy lawman, eh? As long as there's no worry about listening devices from your federal government and mine."

Abadie went to a pay phone by the side of the road. Hubbell didn't have to be told he was calling Colonel Bellamy. The state police had secure lines. Cradling the receiver, Abadie scribbled on a pad. "What'd we do before computers?" said Abadie, squaring himself at the wheel. "Bellamy tapped Interpol's database. Dominic Rocelli Rocca. Sicily-born, American naturalized, age twenty-five. Our boy did time in spaghetti-land on simple larceny. Then he becomes a citizen of New Jersey. How the hell did he get passed Immigration 'n Naturalization? Age twenty-six, arrested Jersey City holdin' a stash of heroin. He does two years ten months. *And then he goes up on manslaughter.* Colonel Bellamy's makin' calls on that. I bet him a stuffed turkey it's a plea down from second-degree murder."

"How much time did he do on that one?"

"Five years. You think he has friends? Since he turned American, the boy's had exactly twenty-three months outside jail. He did landfill work up there. They let him go south like a duck. Imagine what we don't know on him."

"Wife, children?"

"None listed."

It was 9:45 AM when they reached the city. A vast line of cars, vans and pickup trucks wound along the interstate, crawling down ramps toward the Capitol. In the distance, they saw green canopy tents on the lawn surrounding the statue of Huey Long. Doors to the rotunda would be locked till noon.

"People are serving food out there," marvelled Hubbell.

"Regina the event planner," replied Abadie in a neutral voice.

The Capitol and chemical haze from Exxon's towers to the west fell away as the Attorney General's car ascended the Mississippi River bridge and headed down and into Cajun country. A maze of trees and green profusions colored the side of the highway until they reached the Atchafalaya Basin bridge.

Cypress trees loomed across the water like pylons, the green fir branches listless in morning air, the sturdy trunks circled with egrets, pale as cotton. The car floated past a tiny isthmus cushioning a clutch of turtles. As a boy Hubbell had fished secluded tributaries of the Atchafalaya with his father, a protective man for all of his reticence whose descent into crippled silence left the early encounters more precious in the recall. Stamped upon his memory was a topography of riverine passageways, the man and the boy in a boat, paddling like explorers in a new world, casting their lines in bayous shadowed by fan-shaped palmetto leaves with spiked points he knew not to touch, nodding tacitly to men in boots with crawfish nets. The calmest Saturdays came back to him on winds of grace when he shut his law books for the night.

Mermentau, a bare village with a post office, floated past. Hubbell could not get the girl out of his mind, the wild adventure of Sophie and Rex, love-as-a-dirty-secret cutting against an authentic relationship. He realized that to Sophie it had been complicated but a form of love just the same. The Governor's smile popped into his thoughts, and Hubbell splintered his teeth with a punch. *I'm jealous of a dead man!*

"It's down this way," said Abadie, turning onto a road pocked with holes from the weight of heavier loads. The Attorney General's tires began to bounce. He slowed to twenty-miles per hour. Cattle grazed in a green pasture opposite a swamp coated with a yellow-brown sheen from pollen mixed with leaves. A barbed-wire fence cut across the field. A sign on the metal gate blocked the road: Hazardous Materials. Do Not Enter without Authorization.

"These places never have names," muttered Abadie.

The padlocked gate was open. A metal sleeve encasing the call box had been sprayed with a shotgun. "Unhappy locals," said Abadie. The road was empty. "Let's see if Mister Dominic Rocelli Rocca's home holds any sign of life."

It was now ten-thirty. They had traveled ninety miles from Angola.

The waste disposal complex was dormant on Saturday. The first dumping pit, twice the size of an Olympic pool, was a square-shaped lagoon with reddish-purple patches rimmed by a levee. A hundred yards off the pit stood a pyramidal iron base supporting a tubular structure submerged in the soil.

"How far down do injection wells pump?" said Hubbell.

"Thousands of feet. They're safe."

"Christian Fraux doesn't share your opinion."

"No lawsuit has shut one down yet."

"Right. We have to wait for the earth to vomit."

The road made an undulating turn at the second depository lagoon and straightened down a steep incline slashed out of maroon earth and bedded with gravel that made a grinding sound beneath the tires. Two more injection wells arose on the right. A white-shell trail branched off the gravel road toward the next ridge. The Grand Marquis lumbered on, spewing white dust on the dark red canyon walls. The mobile home came into sight on a hill.

"Oh *shit*," said Abadie.

Lines of yellow tape formed a fence around the vicinity of the trailer. Men in uniforms were scouring the weeds and scrub brush behind the mobile home. A man in a suit, writing on a tablet next to a blue Taurus, looked up at Abadie and Hubbell. The door opened to a white Crown Victoria and a man in khaki jumped out, pointing to Abadie, making a pulling motion with his hands.

"Here we go, Henry. Do not volunteer a goddamn word."

Abadie traipsed up the hill and Hubbell followed into a sucking stench of chemicals mingled with heat. James Jack O'Connor met them with a sweat-ribboned brow that made his freckles gleam like decals. "Well, well, if it's not the many-traveled Attorney General."

"Been a while, sport," said Abadie, shaking hands.

"And my new best friend, Henry," smiled O'Connor.

"How's the family, Jack?"

FBI agents were taking photographs of the trash-strewn land around the trailer. A man in overalls, wearing thick rubber gloves, was pawing through a thirty-gallon garbage can, swatting off flies on watermelon rinds. Behind the trailer deputy sheriffs searched the field with a German shepherd.

O'Connor pointed to the trailer. "Stand in the doorway. Don't touch."

Abadie made for the trailer, pausing to shake hands with the Mermentau sheriff. O'Connor pulled Hubbell aside. "You lied to me, Henry. Five minutes after I leave your house the Avoyelles sheriff pulls up at Fraux's mortuary."

"I learned about the call after you did."

O'Connor's scowl melted into a weird smile. "Why, I believe you're telling the truth. Confusion at the top?"

Hubbell broke away and fell in behind Oscar Abadie who presented "my old podna and campaign manager for Mermentau, Johnny Ray Boudreaux" — an olive brown man of fifty with thin nose and wide jaws, quiet in the presence of the FBI. The last thing Sheriff Johnny Ray Boudreaux needed on the morning of Governor LaSalle's funeral was federal agents dragging him into the torment that had invaded his neighbors with rashes, bronchitis and diarrhea, igniting greater wrath than anything in the parish since civil rights. The sheriff hated his impotence over the pounding trucks, the lethal waste they discharged and the seepage of chemicals into aquifers. The local prosecutor was investigating. But the site had a state waste disposal permit and that, legally, was God.

"Dat boy in dare waddn' my people," muttered Boudreaux, "but what dey did on him was somepin evil, yeah."

Abadie and Hubbell peered into blood spatter on the linoleum floor, gobs of blood on walls, flecks and chunks of flesh splotched on the couch and spidery crimson trails that reached the VCR. Strands of black refrigerator tape lay in twisted bloody balls on the floor.

"Dey tied him in dat chair and chopped him sitting up," said Boudreaux.

It was a black leather reclining chair, well padded, the armrests and back wrapped in wire so drenched it looked like the coil was bleeding. The floor was smeared in a maze of bloodbursts. Urine soaked the chair, where the victim had lost control while his hands were being butchered.

"Jesus H. Christ," swallowed Oscar Abadie.

"FBI say dey musta chopped one finger at a time," said Boudreaux. "Imagine what dat felt like, hanh Oscah? I'm tryna figure out how dey manage to tie th' boy down fo' dey chop him." The Sheriff pointed with a hooked index finger. "Icebox tape on the bloody flo. Federal man say dat's how dey shut his mouth. Quiet him yellin' with *heavy* tape. *Um*-mmn!"

Abadie's mouth hung open. Hubbell knew what he was thinking: they didn't just eliminate this Rocca guy — they tortured him to get answers.

"Dey gaddered up the fingers, Oscar. Whatcha teenk dey did with dem fingers? An-a-head. Ho! His head gone. Talk about."

"Slashed arteries distressed the aorta," inserted O'Connor. "That's what your Dr. Willoby says. He's an expert."

The attorneys and O'Connor retreated from the steps.

"What a state," said the FBI agent. "Coroner won't do an autopsy on the Governor or discuss his conversation with the First Lady. A Coroner about to dump in his pants."

Sheriff Boudreaux joined the three men.

"That wise guy lost a ton of blood before his heart died," said O'Connor. "Hits like this are rare for the Gulf South. We find sporadic chop jobs in Queens, Jersey cities, occasionally Rhode Island. Vegas is a theme park."

"I seen one in New Orleans," said Sheriff Boudreaux. "July 1984. World's Fair. Et lunch by that levee at Bucktown, all dem seafood houses. Fella layin' face down with a million holes, fish swimming around the body in lul canal behind whatchamacallit restaurant. But dey never took body pieces, him."

"Semiautomatics are more efficient in a turf war," continued O'Connor. "Quick hit, quick split. When they hurt a man this bad, it's over something personal. A woman. A child. Betrayal. Not usually distribution of power. Somebody had a real bead on this actor."

"Where'd they dump the body?" asked Hubbell.

"Outside Baton Rouge. Willoby figured the corpse was wet three hours."

A man in the field called the Sheriff.

Boudreaux headed out beyond the mobile home.

"This guy was no debutante," continued O'Connor. "Still they managed to tie him down, then cut him up. That's interesting, huh General? No signs of forced entry. Door doesn't even appear to have been locked. Like he was expecting company. Only not the company he got."

He was sleeping, Hubbell realized. If Rocca drove straight from Sophie's house to the trailer, he would have arrived at 4 AM. He imagined the assassin, pumped up, falling asleep at sunrise. Then he awakens with a gun in his ear. "How many people you think killed him?" asked Hubbell.

"So much blood, it's hard to tell. Could have been a single perpetrator. Other questions have more immediacy. Like *how* Mr.

Rocca gained entry to the Mansion. Slipping past state police, slipping out undetected. With a bimbo to boot! How'd he come to work for a dumpsite controlled by Atchison? Who ordered the clip and who ordered the chop? Real questions."

"Makes me wonder about Atchison," murmured Oscar Abadie.

"Silent partner in half this state," retorted O'Connor, the blue tie showing sweat trails. "Look, you guys know some things, and we know things."

"To every time there is a season," said Abadie. "Today we have a funeral."

"Don't play country politician on me, General."

"You've got two murders and no motive," said Hubbell.

"Try this," snapped O'Connor. "Atchison locks up the Senate in waste-pit deals that benefit the mob. He is expanding his turf. Then Rompallo ups the ante: get me out of prison, Senator. Atchison goes to Governor LaSalle, trying to broker a pardon for Rompallo. And Rex says no. I would like to know why. Because a part of the hunter acquires affection for the prey. Maybe there was more good in the late Governor than I was able to imagine. Atchison pushes the pardon, but Rex won't budge. So Rompallo orders the hit and then has the hit man chopped. Good-bye witness trail."

Oscar Abadie was staring with clenched teeth and sweat all over his face.

"But every man has a breaking point," continued O'Connor. "The Senator's going down next week, and when we re-indict him for conspiracy to commit murder, he'll have no choice but to talk."

"Your theory makes sense," said Hubbell.

Thinking: his theory is a bluff. Rompallo didn't order a hit on Rex and he would kill Atchison if he knew the Senator had a hand in the assassination.

Thinking: Jack O'Connor has not mentioned Nobby. FBI has got to be searching for Nobby. O'Connor does not want to contaminate Oscar or me as potential witnesses. They know Oscar was with Nobby in Trinidad. Amelia thinks Nobby was trying to broker the pardon.

"Elvis Banks can't hide forever," grunted O'Connor. "You guys can make it a lot easier by telling us what we need now, when timing is vital."

Abadie frowned.

Hubbell spoke: "Attorney General Abadie has no direct knowledge of any work the Banks' produced, if they produced it, and I have an attorney-client privilege with Mrs. LaSalle that includes all work product."

"I got a subpoena for Mrs. LaSalle," sneered O'Connor.

"I'll accept service at my office the next working day after the funeral."

"I can subpoena you on the toilet, Hubbell."

"And I can flush it down your South Boston throat."

"Hold on, boys!" prompted the Attorney General, stepping between them. "Let's not get all riled up about this."

"*Yeah?*" snarled O'Connor. "What's *your* position on all this, General?"

Oscar Abadie's eyes turned into slits. "Podna, you subpoena the First Lady and I guarantee two US Senators from Looziana will have you working Omaha by Thanksgiving."

"You wish!"

Dogs began yelping in the tangle brush behind the trailer. Men's voices rose like a bee swarm.

"Hey, Oscah!" shouted Sheriff Johnny Ray Boudreaux. "*We found the hole where they buried his haid!*"

FURIES OF THE MORN 23

A gray haze suffused the mid-morning sky while out on the Gulf a muscular thunder cloud formed, auguring some relief from the heat.

Amelia LaSalle had awakened early to the news that a trusty

dispatched by LauraLee had killed two rats in the attic, clearing the way for her to search the final quadrant of Rex's yard signs. She found the strong box wedged between cardboard faces of Senator Breaux and David Duke. The trusty broke the lock with a hammer. Alone in her bedroom the First Lady sifted through stacks of traveler's checks and hundred-dollar bills that came up just shy of $57,000 of which she set aside six-thousand for the St. Anthony donation. Under the money a thick brown envelope read NOBBY.

Her youngest brother Revon, who had driven in from Mobile the night before with his wife and tenth-grade son, was fussing with their daughter, a Vanderbilt sophomore just in on a red-eye from Nashville, wearing a dress that ran halfway up her thigh. Bobby Broussard Junior had flown in from Dallas on a private jet at midnight with his wife and three young sons. The boys made hooting sounds at the tribal masks, cavorting like animals before getting to bed. As Amelia poured through Rex's documents, she heard feet clattering and her mother's plea: "Get dressed for church *right now,* Bobby the Third!"

As the eldest sibling and her daddy's favorite, Amelia carried a natural superiority toward her brothers, though both of them enjoyed good marriages. Regina had told her uncles about the state of Rex's room. Alone at 1 AM with the two men who loved her unquestioningly and had despised Rex for his philandering, Amelia took their questions with a shield of righteousness: "Lipstick smudges are no proof of murder, and whatever it does prove is nobody's business but mine!"

If you can lie to your brothers, you can lie to anyone. Lawyers both, Revon and Bobby Broussard Junior sat dumbstruck. They would tell their wives how Rex died, the wives would tell friends. Servants in the Mansion knew, state troopers knew. Yet the Broussard men knew that without forensic data, no one could dispute the Coroner's decree of heart failure. And if Rex's death was somehow provoked by a bimbo who disappeared, there was no good in serving that to garbage-peddlers in the media.

Amelia's iron-like façade in sealing away the discussion persuaded Revon and Bobby Broussard Junior that this was not their fight, nor did they see it as one fit for Regina, who had guzzled three Bloody Marys before breakfast.

The First Lady decided that the world did not need to know how Rex died. He had violated the boundaries by which good people live. The justice she wanted centered on herself, her own dignity to carry through this horror and steady her resolve. She would deal with the coarsened hows and whys of his demise as they came to her, in her own good time. Fixed on the image of the silver ocean in her dreams, she imagined Rex receding in a liquid plane, waving his arms, crying out words she could not hear, sinking beyond the horizon as the undertow pulled her toward a shore materializing out of fierce light.

She gazed out the window at the Capitol lawn and the leaching sunlight on the statue of Huey Long. Two thousand black folk, robed in shimmering white, swayed on the terrace above the statue, clapping to gospel melodies played by a man on a portable organ next to the massive bronze doors that opened into the rotunda. The sun hovered like a disc above the Capitol lake. She cracked the window to hear the singing:

This little light of mine—
I'm gonna let it shine
Let it shine, let it shine, let it shine.

Once she had been Rex's light. But he ran from the happiness she tried to make. The task now was to utterly remake herself, build a life with prospects of freedom she could not yet imagine. She had her looks and wit; the masks and art work to soften the edge of her long melancholy; and a waiting lover. But the stabbing loss of Rex made her angry at thoughts of Stephen. Kay was secure; Regina was her cross to bear. Watching the gospel singers, Amelia felt a web of life, strands of love from unknown places, settling on her from a spiritual zone barely starting to form. The flowing white gowns and body rhythms rolled like a diaphanous wave while back in the oak grove, where still more singers rocked beneath the mossy limbs, surges of church song buoyed her with a moment of serenity that was so sudden she found herself breathless.

At that moment, the embalmed Governor lay in a coffin wedged in the back compartment of the limousine Christian Fraux guided across Atchafalaya Basin Bridge with escort vehicles from the Avoyelles sheriff. Fraux had been relieved when the FBI disappeared. With Juba snoring on the couch, the mortician had worked alone, stippling the bluish lips with heavy pink, working the brush and cosmetic stick over cyanide splotches to achieve a dark, fleshy color, rubbing in a texture more allied with the pigmentation of a natural death.

Still, Fraux could not pray for Rex. He retrieved lines of scripture that suddenly broke off, the words scattering across a mental desert; he wondered if such a banal waste of talent had drained him of the ability to mourn. He simply could not focus on Rex's soul. As the sky bled gray, Fraux was stricken with fear: what if he got hit with a heart attack, rammed through the guardrail and crashed into the soggy marsh, sinking the Governor with him in murky depths? But lo, the Lord opened a cloud over the steel-girded bridge spanning the Mississippi, and the hearse rose into an ocean of light around the Capitol tower.

The custom of serving food after funerals had magnified for the wake. Coming down the interstate, Fraux saw the Capitol lawn with gospel choirs and tents, long tables, folk preparing shrimp and deep-fried oysters, rice, crawfish bisque in cast-iron pots, a wire-mesh cage where Cajuns with long spoons stirred an enormous vat of jambalaya. Red-robed white folk from an Assemblies of God church had gathered along the western side of the terrace, harmonizing. Several hundred feet farther down, on the road next to the oak grove, ran the bold letters **King Artile and the Zydeco Flames** across a red minivan. Charter busses were dropping more people off. "Musical selections by choirs and zydeco artists will be part of today's ceremony at the rotunda, according to a statement issued by Regina LaSalle," the radio announcer said. "Vice-President Gore is scheduled to arrive at one-thirty. Attendance by Jerry

Lee Lewis and Aaron Neville is unconfirmed at this time. Dignitaries are entering St. Joseph's Cathedral for Mass. Thousands of people have surrounded the foundation of the Capitol where rotunda doors will open after Cathedral services."

Behind the shining blue bubbles of squad cars, a line of school busses curled down the interstate, the parish names emblazoned on yellow panels traversing Fraux's horizon — Calcasieu … Orleans … Tangipahoa … St. John the Baptist … St. Tammany — place names from a geography of freedom strides that had shaped his worldview as a young preacher, raising a family, building a funeral business, using the pulpit to prod his town and state to change. *What we have won is old,* he thought. *Our losses are new and frightening.*

Two-hundred people, mostly media and state police, waited outside the Governor's Mansion with three of Abraham Schoenbaum's limousines in place. The last thing Fraux heard on radio was that Lieutenant Governor Joe Hall "has tendered his resignation to the Speaker of the House, citing reasons of ill health that the *Advocate* and *Times-Picayune* are reporting as alcohol-related."

Robert Lincoln Fraux met his father in front of the Mansion and solemnly shook hands. "Who do you think will become Governor?" he whispered.

"Some thief or another," muttered Christian Fraux.

His son stood by the hearse. Fraux climbed the steps and met Colonel Bellamy, reeking of nicotine, eye pouches heavy, his chin beetled from shaving nicks. "Reverend Fraux, what does the Governor look like?"

"A healthy dead man."

Bellamy left him in the solarium, a room of muted white with fifteen-foot French windows, ferns and rubber trees that rose toward the ceiling. The big window faced Capitol Lake, catching sunlight all hours of the day. On the glass table sat a silver service with beverages, pastries and croissants. Fraux sat in deep cushions of a couch that he reckoned cost ten-thousand dollars.

Regina LaSalle stood by the window, shapely, dark-haired,

wedded to a cellphone. She waved at the visitor: "Help yourself, Rev'nd Fraux. Mama's comin'. You heard Joe Hall resigned?"

"I did, thank you," murmured Fraux, pouring coffee.

Regina turned toward the Capitol. "I don't see the video screens," she said into the phone. "Mr. Eddie said to put them in place before sound check."

Fraux put the coffee aside. With little sleep and long driving over the previous seventy-two hours, his eyelids lowered.

"People on the lawn need those screens to see the ceremony," continued Regina. "No. Absolutely not ... Well, maybe. How many amps does Artile want?" She rolled her eyes. "Tell the band to use amplifiers from the *choirs*."

Fraux nodded off.

"*Too far?* Then alternate the power supply. People in the crawfish booth must surrender their power when the band starts. Y'all are only playing one medley, right?" Regina tapped her foot. "*Well, who regulates the food booths?*"

Fraux's chin sank onto his chest.

"Oh, yes I sure do know who that man is. Daddy said never mess with the Board of Health, it's political suicide ... *Wired differently?* Well, where is Mr. Eddie? This is giving me a headache, Willie Boy. I put *you* in charge of sound."

Christian Fraux opened his eyes.

"Let me speak with Artile!" she exclaimed. "Sleeping in the minivan? Well, get him up!" She turned to Fraux and said in exasperation: "Musicians!"

Fraux reached for his coffee. "Willie Boy the one oughta be sleeping."

But Regina did not hear his words. Fraux marveled at the stuffed leopard across the hall, a creature of feline majesty that seemed to encapsulate an essence of Rex's raging spirit, suggested now in his impulsive daughter.

The glass doors opened and Amelia LaSalle entered in black silk, burnished by crystalline rays of the sun.

Regina disappeared down the hall.

Fraux rose to his feet and engulfed the First Lady's chilly fingers with warm hands. "Good morning, ma'am. I believe that for all the sorrow, today will be a day in which we show the best of who we are."

"I would like to believe that. You have been steadfast, Reverend Fraux. The family is grateful. Please be seated."

Amelia's presence evoked the distant memory of a tiny mulato girl separated from her parents at a carnival parade in Lafayette, nervous yet determined to find her people, holding Fraux's hand for thirty minutes till he located the parents. The First Lady's emotional control in the foyer after the speech had given way to a palpable edginess.

She handed him a slip of paper. "Reverend Fraux, my Regina does not do well under stress. Last night she spoke to several African American ministers and each expects to eulogize Rex in the rotunda. I certainly want a speaker from the community, but three is too many."

Fraux scanned the names. "All are capable orators."

"Whom would you recommend?"

"With your permission, I'd like to do it myself."

"Oh, Reverend Fraux!" Her tautness melted a little. "I would feel so much better. Yes, thank you."

Fraux gave a thin smile.

"What did the FBI say to you?" she asked.

"They offered money for access to the body. I refused."

She closed her eyes in a tremor of fear. "What else did they want?"

"Everything. I told them to call Henry Hubbell."

"Everything …"

"Rex's ties to the black community," lied Fraux. "His relationship to Sutton, Atchison, Doctor Nobby, all about waste! Questions, questions!"

"What did you say?"

"I said — begging your pardon, ma'am: 'None of your damn business!'"

"That's exactly right! None of their damn business!"

Christian Fraux nodded affirmatively as two hard raps hit the door. "Yes?" called the First Lady.

Mitchell Mudd entered. "'Scuse me, Miss Amelia. Revn'd Chris, how you do? General Abadie called. Him and Hubbell are runnin' late. They want to meet here after the wake."

"I see. We are discussing funeral plans."

Mudd sat in a chair next to the divan.

"Reverend Fraux will give a eulogy for Rex." She leaned toward the mortician as if imparting secrets of a blood-line. "And I want people to know that Rex did good things, that he had achievements and ideals."

"I know that's true," piped Mudd, smelling of Old Spice.

"Of course," replied Fraux. "And he was going to stop that catastrophe in Avoyelles. I would be subtle in the reference, as this is a sermon, but a theme of service to the greater good —"

Mudd coughed. "Miss Em, not in no funeral speech."

"What is this?" She frowned. "Explain for me, Reverend."

"Doctor Nobby has a waste plunger polluting soil near the cemetery where Mayor Bobby is buried. People are getting sick."

"It ain't a plunger — And it's further down, over tracks in Blue Line."

"It's one-point-four miles from where Rex will lie," replied Fraux, "unless you bury him at the Capitol next to Huey Long."

"Absolutely not! Rex goes next to my father!"

"Miss Amelia," said Mitchell Mudd. "This is not on point."

"Nobby owning anything could mean trouble," she muttered.

"Nothin' hadn't been proved," countered Mudd.

"I'm sure Rex had documentation," parried Fraux.

"How you so sure?" sneered Mudd.

"He told me in New Roads the other night while you waited in the car."

Turning red, Mudd gazed sullenly at Capitol Lake. The sky was blue. He had persuaded Exxon to cut the smokestacks to clear air for the services. Now, he had to listen to an undertaker tell lies he could not afford to refute.

"Mitchell, I think Reverend Fraux and I need a few minutes. Would you see that Regina and the others head down to the limousines?"

"Sure. But on this other business here —"

"We cannot be late for Mass. Take that phone from Regina. And tell my mother we must head out. Thank you for doing it *now*, Mitchell."

"Yes, ma'am." He stood, glaring at Fraux, and left the room.

"I don't think this injection well belongs in a eulogy, Reverend Fraux."

"I was not suggesting a direct reference. Yet, knowing how Rex was moving on matters of conservation and local safeguards …"

Fraux watched her face form a mask like one of the African carvings that lined her wall, mysterious and impenetrable to him. Who is this woman? Have I pushed too far? Out of another zone, Christian Fraux heard the voice of Rex LaSalle: *I told her you were in a whorehouse brawl. She thinks you cheat on your wife.*

Fraux stiffened.

"He struggled with many issues, Reverend Fraux. Tell me what you saw in New Roads."

"He was emphatic about closing the well. A new turn in his thinking. He was, more than I'd ever seen, animated."

Regina entered, whimpering: "Mitchell took my phone, Mama."

"I'm sorry, darling. Is everyone ready?"

"Bobby the Third can't find his shoes and Uncle Bobby is in daddy's study on the speaker phone to Dallas. I want my cellphone."

"Would you please hurry them up, honey?"

"Mother, I have to work out the video screens."

"Re*gina*. I am occupied."

Christian Fraux had a sudden urge to slap Regina.

"*Yes, mother,*" she grumbled, and left the room.

The First Lady stared at Fraux. "A girl was in New Roads."

"This is true. I never met her. She waited in his car across the parking lot. I had only a glimpse. She had stars on the shoulders of her blouse, blonde hair, jet curls. She looked to be early twenties. That is the total of what I know."

"And Mitchell was in the car with her."

"Yes, ma'am."

Her fingers formed a steeple. "What do you want, Reverend?"

"To stop the injection well in Blue Line."

"That I grasp. Tell me the rest."

"To be your friend and to help. I want you to deal from a position of strength. That will keep the FBI away from you — and me."

"If Rex was unfaithful, how would that affect your sermon?"

"All of us have failings," Fraux said softly. "He was my friend, Amelia. A eulogy celebrates the life that has passed. We don't dwell on the sins."

"Tell me the gospel truth of what you can say about him."

"That he built bridges between the races. Helped old people and teachers. A Governor the likes of which we will not soon see. A figure of history."

"Very well, Reverend. You stick to that line of oratory and let me talk to Oscar about that injection well. It doesn't sound good to me."

"Fine. But remember that I gave him fifteen hundred to stop that well."

Never promise what you cannot deliver, her daddy had always said. The sudden recall of those words caused a stiffening in the First Lady. She noticed the sweat beads along Fraux's brow, and sensed his nervousness in confronting a white woman with looks and power.

"You were with Willoby and Hubbell. What else should I know?"

As he recounted the arrival of the chopped up body at the morgue, Fraux realized that the voice of the Governor that had run through his thoughts moments earlier was a fluke. Chris Fraux was no whacko!

Fraux's words were done. The First Lady stood.

Fraux stood.

The First Lady crossed her arms and sat down.

Fraux sat down on the edge of the couch, next to her chair.

"All right," she said to mental images of mob carnage and a wind of raw wickedness, "if the FBI thinks the mob killed the murderer, do they think Rompallo is behind this?"

"I have no position on that, ma'am. I am not a detective."

"Tell me your opinion then."

"My opinion is you will be late for church if we speculate about plots. Focus on your husband, the good he did. Put the other matters aside for now. God will not abandon you, Amelia. You have fought the good fight."

"Thank you for that, Reverend." Her lips trembled. Her skin ran pink to scarlet so swiftly that Fraux thought she would hyperventilate.

"But what about the damned girl?"

Her eyes overflowed — the widow of his ally, the daughter of Miss Della who had given to his cause. Her down-curled lips and the mascara trailing thin lines bestirred Fraux. With the sweep of a violin arpeggio, he sank to one knee and withdrew a handkerchief, dabbing her salty cheeks as she buried her sobs in the silk cloth, clutching his wrists as no white woman had ever done.

"You must rise above this, Amelia. You must show *grace*."

She drew back from the drenched silk, releasing him as the cloth passed from his palms to hers. She wiped her face. "Forgive me."

"There is nothing to forgive, ma'am. Life forces us to seek. The lucky ones prove Saint Paul right — in finding we are made new."

The First Lady blinked. "I need all the help I can get making new."

"You have it within you more than you know," he asserted.

Then she was gone. Fraux felt a bolt of fatigue, and poured himself more coffee, wondering what had possessed him to volunteer a eulogy or gamble with a rumor from his state representative, Clyde Buzby, of legal action on Nobby's well.

The media drama began with the family's departure from the

Mansion: the children entering limousines with the First Lady's brothers and their wives; Kay walking slowly, leaning on her husband; Miss Della on Regina's arm; and Amelia LaSalle in a solitude of dignity that disseminated via networks and the wire services in pictures across the land.

Two thousand people jammed the Cathedral. Christian Fraux orchestrated the pallbearers on each side of the casket: Revon and Bobby Broussard Junior in front, House Speaker Walter Sutton and Representative Little Joe DuBulio in the middle, Representative John Burns Logan and Mitchell Mudd bringing up the rear. At Fraux's signal, the men began the slow escort down the aisle. The Archbishop of New Orleans and the state's six other bishops, wearing robes of watered silk, formed a purple fan around the altar. The solemnity of incantations by Benedictine monks in the choir loft calmed Amelia, sitting in the first pew between her mother and Kay. As the Archbishop raised the chalice, Amelia prayed for Rex's soul, for the healthy birth of Kay's baby and a harmony with Regina that had long eluded her. Returning from communion, she saw them in fleeting mosaic, row upon row of dark suits, white shirts, red ties, the House and Senate mammals who fed on what Rex had left, and in the middle of them, Senator Clifford Atchison, his face awash in sweat.

24 GHOSTS OF LOVE

At 11 AM, Sophie Thibodeaux reached the ladies department at Maison Blanche. The floor was overrun with customers, most of them over fifty, trying on dark dresses. A sleek thirtysomething saleswoman with jet black curls floated in her center of gravity. "Somethin' tells me you have important business and not much time."

"Is it obvious?" murmured Sophie.

"Based on your confident appearance, I would say so."

"Well, I need something appropriate in black."

"It's a seller's market due to the funeral," said the sales clerk, leading Sophie to a row of size fours. "Senator Atchison's wife came in yesterday."

Sophie perused the racks. "It must be hard for that woman."

"She went with a black Chanel suit. But she needed the flattering. A dress'll do you better."

"It's sure hot out."

"They say it's gon rain with a temperature drop."

Sophie selected a Donna Karan black silk, which at $300 was beyond her budget, but saying farewell to Rex required something special. Her wardrobe, heavy with designer jeans, ran to skirts in earth tones and blouses in various shades of the sky. The dress made her feel poised. "Maybe I need to try the cream blazer there."

"That's a front line combination."

The woman went to check on other customers.

When she returned, Sophie was standing at the mirror, wearing sunglasses to prevent her eyes from flooding.

"You and half the state are going to that funeral," said the woman. "I've made twenty-four sales this morning. That Rex was a honeydripper. You sure have lovely hair."

"Thank you," she whispered.

In the five days since Arabel's visit, Sophie had replayed the memory of Nobby's wife, the rockarolla big momma, showing up on her doorstep at dusk unannounced. Jittery, smoking Kools in a chair, Arabel had cracked-egg eyes and leaky nostrils. *It's ugly, sugar. In this state the big boys do anything.*

Sophie had lied to Nobby about her meeting with Arabel out of a raw instinct for survival. Withholding the information from Hubbell was a precaution.

Arabel had sat on the back deck next to the hot tub. Sophie made a pitcher of iced tea. Arabel drained three glasses in a row. The woman had more chemicals in her than a drugstore. *You know why Nobby hired you, baby?* Sophie shrugged. *Nobby was in a hard blue funk after months of bein' stiff-armed by Rex. I never saw two men fight the way they did. That CD was stuck in a groove. Nobby saw you as a way of getting' unstuck.* Did Nobby tell you this, Arabel? *Nayo. He didn't need to. You have natural endowments, sugar. Don't blush. This is you an me talkin'. When Nobby said Rex fell for you like stars on Alabama, I did start to wonder. Suddenly Rex was callin' Nobby all hours, just like days gone by. Podnas laughin' and schemin' and then Nobby had leases out in Mermentau. Suddenly this, suddenly that. Too suddenly. Nobby used you to lure Rex, sugar. I should have tole you so before.*

Why are you telling me now?

I have made my last chili omlette!

Through Arabel's screen of Kool smoke, Sophie reconstructed the early months after she met Rex. Nobby disappearing when Rex showed up at clubs. Nobby giving her money "for wardrobe — standard operatin' procedure in this bidness." Nobby handing her the deal to manage King Artile and the Zydeco Flames folded into Rex materializing at dancehalls in revolving disguises with hair slicked back like Elvis. For two years, none of the Zydeco Flames suspected that Bobby Joe — who waited while she collected the money, paid the band and made sure Artile and his party got in the minvan — was their Governor. Eventually the band members became hip to the relationship, but Artile and his boys were faithful to Sophie for guiding them well.

When Nobby gets back from Trinidad, there will be no chili omlette.

You should get in detox and recovery, Arabel.

Nobby's the one needs that! I never signed on as a silent spouse on some shithouse for big oil. Yesterday we got served with a lawsuit over a baby born malformed near Mermentau. My name on that legal paper! Those waste wells were the Senator's idea. Ever eat supper with Clifford Atchison? I guess not. Deacon at First Baptist, that man will carve the skin off your thighs and smile. I tole Nobby: that Atch is an evil, evil man. Nobby laughed. He told me there's no such thing as evil. Nobby didn't laugh when he drove me to the hospital.

Was he taking you to detox?

Nayo. She lit another Kool. *Sexual accident. My right nipple took stitches.*

"How 'bout some matching pumps?" said the saleswoman.

"Just pack the outfit I came in, please."

"Not a problem. Cash or charge?"

As she fumbled for her Visa card, she brooded on the fact that only Mitchell and Nobby knew that Rex visited her house. Nobby could plan anything. How many people had been spying on her? Who *were* Nobby's people?

She got into the Mazda wondering if Henry Hubbell was who he seemed — sturdy, reliable, a gentleman; or would his identity change as Rex's had in hunting her slowly, artfully, eliciting the deepest secrets of her life, the better to place himself at the center, while his quest to *be loved* escalated into the desperate intensity of a force that had no bounds. The salesgirl called him a honeydripper. Did the woman know she was one in a trail of women sweetened by his past? Probably not; the girl wanted to sell her a dress. An hour before his death, Rex was exhausted from the political rally, but lying in bed, he pleaded: "Let's make love for old time's sake!" *I am bored with him,* she thought then.

Driving down Government Street, she tried to picture Hubbell, so stiff, so arch, dancing to the zydeco. What are you doing? she asked herself. Analyzing fantasies just to keep a grip. Observing the sides of myself from an inviewing window. *Rex, darling:* I grieve for you and I know that grief will be with me for a long time. But I believe we are put here to find love in a world ruled by forces we will never understand. I will not let visions of you drag me down a mud pit.

The massive Capitol came into view, aglow in the late morning haze. Parking slots in front of the post office were empty. It was Saturday, no need to put coins in the meter. She hadn't checked her PO box in days. She was expecting advance copies of the Zydeco Flames' new CD and a contract for the recording mix to be done in Nashville. In the glass plate of the postal box she saw a yellow slip of paper, which she signed and gave to the clerk at five minutes before noon.

"It's two big boxes, Miss Thibodeaux. You'll need some help."

The cardboard boxes were so heavy that the postal clerk put them on a wagon, rolled them to her car and hoisted them into her trunk. She thanked him and offered five dollars for which he thanked her. No return address on the boxes. Seventy-five dollars in postage paid from Mobile, Alabama.

Arabel on the run.

Sophie found the last slot in a You-Park-It six blocks from the Capitol. She opened the first box and stared at the neat folders. Ten minutes later, the parking lot attendant startled her. "Five bucks if you plan to park, lady." She handed him the money and was glad she had bought the blazer. The air was turning cooler.

She was agog at the totality of Nobby: folder after folder bearing Arabel's crisp lettering on receipts to so many political names that the file tags seemed like rosters in a phone directory. Mortgages, contracts, maps, blueprints.

Sophie shut the trunk and made a slow circular sweep with her eyes, checking to see if anyone was watching her. No one she could detect. Herds of people were parking and heading to the Capitol for the services. She shut the trunk and began the slow walk toward the near side of the great lawn, numb and trembling, thankful to Jesus for sparing her life. Just then the van of the Zydeco Flames came in sight.

25 EULOGIES

Images of Arabel came to Nobby in the half-sleep of hot towels blanketing his face. Her raven hair tied in a green band, the emerald cape of a Bombay princess draped on that curvaceous six-footer. His blind date. Krewe of Bacchus ball, Mardi Gras 1985. Magical figures they made! He was Zorro, black shirt with bolero tie and snakeskin boots that made her murmur: "Was-it-you shot the rattler on those boots, big boy?" And who are *you,* Miss Lady? The Neville Brothers sang "Iko Iko." He spun her around a floor of two thousand dancers. Entranced by her wit and Amazon beauty, he hungered for her breasts and dreamed of lathering them in champagne long before she let him.

Nobby's face soaked beneath the towels. Fluids seeped over his scalp.

Foiled at Sophie's house, he had driven fifty miles to Lafayette and withdrawn $800,000 from his safety box in the Security Center and locked the money in the attaché case that never left his side. He deposited his car in a parking-tower slot that he prepaid every six months; he crossed Jefferson Street to the Avis office and got another car on the credit card of Joseph Benbow, whose identity he occupied at the Lafayette Hilton, with a room overlooking the Vermilion Bayou and memories of torrid nights gone by.

At 6:45 AM he had summoned room service: Eggs, grits, ham, tomato juice, coffee. "Fast, please. Important bidnessman on the move."

The bellboy left with a ten-dollar tip. Cool beads dotted the glass of red juice. The day of Rex's wake. I didn't bargain for this, he brooded. But then, maybe I did. The genius of America is that with enough money, anyone can remake himself.

The week before, he had driven up the winding road to Angola prison, palmed five hundred to Warden Joe B. Carson and sat alone with Rompallo in folding chairs beneath a sycamore far back of the dorms. *I hate to tell you this, Mr. Luigi, but Atch been talking his mouth. That Senator visited Rex. I'm hearing that he gave him blueprints for the toxic pipeline in exchange for Rex talking the judge into going easy on him. When I pressed Rex about your pardon, he said the Feds wanna know what Rex knows about Rompallo, Atch and waste. Rex can't sign the pardon with so many trails involving the double-crossing Senator.*

Rompallo's eyes had tightened. His brows, thick and streaked with silver, coiled down a forehead that resembled an anvil. *Ah sent a message from Lul Joe D'Bulio to Atch: Doan talk, Senator, and nobody hurt you. Hunh. Atch think he kin snitch? I ain't no pussy. Atch needs a lesson,* grumbled Rompallo.

Nobby nodded sympathetically. *I think that's a logical step, Mr. Luigi.*

Setting Atchison in Rompallo's cross-hairs freed Nobby to preserve his own viability.

"See what you think, Mister."

The hair-salon gal turned his chair to the wall mirror. His eyebrows and hair were deep brown-red, the silver totally gone. His hair sat low, the color returned like in varsity days, before his pompadour.

"You done good, sugar."

"For twenty-eight dollars, we guarantee the color you see on you now, Doctor. Shampoo is seven dollars extra."

He handed her four tens. "One shampoo, keep the change."

The rented Town Car shot across Atchafalaya Basin. Nobby stewed about Atchison. *All the money we made, and he done a double-cross, went behind my back to Rex after I entrusted the Governor with the waste pipe plans. If Atch hadn't blabbed to Rex, everything woulda been fine. Instead, he put Rex in a position of knowing too much. Explaining that to Rompy would not be healthy for me. On top opf that, Rex woulda sandbagged me if the Feds started questioning.*

Nobby had new hair, sunglasses, a dark blazer making his image harder to detect. *All the disguises Rex wore, yes Nobby would miss him. But survival is an enterprise and the ledger must be kept. All the wildness that came over Rex, mad for sweet Sophie in blue jeans. Smart business dictated Nobby's avuncular treatment of the gal.* Making love with Arabel he often fantasized Sophie tied at the wrists, spread-eagled on his bed, and Rex, in chains, forced to watch.

Men who chopped up Rocco boy got to have hot hands for Nobby. Who ever heard of havin' to bury a man's fingers in your backyard? What a bunch of mess! This ain't Kansas, Toto. Time to balance out the scales. Costa Rica has good real estate, plus no extradition with Uncle Sam. Good place to hide. Money in a Caymans bank: wire out what I need, when I need.

The Town Car descended the Mississippi River bridge, and there was the Capitol, dark and solemn in the heat. Twenty-thousand people formed a radiant blanket across the lawn. Nobby parked ten blocks from the Huey Long statue, caught a shuttle bus to the lawn and began foraging into the crowds on a knee that felt as strong as steel.

What a turnout for Rex!

Rainbow hues of the human experiment: Pentecostals in silk shirts, Afros in pinstripe, polyester Cajuns, Indians in seersucker with straw hats, a covey of Vietnamese nuns waiting for free plates served by Negresses from Mount Olive Missionary Baptist Church at the fried chicken booth. Aromas of barbecue and lemon, deep fry and smoked andouille sausage. Monster video screens on the terrace showing Mass over at the Cathedral. Live gospel action on the lawn. Long lines waiting for the rotunda. Somebody dipped into Rex's slush fund for all this free food. Regina, he reckoned.

Darkness tinted the sky. *Goan get us some rain,* figured Nobby. Rex, boy, we had us a march. The ending waddn't what I preferred but no one can predict how the big wheel spins. All these food booths. Folks serving oyster dressing. Now the buttery garlic scents. Now stuffed mirliton. Lo, I see Omar the Pie Man. So much to choose. Think I'll have me a cup of alligator stew.

The gospel singers, clapping like a train carrying Jesus, sang to the sky.

The fault's not in the Lawwd …
Oh, no!
No, the fault's not in the Lawwd.
It's in ME!

Nobby cringed. Why don't you Negro people sing some other words? Who says the fault ain't in God. It was God made my daddy leave and God called my momma young and God bust my leg at LSU and goddamn I hadda become a rockarolla pitch man 'stead of a pro-ball player. God picks his choices and makes his mistakes. He picks the handsome over the ugly, the nimble ones over the clubbed feet, the naturally strong, excellin' people over the victims of their own weakness. God has his preference list just like we do. That's the mystery these Christians miss: why God's like us. Because God gives power to man. It is up to us, the ones born low, crawlin' up from the caverns, graspin' power to compete with God, using what tools, what means, what levers we got to find the great leveler, to make the high-born and the low-born come up equal.

Rex had his queen-of-the-bayou wife. He had Sophie, first among chickywawas. Had Mayor Bobby as his startup guide, and I never had nobody like that. Who was Domainge but a big boy with a bad knee, hungry for a share of what Rex could achieve? Knowin' I waddn't near as smooth or pretty, I hung close 'cause the man was an escalator to the sky. But Rex laughed at me. Oh, yes, he did. He laughed many times. And never *once* imagined that I had feelings or that the clowning big boy covered a heart bleeding with desire for some triumphs like Rex had, or just some natural love.

Where is Johnny Adams when we need him? Best bluesman in Looziana. Sing one for the Governor, Johnny.

I won't cry
And I won't shed a tear
I'll keep on loving you
Year after year …

He could sing that song for Arabel. I wonder if she did cry. Stole the furniture, all my papers. Plus a pound of cocaine. Cold-blooded woman! Nose candy's why she never got jealous. Them snowbluffs made our bodies groove. Supremely coked, Arabel let me tie her wrists to the bedposts. I never meant to bite her so hard. Told her she didn't need a stitch but blood on her titty made the woman wail.

Rex told Nobby they shared sorrow in losing their daddies young. *Yes, but my daddy disappeared, Rex. And you had Mayor Bobby when you were older.* Yes, admitted Rex, it was different. Rex was going to be Domainge's agent for a pro-ball contract till Alabama crushed that knee. All these religious singers in their flowing robes were appropriate for Rex. Man knew more people out of Africa than the missionaries. Rex loved their churches and was a soft touch for the harmonies. He got their vote, too. Every time.

Four hundred ROTC cadets from LSU in pressed khaki and spit-shined boots filed up the middle of the lawn, taking parade rest positions between the red-robed gospel Negroes and some hundred 'n fifty white folk in a fusion choir from Assemblies of God, robes of royal blue, floating harmonies of their own. Everybody singing in homage for Rex. Some kinda floor show, this. Red was the color of Nobby's hair and the moon bleeding over Trinidad.

He saw the meat-packers gathering on the terrace, just come from church. John Burns Logan, needing nobody's money but his own, standing with his long-legged wife and scrub-brushed kids. And Nobby's poker-playing podna, DuBulio, who wouldn't get squat outa that flag-burnin' bill now. Pfft. Look at Frampton with his patent on virtue. In a suit Nobby bought him at Rubenstein's. Woodruff with his daddy's money and Buzby like a hammer for injection wells keeping Looziana safe for oil. You can put those boys up against any state legislature, thought Nobby, and we would win.

At the edge of the terrace, alone with his wife, stood the outcast Atchison. The sorry lard-ass made a mess of everything by confiding in Rex. There comes a crossroads when all a man does must be gambled in the blinding fire of a moment. Rex knew too much. Atch won't talk now. He saw what happened to Rex. What Sophie knows is a problem.

A long haired Negro-Negro-Negro moved across his field of vision in black jeans with a sequin-spangled shirt and cowboy hat of midnight felt. Hey, now, sleepy-eyed bucko: Willie Boy the rub-board player will lead me to my prey. Sophie, oh Sophie!

Nobby tracked Willie Boy out of jambalaya mist into a forest of mourners and the letters **King Artile and the Zydeco Flames** while a WBRZ camera crew followed Joanie Charlot threading her way through gospel singers and minions at the food booths, her producer wielding a boom mike as Joanie sidled up the stairs, weaving toward the rotunda where Speaker Sutton stood like a Trojan, waiting in the doorway.

The LaSalle caravan arrived.

Reporters converged as the lead limousine halted. Christian Fraux, in dark suit with poker face, stepped out as a dozen state troopers removed the casket. Fraux handed the keys of the hearse to his son as the second vehicle arrived. Colonel Bellamy opened the door for the First Lady, followed by Kay, her husband and then Miss Della, tottering, with a hard grip on Regina's arm. After the third limousine arrived, and the parties of Revon Broussard and Bobby Broussard Junior debouched, the family formed a column behind the First Lady, flanked by Bellamy, and began their procession up the forty-eight steps.

As the television cameras tracked the family's climb to the great doors where Speaker Sutton waited to welcome them into the rotunda, Christian Fraux trailed off to the left, disappearing into the congestion of people and voices settling into a hum.

The Senate cloak room had become a sacristy for ministers from African American churches that had powered Rex LaSalle's electoral base. Fraux found five men in radiant robes, eyeballing one another in a circle knotted by the crossed promises of Regina LaSalle the night before. "Not two weeks *past,* he stood in *mah* pulpit," boomed Reverend Cambronne, "proud as a lion, speaking to my people! And there is a reason, my brothers, a *serious reason* —"

"Why Gina called you after she called me?" scoffed Bishop Axleforce, a Full Gospel leader of New Orleans, his congregation twice the size of Cambronne's in Lafayette. "A girl in distress reaches out, seeking solace. *Men* must resolve these differences! I knew Rex LaSalle as well as any Aframerican. I stood with him at the first NAACP meeting he addressed. I introduced him then, Brother Cambronne. He ate at my home!"

"And mine!" cried another.

"He swam in my swimpool with my *grannnchildren!*" came another.

Fraux inserted himself into the circle; he raised his hands and eyes. "Beseeching God for blessings bestowed on our fellowship, we bow heads and ask for grace!"

The prayer caught the preachers off guard; they had no choice but to bow their heads.

"Precious Lawd," intoned Fraux, "we thank you for the generosity of Amelia LaSalle, her contributions to churches of our people long known."

"*Yes-Lawd!*" responded Bishop Axelforce, wondering why Chris Fraux was here and where he was headed with all this.

"Her visits abundant in the memories of us all," continued Fraux.

"*Have mercy!* " trumpeted Cambronne, turning to make eye contact with Bishop Axelforce, who rolled his eyes and shrugged.

"A time of burden and a time of grief," continued Fraux. "And the foolishness — yes, my brothers, the intemperate nature of a young woman, in her sorrow, imbibing spirits in the night!"

Axelforce's head went up like a jackhammer.

"And making promises her mother did *not* approve!" declared Fraux.

Ten eyes converged on Fraux. "I have come at the widow's behest."

The Bishop jabbed a finger toward him. "You sayin' she wants you to preach the eulogy?"

Fraux bowed his head. "Beseeching you furthur, Lawd, who carried us to freedom's fount, for guidance … on today … and unity among our brethren."

Again, the five heads ducked in prayer.

Fraux: "… *reconciliationnnnn* — praising Christ Jesus for patience, for wisdom, thankin' Him for charities of the purse …"

Fraux held up a white envelope.

"… and the contributing concerns of the First Lady, Missus Amelia …" He opened the envelope — "Broussard" — withdrew a quarter-inch of hundred-dollar bills — "*LaSalle*"— from the thousand cash he ritually carried to all political events in case of emergency, his incantation slowing to a cadence somewhere between a prayer and hybrid sermon for he knew from years in the pulpit that until "Amen" the prayer is not done and a line of oratory must resolve itself thematically in the Word.

"Thanking you, Lawd, for the understanding of our leadership, here gathered, we pause. "He handed two one hundred dollar bills to Bishop Axelforce. "Bestowing gracious measures of appreci*ation* from the bereaved family, to our brethren —" He gave two-hundred to Cambronne, passing pairs of hundred dollar bills in turn to each man. "These emoluments … of the heart …"

"My my my," sang Reverend Cambronne.

"Generosity from the First Lady," purred Fraux.

"Lord-have-mercy!" uttered Axelforce.

The preachers fell silent.

"… *and expectations,*" boomed Fraux, "of a ritual to achieve the dignity, and purpose, which she, a widow in grief, has envisioned for today."

Out in the rotunda, a peal of bugles broke. A brass ensemble from Tulane University began "Battle Hymn of the Republic."

"Brudder *Frauuuuux*," came Cambronne in sing-song tenor, "thanking Jesus, praising the Lawwd, but the hour is late —"

"Yes-Lawd!" sang Axelforce. "Late, late."

"What does Missus LaSalle want?" asked another preacher.

"She wants me to wear a robe and eulogize Rex on behalf of our people," answered Fraux. "She has given me this charge and apologizes for her dysfunctional daughter."

Clearing throats, coughing, the men eyed one another as the money sank in their pockets. Silence draped them like a fog. The brass melody filled the great room beyond them. Outside, a thunderclap hit the sky.

"Very well, then," said Reverend Cambronne. "Take my robe, Chris."

It was a red robe shimmering like a cardinal's cape beneath the klieg lights as Christian Fraux made his entrance into the rotunda, leading the procession into the day's pageantry. Buglesong ebbed. Lush organ chords drew people into a sway with the solemn tones of "Just a Closer Walk with Thee" and a scene that provoked debate at offices of the Associated Press, owing to a reporter's description of "African American ministers, like magi in flowing robes, filed past the open coffin." (*Cut magi!* thundered the bureau chief. *We never had anyone at Bethlehem.*) Each preacher murmured prayers before the body, with stately bows to the First Lady.

Della Lee Broussard fainted.

"Mother!" cried Amelia as the old lady fell into the arms of Regina. A surge of gasps rose from people in the arena where Rex LaSalle lay in state, draped with flags of Louisiana and the USA. Colonel Bellamy cleared a circle and fanned her with his hands. Miss Della regained consciousness. Leaning on Regina, she sighed: "It's this godawful heat."

But the heat was on a tailspin as the blackest cloud in memory unfurled across the sky, a mammoth field of midnight blotting out the light. Air streams poured down from the deepening darkness, mottling the shiny green oak leaves as branches shook in the sough of wind. A jolt of lightning split the sky with jagged silver lines and rainfall beat down on the lawn. A caterwauling rose among the gospel singers and a current of terror charged through the Pentecostal minions watching the video screens, another crash of thunder ignited a stampede of people, clutching their robes knee high, scattering through the oaks, tromping over blossom beds dried by the weeks of heat, a herd of beings breaking for the food tents. Torrent lines whipped the earth, driving the ROTC cadets into tents with singers and other mourners seeking shelter.

Another thunderbolt crashed into a satellite dish outside the Capitol with a fiery silver-blue burst that throttled the truck beneath it like a child's toy. The large video screens on the terrace shorted out in the sheets of rain and toppled over, shattering glass that the wind whipped into a geyser. People screamed as the storm slashed the Capitol.

Security forces locked the basement doors after the casket had come through. A tide of men and women and children sloshed across the terrace, pushing at the huge bronze doors, pressing into the dense-packed rotunda, and still more people came, wailing in the rain, a mass of bodies that lit up like phosphorescent waves each time a jagged arch of lightning crawled across the sky. State troopers and police officers formed a rampart, forcing people into House and Senate chambers behind the rotunda, driving them up the stairwells for hallway space on office levels as the rain raged and flash floods sucked branches and leaves into the food tents.

A thunderclap hit again, and then another and another; serrated lines lit the sky like spidery fingers until a gigantic blast killed the electricity, and a cavernous aftershock plunged the rotunda into darkness.

"Governor LaSalle was known for his galvanizing presence," noted the Archbishop of New Orleans, at the podium with a dead microphone, bestirring nervous chuckles among five thousand souls. "We expect light soon," he called above the din, handing the next segment of the ceremony to the choir leader of Lazarus Full Gospel Church, a black lady timorous of thunder, sensing something bad in the offing as she thanked the Catholic prelate and expressed her condolences to the LaSalle family in a wind sprint of forty-five seconds upon which the hundred voices of her choir began:

Ama-zinnn grace
How sweet
the sound …

It comes upon me gently now, thought Sophie Thibodeaux of the lyrics, a part of myself I cannot expunge.

Huddled behind the elevator, helping King Artile adjust his gold lamé cape, she felt an echo of the spirit that was present the day five hundred believers celebrated Reverend TJ Thibodeaux's dedication of Jesus in the Big Woods, wrought of loblolly pine.

… that saved a wretch like me
I once was lost
but now, I-am found

Maybe Hubbell is right, she thought: there is a purpose to suffering, light beyond the sorrow, promise in time yet lived. Reverend TJ Thibodeaux never knew about Rex, but the dreams of my stepdaddy with a telescope hiding behind my dorm haunted me:

TJ with field glasses up top Tiger Stadium: TJ with a tape recorder hiding behind sound systems when Rex and I danced. "*Be sure your sin will find you out,*" his sermon words that invaded my sleep had ebbed with therapy, only to come back like a soundtrack as I cut distance from Rex.

A thunderbolt whipped the black sky; again the bronze doors heaved. Sopping wet, people herded past Colonel Bellamy, trailing water into the crowd as state troopers forced the doors back shut.

"Seem like God be mad," said King Artile.

"Talk about," said Willie Boy.

"Y'all hush about the Lord," said Sophie. She smoothed the king's cape. "Find salvation in that choir, Artile."

… was blind
but now I see.

I was never really lost, she realized. Just caged in the obsessions of that corn-pone Jesus-builder. May the Lord grant rest to TJ Thibodeaux's soul. In all the holy madness, he gave me space to read and roam after Molly died. *Your stepdaddy's loneliness relied on that hidebound preachin',* Rex had said. *Sinners before an angry God was the only way that man from Pentecostal woodlands could process what the world did to him every night on television.* She knew it was true the moment Rex said it. TJ had been at war with the world outside his tiny radius. But Rex, you were afraid that TJ would expose you if he learned about the Governor and his daughter. *You* were the sin in those dreams, Rex, and I could not bring myself to face it.

Through many dangers
toils and snares …

Church folk had lowered TJ's coffin into the earth. My stepdaddy and stepmomma sleep in soil with twin crosses below a sixty-foot Jesus. That is one core issue. At the funeral, Rex stood by me, ephemerally died black duckbill hair and a baggy suit, thick glasses, introducing himself as "Sophie's frien' from LSU, Bobby Joe Fandall." You made a wholesome impression, Rex. None of those pine village folk realized the Governor had come with Sophie to bury her stepdaddy, who fell off the shoulders of Jesus while arranging the neon thorn crown and hit the ground dead on the spot. Oh, you always succeeded Rex! And now it's your last hurrah, sensations of your spirit calling me, beckoning a companion for that lonely zone. Rex, I can feel you, groping in the catacombs, palms moving along ice walls into the arena of collision with TJ, trying to keep out of God's sight. Two men who never met, floundering in a Neanderthal tar-pit like television wrestlers up to the knees in mud, angels gazing down on wild soft punches, mud-caked bodies fearing loss of your souls, these poppas all hot and bothered: my stepfather of the world lying beyond Big Woods, which made him denounce what he could not understand, and Rex, trembling, sputtering nonwords, a contrition beggar shadowed by a fear going back to when he was thirteen and his own daddy died. *You can't get too close to love. People will always fail you. I learned that real young, Sophie. I had training for politics.*

"We thank our brothers and sisters for those sonorous modalities," came the voice above the storm racket, a baritone without amplifier.

"And we have an announcement," continued Christian Fraux. "With *regret,* the Vice President is unable to join us. The inclement weather has prevented Air Force Two, and Al Gore, from landing … in Looziana."

Rain sheets pummeled the huge bronze doors as people outside clamored to get in. Water whipped a grimacing Colonel Bellamy each time the doors heaved inward; he allowed clusters of people into the building, shaping them into a line that wound snakelike around the mourners massed in the rotunda with state troopers prodding them up the stairs and farther back to allow space for more drenched, shivering people pleading to be let in.

With electricity down, the rotunda was like a room of phantoms.

"All who have cigarette lighters, light them!" cried Christian Fraux.

Flashes began to flicker, a sea of tiny lights bathing the room in auras of gold.

"The Lord is light and he shines into our dark," rose the voice of Christian Fraux above the coughing and scrape of shoes on marble as soaked people moved in from the chilly storm. Television crews with battery packs had taken stations in the crowd, training viewfinders on Fraux, experimenting with light kits to capture the rare colors of the flickering lights.

"Who was this man, Rex LaSalle?" Fraux called out.

Sophie craned to see Christian Fraux, his red-draped forearms in upward curls like a painting by Tintoretto. Arrayed behind him, Miss Amelia and the family seemed like icons in the glow of lighters.

Colonel Bellamy heaved against the bronze door like a reed bent to the wind. Sophie saw a hand, then an arm, worm its way through the crack left by the enormous door, and then the body belonging to Henry Hubbell entered the room, hair-drenched in a suit soaked to his skin. She stood on tiptoes to see this strange new man. *Episcopalians seem so detached, intellectualizing scripture, unlike my people for whom it is a rushing river ...*

Fraux continued: "We are born in sin and shadowed by iniquity, and we seek a road of grace from the cradle to the grave."

"*Yes we do!*" echoed Bishop Axleforce.

"In Psalms, number one hundred and thirty-seven," resumed Fraux, "the Israelites are captured. They have hung their harps on the willow tree. *And the Babylonians ...* demand — that they sing!"

"Say it now, Brudder Frauuux," came Reverend Cambronne.

"How could they sing of Zion?" cried Fraux. "In a strange land, how could they sing ... without mirth?"

The First Lady and her entire family were fixated on Christian Fraux.

"We today are like those captives. Sorrowful. Perplexed by the loss of our leader, we confront a cold world. And the challenge, my brothers and sisters, is to prove our faith in God. How do we sing the Lord's song in a strange land?"

"*Thaatttt's right,*" purred Jimbo Jenson Junior.

"Rex LaSalle was a sinner," announced Fraux. "We share that with him — the imperfection that marks us as subjects of the Lord.

Now perhaps … some would say … that because of his *powahhh*, the potential … for wrongdoing … was greater. My my, yes. Certainly an interesting propo-*sition!*"

Fraux paused.

"And troubling! Oh yes, quite troubling indeed for those who would pass judgment on a man's life." Fraux dabbed his forehead with a handkerchief. With the power outage, the air conditioning was down and the only coolness came from gusts of the rainstorm when the rotunda doors heaved open, only to be shut by the state police after a few more people trickled in.

"But judgment belongeth to the Lord, my brothers and sisters, and we have come to *praise* the Lord!"

"Say it now!" cried Bishop Axleforce.

"To praise Him and to act as intercessors on behalf of our brother Rex. 'Regard the prayer and supplications of your servants, Lawd.' I have the Third Book of Kings, Chapter Eight."

"Y*es-Lawd!*" echoed Reverend Cambronne.

"The Lord used Rex LaSalle to achieve good ends."

"Have mercy, Jesus!" exclaimed Jimbo Jenson Junior.

Christian Fraux was censoring his sermon: Sophie realized it in the recall of King Solomon's prayer from the mental drumbeat of her stepfather's pulpit ("For if heaven and the heavens of heavens cannot contain thee, how much less this house which I have built?") The house Rex built had spiritual cracks. African masks, paintings, metal ostriches, Mexican stone gods, all that beauty arranged by the First Lady, and he fled the love in that house, a realization that crept upon Sophie in the final months as her own love for the Governor died. Rex, you can't create true love out of costumes and secret plots. The little daily realities add up. How do two people make their lives work together, Rex? *Why you wanna know so much about my marriage — are you jealous, Sophie?* He did not have the emotional texture to see why she was curious about the relationship of a man and woman whose lives were not ruled by Solomon and Judges and Leviticus denouncing homosexuals and scripture rivers leading to end time. She asked him what kinds of things he and Amelia talked about at breakfast. There must be ways y'all keep the harmony. Like what y'all discuss — you know, just *things*. What do couples do, Rex?

At that he had laughed: *I'm just a Roman from Ville Platte.*

"Like the Children of Israel," cried Fraux, his voice ringing through the rotunda, "we must take these harps down from the willow tree and use them to make song!"

"Sing it, Brudder Fraux," came Cambronne.

"I have Psalm Fifty: 'Let me hear the sounds of joy and gladness … Give me back the joy of your salvation and a willing spirit to sustain me.'"

Christian Fraux was doing it again: He left out *the bones you have crushed shall rejoice. Turn away your face from my sins and blot out all my guilt* — he was sanitizing Rex in the lines cut from scripture.

"And our Governor was, a willing spirit. He leaves us much proof of his volition. Evidence of the concerns he expressed, the things he made and built."

"Yes-Lawd!" sang Jimbo Jenson Junior.

"The *roads* that Rex LaSalle put into communities, where only dusty paths had been before!"

"Say it now!" bellowed Reverend Cambronne.

"Paths that turned to mud when rain tumbled down as it does today, trails stretching back across years of suffering that he, as Governor, knew must be healed. Trails of mud became concrete. Tears of sorrow become tears of joy!"

"Say it now!" chimed Jimbo Jenson Junior.

Sophie watched them in the fluttering glow of lighters: Amelia LaSalle, nodding. A faraway gaze in Kay's eyes. The grandmomma gripping Regina like she was the last soul on the planet, and both of them riveted on Fraux like each word was a diamond.

"And he wanted something else!" exclaimed Fraux.

"Yes he did, sweet Jesus!"

"Oh, Jesus *is* sweet, Reverend Cambronne! And Rex LaSalle wanted to cleanse this land and purify our waters! He heard the cry of Genesis: 'The Lord God caused growth from the virgin soil all kinds of trees pleasant to the sight and good for food.' And he worried, *oh* how he *grieved* in his late days over the desecrations of our earth and the spoliation of our water!"

Reporters won't check the Book of Genesis, Sophie knew.

Fraux left out the part about the tree of good and evil growing from the same soil. When Rex got in his car in New Roads we sat in the dark coolness as Mitchell drove. Finally I said, what were you discussing with that preacher man back there? "He says they are putting garbage on the threshold," Rex replied with a distant weary gaze. "*Power is the ability to change what people see, make them think the images mean something else.* I thought civilization was gaining, but here, Chris Fraux comes whisperin' the last days of Pompeii. He's ahead of the people, sugar. The people! What a concept. The earth cries, and they wait for TV to make it real."

Fraux's words carried through the rotunda: "A man of multiple dimensions! Rex LaSalle held up a mirror, forcing us to question ourselves."

Christian Fraux shouted: "Will Louisiana become Babylon?"

The First Lady's mouth dropped. Miss Della opened her eyes. Five-thousand people gawked.

"Will we lose ourselves to cracking smoke beneath the earth, the loss of waterbeds and rich land by these chemical behemoths? Or will we follow the path of Rex our brother, Rex our leader, fording troubled rivers, telling us to protect the sanctity of our shores and take our harps from the willow tree. We must take back our song!"

"Take it back!" cried Bishop Axelforce. "Play the harps!"

"Let us remember our departed brother who protected the earth, and who tuned our harps and taught us to play the precious melodies of life!"

Ten-thousand hands thundered in applause.

"Now we have an interlude," said Fraux, "a different kind of repertoire ... by one group, among the countless many whose talents he championed. Artile?" Fraux paused. "It is hard ... without the light ... We call upon the Zydeco Flames to come forward."

Proud in his gold cape, King Artile wore the crown that Rex

had fixed upon his head in a ceremony after the Grammys. With the electricity out, he began a hand-patting on the side of the accordion, a percussive rhythm igniting the crowd in popping palms as the saxophone honked and Willie Boy hummed the melody, thimbled fingers thrumming the washboard. *"Calinda ... oh, Calinda,"* sang Artile. Sophie knew why music became her salvation, the rhythms completed her without Big Woods retributions, a cry to God of joyous song arching over the coldness of a world divided by scripture.

Hot breath hit her ear: "Start movin' backward. Slowly."

The cold shaft burrowed into the base of her spine. "Muzzle's got a silencer, Sophie. One word and I'll spray this crowd with your insides."

Her body felt like ice. Following the push of the muzzle she stepped away from people purring to the zydeco, beyond the light flickers warming the rotunda. A crash broke across the sky, dimming the web of flares as Nobby guided her toward the stairwell.

In the yellow haze, Hubbell saw the bulk of Nobby, moving sideways with Sophie like a shield. Hubbell maneuvered past a potted palm, eye trained on Sophie as they retreated toward the elevator.

They were gone.

Hubbell cut diagonally through the masses swaying to the zydeco and pushed on, reaching the elevator. No electricity: they could not have taken it. Storm-soaked people were streaming upstairs to gray light filling the windows of the office floors. Hubbell peered down the stairwell into the basement and stepped into pitch black.

At the bottom step, sewer water seeped into his shoes, soaking his ankles in the quiet stench of a current broken by sloshing shoes fifty yards ahead. He heard a thump and creak. A door swung open. In the flash of rain sky spilling through a window, he saw them, spectral figures as the door shut behind them. Hugging the wall, Hubbell crept through the slosh of fetid mud pushed back from the sewers. He hung flat against the wall, cadaver-cold to the feel of his chest and cheek, moving his feet through the sluices down the hall till he reached the door with the glass panel emblazed Men's Room.

Fingers slipping over the knob, he listened, and heard nothing. This had to be the room they entered. The next one was down the hall, out of sight. Turn the knob, Henry ...

Window light framed Nobby, big as a bear with red dye dripping down his forehead. "Come in, boy. I can shoot her easy as you. This gun is silent as a lamb."

Sophie was Nobby's shield. He stood between the row of sinks and toilet stalls, the pistol trained on her cranium, his free hand gripping her neck, pushing her head on her chest. "Edge in slow now, boy."

Hands dangling, Hubbell stepped into the puddled aisle of the checkerboard tile. The room was lit in grainy film from the window above their heads, light seeping through mud backed up from the flower beds outside.

Nobby forced Sophie onto her knees.

Three urinals lined the wall behind him. The big man made a semicircular shift toward the toilet stalls, forcing Hubbell against the urinals that smelled of ammonia.

"You're breaking my neck," gasped Sophie.

"We'll cut you some slack, sugar. Keep your arms folded. *Both y'all!*"

Hubbell crossed his arms on his chest.

"You, boy. On yer knees. Now!"

Rough patches of silver showed in Nobby's hair as the crimson seeped down his neck and forehead. He hovered like an Oceanic totem. Sophie drew her thighs together. Hubbell knelt across from her in the stinking water and said: "She doesn't have what you want, Domainge."

"Nobody called me that in a way long time. Say what you know, boy."

"You can meet Arabel at the airport."

"I ain't playing shrimp on your bait line, boy."

"Rex made her clear out. She wants you."

The roar of the rain drummed the long windows level with Nobby's neck. Resting her palms on the dirty floor, Sophie looked at Hubbell with requiem eyes. He said: "Old man in Angola wants to go home, Doctor. Amelia wants this mess buried. Rompallo says if you leave Dodge, the butchers won't follow."

"Makes sense. Avoid trouble all around."

Sophie's heels shot up in a backstroke hammering into Nobby's groin, knocking him away. Hubbell lunged with an elbow to Nobby's throat. Nobby bounced back like a medicine ball, slamming Hubbell onto the tiles.

"Stop it, Nobby!"

In the doorway a man with a black mask pulled over his face wore a black suit with black gloves and pointed a .357 Magnum.

Nobby stepped back.

Sophie jumped to her feet.

The door swung shut behind the invader.

"Get up," hissed Sophie, pulling Hubbell to his feet.

Nobby tottered two feet to their right.

The invader entered the narrow space between the wash stands and the latrines, the gun trained on Nobby's face. "Dump the gun."

How did this guy get in? wondered Hubbell.

Nobby lay the gun on the porcelain sink.

"Into the stall, Doctor."

The invader took Nobby's gun, and with his own larger weapon, pointed him toward a stall. "In there."

Nobby lumbered into the toilet.

"Sit on the john, Doctor Nobby."

"I know you, podna. Five-hundred-thousand. Cash money. No questions."

"Sit," commanded the man, training the shaft on Nobby.

"Trunka my car. Five … hundred … thousand —"

But the man shot Nobby through the mouth.

The silencer made a pump, his head pitched back, blood exploding on the wall. Sophie squealed. Hubbell covered her mouth with his hands.

Upstairs, five thousand people were clapping to the zydeco.

"Do not look. Do not make a sound," commanded the shooter.

Hubbell held Sophie to his chest, her body shuddering.

"Go to the door and do not look back," said the shooter. He entered the stall where Nobby was wedged against the blood-spattered wall, teeth shattered from the bullet blast and eyeballs rolled into his skull. The gloved man slipped Nobby's weapon into a lifeless hand. He stepped out of the stall and opened the window, unleashing a river of rainwater and mud from the flower beds.

"Leave to your right," commanded the man in black.

Hubbell's fingers turned the knob, shaking frenetically.

"And remember," came the voice. "This never happened."

26 INTERROGATION

Out of the basement streams, Henry led Sophie into the torrents and down the lawn sloping beneath bronze-fisted Huey Long. Water slapped at her thighs, rain lines piercing like needles. Mush crept over her ankles like an organic suction as they pushed into the current, avoiding shards of wood and chunks of the screen from skeletal remains of the jambalaya tent. Shattered booths where people had been serving shellfish and meats sank into a cavity of mud.

Reptile gills rose to her right, and then a stuffed maw, dripping foam, and the reddened black debris of crawfish shells snagged in jagged teeth.

"Henry, that's a bull gator there — watch out!"

Hubbell hoisted her into his arms and pushed through the flood, cutting wide of the giant reptile devouring the seafood booth. Rain beat down as he sloshed through the oak grove, abandoned by gospel singers, with Sophie in his arms, hands around his neck, shivering in the wetness that seemed almost freezing. The lawn stretched on like a swamp. "Where is the car?" he croaked.

"In the lot behind Natural Resources Building, honey."

They slogged across the flooded grass behind gospel singers and food people in weary flight through knee-high waves. Ahead, on slightly higher ground, the tires of moving vehicles spewed long spits of mud. Men on foot trudged like soldiers; ladies held hems above the sucking ooze. A van puttered along in slow motion, waves lapping off the running board.

"I can walk now," she said.

He set her down on the mushy incline that emptied onto a street where flood streams carried branches and flotsam from the food stalls. At last they reached the parking lot. Hubbell started the Mazda; heat rushed from the vents.

"Nobby's files are in the trunk. Arabel mailed them. I got 'em at noon."

He nodded vacantly. "I'll read 'em at home." Silence filled the space between them like a corpse. Hubbell peered through the wipers whipping rain off the windshield and steered the car up a winding boulevard. His clenched jaw reminded Sophie of a Gulf War vet she'd met on a blind date for a football game; he stared at collisions on the field with no emotion, never moving his body.

Women want men to be strong — not to let you down. Rex had the bravura confidence that aligns with power, but she saw him desperate for a love that she could not requite. A fugitive from himself, Rex wanted her to keep on giving.

Floodwaters receded on the road that led to a high street showing no sign of the storm tides that swamped the city. Rainfall was running like a generator as they entered his house. She went immediately to the bathroom and spent fifteen minutes in a burning shower, trying to expunge her mental image of Nobby's scalp dripping red before the masked man shot him in the toilet stall. *Hubbell and I are accomplices.*

She found him on the living room couch, in gray sweat pants and a blue Red Sox jersey, going through the folders Arabel had sent her. Audio on the TV was low, just enough to hear vocal patterns of the anchorpeople. Coverage moved from taped scenes of the wake to live footage of helicopter angles on the mammoth flood, mile upon mile of city streets with half-submerged cars, water lines bisecting stop signs, black people in one neighborhood sitting on house roofs, waving to the viewfinder. The coverage cut between the deluge and candle glow in the rotunda, voices humming, bodies shaking to the zydeco. Hundreds of handheld lighters formed a golden halo around the First Lady and her family, like people everyone should love.

"Have the cameras shown us?" she asked.

"Not that I've seen." He studied a document. "These are the Mermentau leases. Why did Arabel send you all this?"

"She must have seen the news. Figured out Nobby had it in for Rex."

Nestled into the couch next to him, she wore black jeans, a pair of his thick white jogging socks and a Zydeco Flames T-shirt.

"No coverage of Nobby yet," he muttered. "But it's inevitable."

"What then?" She curled her legs around him.

He rummaged through the files.

"So, Henry. Cat got your tongue?"

"What do you think happens?" he snapped. "I become material witness to a homicide. One more insect in this endless net. And I get disbarred!"

"They can't do that. I'm your witness. No one knows what happened unless that killer talks — whoever he is."

"*They?* You think 'they' can't? They killed Rex, they killed Nobby, they killed Rex's killer. They can do anything in this God-abandoned state."

Her body went tense at his anger, this man who believed in law and duty. Yet his rules-based approach to life had given her something, as if pulling out a love ballad from pew-thumping melodies. He had a center, a sense of right and wrong that comforted her.

"I want to thank you for all you've done, Henry."

"You're welcome. Why did you kiss Rex on the legs?"

"I didn't," she sighed. *Here we go again.* "Mitchell and I saw the lipstick when we laid Rex on his bed."

"You're saying you didn't kiss him."

"I think the killer used lipstick to make it seem like a woman was there. We were in a panic to leave. Maybe we should have wiped it off."

He went back to Nobby's files as TV coverage spun scenes of Rex blowing kisses from a Mardi Gras stand; greeting Pope John Paul II at New Orleans airport; doing the two-step with Linda Rondstadt at Jazz Fest; now taking the oath of office. Watching the mosaic left Sophie hollow. The Governor who loved her, craving the adoration of so many others, pursuing her to rejuvenate himself, the weight of his needs stunting her quest for a new plateau, a life with love in balance.

The facts on Nobby, Atchison and the mob were at Hubbell's fingertips. The anger swelling inside him was palpable. Unlocking all these dirty secrets was enough to overwhelm even a hardbitten attorney, and she detected a man in confusion about how to find life and make his way with happiness.

She reached down into the files and captured his hands, pulled them into her palms and locked her eyes into a straight line with his.

"I don't blame you for being furious, Henry. I have never seen anyone get killed and I will never forget it either. But you said something last night that I can't just erase. You and I are here for a reason. We found each other. Despising Rex does no good for you, or me. Number one, the man is dead. Number two, what he and I had was finished before he died."

She wrapped her hands behind his neck and met his lips with long slow heat, feeling his resistance thaw, his arms curving around her back, the fingers kneading her with firm strokes that made her moan. Where did this guy come from?

"It feels like I've been running toward you all my life," he whispered.

The words raced her heart. Jumping into relationships was not her style, but the speed of violence over forty-eight hours had sent her into a free fall and suddenly she had found a new man, a man who showed value. He was younger and more naive than Rex, but he had a stunning mind and a decency that made her want him even more. She traced his lips with her fingertips, wondering if all this revolution could really deliver love.

"Henry, I have got to shoot straight with you."

She pulled herself up on the couch. "You have a good job. But Baton Rouge is a dirty place to me. I want to get out of here."

He moved closer. "So do I."

The telephone began ringing.

"Are you serious?" he demanded.

"More than you can begin to imagine."

She took a deep breath. He gathered her face in his hands and drew her toward him. Files spilled on the rug, the phone rang on, till suddenly tires rumbled outside and someone was pounding the front door.

She jackknifed off the rug; he scooped the files into his arms and deposited them in the boxes Arabel had sent. "We've got to keep these in my study." She helped him carry the boxes down the hall.

The temperature had dropped. In the chill of the house, Sophie was determined to hide no more. She took his hand and walked with him up the hallway, standing at his side as he opened the door.

In the rainy mist, Mitchell Mudd held an umbrella over the First Lady. Draped in a black cape, sparkling from the rain, Amelia LaSalle had a radiance that made Sophie see at once why Rex had loved her. Sophie froze at the knees.

"How quickly we make friends," said Amelia.

Mitchell Mudd stood like a statue with the umbrella.

The First Lady scowled. "Mr. Hubbell, I thought you were honorable. But this" — pointing to Sophie Thibodeaux — "is betrayal without bounds."

"You have no right to make such judgments," he replied.

"No right? I guided you toward *that*" — shaking her finger at Sophie like a scolding preacher. "Oscar told me where she woke up this morning."

"You sent me to find her, Amelia. And I thank you for that. Rex was a pirate but thanks to her I appreciate him more objectively now. We found the killer. You buried Rex with dignity."

"*Pirate?*"

Sophie saw it coming but Hubbell missed the arc of her hand until it slapped him on the cheek with a full-throttle *whack!*

"Don't you ever speak ill of my husband, young man! The funeral — we were stuck in that God-forsaken Capitol three hours. I came home and that FBI creature arrived unannounced."

"What did O'Connor want?"

"Rex's records, all kinds of information. Thank God Oscar got rid of him."

"That's a radical move for O'Connor," said Hubbell.

"He came," she bristled, "to tell me that Doctor Nobby was found dead. He shot himself or someone shot him in the basement of the Capitol."

Hubbell raised his eyebrows. "I think Mitchell and I need a few words on the porch, ma'am. Come in. Sophie, would you make coffee?"

The First Lady advanced like a praying mantis, edging Sophie into the kitchen.

Hubbell stepped onto the porch. Rain dribbled off the eaves in a silver glow of street lamps. He saw the moisture of Mudd's whiskers and inhaled his deepening odor. The women were out of earshot.

"You put Rex in his bed at four in the morning," said Hubbell. "You got to Angola by dawn, and made it back to Rex's office for 9 AM. Nobody else could get into see Rompallo without cover. But you know the warden because he and Rex fought roosters together."

"That don't mean nothing," snorted Mudd.

"Do not — *ever* — hassle me again. You understand, Mitchell?"

"Meaning what?"

"Rompallo gave you the map to the hit man. You left the Mansion just after meeting me yesterday morning. You shot over to

Mermentau, pulled Rocco out of bed with a gun on his neck. Tied his wrists and chopped off his fingers till he told you Nobby paid him to kill Rex. Then you sawed off his head."

Mudd grinned. "You got some active imagination."

"The tough part was the Scotch by Rex's bed. Then you showed me shaky fingers, said you were in AA — and it hit me. You needed that drink, and you knew that leaving the glass would confuse the bedroom scene."

"I don't admit to that."

"But you do admit killing Nobby. Your body language, your voice. I saw you fire the shot. So did Sophie."

Mitchell Mudd blinked. He made a sucking sound.

"Talk issues, Hubbell."

"I have one issue, Mitchell."

"You want the girl."

"That's right, and I don't want any interference."

"You don't snitch on me, Hubbell, and I won't spill on you."

"It's a deal."

They shook hands before the flash of oncoming headlights.

In the kitchen, Amelia had Sophie cornered by the coffee maker. "I understand you were with my husband when he died."

"As God is my witness, ma'am, I had no role in Rex being murdered."

In the First Lady's face and regal brow, Sophie saw impressions of Regina, a resemblance of Kay, a totality of the LaSalle women that engulfed her in a discomforting sense of common purpose, despite the guilt. The First Lady inched closer, so near to her body that Sophie whispered: "I am humiliated, ma'am. I have sinned and I ask your forgiveness. My people call this backsliding. But never, on my soul, was I plotting a state of divorce. What we did was wrong, and I know Rex felt terrible about the hurt he caused you."

Staring at the creamy skin and honey-hued hair of youth, Amelia experienced an out-of-nowhere tremor, some inchoate working of the heart stirred by a mental picture of Rex, solid at her side when Mayor Bobby Broussard died, the priest dousing holy water on her daddy's coffin, the comfort of Rex the day they buried Bobby in the Avoyelles cemetery ten years ago.

Rex had buried the love for Amelia long before he died. A bolt of chill penetrated her shoulders and rolled down her spine. *I will not let this anger seep in like something toxic and destroy who I am supposed to be.*

"What did my husband want?" she said calmly.

"Oh he loved you very permanently, ma'am. It did take me a while to see that. I learned that he was more afraid of losing what he had than accepting limitations about himself. He was one restless bearcat. If anyone asked, 'Sophie, on your life, *who was Rex LaSalle?*' I would say a dreamer who wanted positive affections without accepting the consequences for his actions."

The First Lady raised her eyebrows. Sophie met her gaze with a brow of pain. The agony of Rex's roaming flooded Amelia again. "You lasted longer than the other ones," she said tartly.

"Yes, ma'am." Sophie blushed. "Truthfully, I don't know why."

The rage inside Amelia was hardening like mortar; words would not come. Stricken by the verbal loss, she opened the cabinet and pulled out a tin of coffee. "Fill it halfway," she said brusquely.

"Oh, absolutely, ma'am." Sophie's fingers shook as she poured the coffee grinds, spilling dark dots onto the counter.

"Don't slop up the man's nice kitchen," admonished the First Lady.

Sophie cleaned the counter. Amelia stood twelve inches away, ravenous for words to appropriate the moment.

The line of coffee dripping into the pot sent a warm aroma of familiarity into the icy space between the women. Sophie withdrew mugs from the pantry and spoons from a drawer.

"You have every reason to hate me," Sophie said to the First Lady. "If you can find it in your heart to forgive me, I would do anything in return."

Amelia crossed her arms and retreated to the refrigerator.

"The press will dig like garbage scavengers now that Rex is

gone," she said. "I need to know something. Did he ever play tape recordings for you?"

"Oh, all the time. The Nevilles, Zydeco Flames, Jerry Lee, you name it."

"What about politicians?"

"Oh, no ma'am. He only played music."

The First Lady smiled. "You must have had warm times," she said acidly.

"He always said it was away from the action."

Outside the house, they heard tires crunch on wet asphalt. Sophie poured the coffee and followed the First Lady into the living room.

Jack O'Connor stepped out of his Taurus, keen to a system that dismembers one killer and leaves a bagman dead in a toilet with a lagoon of mud on the floor, federal agents photographing a hundred angles while Bellamy kept the press at bay. In this state, all the people were the same, thought O'Connor: just a species apart, even reporters and reformers suck the same ozone. I can't put Rompallo near Nobby's death!

O'Connor bounded onto the porch, badge-flashing in unison with his partner Joe Dymally. At the coupling of Mudd and Hubbell, the FBI agent smiled. "Been a hard day, friends. Record rainfall and one more homicide for the great state. How 'bout us fellows talk inside, Henry?"

"Not your buddy."

"We work in pairs."

"Not in my house."

"I can arrest you now, Hubbell."

"That would be a mistake, Jack. My client is inside."

O'Connor frowned. O'Connor nodded. He wanted face time with Amelia LaSalle the way a prisoner wants sex. O'Connor ordered Dymally back to the car just as a new vehicle emerged from the rain, long and black like a battering ram.

Attorney General Oscar Abadie stepped out of the limousine with Speaker Sutton, whose driver remained in the car as the two elected officials crossed the sidewalk in a cool drizzle. The tall, white-maned Speaker climbed the stairs, gripping Abadie's elbow. A surge of adrenalin shot through James Jack O'Connor. Never in his career had every target of a probe knowingly gathered under the same roof; this was better than videotaping mobsters.

Hubbell opened the door. Mitchell Mudd stood aside in deference to the Speaker, who scowled at Hubbell as he lumbered into the living room with Attorney General Abadie. Hubbell followed with James Jack O'Connor bringing up the rear.

The spectacle of Sophie Thibodeaux, full ripeness and youth, seated on the couch next to the First Lady, prim and elegant with coffee on her lap, caused an audible suction of breath from the politicians and the FBI agent.

A tense silence descended on the room.

Mitchell Mudd assumed a guardian's stance behind the First Lady. Hubbell brought a chair from the dining room for his boss and another for Speaker Sutton, whose bitter stare the young attorney returned with a cheery, fuck-you grin. Hubbell sat on the arm of the couch next to Sophie.

The FBI agent occupied the rug, standing with confidence. He scanned the semicircle from Sutton to Abadie, Mudd to the First Lady, then Sophie, then Hubbell.

"Well, friends. Doctor Nobby is dead in a men's room. Mr. Mudd, you threatened to kill him six months ago."

Amelia gasped.

Mudd sneered: "Cut through it, bubba! Nobby paid me on the squawk kill. You say I'd powder a dude over slow pay on a cock bet? *Pahhh.*"

O'Connor backed off a beat. "Miss Thibodeaux, we found signs of a struggle at your house. And your car tires were slashed."

"She says nothing without an attorney," interjected Hubbell.

"And who is yours, counselor?" smiled the FBI agent.

"I don't need one. But you need arrests so you can move up to Washington where democracy is clean. Cracking a murder is tough with one guy carved up and his paymaster dead in a toilet."

"Start a manhunt!" boomed Oscar Abadie.

The FBI agent fired at the First Lady: "Do you take comfort in a trail of blood and unanswered questions about the mob killing your husband?"

"Calls for an opinion!" piped Oscar Abadie. "Hers and yours."

"My client," said Hubbell, "has no knowledge of organized crime nor any direct proof of who killed the Governor."

"So we admit he was killed!" chimed James Jack O' Connor.

"No one admitted nothin'," stewed Attorney General Oscar Abadie.

James Jack O'Connor was grinning like a fox.

"You need Nobby's files," announced Hubbell.

"I'm sure I do," replied O'Connor, surprised.

The First Lady knew Hubbell would not lie about documents to an FBI agent, and the reality hit her like lightning: Arabel had turned on Nobby and given files to Sophie. The protective shroud she had felt that morning at her window, mesmerized by the gospel singers on the Capitol lawn, thickened as she pictured Rex, positioned on a grid of power they still shared as mates. Protecting him had become her battle against the Federal forces.

"Those files gain value," the First Lady stated in a firm voice, leaning forward on the couch, eyes trained on the FBI man, "if they corroborate plans for a toxic-waste pipeline and a map of land deals with the Mafia."

"The client without knowledge of the mob," chuckled O'Connor.

"What the Governor may have shared anecdotally with his wife is hearsay," said Hubbell, protecting his client. "But if Doctor Nobby's files reveal fraudulent representation to landowners, violation of pollution laws, a conspiracy between Rompallo, state senators and toxic-waste dealers, that's rocket fuel, Jack."

"We've got Atchison nailed. Rompallo's in the state pen."

"You don't have his organization," said Hubbell. "You don't have toxic-waste dealers who pay to make the earth swallow. You don't have contractors in bed with the mob. You don't have their friends in our polluted legislature."

"And you're saying you possess such documentation."

"That's right. But you'd better wait till the jury convicts Atchison before you accept custodianship of Nobby's files."

Jack O'Connor opened his mouth and said exactly nothing. The six people in his net, in this room, had just witnessed his being told of the existence of documents involving Senator Atchison, documents which the us Attorney under law would have to share with Senator Atchison's defense team.

"You're close to convicting Atchison," said Hubbell. "Anything you take from here has to be disclosed. That will force the judge to halt proceedings."

"And call a mistrial," said Oscar Abadie.

The FBI agent held out his palms like a politician signaling quiet from his followers. O'Connor had to process the reality at hand. He knew that Atchison had squeezed contractors and doled out money to greedy senators. He had no idea that senators were central to a plan for a toxic-waste pipeline. The prospect of mob-friendly contractors in bed with other state senators was a pump to his testosterone and a big reason why the FBI agent loved Louisiana.

"Who do you think sucked Atchison into the waste business?" said Hubbell. "Who do you think cemented the fat Senator's career to Rompallo?"

No one said Nobby's name.

Hubbell continued: "Atchison was afraid Rompallo would have him killed if he testified or cut a plea. So he went to Governor La-Salle, begging help, leaking everything about his ties to Rompallo and Nobby. When the Mermentau people filed suit, linking Nobby and Atchison as owners of the waste dump, Nobby realized that he would be the prime suspect if Atchison was murdered."

"So Nobby switched the target," gasped O'Connor, startling himself at the assertion. "He had Rocco from the black lagoons kill Rex — instead of Atchison."

"They were the two people who could do Nobby in," Hubbell

explained. "And by killing Rex, Nobby figured he could guarantee silence from Atchison."

No one spoke. Sutton's face was hard as granite. Oscar Abadie gazed bitterly at a corner of the room. Sophie sat with fists on her lap, looking at the First Lady, drawing confidence from her imperial silence. Mudd stood at attention. The First Lady stared at O'Connor with beady eyes.

Her stare said something to the FBI man: Husband dead, the gal pal sitting next to her, this woman is working double-overtime.

"I don't see why we need to hide the truth," O'Connor said.

"Because the media will destroy my husband's memory!" snapped the First Lady. "You put out gory details of a homicide and people will think the mob killed Rex in retaliation for something. Trampling a dead man's reputation is cheap, Mr. O'Connor. I deserve better. So do my daughters. So does this state. You people tried to demolish Rex when he was alive and you failed. Don't start again. Tactics like that are a barrier to the work I have to do."

"Meaning what?" said O'Connor, coldly.

"This state is out of control. Someone has to pull it together."

Speaker Sutton swiveled his head toward Abadie, who shrugged.

Hubbell smiled, imagining Amelia with all those tapes of politicians.

Sophie was transfixed at the woman whose complexities had never registered on her in all the time with Rex. The First Lady was utterly unique; she had never met a female who was commanding, elegant and sexy all at once.

"You intend to be Governor?" asked O'Connor.

"With the support of General Abadie and Speaker Sutton," she replied, "I will serve out my husband's term and decide later on seeking election in my own right."

"Everyone supports Miss Amelia," announced Mitchell Mudd.

"I'd vote for her," said Sophie Thibodeaux.

"We have a leadership vacuum," groused Abadie, craving Jack Daniels.

The Speaker cleared his throat. "Amelia and I are friends."

O'Connor: "Does the state Constitution allow this?"

"That's not an issue," the Attorney General said dismissively.

"In that case," said O'Connor, "I'd like to speak with you, ma'am, and your designated legal counsel."

"In my study," said Hubbell.

O'Connor and the First Lady followed him down the hall.

Around Sophie Thibodeaux converged the domination of men: The height and pulsing anger of the Speaker; the meat of Oscar Abadie and his moody detachment; Mitchell Mudd, the volatile man who knew her secrets.

"Rex dug his own grave," snorted Sutton. "Oscar, I see no reason to sacrifice some senators to censor news about Rex and his bimbo."

"*You dirty old man!*" hissed Sophie, springing off the couch and swatting the Speaker on his face. Sutton tottered in his seat, stunned by her act of treason.

The Attorney General jumped between them: "Sit down and control yourself, young woman, or you'll get arrested!"

"You people are too sleazy!" she cried and stalked off to the bathroom.

Mitchell Mudd sat on the couch, drawing one knee over the other. When he saw the splotch of Nobby's blood on his right shoe lace, Mudd stood and repositioned himself behind the couch.

Abadie huddled with Sutton, talking quietly.

Meanwhile, in Henry Hubbell's study, James Jack O'Connor sat behind the oaken desk where Forrest Hubbell had drafted epic petitions that sent Negro children into white schools. Surrounded by books and photographs of France, the FBI agent experienced a cloud of blissful reality.

"Tell me, Henry: Nobby's documents support how many indictments?"

"Thirty-five, forty people, multiple counts. You get the files on three conditions. One: we bury the Governor and all information on his death. Nobody investigates. Two: no subpoenas or prosecution of anyone in this house, plus Doctor Willoby, Colonel Bellamy, the Banks brothers and Christian Fraux. Three: Immunity to Nobby's wife. She doesn't even know she's in this yet."

"And in exchange we get what?"

Hubbell leaned down the length of the desk. "The six senators, DuBulio, eight other representatives, the insurance commissioner and head of the Department for Environmental Quality. Nobby's money glued everybody on this project. Hell, you've got the Voting Machines Commissioner tied to Nobby, why I don't know. Your problem is deciding who *not* to indict. You could sink so many that Clinton would have to appoint a special master to fill in till new elections."

"The President will do no such thing!" snapped the First Lady. "I'm going to take over with appropriate measures to make this stable clean."

The freckles on O'Connor's face reminded Amelia of a reptile. How he enjoyed his conquests! She knew how his kind worked: matching crimes and sentences, calculating tradeoffs, molding witnesses to bring down bigger prey. And he couldn't raise the money to run for constable.

"I like the sound of it," grunted O'Connor. "We'll need a power structure so the electorate feels secure. No disrespect, ma'am. Your husband and I had our differences, but that's water under the bridge."

"Just keep out of my life," said the First Lady.

"I need to question Sophie Thibodeaux," said O'Connor.

"That violates terms of our deal," said Hubbell.

"It's the Governor's call," said the FBI agent.

"I need a word with my client," said Hubbell. "You wait down the hall."

Hubbell guarded the door until he saw that O'Connor had returned to the living room. The First Lady stood next to a Cartier-Bresson photograph of a proud, smiling boy walking with a bottle of wine down a winding French street. Arms folded, Amelia was showing serious agility.

"We both have reasons to protect Sophie," said Hubbell.

"Pray tell, counselor: what is mine?"

"If the FBI grills her, O'Connor gains serious leverage — information on Rex's sex life. He'd use it in a heartbeat to compromise the deal before we cement it. Move quickly. Give a press conference tomorrow and announce your intent to assume the governorship. Deflect foul-play stories by speaking sympathetically of Nobby. Rex's college buddy who took his life in self-pity. Wife and furniture gone. Pathos, blood, broken love — the press will eat it raw. Show O'Connor you mean business, and the rest of us can get on with our lives."

The coil between love and hate had wound through her since Rex's death, blurring the extremes; she wanted to let go, move on, make new, but the temptation of vengeance was almost erotic. "And what if I let the FBI interrogate her?" retorted the First Lady.

"Then I give the *Times-Picayune* documents from Nobby's files on the purchase of land where the Governor's Mansion stands."

"The Mansion is on state land."

"Nobby got it from Rompallo. Great headline: Mob Brokered Governor's Mansion. I need to sanitize Nobby's files before giving them to the FBI."

Amelia was baffled by the turn of Hubbell's mind. His arch rectitude had melted into something more rash, more political. "Why do you want that girl?"

Unable to admit his retrospective jealousy toward Rex, Hubbell lacked the emotional vocabulary to mollify the First Lady or begin to explain the mystery that had come upon him like a cosmic force.

"She wasn't here before," was all Hubbell could say.

The blunt simplicity of men, the dense way they hunted pleasure, the predictable way that sex lifted their eyes, was all of a piece to Amelia. Hubbell had his own bed to make. Rex died a fool and she would bury him a hero.

A pinch-lipped James Jack O'Connor met them in the hall.

"Leave the girl alone," muttered the First Lady.

Sophie had just taken her seat on the couch when Hubbell rejoined the group. Walter Sutton rose to the full expansiveness of his six-and-a-half-foot frame, shaking with hostility. "Amelia, Oscar and I been talking!"

"So have I, Walter. We have negotiated a clear understanding with Agent O'Connor that provides security to everyone in this room. On that basis, I see absolutely no use for further debate."

Sutton's lips trembled; his cheeks turned mauve.

"This has been a terrible crisis for our state," the First Lady continued. "But we shall carry through. Now, if you'll excuse me, gentlemen."

She fastened her silk cape. "Come, Mitchell."

Mitchell Mudd opened the umbrella and ushered her out to his car.

The FBI agent paused at the door. "Hubbell, everyone in this room knows that if Nobby's files don't deliver, the deal is off and you are history."

Hubbell nodded.

James Jack O'Connor glared at the Speaker and the Attorney General. "You're the two luckiest bastards I ever saw."

As the FBI drove away, Speaker Sutton went red with rage: "I knew you were a Communist, Hubbell! But I never thought you were a goddamn radical! You realize what those five senators'll do to you, boy?"

"Simmer down, Walter," said Oscar Abadie. "I'm not thrilled about this either. But the FBI agreed not to go after you or me. If we don't talk, the senators won't know how the Feds turned them into meat. It also means that any information in Nobby's files about us won't be used against us."

Sutton snarled: "Hubbell, I'd be real happy if your legs got amputated."

Hubbell smiled. "You wouldn't want the FBI sniffing out payments to our just-resigned Lieutenant Governor, eh Mr. Speaker?"

The Attorney General buttoned his coat and pulled back his shoulders. "I have no time for unsupported allegations on Joe

Hall. Man's in bad health. At some point we in law enforcement must show some charity. Let's go to Ruth's Chris Steak House, Walter. I need some supper."

With a parting scowl, Sutton descended the porch stairs alongside Abadie. Through the drizzle they made their way to the limousine where the driver held Sutton's door. They sat in the back and stretched their legs. Sutton inserted a key in the leather armrest and withdrew a fifth of Wild Turkey, two glasses and an ice bucket. He poured a stiff one for himself and his comrade.

"That girl goddamn hit me, Oscar."

"Suck it up, Walter. We got too much else to worry over."

"I never liked that boy's daddy," sulked the Speaker.

"Ah, Forrest was all right."

"Goddamn, Oscar. How'd that boy pull off all that crap back there?"

The Attorney General shrugged. "He went to Harvard."

They buried Rex the next afternoon under blue skies in the graveyard of Avoyelles. A dry chill marked the autumn air. Mourners formed concentric circles beneath a sycamore whose yellow leaves plastered Mayor Bobby Broussard's tombstone. At her grandmother's urging, Regina peeled off the leaves before the Archbishop sprinkled holy water on Rex's coffin. The crowd numbered about three hundred, of whom half were related to the First Lady.

The interment itself merited scant coverage. A handful of reporters stood a respectful distance from the family; two television cameramen were outside the cemetery gates. The Sunday newspapers and morning programs were saturated with accounts of the ferocious storm, the music and drama of the wake. The longest quotations and sound bites were from the sermon of Christian Fraux. The *Times-Picayune* called it "a day of history and passion, befitting the colorful man whose repose seemed a counterpoint to the tempest swirling outside. One floor below, an old friend of the Governor's, mired in legal and personal problems, died of his own hand."

There were no visuals of the bloody room where Doctor Nobby was found. Dr. Willoby pronounced it a suicide. The chief of police overruled protests from his own homicide division for a deeper probe after consultation with the FBI. At a press conference Sunday morning, Amelia LaSalle had spoken eloquently of Nobby. When asked about his missing furniture, the First Lady opined that "the breakdown of his marriage added to his grief. Perhaps it pushed him over the edge. Who can say?"

Nobby's death thus became a footnote to history. As Rex often told Sophie: *The great power is the ability to make people believe that something false is true.*

The night before, after a hurricane of lovemaking, Hubbell bolted out of sleep at three in the morning rattled by a dream of floodwaters squeezing his neck and sawtooth maws of a bull alligator coming straight at him. He sat up in bed to a flooding *deja-vu* — the deserted affections of youth; heartsick and entombed with bitterness toward a state drenched in beauty and crimes of obedience. She whispered his name. For a moment he thought Sophie had read his thoughts, could see how terrified he had been of the hold that his past still had on him. Under a lush moon, she nestled on his chest, her hair soft as ermine.

"Talking in your sleep," she murmured.

He lay quiet until she slept again, wondering what he might have said, curious if the body chemistry between them had blinded his faculty for reasoning. But he had been alone so long, and suddenly here she was, a pool of joy and mystery, drawing him into a reckoning of himself.

Eight hours later, on the drive to Avoyelles, he asked her if love with Rex had been an illusion, like the beauty that lies behind a pane of glass. Arms crossed, she frowned at the road. "It was not illusion," she reported. "It was overpowering, at first. Maybe that's because I didn't know enough about who I wanted to be, only that I didn't want to be trapped by the past, all that crazy Jesus-business back in Big Woods. When I realized how much was missing with Rex — no chance of a life force — I knew it had to end."

"You told Rex that?"

She shook her head no. "I tried to let him go more gently."

Hubbell realized how ignorant he was of love. When they reached the cemetery, he had a raging desire to touch and hold and hug her again, but she had grown remote with proximity to Rex's gravesite. She insisted he give her some time alone in the cemetery before people arrived. He left her among the tombstones and drove out to the big house for final matters.

The Mazda swung through Blue Line, past Fraux Mortuary and St. Joseph Square, heading for the sugarcane fields outside of town. He drove up the road to the Broussard estate, lined by rain-freighted pecan branches. The Attorney wondered how Bobby Broussard had managed to govern Avoyelles all those years he lived outside its limits.

A scent of evergreen and wet pine needles soothed his nostrils. Pale columns of the porch were streaked with lines where rain had scoured the dust. He wiped mud off his heels on a mat. A set of workers' boots rested by a bronze bucket where umbrellas had dried. He rang the doorbell. LauraLee met him with indifference. He doubted that the First Lady had imparted secrets of Henry and Sophie to her maidservant; rather, the women behind great women achieve a knowledge by crafty intuition.

"Miz Amelia say for you to sit in May Bobby study and don't come out till she call for you."

"Well, thank you."

"Well, you welcome."

Time had stopped in Mayor Bobby Broussard's study. Photographs of Miss Della, children and grandchildren formed a chronology of the heart, the images arranged along walls like decals of memory. His absence, the years since his death, seemed forgotten by the room. For a moment, Hubbell thought the portly man in the photograph, holding a crooked trout next to a beaming, ten-year-old Regina, would step out of the frame, slap the fish upon the desk, grab Hubbell's hand in a paw of confraternity and plop down for a swill of whiskey by the fireplace. Three rifles, unoiled in years, lined a rack above the bookcase. An aura of lordly contentment suffused the room.

He sat in a rocker by the burning logs and wondered what he had been fleeing so many years. Was it merely a scarred memory of youth, sutured with unanswered questions about his father? Sophie's yearning to draw some enduring truth from scriptural tyranny had forced Hubbell to assess his own flight, not from mediocrity, as he had long told himself, but from a fallen world, one of his own making, a world lacking the possibility of tiny redemptions that allow life to succeed. How was it that Bobby Broussard had been so happy in the land Hubbell wanted to escape? Was it merely that the old mayor had demanded less of his surroundings or had he mined some deeper vein of wisdom?

In a world devoid of heroes, there must be some few in whom we invest a belief in goodness and genuine conviction.

Henry wondered then: had Forrest Hubbell deceived his wife and son? Warmed by the fire, he realized that Oscar Abadie had planted the question on the day of his father's funeral. When Hubbell told him that society had paralyzed Forrest, Oscar had ignored the remark and kept on talking. Now the seeds of doubt began to sprout. Had the belief he and his mother held sacred, that sinister people destroyed the man they loved, been a convenient fiction? Had Henry hidden from a reckoning, that their lives had been cheated by his father's quest for — something: what? In the eighteen months since his father's death, he had never questioned Oscar Abadie about Forrest's motives.

What would his father think of his harboring knowledge of three murders that would never be solved? He had done what his client wanted. Some rough justice had occurred: the killer had been killed, and Nobby the conspirator murdered too. It was easy to believe that Mitchell Mudd would never kill again: the avenger would lay down his arms and like some oily Cincinnatus, resume his toil as a cog in the machinery. From a circle of conspirators, Hubbell had learned the art of secrecy; instead of feeling guilty, he was in love — loving the idea of Sophie as much as the mystery she presented, of whether love could endure.

Christian Fraux entered the study, shook hands and took a seat opposite him at the fire. Fraux stretched out his legs and yawned.

"Your sermon yesterday was quite compelling."

"The media has been calling nonstop," chuckled Fraux. "After a life of anonymity I am suddenly in demand. My wife spent fifteen minutes on the phone with Dan Rather!" His shoulders shook with laughter.

"You should have leverage with the new administration."

"Well, I think God smiled."

"She's shutting down the injection well?"

Fraux nodded.

"I'm glad of that, Reverend."

"And I'm glad it wasn't necessary for you to put pressure on your boss. Save that leverage for some time when you really need it — or until *I* do."

Hubbell smiled.

"Such sordid business," muttered Fraux, palms open at the fire.

"After the legal struggles you have known, there must be some misgivings about the concealment of recent crimes."

"My image of justice is a blindfolded goddess holding empty balance scales." Fraux paused. "What goes around, comes around."

The crackling of logs seemed like applause.

"Reverend Fraux, about my father ..."

"Ah."

"Did he ever say why he joined your cause?"

Fraux peered contemplatively at the fireplace. "The leadership was suspicious of his overtures. We invited him to a secret meeting, where he spoke of his belief in the Constitution. Your father was a persuasive orator, of course."

"But what made you all accept him?"

"Well, I can only give you my opinion, and I had a great admiration for your father, utmost respect, yes …" As he lapsed into the cadences of a sermon — "superb intelligence … a master psychologist of the courtroom" — the young attorney realized that Christian Fraux had made his money at burials and wakes, where great things are said about the worst people.

He saw that Fraux was unable to say what he *felt* about Forrest Hubbell any more than Oscar Abadie had been willing to divulge his deeper feelings. In his stirring eulogy, Fraux had masked whatever he personally felt about Rex in a grandiose praise-song that ended up crying for environmental justice.

"Did any pivotal event drive my father into your camp?"

"Yes," answered Fraux. "When Dr. King received the Nobel Prize for Peace."

A log crumbled, shooting sparks up the chimney. Henry wondered if an unquenched ego had caused his father to make the move that ended up wrecking his health and devastating his family.

"When a man's instincts are sound, Reverend Fraux, but the reason — ah, the motivations … Why can't I say what is on my mind?"

Fraux folded his hands. "You wonder what it means to do the right thing for the wrong reason. Applied to one's father, that is a frightening question. Betrayal from the past, how do we handle that? But flaws are magnified in those we love. Pride, now that's a common sin. It's the stew meat of politics."

"You found him overly proud?"

"You ask what I thought of your father?"

"Yes, that's something I want to know."

"I enjoyed his company. He was never much on small talk. He was curious about blacks and asked many questions about our attitudes. He wanted to be sure that teachers and folk with good jobs were not intent on violence. *He didn't want to get double-crossed.* Most liberals weren't so cautious. And so I befriended him. He was arrogant, but we shared some laughs. He was the most guarded man I have ever met. Exasperation was his dominant emotion. He was more persuaded of his rightness — and the ignorance of white people fortified that — than by a passion for my people. I don't impugn his moral baseline. For him, the law was God. Forrest was, well, aloof."

"Why did you work with him?"

"I thought he could deliver. His motivations were secondary to me."

"What did he really want?"

"To become a federal judge."

"He never told my mother or me that!"

Fraux shrugged. "I never faulted him for it. He spoke of the federal bench as an almost mystical calling. His desire was transparent, at least to me."

His father's speech, so labored after the stroke, had framed Hubbell's teenage years with sadness. Forrest's decline permeated his imagination and had driven him far from Louisiana. What he had sought, in coming back, was to achieve a delayed retribution. Now he shut his eyes, realizing that it was an equilibrium of himself he had been seeking.

"I used to worry about the motives that give rise to justice," Fraux confided. "These days I fret about civility, the coarseness and criminality that spike our hearts. Your father's decency was genuine. Weigh his achievement against any disillusion you have. Few people leave fingerprints on the world."

LauraLee entered. "Miss Amelia ready for you now."

As Hubbell rose, her face brightened and she spoke to Fraux in a sing-song voice: "Would you like some coffee, Rev'nd?"

"Why, thank you, LauraLee."

Hubbell left them in the study and entered the dining room, where Amelia sat alone with a legal tablet at a long mahogany table. She wore bifocals, which surprised him. "Sit down, please, Mr. Hubbell."

"Thank you, ma'am. I want to apologize for my remark last night about the Governor."

"Yesterday was harrowing for all of us. Politically, things succeeded." She lay her bifocals on the tablet, pondering the spiritual peace she had felt before the burial mass, yet convinced that she had made a decision consistent with her journey. She had lived her years among powerful men and what she wanted now was to exercise power of her own. The waves of light and rolling peace she had felt watching the gospel singers held out a promise of serenity. But the crush of events had pushed her onto a stage she could abandon or use in making a suitable drama of her own life, one without disguises or folly.

She spoke in a firm, yet maternal way: "It is who you are, internally, that concerns me. I never dreamed you would get so close to that girl." She strummed the tablet with her fingers. "On the other hand, I can appreciate mistakes made in a blind moment, and I am prepared to offer you a position. Mitchell Mudd is opposed to this. He is threatened by your intelligence. That is the part of you I value most. In this business we must mend fences."

"I have no desire to assist you further."

The light faded from her eyes. "You really mean it?"

"Yes, ma'am. I just want closure."

"Well then," she sighed. "How much are we talking about?"

"There is no bill. Just make sure your people respect the terms I hammered out with the FBI. No reprisals and I'll keep my end."

"I am not a woman driven by revenge, but there may be problems with the FBI, or unforeseen —"

"Oscar can handle that. He can call me if anything arises."

"Call you?"

"This morning I resigned by e-mail, effective immediately. I'll have my house on the market in a few days."

"Where are you going?"

He frowned. "New Orleans, I imagine."

She lay her hands on the table. "You want *nothing* else?"

He saw the concern on her face. "There is one ... ah —"

"Yes?"

"— crucial matter in need of resolution."

She raised her eyebrows.

Say something for Albert Jackson Tremaine, boss!

"An informant who proved quite useful. A man who took serious risks in light of — Rompallo," he said gravely. She wrote the prisoner's name as it came off his lips. "A gubernatorial pardon would satisfy the balance sheet."

"I'll have Tremaine moved from Angola and sign the pardon soon as I'm sworn in."

"Thank you, Governor."

An edgy silence hung between them. He stood.

"Thank you," she said. "One more thing."

She came around the table. He never expected her to hug him; he was startled by the warmth of her embrace. An ocean of sensations flooded up.

"Good luck to you, Henry. And God bless."

Her tenderness melted an emotional shield of lawyer's years wrought from the defensive strategies of an only child — he began to weep, covering his eyes. She patted his shoulder.

"I knew there was more to you," she whispered.

She left him in the room to compose himself. He had no memory of how long it took to leave the house or if anyone saw him go. At the burial service he avoided eye contact with everyone, standing well behind the Archbishop as he said: "Know, man, that thou art dust, and to dust thou shalt return …"

He never saw Christian Fraux again.

In the shadows of a moss-limbed oak, he watched the mourners file down soggy lanes toward their cars. The First Lady paused by the grave, leaving Hubbell to wonder if the grace she had shown through the crisis was a quality he might emulate in the days and years ahead. Under the firmament's blue canopy the coffin lay in wet Louisiana soil. These latitudes, so gorgeous, so cursed, will manifest seductive charms like the great gilded promise of democracy a thousand times and then again.

He scanned the lanes of country headstones and spotted Sophie in a corner, seated on a sarcophagus thick with vines, a clutch of goldenrods in hand. She had been crying, but on seeing Hubbell began to smile. The loam of parish souls lay still in a silent noon. He reached down and took her hand, realizing how much more she meant to him than an hour before.

The force of life comes with shuddering fall, and the burden on each of us is to make our lives complete.

THE AUTHOR AND THE ARTIST

Jason Berry is renowned for his pioneering investigative reporting on sexual abuse in the Catholic priesthood. *Lead Us Not Into Temption* (1992) was the first major book on the church's crisis and is still used in many newsrooms. He has worked as a consultant for ABC News and is routinely interviewed in the national media about Catholic church issues and his native city, New Orleans. *Vows of Silence* (2004) prompted a Vatican investigation and demotion of one of the most powerful priests in Rome. The author directed a film documentary based on that book which has been distributed internationally. Mr. Berry is also a cultural chronicler of New Orleans, in such books as *Up From the Cradle of Jazz*, a grand history of popular music. His play, *Earl Long in Purgatory*, won a 2002 Big Easy Award for best original work of theatre. In that same year, he was named Humanist of the Year by the Louisiana Endowment for the Humanities.

The author has received Guggenheim and Alicia Patterson fellowships for his research. The comic novel *Last of the Red Hot Poppas* marks a new turn in this writer's varied career.

The art gracing the cover is the work of **Leslie Staub**, a New Orleans native whose naive-art style neatly captures the dark comedy at the heart of *Last of the Red Hot Poppas*. Ms. Staub has had her art work exhibited across the US and has illustrated several books, including *Lives: Poems About Famous Americans* (1999) and *Whoever You Are* (1997) by Mem Fox. Ms. Staub had to leave her beloved New Orleans after Katrina and is currently residing in Durham, NC.

A healthy heaping of Jannon Moderne
Sprinkled with a dash of Fedra Sans
Bound with various papers from the Orient

And a set of hyperperfects
for the king who was anything but.

6 21 28 301 325 496 697 1333 1909 2041 2133
3901 8128 10693 16513 19521 24601 26977
51301 96361 130153 159841 163201 176661
214273 250321 275833 296341 306181 389593

cm